MAGNUS

the

MAGNIFICENT

LESLIE TURNER WHITE

MAGNUS

the

MAGNIFICENT

A NOVEL

CROWN PUBLISHERS · *New York*

This book is
dedicated to my friend and shipmate

REAR ADMIRAL CHESTER H. JONES, U.S.C.G

"Bos'n" of the Schooner *Able Lady*
and "Port Captain" of *White Anchors*.

Foreword

THERE has been a surprising amount of verbiage and nonsense propagated about the origin of Magnus Carter, as is often the case with men who have vaulted precipitately from obscurity to fame. Most of his chroniclers have been at great pains to prove he was of gentle, if not actually noble, birth. No less a personage than Robert Dudley, Earl of Leicester, the Queen's favorite and the most influential and hated man of England in his day, is guilty of this distortion of truth. In his now-famous secret letter to Mr. Secretary Walsingham, after elaborating on the courage and intelligence of Magnus, he declares categorically that Magnus Carter was "well born."

My Lord Leicester may have done this in self-protection, not wanting to sponsor a man of mean birth, for his own background being what it was, he was unduly sensitive to the importance of good breeding. Or (to give the much maligned earl the benefit of the doubt) he may have meant it as a kindness to Magnus. Yet whatever his reasoning, he knew better, for Magnus Carter was the son of a common actor in the earl's own company of players, with the status of a servant to keep it from being worse, for during this period play-actors were social outcasts, being classed with "rogues, idlers, vagrants, tellers of fortunes, tinkers and such as gad about the country."

On the other hand, we have the *Testimonio* from the archives of the parochial church of La Guardia, Spain, in which Frey Alonso de Cigales swore before the Tribunal of the Holy Inquisition in 1584, that the "arch heretic, Magnus Carter, is an English gentleman." It is possible, though highly improbable, that this crafty Jesuit believed this, for he had (unfortunately) sufficient avenues of information for getting facts out of England. There are two conceivable explanations for this error: either he hoped to elevate his own stature by the alleged importance of his victim, or someone else (possibly

7

Tim Prettyman) told him the lie in an attempt to save Magnus from the stake.

Yet even the meticulous Richard Hakluyt, who was personally acquainted with Magnus after he had been honored by the Queen, is said to have perpetuated the myth in his classical work *The Voyage Made by Magnus Carter, Esquire and Afterwards Knight, to the Indies of Nova Hispania, In An. Dom. 1585–7.* Tragically enough, this report was destroyed, along with other priceless documents, during the Reformation, and all that now remains are a few lengthy excerpts incorporated in the tedious memoirs of the Elizabethan gossip, Sir Leffingwell Orr. It is to these we are indebted for Hakluyt's quotation of the testimonial of Sir Francis Drake, another staunch friend, that Magnus "doth discover the address and Noble countenance of a lord."

While that wily old sea-dog Drake may have straddled the fence a trifle, he did not perjure himself in his statement. Magnus *was* extraordinarily handsome—tall, supple, with the grace and bearing usually attributed to princes yet seldom found in them—and his wit was as keen as his blade. His hair was nearly as red as Queen Elizabeth's own flaming tresses, and his falconish features and piercing eyes were sufficiently like Lord Leicester's to encourage the Spanish ambassador to insinuate to his master that he suspected Magnus of being "a bastard beget of that whore Elizabeth and her paramour Leicester."

However, the bald facts, if less spectacular, are more palatable. Magnus was born somewhere in Devonshire in the wagon of strolling players in the year 1565—the month being unknown. Historically, his parents remain mere shadows. His actor father must have had some smattering of education, for Magnus was early taught to read and write—quite an accomplishment for one of his class. There is no record whatever of his mother.

Of his childhood, I could find no trace until his fourteenth year when he ran away to sea, but it is a fair inference that it was from his early stage experience that he acquired his *savoir faire* and sense of dramatic timing which stood him in such good stead in later life. The next five years, from mimic to mariner, are unfortunately shrouded in mystery. His detractors claim that he became a common pirate, but then starry-eyed pedants and rocking-chair philosophers have made the same charge against his immortal contemporaries, Hawkins and Drake, a lie built on half-truths. Magnus was no angel, nor was he all devil; the truth doubtless lies somewhere between the two extremes, or it might be more accurate to say he was a little of both.

Men must be judged in the light of their own times, not ours. Like

8

Hawkins and Drake, Magnus was a product of his era. Technically, perhaps, they might have been deemed pirates if there had been peace, but there was no peace during the sixteenth century; Spain saw to that. Ruthless, rapacious and arrogant, she was determined to loot the New World and subjugate the Old. Englishmen were seized by the Familiars of the Holy Inquisition, whipped, starved in dungeons, burnt alive or sent to the galleys, while King Philip plotted to dethrone their Queen. England, having neither power nor money with which to defend herself had only courage and these so-called *pirates*—practically her only navy.

So it is this magnificent breed of men she can thank for her existence. By sheer dauntlessness and seamanship, they reclaimed the world from Spain and brought freedom to the seas. To them we owe our heritage.

L.T.W.

Book One

ENGLAND

Chapter 1

A TAVERN, even though standing on the hills of Devon within sight and sound of the sea, is not a fighting ship, and no amount of work or pretense could make it so. Tim Prettyman conceded that point. Yet it helped assuage the nostalgia somewhat to keep the place as trim and neat as a good ship should be. He insisted the planked oak floors be holystoned as white as decks, and at least the pewter and coppery utensils could shine. Such detail created a sympathetic setting for his dreams of past glories, and now, as every morning, he worked off the worst of his discontent by rubbing vigorously on a tankard until its ruddy glow reminded him pleasantly of the coppery sunsets he had long ago witnessed on the Spanish Main. For every man reaches an apex in life from which, henceforth, he dates time, and old Tim elected for that honor the great days when he had been a Master Gunner under Francis Drake, instead of the paunchy, one-legged innkeeper he now was.

This morning his mood was blacker than usual, for it was October already—in the year 1584—and the raw cold of approaching winter crippled the toes of his left foot. Though the pain was intense, there was nothing he could do to relieve it, since the foot in question had been sawed off years ago aboard the *Pelican* and consigned to the tepid waters of the Main. It brought no relief to massage the stout brass-bound peg leg the ship's carpenter had fashioned for him; the ache was in the missing limb.

Yet the ache begot other aches, more poignant still, so he paused in his chore to gaze wistfully through the mullioned window, where, beyond the rooftops of Plymouth, the Sound lay veiled in a thin purple mist that scattered slowly before a land breeze. A little lower, St. Nicholas Island emerged from the touch of mystery lent it by the fog to shimmer sleepily in the cold sunlight. A few fishing smacks minced fussily out of the Catwater to beat around four stately old ships that swung restlessly to their hawses, as if eager to follow the tide into the Channel, that peerless high-road to adventure.

13

What a day to sail for the Indies to yank King Philip's beard! A fair wind, a fair tide, and the season of the hurricanes, or *furicanos*, as old John Hawkins called them, was over. Wistfully, Tim recalled the old seaman's rhyme:

> June—too soon.
> July—stand by.
> August—you must.
> September—remember!
> October—all over.

Aye, mused Tim, it was all over; both the *furicanos* and his own adventuring. He was nothing but a peg-legged old cripple, doomed to eke out his days doing a woman's work. Yet his bitterness was not derived entirely from self-pity. None of these proud galleons now rotting under the shadow of the Hoe were going south. Those grand old days were also all over. Queen Elizabeth—God forgive her naïveté!—was trying to pacify the Spanish dragon. Her magnificent sea-dogs wore muzzles. Drake, the great *Drake*, wasted his skill in Parliament, and Hawkins, whose very name was enough to give Philip apoplexy, was chained to a desk as Comptroller and Treasurer of the Navy. Tim spat an oath. *Navy?* Why, England had no navy worth the name, and all that stood between her and the strangling arrogance of Spain were a few unknown youngsters who challenged her might in their cockleshells. Aye, these were sorry days!

His reverie was shattered by the rumble of a coach crossing the courtyard. He sat a moment longer with the tankard on his apron, reluctant to leave his dreams, when his wife shrilled his name in a voice that invariably set his teeth on edge.

"*Ti-im-oth-thee!*"

There was no denying that screech. The coach had come to a halt now, and by the time he settled the tankard and limped into the common-room, his wife was already welcoming the coach's occupant, a tall, elegant figure closely followed by two dark, foreign-looking seamen who staggered under the weight of a sea chest.

Since such magnificence seldom graced the modest White Anchors Inn, Mistress Prettyman attempted an unfamiliar curtsy that almost upset her.

"Yer 'umble servants, m'lud!" she babbled with a warning glance at her husband.

But old Tim was in no mood for obsequiousness. Furthermore, the newcomer looked Spanish, and a Spaniard to ex-gunner Prettyman was anathema. He scowled at his groveling spouse, whose un-

14

gainly carcass reminded him of a huge sack of potatoes tied around the middle with twine, then gave his attention to the visitor, who imperiously surveyed him along the ridge of a prodigious nose.

Tim started automatically to make a leg, then caught himself in time. Damned if he would dip his colors to a "furriner"; for all he knew, the rakehell might be a spy. Under a plumed hat he wore a thick green wig, and his pointed beard was dyed the same color after the Continental fad of the day, and (thought Tim) probably perfumed. His short cloak was of scarlet velvet with a fur collar and under it was a richly brocaded doublet. His long legs were sleekly, almost indecently, encased in silken hose. One hand rested lightly on the jeweled pommel of a dress sword while the other waved a perfumed wisp of lace back and forth under his nose, as if the odor of the place offended him. His pale eyes shifted from one Prettyman to the other.

"Who is in charge here?" he lisped in an affected voice tinged with a strong Castilian accent.

Tim muzzled his distaste to growl, "I be, m'lud!"

"Well, look to your manners, my man!" snapped the visitor. "Must I stand here all day while you gawk at me? This hovel was recommended as a place where I could find peace and privacy, and quarters suitable for a gentleman! It appears I have been misinformed."

Before Tim could frame a suitable retort, his wife wriggled around in front of the guest.

" 'Tis the God's trufe, m'lud! We've a royal suite, we 'as, m'lud, w'ere King 'Arry 'imsel' onc't styed—God rest 'im!" She transfixed her husband with her small myopic eyes. "Come, Mister Prettyman, show 'is ludship the parlor! Per'aps 'is ludship would fancy a pint o' sack?"

The stranger's face lost its severity and he doffed his hat with a flourish.

"Bless you, señora. I own that is thoughtful. As a matter of fact, I shall fancy several pints, to be followed by one of your famous dinners." He saw Tim turn toward the taproom, so he shouted after him: "Ho there, my man! Fetch an extra bottle of your best vintage for your pretty wife. The *best*, you understand!"

While Tim stopped in astonishment, the visitor bowed to the woman. "Señora, I pray you will drink to Don Ruster, a poor homesick wanderer?"

Mistress Prettyman was near to swooning. A flabby ponderous woman with the face of a broad-axe, no one had called her pretty for at least two score years.

"Marry!" she giggled. "Oh, aye, ye'll 'ave the best, yer Grace, an' God bless ye!"

15

Tim made a grimace of disgust and stomped toward the staircase. "Don't stand there vaylin' yer tops'ls, Mistress Prettyman!" he snapped. "Send Kate up wi' the sack, then lay yersel' a course fer the galley. This way, yer ludship!"

Drunk with flattery, the old woman waddled off to the scullery, caterwauling for the serving girl. The visitor spoke in Spanish to the man guarding his chest, then followed Tim up the stairs to the private suite on the first floor. The two seamen deposited the heavy box near the foot of the bed and took their leave, while the elegant gentleman proceeded to examine the room.

Watching him, Tim was struck with a sense of foreboding, strongly mixed with resentment. It was difficult to separate the two, especially when the foreigner lingered at the window overlooking the harbor. The Spaniards hated Plymouth above any port in England, for it was the sea-dogs of Devon who most harassed them. Like most experienced seamen, Tim felt certain it was only a question of time until Spain would send a fleet to assault England.

Once again the strident voice of his wife broke in on his thoughts. Mumbling a promise to have the sack sent up immediately, he backed out of the room.

He found the woman waiting for him at the foot of the stairs. "More trouble!" she hissed at him. "I warned ye not to keep such vulgar company, Master Prettyman, w'at gives my place a bad nyme!"

"Avast, Mistress Prettyman! Stop blatherin', an' tell w'at's ruffled yer tail feathers!"

"*Bailiffs*, 'at's w'at! The Justice sent 'em! 'E s'ys 'at dirty smuggler, 'at pirate, 'at clown, 'at vagabond ye waste my best victuals on . . ."

Tim beamed for the first time in months. "Glory be!" he crowed. "*Magnus Carter* be 'ome!"

The woman sniffed. "So s'y the bailiffs! I swore we uns don't 'ave no truck wi' such varmints, but . . ."

Old Tim was not listening. He hobbled to the front windows and took a quick glance at the ships anchored in the Sound. Then squaring his shoulders, he swung on his spouse.

"W'ere away, Mistress Prettyman? Show me the lubberly swabs, an' as God's me life, I'll larn 'em to 'ound an 'onest man!"

The woman's virulent reply was drowned by a loud commotion from the kitchen—the sharp curse of a man, a blow, the raucous screeching of an angry macaw followed by the thud of a falling body.

"God preserve us!" wailed Mistress Prettyman. "They've caught

16

'im in my 'ouse!" She started waddling toward the kitchen, but for all his wooden leg, Tim got there ahead of her.

His first confused impression was of two startled hounds fighting a wild cat. One of the bailiffs was stretched on his back, yelping for assistance and trying to ward off the slashing fingernails of a very blond and very angry girl who had straddled him. His companion was circling cautiously, trying to get behind her.

"Pinch my backside, would you!" screamed the girl, clawing his face and kneeing him at the same time. "You dirty, evil-minded catchpoll! I'll teach you to keep your filthy . . ."

"Fer Christ's sake, get the bitch off'n me!" howled the victim.

Tim stopped short, delighted, but his wife threw up her hands in horror.

"Kate! 'Ow *dare* ye!"

Kate laid four neat furrows down the bailiff's cheek. "No stinkin' thief-taker can fondle my bottom!" she raged.

"Leave 'er be, Mistress Prettyman!" warned Tim. " 'Tis a seaman-like bit o' boardin' she's doin', damme if else!"

But the old woman disregarded his counsel. Snatching up the bailiff's stave, she belabored the girl across the shoulders until she had to give up the fight.

"Out to the scullery w'ere ye belong!" shrilled Mistress Prettyman. " 'Tis not the first time yer bottom's been fondled, ye bad-tempered vixen! Aw'y wi' ye!"

As the girl retreated before the onslaught, Tim bellowed encouragement.

"Ye careened 'im neatly, Katie me girl! Now I'll finish the job!" And as the girl backed into the scullery, he bore down on the disconcerted minions of the law.

Before his advance, the subdued bailiffs edged together and gripped their staves, for despite his peg leg Tim Prettyman presented a formidable appearance, with his tremendous torso balanced on his slender, unmatched pins. His head was bald, save for a girdle of iron-gray hair that spanned the crown from ear to ear, and his hide was the shade and texture of a crocodile.

" 'Azy now, 'azy, good Master Prettyman!" cautioned the taller of the pair. " 'Is Honor won't be pleased to 'ear 'ow ye . . ."

"Scuttle 'is Honor!" thundered Tim. "W'at brings ye lecherous swine aboard the craft o' an 'onest man?"

The tall bailiff glanced at his blocky companion, but that worthy was too busy mopping blood from his face to carry the burden of explanations. The tall bailiff sighed, and went on: " 'Is Honor 'ad information that the smuggler Magnus Carter slipped into Teign-

17

mouth 'arbor on last night's 'igh tide, an' was 'eaded o'rland to stop 'ere at White Anchors!"

"By God, I wish't 'e 'ad!" vowed Tim. " 'Tis proud I'd be to clasp 'is 'and, that I own."

"But 'e didn't!" babbled his wife. "We runs a respeckable . . ."

" 'Old yer fire, Mistress Prettyman!" blazed Tim. "Cap'n Carter be my friend, an' if 'e drops 'is 'ook in my cove, by God 'e's welcome!"

" 'E's a bloody criminal!" muttered the squat bailiff.

"Would to God England 'ad more criminals like 'im!" Tim retorted. "Instead o' a mess o' barkin' ol' shrews an' piddlin' tip-staffs w'at can't keep their paws off'n a wench's arse!"

The bailiffs squirmed and exchanged glances. "Blime, if 'e ain't 'ere, 'e ain't 'ere," the injured one observed sagely.

" 'E ain't 'ere, God's trufe!" echoed the old woman.

The tall bailiff put three paces of floor between himself and Tim, then tried again.

"Now, Master Prettyman, ye won't be arter wantin' trouble o'er no pulin' pirate, 'at's plain, so if this 'ere Cap'n Carter shows 'is fyce, just send a pot-boy an' we'll . . ."

"Sheer off!" bellowed Tim, starting toward him. "An' if ye lousy catchpolls lay athwart my hawse again, I'll sink ye, on my oath!"

The bailiffs took the hint and scuttled out of the inn. Mistress Prettyman glowered at her husband, and sensing intuitively that he was in no mood to be bullied, she dissolved into tears.

" 'Ow brutal ye be!" she wailed. "Not a bit like poor 'Erman, me first 'usband. 'E was good an' kind an' . . ."

"Aye, an' if ye 'adn't nagged 'im to death, 'e'd still be 'ere!" snorted Tim, and limped into the common-room. Despite his show of temper, he was secretly in excellent humor, for the news that his friend was back in England had buoyed his flagging spirits. He retraced his steps to the window, for he found it easier to think when staring at good salt water. So Magnus was in Teignmouth! He wondered what to do about it. It would be futile to ride over to seek him; the scamp was as elusive as a will-o'-the-wisp. On the other hand, Tim knew the treacherous disposition of his wife too well to want the boy to come to the inn; Mistress Prettyman would betray him at the first opportunity. The wisest course, he decided, was to do nothing. After all, Magnus also was acquainted with the idiosyncrasies of Mistress Prettyman, and he would know better than to walk into a trap.

While he was standing there, quarter-deck fashion, he heard the door above open, then the accented voice of his guest.

"Host! Oh, Host!"

Tim spat angrily and stomped toward the stairs. "Comin'!" he growled.

By the time Tim reached the upstairs parlor, the visitor was stretched languidly in a chair.

"See here, my man," he said imperiously. "What was all that brawling about below?"

"A couple o' knaves badgerin' the barmaid."

"H'mmn! I trust I have not entered a den of ill-repute."

Tim controlled himself with an effort. "Ye're aboard an 'onest craft, stranger, an' ye can lay to 'at," he retorted bluntly. "Howbeit, peradventure ye don't favor the 'oldin' ground, ye can shift yer anchorage an' welcome."

The other stroked his beard reflectively, then gave a short, hard laugh.

"From your salty vernacular, I gather you are a seaman, host."

Tim evinced surprise. "Damme, I don't know w'at I said to gi' ye 'at ideer, yet I own 'tis true enough. Served me time afore the mast, I did; three an' thirty years o' it."

The guest shuddered. "*Santa Maria*, what a rugged existence! Forgive my inquisitiveness, host, but your leg—did you lose it at sea?"

Tim's jaw began to jut, for that leg was a sore point with him. "Nay, I didn't *lose* it; I *traded* it, in a manner o' speakin', fer the lives o' six Spaniards, though to speak true, I sought to colleck a higher price."

The tall man sprang from his chair in indignation, then recovered his poise.

"Since you do not know my nationality, I presume I must overlook the effrontery," he rasped. "However, I certainly hope you were not of those misguided souls who pillaged the seas under that piratical dog Drake."

The old man turned livid at this heresy. It took him a full minute to find his voice, but when it came, it came full blown.

"*Piratical dog!*" he trumpeted so that the windows rattled. "By God, I don't know 'oo ye be, an' damme if I care. But this I'll state: no perfumed furriner can stand on my deck an' call Cap'n Drake a dog! Ye take 'at back, else by God, I'll . . . I'll . . ."

The guest gave ground before the blast and dropped his hand to his sword hilt.

"You will *what?*" he challenged.

Tim was already staring wildly about him for a convenient weapon. Seeing his old cutlass hanging on the wall beside the washstand, he stomped over and ripped it down. He made a couple of preliminary passes to flex his sword arm, then turned back.

19

"Now, by Neptune, I'll larn ye to respeck . . . !" he began, then his words trailed away from a jaw gone slack.

The tall man stood in the center of the room, laughing at him. The green wig, the false beard and nose, were precisely spread out on the table. Instead of facing an arrogant Spaniard, Tim found himself gaping at a familiar, lithe, red-headed youth.

"*Magnus!*" gasped the old man. "Magnus, by God!"

The young man grinned. "Well, you crusty old shell-back, I'll swear this is a fine way to greet a friend, with a cutlass in hand!"

With a delighted bellow, Tim flung the weapon onto the bed and hopped forward to throw his arms about the other.

"Magnus, Magnus, ye crazy clown! Sink me deep in forty fathoms, ye be as welcome as a Spaniard's death, I vow! Damme, I should 'a guessed 'twas ye, but ye've growed. By God, ye be tall-sparred! W'at's yer age an' tonnage now?"

After the bear's hug, Magnus had to gasp for breath.

"Almost twenty years, and nigh unto thirteen stone."

Tim backed away for a better look at him and nodded admiringly. "*Don Rooster*, be it?" he chuckled. "Aye, 'tis a fittin' nyme fer a young cockerel 'oo can ruffle the ol' 'ens so. But damme, younker, won't ye ever forget yer clownin' an' play-actin'?"

Magnus, having chucked off his appendages and removed his cloak, sword and ruff, stretched lazily on the bed.

"I don't seem able to, Tim," he confessed. "On my oath, I find more necessity for play-acting *off* the stage than I ever did *on* it." He grinned at the bewilderment on the other's face. "Perchance it was a cruel jest to play on your good wife, but I didn't want to walk into the arms of those damn thief-takers."

"Then ye knew they was 'ere?"

"Aye, I passed them trudging up the hill. I was sorely tempted to bring them along with me, but I was half afraid you might recognize me despite my disguise."

Tim slapped his good leg heartily. " 'Twas well done, I grant ye. W'en ye 'ove 'ull-up, I'd 'a swore from the cut o' yer jib ye was a bloody Spaniard."

"You say the bailiffs ran afoul of the barmaid! Was it Kate, or is she still with you?"

"Aye, 'twas Katie, an' a proper maulin' she gi' 'em!" laughed Tim. " 'Ad one o' 'em on 'is beam's end an' would 'a dismasted 'im if the ol' woman 'adn't rammed 'er!"

"Bless the wench! Is she as buxom and pretty as ever?"

"Aye, lad, she's nice lines! A good clean run, wi' plenty o' sheer an' a beautiful tumble-'ome. A mite 'ard in the bilges, but she's got the prettiest stern in the fleet, I'll swear!" His face darkened.

"But tell me—w'at brings ye 'ere, laddie? Though 'appy I be to see ye, sink me if else, I wonder ye risked it. Means 'angin' in chains if caught!"

Magnus stretched sensuously in an excess of self-contentment and folded his hands behind his short red curls.

"I won't ever be caught by those coxcombs, Tim," he chuckled. "Soon my ship sails away and Captain Carter the smuggler vanishes for good."

The old man's ruddy face lengthened. "Aye, 'tis best, methinks, though in all truth, I 'ates to see ye go. Would to God I 'ad me underpinnin' an' could sail wi' ye."

"Oh, I'm not sailing with her, Tim! I've turned her over to the crew. I'm quitting the sea."

Tim collapsed into a chair. "Swallowin' the anchor, ye say? Ah, yer just gammin'!"

"No, I'm serious." Magnus laughed and waved a hand at the sea chest at the foot of the bed. "I've enough gold bagged in there to buy me a respectable berth ashore. I'm going to be wed."

Tim raised his hands in protest. "A lubber *an'* spliced! Not both, by God!" He thumped his peg leg on the floor to punctuate his argument. "Avast, lad, ye're 'eaded fer the reef! Look w'at 'appened to Cap'n Drake—a bloody country squire eatin' out 'is great 'eart amongst the ol' wimmen o' Parliament! Look at proud ol' 'Awkins, rottin' on the beach! Look at *me*, Magnus, the best bloody gunner w'atever 'ulled a Spaniard—wipin' mugs an' emptyin' piss-pots!" He mopped his face, almost overcome by his own emotions. "Why, sink me if I wouldn't almost as soon see ye 'angin' in chains as wed, fer 'pon my oath, 'tis practically one an' the syme!"

Magnus hooted merrily. "What oratory, Timothy! I vow you'd shame a bishop! Yet coming from a well-fed old benedict with a sweet and ever-loving spouse to pamper your every whim, this tirade against connubial bliss astounds me!"

Tim reddened. "That was a foul thrust at a shipwrecked ol' sailor w'at loves ye like a son," he chided. "Ye could 'a said a-plenty wi'out sayin' *that!*"

Knowing Tim's story as he did, Magnus cursed his thoughtlessness in bringing up his wife, for it was the one subject in which the old man could find no humor. And Magnus could not blame him for that. Crippled in the service of a country that made no provision for wounded seamen, he had come ashore, with all the romantic illusions of an old tar, to seek a sinecure. He had been fair game for the Widow Bodilly who, having nagged one spouse to death, was seeking another victim. Tim had been expertly brought to gaff, and as he once phrased it: "W'en the battle-smoke cleared,

21

there we was—jined by a long-splice!" Marriage and a wooden leg were two cables which, in his vernacular, he couldn't "slip."

Magnus walked over and laid a comradely hand on the old man's arm.

"I'm sorry, Tim, so help me!" he said in quick sympathy. "I didn't mean to pour salt on your wounds. Please forgive me, old friend."

Tim sniffed. "If it 'ud be a lesson to ye, I'd not mind. Believe me, a seaman's got no business on the beach, an' by God, if I 'ad me two shanks, I'd leave the ol' she-bear to 'er ever-lastin' snarlin' an' go to sea if I 'ad to straddle a log to do it. That's the God's trufe!" He paused as someone knocked on the door.

" 'Oo be it?" he growled.

Magnus had made a dive for his disguise when a cheery voice called from beyond the panel: "It's just me with the sack, Master Tim!"

Tim hobbled erect and gave Magnus a questioning glance. "It's Katie!" he whispered.

Magnus grinned. "Let her in and say nothing." As Tim fiddled with the bolt, he walked to the window and stood with his back to the door. After a brief pause, he heard the girl come in and set the tray on the table.

" 'Oo ees eet, señor?" he asked, without turning.

"Me servin' wench wi' the sack, m'lud," rumbled Tim respectfully.

"Santa Maria! Ees eet the wan w'at was fighting, señor?"

"Aye, m'lud, the very one!"

"H'mmn! An' w'at deed you fight about, leetle girl?"

After a moment's hesitation, Kate said, "The lout got impudent with me, sire."

"So? W'at deed 'e do?"

Silence greeted this query until Tim growled, "Speak up, Katie! Tell 'is Grace w'at the varlet done to ye!"

"I'd rather not," the girl demurred. " 'Tweren't decent!"

" 'E fondled 'er keel, m'lud," Tim reported solemnly.

"So? Ees that not pleasant?" demanded Magnus. "Would you scratch me, leetle girl, if I fondled your w'at-you-call keel?"

"You're bloody well right I would!"

"Katie!" roared Tim. "You know naught 'oom ye address!"

"What's more, I don't care!" cried Kate, on the verge of tears. "Nobody pats my bottom-cheeks without I say so!"

"Not even me, señorita?" persisted Magnus, turning slowly.

"Not you nor nobody . . . !" She stopped short, rooted in astonishment.

22

Magnus grinned admiringly. As Tim had so succinctly described her—Kate had "nice lines." She was tall, seeming taller because of the coronet of plaited blond hair atop her head, and full of tempting curves. A low-cut bodice gave something more than a glimpse of ample breasts, and her slim waist sheered off into generous thighs.

"Well, if I can't fondle you a bit," laughed Magnus, "then by my troth, times have changed around here."

"*Magnus Carter!* You tricky devil!"

Squealing delightedly, she flung herself into his arms and kissed him a resounding smack. He in turn caught her around the waist and swung her clear off the floor.

"Oo-oo, Magnus, Magnus!" she screamed. "It's wonderful to see you again!"

"Belay that carronadin'!" warned Tim. "Else ye'll rouse the ol' woman! W'at think ye o' Don Rooster, Katie?"

"I'll swear the name fits the gamecock like his hose!"

Magnus slapped her buttocks and wriggled out of her grasp.

"By heaven, girl, give me sea-room, else I'm liable to forget your master is gawking at us!"

Kate, flushed of face and bright of eye, swung on the old man.

"Master Tim, I'll trade you twelve months' wages for one half hour alone with Magnus!"

"Ye're a brazen 'ussy!" chortled Tim. "Yet, damme, I've a notion to oblige ye, fer 'tis the very medicine 'e needs, the grinnin' idjit!"

Kate caught the excess of feeling in the remark and glanced wonderingly from one to the other. "Idiot? You call our Magnus an *idiot!* Why, Master Tim, I'm ashamed . . ."

"Aye, a four-ply idjit!" grumbled Tim. "'E's goin' to marry up wi' a woman!"

Kate turned laughing eyes on Magnus. "And pray—why not? A lively stag like him shouldn't be at large to break hearts everywhere he roams. Aye, married he should be, for I can vouch as to what a bed-fellow . . ."

"Now, now, Kate!" Magnus cautioned hastily. "Watch your tongue, else we'll both get thrown out of Master Prettyman's respectable establishment."

The girl favored old Tim with a sardonic glance that reddened his ears.

"I wouldn't worry about *that*, Magnus. Master Tim is remarkable human himself."

Magnus' knowing laughter was interrupted by a baleful wail from below.

"Kat-tie!"

Tim sighed relievedly. "There's the ol' woman arter ye, Katie. Better slip yer cables an' begone."

She hesitated, looking wistfully at the younger man. "Peradventure, I'd better. Are you staying long, Magnus?"

"A few days, perhaps. It all depends."

She colored slightly. "I'll be seeing you again, won't I?"

He lowered one lid perceptibly. "I'm counting on it."

"Kat-tie!"

The girl made a face. "That's all I hear from dawn to darkness. Kat-tie! Kat-tie! It's enough to make me hate my own name!"

"Get along wi' ye!" Tim growled impatiently. "An' don't betray 'im!"

She blew them both a kiss and crossed to the door. "Don't worry I'll see you anon, Magnus."

After she had gone, Magnus stood staring at the closed door. "By God, there's a girl for you, Tim. It's a wonder you haven't bedded her yourself."

The old man exhaled regretfully. "Aye, she's true blue, that 'un! An' bed 'er I'd like to, yet she's too lively a craft fer a peg-legged ol' sailor. She'd 'eave me overboard on the first wave!" He reached for a bottle of sack and drew the cork. He passed it over to Magnus and opened another for himself.

"Well, 'ere's 'appy sailin', matey!"

Magnus drank to the toast. "That's good wine," he approved, lowering the bottle.

"It should be. 'Tis of the last batch ye brought from France. Fill yer cask, laddie, an' I'll rip the 'atches off'n another." He suited the action to the word. " 'Ow come the bailiffs was seekin' ye? Did anyone know ye was landin'?"

Magnus shook his head. "Only Jethro Maynard. I wrote him from . . ."

"*Maynard!* God A'mighty, man, 'tis a wonder ye weren't met at the quay by all the catchpolls in Devon!"

Magnus frowned. "Easy, Tim! Maynard is my friend, aye, almost a second father. He'd cut his tongue out before he would betray me."

"*Bilge!*" snorted Tim. "I allus said readin' an' writin' 'ud get a body into trouble!"

Magnus found his hand trembling. "What are you implying, Tim?"

"Jes' this—Jethro Maynard never got your letter, though 'tis likely the Justice did. 'Ow long since ye've been 'ome?"

"Three-and-twenty months. My God, has anything happened to

24

the Maynards?" Magnus sprang to his feet and stood scowling at his host. "Tell me the truth!"

"'Tis nothin' to quarrel wi' me about!" grumbled the old man. "The truth be that Jethro Maynard got 'imself exiled to France fer Roman tendencies!"

Magnus groaned and walked heavily to the window. The mist still wreathed the crest of Mont Edgecombe, but the Sound sparkled with sunlight. Yet to Magnus there was no beauty in the panorama.

"The poor addle-pated fool!" he fumed. "Why couldn't he have kept his mouth shut! Now I'll have to go to France."

Tim's eyes widened. "Magnus, Magnus! Ye ain't takin' up wi' *papists!*"

Magnus shrugged impatiently and took a nervous turn around the room.

"I don't give a damn if he's embraced the Devil!" he snapped irritably. "It's his daughter Rosalind I've come home to wed."

Tim took his head between his hands. "It gets worse and worse!" he groaned. "Ye're too late, lad, the chit be as good as wed already!"

"Wed?"

"Aye! 'Ere's the way o' it: w'en Maynard 'eard the Queen's men was arter 'im—eleven months past, it was—'e 'ad to leave in such an 'urry he couldn't take the girl. So 'e left 'er wi' 'is brother-in-law, Sir Gregory Duane, 'oo 'as the big manor 'ouse off the Tavistock Road."

Magnus gave a short dry laugh of relief. "Why did you not say so in the first place!" He reached for his ruff. "I'll go see her at once."

"Avast, lad, avast! Ye ain't 'eard the worst. I tolt ye she's almost wed!"

"You're bloody well right she's almost wed!" jeered Magnus, adjusting his ruff. "Maynard promised her to me!"

"But Maynard's naught to do wi' it now!" Tim protested. "Sir Gregory 'as taken charge o' the chit, an' 'tis common knowledge 'e intends to marry 'er off to a Sir Peter Beckles, a court fop an' favorite o' Queen Bess—God bless 'er!"

Magnus snorted. "A pox on Sir Gregory and his court fop! Rosalind and I have been sweethearts since childhood, and I've had her father's blessing these two years past. Until now it was merely a question of gold, and . . ."

"An' now 'tis a question o' politics," cut in Tim. "Hark ye, boy— w'ilest I know naught o' Sir Gregory's game, some as say 'e too 'as been playin' wi' the papist traitors, an' 'at 'e's 'andin' Rosalind over to this Beckles to assure 'imself an ear at Court. Howbeit, much 'as 'appened since ye went away, an' 'tis certain a tough ol' rooster like Gregory Duane won't welcome no interruption to 'is plans."

"Curse Duane and his plans!" scoffed Magnus, tightening the points of his hose. "Can you give me a good horse, Tim?"

"But ye ain't eaten yet, laddie!"

"You've given me all I can digest for the nonce," Magnus growled ruefully. He buckled on his sword. "Get me a horse."

Tim heaved himself out of the chair with obvious reluctance.

"I'll get us a couple o' nags an' go wi' ye."

"I prefer to travel alone. Tim!"

The old man squared his jaw. "Sobeit! But this I'll state: ye're a selfish, pig-headed fool. May God 'elp ye, because ye're goin' to need it, I'll warrant. 'Tis plain, 'twas Sir Gregory 'imself 'oo got 'old o' yer letter to Maynard an' set the bailiffs arter ye. 'E'll be on 'is guard."

Magnus paused in his preparations. That was a contingency he had not foreseen. Tim snorted maliciously and unbolted the door.

"An' don't ferget yer snout an' w'iskers, *Don Rooster*," he grunted. "Ye've got another enemy downstairs!"

Chapter 2

Magnus galloped out of Plymouth in a lather of impatience, but on reaching the high country, the chill, wintry winds sweeping across the open moorlands cooled his nerves. Then he chided himself for acting like an hysterical woman and began to deplore his folly for having left the inn with an empty belly. He drew rein, and after jamming his disguise into his saddle-bags, proceeded at a walk while pondering a course of action.

He assured himself the whole thing was a misunderstanding which a talk with Rosalind would quickly clarify; an irritation, but nothing over which to get emotional. However, it would be poor policy to burst in on such a personage as Sir Gregory Duane and demand his niece forthwith. Precipitancy of that sort might well prove fatal if, as Tim Prettyman suggested, it was Duane who had intercepted his letter and turned it over to the Justices. And while

26

it galled Magnus to contemplate it, he decided he had best use circumspection until he found out what it was all about.

In this mood, he searched his memory for what few facts he had about Sir Gregory. They were scant. The old knight was known to be an austere, unfriendly recluse who late in life had married Jethro Maynard's older sister. His choleric disposition was attributed to a malignant disease allegedly eating away his vitals, and local rumor had attached many dark deeds to his name. He had acquired his title from King Henry, before the latter's break with the Pope, and was suspected by his neighbors of papist tendencies which, though a heinous offense in the eyes of Puritan-minded Devon folk, was a matter of supreme indifference to Magnus Carter.

What disturbed and irritated Magnus most of all was Maynard's exile. Why in heaven's name, he asked himself, hadn't the good-natured imbecile sense enough to worship as he pleased in private and keep his mouth shut in public? Quarreling over such trivia as religious ritual seemed the height of folly to Magnus, especially when there were so many other important issues to quarrel about. But, unfortunately, that was characteristic of Jethro Maynard. Like so many ardent men, he was flighty and unpredictable; impulsive in his sudden affections, intemperate in speech and impetuous in action.

Viewed in retrospect, Magnus was forced to admit, ruefully to be sure, that Maynard's very friendship for him had been indicative of these selfsame traits. He had gotten the boy, a stranger then with a bad reputation for wildness, out of a serious scrape, taken him into his home and subsequently tolerated his suit for his only daughter—to the horror of his friends. And while Magnus was eternally grateful for this bounty, he was now objective enough to concede the folly of it.

Yet folly or not, Magnus had justified Maynard's confidence. The one stipulation Maynard demanded was that Magnus delay his marriage until he was financially able to care properly for Rosalind. To this Magnus had acceded. It had taken him nearly two years to garner enough gold to live up to his end of the bargain, and now that he had, he meant to collect his bounty.

As for Rosalind herself, Magnus had no doubts, for in his sight they were wed already, and it was the precious recollection of the night she had spent in his arms which had sustained him through the long months of separation. All the crusty old knights of England could not eradicate that.

The remembrance rekindled his impatience, and he spurred the gelding into a gallop. The moors vanished and they swept across a fertile valley. The trees grew thicker and the hillside took on the

27

gorgeous scarlet coloring of autumn until, on topping the summit, the towers of the gray castellated manor house loomed in the offing.

Magnus guided his horse off the road, and reining in, sat sideways in the saddle to survey the place. Set in a grove of oaks and beeches, and ringed by stables and out-buildings, the dark pile of century-old masonry gave the impression of a gigantic sepulcher. The imposing courtyard was surrounded by a high stone wall, broken only by a turreted gatehouse. Beyond this quadrangle stood the mansion. Not even the splash of sunlight on the oriel windows softened the austerity.

A trifle daunted by the all-enveloping stillness, Magnus urged the horse into a walk. He reasoned that, since the manor house was not on the main road, strangers would be viewed with suspicion, so he kept warily in the shadow of the trees until he had worked his way around behind the stables. There he dismounted, tethered his horse in a thick grove and continued afoot.

Where the footpath crossed a turnstile, he paused, at a loss how to proceed, and sat on a fallen log to consider various expediencies. The notion to use his disguise he instantly discarded; that might fool simple rustics like the Prettymans, but it could not be expected to deceive a sophisticated nobleman. On the other hand, he could not march boldly up to the gatekeeper and demand admittance, for doubtless all the men-at-arms had been warned by Sir Gregory to keep an eye out for him.

Thus balked, he was beginning to contemplate the wisdom of retiring from the scene and seeking some less direct method of communicating with the girl, when a sudden whistling brought him hastily to his feet. He had just time to back into the thicket before a diminutive pageboy came sauntering along the trail with a hooded falcon on his wrist.

He appeared to be a clean, open-countenanced lad of about twelve years and his eyes were alert and intelligent. Playing a hunch, Magnus stepped out of hiding.

"Hello, younker!" he said genially.

The boy was so startled that the falcon had to spread its wings to steady itself, and for a moment Magnus feared the lad was going to bolt. But seeing Magnus' friendly smile, he recovered his poise and muttered hesitantly, "Your servant, sire!"

"It appears I've lost my way," Magnus explained. "Is this the road to Tavistock?"

The boy smiled relievedly. "Oh, no, sire, you missed the turn half a league south'ard. This is Sir Gregory Duane's holdings."

Magnus feigned amazement. "Did you say *Duane?* By my troth, does not my lady Rosalind Maynard reside with him?"

The youngster's face lighted. "That she does, sire! I was hawking with her ladyship only this morning."

"Bless me, think of that!" marveled Magnus. "I used to know her very well! It would be a pleasure to see her again." His shrewd eyes saw the lad evince nervousness, so he added casually, "I take it, from your tone, you are fond of her, younker?"

"Aye, sire! She's very kind to me."

"Well then, that makes a sort of bond between us." Magnus laughed, and fishing a gold coin from his pocket, hefted it significantly. "Would you do her a great kindness by taking a message to her?"

The page flushed. "Oh, sire, I'd like to oblige, but my master is terribly strict about such matters and he gave special orders only the other day that under no circumstances were strangers to be admitted without his knowledge. He'd have me whipped if I disobeyed!"

Magnus chuckled and slipped a ring off his finger, which he handed with the coin to the hesitant youngster.

"I tell you what—we won't endanger you by disobeying any orders. You just hand this ring to our lady and tell her you found it by this stile—that, and nothing else. You can manage it without embarrassment, I'm sure."

The boy faltered, staring at the objects in his hand. The falcon ruffled its feathers indignantly and settled down. After a lengthy pause, the little fellow nodded.

"I think I might do it without risk, sire."

"Splendid! You're a good lad! Just hand it to her privately, and I'll see that you get another piece of gold."

"Oh, thank you, sire!"

"But as you love her—*tell no one else!* You understand?"

"I wouldn't dare!"

Magnus sighed softly. "Then begone, and God speed you!"

As the page disappeared in the direction of the house, Magnus retreated into the grove. But waiting came hard, for patience was not one of his virtues and he tormented himself with possibilities. He had no illusions about his predicament. If the youngster were indiscreet or served him treacherously, he would be extremely fortunate to escape with a whole skin. He debated the advisability of bringing his horse closer in case of need, but he dreaded to leave his post in the event Rosalind should come. Furthermore, if so near to the stables, the beast might whinny and betray him.

With the passage of time, his hopes waned. She wasn't coming! Perchance she had failed to recognize the ring she herself had given him to pledge their troth; perhaps she did not grasp the significance of the message? After all, he brooded, she was only a child—fifteen, no, by God, she was seventeen now! Nevertheless, she was still young and unworldly.

Unaccustomed to nervousness, Magnus didn't know what to do with himself. He paced restlessly back and forth until he had worn a track in the woods. He loosed his sword a score of times, and as often toyed with his poniard. He convinced himself something had gone awry. Doubtless Sir Gregory had discovered the subterfuge and was this very moment berating Rosalind before turning loose his dogs and men. The possibility was more than Magnus could stand. Better by far to ride up to the mansion and beard the old lion in his den than sulk here in the forest!

He had actually started for his horse when the sound of running footsteps stayed him. Hand to hilt, he turned back, keeping to the shelter of the trees. It was Rosalind—hurrying down the shaded path toward him! Still hidden from her view, Magnus stood lost in admiration.

She was small, yet perfectly proportioned. Every facet of her person reflected style and breeding—from the silky black hair frizzed atop her head and laced in place with pearls to the elegant gown of scarlet velvet with its drum-like French *vertingale*.

Magnus caught his breath. Could this enchanting woman have flowered from the budding child he had kissed farewell less than two years ago? It seemed incredible! Yet those flawless features— the wide, trusting eyes, the piquant nose, the full-lipped mouth— could belong to no one else. Until this moment, he had been half-fearful lest in memory he had idealized her overmuch, but in the reality she beggared even his romantic imaginings.

The gay, rollicking greeting he had planned evaporated and of a sudden he found himself overawed by her breathtaking maturity. For perhaps the first time in his life, Magnus Carter became self-conscious. Then as she paused by the turnstile to look anxiously about, his confidence returned. Removing his hat, he stepped into the open.

"Roz!" he called softly.

Turning swiftly, she stared at him a moment as if unable to believe her eyes.

"Magnus! Oh dear Lord, it's really you!" Then with a cry of pleasure she was in his arms.

He kissed her tenderly at first; then, with the feel of her body next to his own after the years of separation, his natural ardor soared until she had to tear her mouth away to breathe.

"Oh, Magnus, Magnus, I can't believe it's true!" she gasped. "It has been so awfully long!"

30

Without reply, he placed both hands on her shoulders and held her at arm's length while he devoured her with his eyes. She flushed under the intensity of his gaze.

"Why do you stare at me like that?" she laughed.

"I'm trying to adjust myself. On my oath, Roz, you are more beautiful than even I remembered! No, don't speak for a moment. Just let me look at you!"

She colored prettily. "Then you are not disappointed?"

"*Disappointed?* Good Lord . . . !" He pulled her hungrily toward him and she again surrendered ardently to his embrace.

Finally she drew back her head, laughing half-hysterically. "Let me go a minute!"

"I'm never going to let you go again!" he vowed, but she struggled laughingly away.

"Wait, you goose!"

She stepped back a pace, and after a hurried readjustment of her costume, called softly, "Donnie!"

The head of the little page popped from behind a tree.

"Aye, my lady?"

"Sit here by the stile, like a good boy. I'm going for a little walk. If anyone comes this way, you give me that hawk-cry of yours."

The youngster beamed. "Depend on it, my lady!"

Intoxicated with happiness, Magnus tossed the boy a handful of coins.

"Amuse yourself with these, younker."

"Bless you, sire!"

Rosalind linked an arm through one of Magnus'. "Now we're safe," she whispered. "Let's go down by the brook."

Too full of emotion for talk, Magnus could only nod his head. The past and the present had intermingled into a strange, dream-like confusion. During the interminable months of separation, he had envisioned this reunion so graphically that now, paradoxically, the reality itself seemed unreal.

Together they moved slowly down a cloister of aged oaks while he savored the loveliness of her—the perfume of her hair, the sibilant swish of her garments, the grace of her every movement and, most potent of all, the tender pressure of her arm.

"I nigh fainted from surprise when Donnie handed me your ring." She laughed happily, and to his hungry ears it sounded like the music of silver bells. "He was so adorable about it. He suspected you were a fairy prince. My love, you are as bronzed and lithe as a savage!"

"And you," he murmured, "are almost too wonderful to be human!"

31

She raised twinkling eyes to his. "*You* know I'm human, Magnus!"
His pulse quickened. "I'm glad you haven't forgotten that."

"Forgotten? Oh, Magnus, as if I could ever forget that night!
I've thought of it a hundred times! It was like climbing to a lofty
mountain, then suddenly soaring through space into a warm valley
of sleep! I'll always treasure every moment of it!"

He drew his arm out of hers and put it around her shoulder. "If
such moments are treasure to you, sweetheart, I'll make you rich
beyond all count of man," he told her huskily. "For I'm home to
stay. I swear it!"

She trembled slightly, but made no comment. They walked in
silence onto an ancient bridge spanning a gorge. Rosalind leaned
her forearms on the crumbling rail and stared down at the brown
water foaming over the rocks.

"Have you heard what happened to Father?" she asked finally.

He nodded. "Aye, and I'm sorry about it. When we are married,
we shall go to France and visit him. I don't care what the Queen's
ministers . . ."

Sighing, she turned slowly to face him. "Honey sweet, I'm afraid
we cannot wed."

It took some time for her meaning to penetrate his happy
delirium.

"Cannot wed? What are you trying to tell me?"

His voice had risen unconsciously, so she laid a soft hand over
his lips.

"Don't shout, lover!" she pleaded. "Listen to me! Please!"

He wrenched his head away and caught her by the arms. "Tell
me!" he demanded. "Have you changed toward me?"

"Magnus Carter! Are you daft? As God's my witness, I love you
more than ever—if that's possible! Now stay until you hear what
has happened since you went away."

He exhaled in a long quivering sigh. "I'll listen," he said grudgingly, "but I don't care what's happened. It has nothing to do with
us."

She gave him a tender, almost maternal smile. "I'm afraid it has,
darling. You see, when Father got into that awful trouble, he had to
flee so precipitately he couldn't take me with him. Uncle Gregory
agreed to give me a home and was appointed my guardian. That
changed everything."

He snorted impatiently. "Bah! Your uncle can't interfere with us!
Your father agreed to our marriage on the single condition that I
made enough money to settle down and care for you properly. Well,
I've done that! So Sir Gregory Duane can nurse his sick belly and
be damned!"

32

She stamped her tiny foot. "Magnus, are you going to act like a headstrong child, or will you listen to me?"

"Go ahead!"

"It has not been easy for me, I can promise you that! It has been like living in a big prison, and I used to pray every night that you would come and take me away. But you never even wrote . . ."

"I wrote at least once a month!" he interrupted heatedly.

"Well, I never received your letters. I thought something must have happened to you. Uncle tried to be kind to me, in his peculiar way, then decided that I should marry. I told him Father had promised that I could marry you, but he just brushed my wishes aside and brought up the name of Sir Peter Beckles."

"Aye, I heard about *that!*" growled Magnus ill-temperedly.

"You are making it very difficult for me, Magnus," she chided. She paused so long, he prompted her: "Well, let's hear the rest of it!"

"I refused, of course, and we had some stormy scenes. I assured him that I loved you, and only you, but he grew angry and forbade me ever to see you or mention your name again."

"He did more than that!" fumed Magnus. "He intercepted my letter to your father and sent the bailiffs after me."

Her eyes widened, then she shook her head. "I'm not surprised. I, too, wrote to Father, reminding him of his promise and begging him to intercede with Uncle Gregory. I never received an answer."

"Jethro Maynard is not the man to go back on his word!"

"Oh, I know that! I also know that he has written to me. Donnie, the page, saw several letters from France addressed to me, but Uncle refused to let me have them. I guess he means to hold them until after the wedding."

Magnus went wild with fury. "By God, he can't do that! We'll get married right away! You are a woman with a right . . ."

"Darling, darling, please cool down! You know I'm not of age. Uncle is my legal guardian and he would have the law on us!"

He stepped away and took an angry turn about the bridge. "God's life, this is ridiculous! I have it! I'll go to France and get a deposition from your father! That will settle the matter once and for all!"

She made a helpless little gesture with her hands. "Dear Lord, I wish that were possible! But there isn't time. Uncle and Sir Peter are settling up some private business they have here and we are all leaving for London the day after tomorrow for the wedding. You see, Sir Peter has been appointed to a diplomatic post in Spain and we must leave . . ."

"You're not going to Spain and I don't want to hear that dog's name again!" shouted Magnus, beside himself. Suddenly he was struck by an idea. "Look, where are those letters from your father?"

She glanced at him sharply. "Why . . . why I suppose Uncle has them locked in the solar! But merciful heavens, you are not dreaming of . . . ?"

He smiled without mirth. "Exactly! Tell me—where are Duane and this court fop now?"

She toyed nervously with a wisp of lace. "They left this morning and are expected back late tonight. But, my honey sweet—it would be utter madness to attempt it!"

A ghost of humor softened his smile and he took her into his arms.

"Sweetheart, my *madness* is all for you!"

She kissed him passionately. "Oh, I love your recklessness in spite of my better sense!" She laughed excitedly. "I wish we were married right this minute!"

Once again Magnus felt the blood begin to pound in his veins. He scanned the sun, now settling over the grove, and forced temptation aside. Having waited two long years, he could wait a few hours more.

"Will you help me?" he asked.

"You know I will—any way I can."

He drew away from her and put his dagger into her hand. "Come —draw me a plan of the house in the dirt."

She went down on her knees and, with a tremulous hand, traced a rough sketch of the floor plan on the ground.

"The solar is here on the first floor, right over the cellar," she explained breathlessly. "I'm almost positive the letters are locked in Uncle's desk."

"Good! Now where is your bedroom?"

"Here—over the buttery." She looked up at him. "Sweet Lord, you're not intending to . . . ?"

Laughing, he lifted her to her feet. "Not tonight. What I want to know is—can we see your window from here?"

"I believe so. Yes, it's the last in the top row; the one furthest away!"

"Now about the servants: when do they retire?"

She shuddered slightly. "They are usually in their quarters by nine of the clock. That is, all but the gatekeeper."

"Splendid! When they have all turned in, will you slip down and unbolt the front door?"

"Oh, yes, Magnus! Then we can . . ."

He silenced her gently. "No, I'll handle this alone. When you unbolt the door, go back to your room and set a lighted candle in

34

the window where I can see it from here. Leave the rest to me. Agreed?"

She put her arms about him and leaned her forehead wearily on his shoulder. "Oh, my love, I'm afraid! What if you should be caught? Uncle is so ruthless and . . ."

He chuckled with mounting enthusiasm. "*Me* caught? Don't be ridiculous! Why, half the catchpolls in England have been trying to catch me these past two years!" He kissed her fears away. "Come, sweetheart, we must be getting back. I have some figuring to do."

Chapter 3

AFTER Rosalind had reluctantly left him, Magnus reconnoitered the grounds. The high stone wall surrounding the courtyard at first appeared impregnable, but a closer inspection disclosed a jagged rift on the west portion which would offer sufficient hand-hold to an agile seaman. This would get him into the quadrangle; how he was to get out was a problem he dreaded to consider.

Sturdy old vines had fashioned a web across the front of the solar's wing, and, for a while, Magnus pondered the practicability of attempting an entrance through the big oriel window. Eventually, he decided against it. The window would doubtless be locked and the noise of forcing it might attract attention. No, his original scheme was the only feasible one; he must enter the manor by the front door. If he blundered into a servant—well, since he could expect no quarter, he would give none.

He returned to the bridge and, squatting on his haunches, studied the plan Rosalind had drawn until dusk blotted it from his vision. Then, shaking his head, he moved to a position that afforded him a clear view of her window. It was not the personal danger that troubled him; it was the possibility of failure.

Thus began his devotional watch. After a while, the impetuous song of the rushing water began to join voice with his own mounting impatience. *Hurry, hurry, hurry!* Twilight gave way to darkness and Magnus' shadow abandoned him. A few timid stars peered from the glowering sky, but were quickly obscured by black clouds. The wind commenced to moan, softly at first, then with vigor.

Magnus' apprehensiveness increased. *Man* he did not fear, but this was the legendary *Abbot's Way* which every West Countryman knew to be the haunt of the *yeth-hounds* and the *ghost-lady's* phantom coach which, guided by headless horsemen, roamed the territory on such a night as this in search of victims. Let strangers scoff; Magnus knew these things to be so. With a shudder, he recalled the last verse of the ancient rhyme:

> I'd rather walk a hundred miles,
> And run by night and day
> Than have that carriage stop for me,
> And hear my ladye say:
> Now pray step in and make no din,
> Step in with me to ride,
> There's room, I trow, by me for you
> And all the world beside.

Shuddering, he drew his cloak about his shoulders and fondled his sword hilt. He tried to keep his mind on Rosalind and the precious moments they had just spent together. But when he realized how much depended on his success in recovering the letters from her father, he was tortured by anxiety.

The rain began, tentatively, then with confidence. Lightning scrawled a blazing challenge across the sky. Somewhere in the distance, a mastiff bayed dismally. Magnus took shelter under an oak, but restlessness drove him into the open again, and he strode up and down the bridge, a victim of his imagination.

He concluded Rosalind had changed her mind; she wasn't going to help him. She was like her father—unpredictable. He cursed himself for letting her get away from him after he had held her in his arms; he should have spirited her away and arranged the details later with her father. Now he had missed the opportunity!

But had he? Why not go up to the manor, now that old Duane and this damned Sir Peter were both absent, and bluff his way past the gatekeeper? Aye, by God, he'd do it! What were a handful of oafish men-at-arms to Magnus Carter who had boarded Spanish galleons when the odds had been three to one?

He was on the verge of leaving his post when a candle gleamed abruptly in the darkness! To his overwrought nerves, it blazed like a tar barrel.

With the end of suspense, his nervousness vanished. Having

studied the landmarks carefully, he was able to move through the darkness with certainty. He scrambled up the bank, crossed the unused moat and groped his way along the wall until he relocated the cleft. A few moments later he reached the top.

He lay flat on the cold stone, listening for the growl of a dog, but heard nothing save the spatter of rain on the flagstones and the thumping of his own heart. Edging over the rim, he hung briefly by his hands before dropping into the courtyard.

Sword in hand, he followed the masonry until he reached the front door of the house. There he paused again, before setting his shoulders against the stout oak timbers which had been built to withstand an enemy. To his intense relief, the door gave grudgingly, and a widening rectangle of light shimmered on the wet flagging.

He sheathed his sword and unlimbered his dagger. Cautiously scraping the gravel and mud from his feet, he eased inside and closed the door.

After the abysmal blackness of the outside, the candle-lit interior seemed blinding. He crouched in the narrow entrance porch until his eyes readjusted, then moved soundlessly to the screens that marked the lower end of the great hall.

Blessedly, the hall was empty. It was a bleak, lofty room, going clear up to the roof and dividing the manor into two halves. Dark wainscoting robbed the few candles of their strength and left the space above the beams in shadow. Along the inner wall stood a row of gleaming suits of armor, leaning on upright lances like spectral sentinels.

Magnus grimaced ruefully and tiptoed the length of the planked floor to the newel staircase leading to the solar, the private sitting room of the master. Gaining the door without event, he took a last glance behind to make certain he had not been observed, then slipped inside and closed the door.

The solar was softly illuminated by a hanging candelabrum. Magnus rested a few moments to catch his breath. Fortunately, heavy velvet drapes had been drawn over the oriel windows facing on the courtyard, so he was not likely to be seen by anyone on the outside. However, since his first step was to secure an avenue of retreat in the event he was surprised, he examined the room with care.

On the front, the solar was largely taken up by the oriel. The west wall had no windows and was paneled entirely save for a tremendous fireplace, large enough to stand in. The mantel was supported on either side by a marble griffon, and in the space above was an elaborate carving of the Duane crest.

Directly across the room from the fireplace was a massive desk, over which hung a French mirror. Magnus grinned optimistically.

If Rosalind had been correct in her surmise, those precious letters were in that desk.

The remaining, or rear wall, was hung with tapestries, except for a small, leaded window. To Magnus' chagrin, he discovered it opened only into an inner court which, being walled on the ground floor by the kitchens, scalding-room, brew-house and buttery, would have no outside exit. He might as well be trapped in the solar as in that quadrangle.

Disappointed, he moved over to the desk. As Rosalind had forewarned him, it was securely locked. He forced the point of his dagger over the edge of the middle drawer, directly above the lock, and gave it a wrench. The lock held.

Cursing softly, he tried again. But as he braced himself for another effort, he had a sudden premonition he was not alone in the room. The sensation was devastating! He found it difficult to breathe. Then a vague flicker of movement above him caught his attention. He raised his head—and found himself staring into the face of a man!

Magnus froze, immobile, too startled to help himself. The hair tingled along his nape and he was certain his heart had stopped beating. The gaunt ascetic features of the other seemed to belong to a bird of prey. He couldn't believe it was a human face, and for a fraction of time, he feared one of the marble griffons had come alive.

Abruptly it dawned on him that he was staring into the huge mirror, and that the creature—whatever it was—stood *behind* him. With a sharp oath, he sprang to his feet and turned with the poniard in his hand—

The room was empty!

He felt suffocated. Rather would he have faced a company of armed men than that haunted blankness. He glared about in panic. Had his imagination tricked him? Turning back to the mirror, he tried to calculate where the *thing* must have stood, but all he saw now was the sooty blackness of the hearth. With his dagger poised, he warily approached the fireplace and peered inside.

There was nothing there. Not even an ash marred the cleanliness.

He began to doubt his sanity, and the impulse to flee almost overwhelmed him, but he stifled it. After risking his neck to get this close to the object of his search, he did not intend to be frightened away by ghosts. He ran his fingers over one of the griffons to make sure it was still marble, then chuckling at his own gullibility, he returned to his task.

However, when he again dropped to his knees before the desk, his breath was jerky and his hands trembled clumsily. From far

38

away came the bark of a mastiff, and the fear that it might herald the return of the Duane party made him work with a desperate urgency. Yet despite his impatience to be finished, he found his eyes straying from time to time to the mirror overhead. But the apparition did not reappear.

At last the sturdy lock yielded to his skill and the drawer slid open. He came erect with a relieved sigh. Inside were two thin packets of letters, carefully bound with ribbon. Choosing one at random, he held it closer to the candelabrum.

The creak of a stair beyond the door set his nerves on edge. Had he imagined that, also? He stood perfectly still, his head cocked. No—there it was again! In despair he snatched up the other packet, shut the drawer and sprang for the oriel. He had barely secreted himself behind the heavy drapes when the door opened slowly and a figure sidled into the room.

Tensed, Magnus appraised the newcomer. Of one thing he was certain: this was not the man he had seen in the mirror. He was short and stocky, with blunted features, and though he wore the dress of a gentleman, his actions were those of a thief. His soft-soled slippers made no sound on the heavy rug and he kept glancing over his shoulder in the manner of a nervous bird.

Magnus watched him, mystified. He went directly to the desk, appearing surprised to find it unlocked. Opening the main drawer, he rummaged among the loose papers within, holding each in turn to the light. His low grunts of disappointment were audible.

Though his conduct was furtive, the fellow seemed in no hurry, but to Magnus, crouched like a trapped animal behind the drapes, the passing moments were agonizing. Then once again he heard the bark of a dog, and with it the sound of horses. He turned his head. Through the window, he could see the link-bearers lighting horsemen through the main gate.

Frantically he peered between the curtains, expecting the other marauder to flee, but either the rain or the heavy drapes deadened the noise of the riders to the man in the room, for he continued his examination, apparently oblivious of his danger. Not finding what he wanted in the desk, he began moving along the walls, tapping the wainscoting as if seeking a hidden panel.

Magnus did not know what to do. It was now too late to escape through the window and climb down the vines, for the courtyard was already teeming with dogs and men. He wondered if it would be possible to overcome the stranger.

Then to his everlasting horror, the man swung around and moved directly toward the oriel. This act took the decision away from Magnus and removed his doubts. While he had not counted on a killing, there was nothing for it but to make one quick thrust and take to his heels. If he was successful in that, there was a fair chance that Sir Gregory would not come to the solar after his long ride, and Magnus might effect his exit later. Howbeit, if the thief screamed in the dying, Magnus was undone. He cautiously raised his poniard and waited for the other to come within striking distance.

But the fellow dawdled uncertainly, and before he quite reached the oriel, the door burst open and three armed men rushed into the solar.

"There's the dastardly spy!" rasped the oldest of the trio. "Seize him!"

So complete was the surprise, the two younger men sprang forward and seized the thief before he found his voice.

"Sir Gregory! Sir Gregory!" he protested. "I am no spy! I am your guest!"

The old man who had spoken first closed the door and stood with his back against it, leaning on his sword. From the sunken, feverish eyes, emaciated legs and swollen belly, Magnus guessed him to be Sir Gregory Duane.

The other pair, he did not recognize. One was a veritable giant in a rough leather jerkin and the livery of a man-at-arms, but the other was a tall, virile courtier with black wavy hair and alert eyes. He was magnificently costumed in a blue Venetian cloak over a peascod doublet of rose-colored velvet.

Having drawn no response from Duane, it was to this man the prisoner now appealed.

"In God's name, Sir Peter, don't scowl at me as if I were a thief! I came down here as your companion!"

Magnus whistled soundlessly. So, this *magnifico* was his rival—the great Sir Peter Beckles!

Beckles was frowning. "Howbeit, that does not explain what you are doing in this room, Moley."

"Explain?" cried the man. "Great God, is there anything amiss in a guest walking into a solar? What have I done to be treated as a common criminal?"

"That remains to be seen," wheezed Duane. "You claimed to be too sick to ride with us today, yet on my return, I find you prowling in my private sitting room. A suspicious circumstance for a stranger, I trow."

"Surely not a stranger, sire! Sir Peter can vouch for me!"

The stern old knight shot a sidelong glance at Beckles, who merely shrugged.

"As I told you, sire, he came recently from France bearing letters from our comrades Arundel and Fitzherbert, and offering himself

40

as an experienced courier. He goes by the name of Roger Moley."

"Goes by?" echoed the prisoner with a fine show of indignation. "Do you even doubt my name, Sir Peter?"

Breathlessly taking it all in, Magnus felt a grudging admiration for the fellow's nerve. His predicament was certainly unenviable, for there was something inexplicably foreboding in the attitudes of the new arrivals; it was almost as if they had *expected* to find him there. No one bothered to answer Moley's last question, and in the portentous silence which followed it, old Duane locked the door, pocketed the key, then limped painfully over to the desk. He tested the drawer before glancing inside. With no change of expression, he pushed a chair into position facing the prisoner and eased his sick body into it.

"So," he began with deceptive mildness, "you came from France to offer yourself as a courier in our Cause?"

Moley's shoulders straightened slightly. "Before God, that is the truth, sire! I have been trusted in that capacity in the past, yet peradventure you are not satisfied with my credentials, I'll cheerfully withdraw my offer."

"Not so fast, not so fast!" growled Duane. "We may have done you an injustice here, and a faithful courier might, perchance, be of use to us. Let's not be hasty. I presume you come well recommended?"

"Why, I gave Sir Peter letters from . . ."

"I know, I know," Sir Gregory interrupted. "Yet methinks letters could be forged. We have to be careful. Are you acquainted with others in France in addition to Arundel and Fitzherbert?"

"Certainly, sire! I am familiar with nearly all the faithful."

"Jethro Maynard?"

Magnus winced at the name, but Moley only smiled. "Your brother-in-law? Oh, yes, Sir Gregory; I stayed at his home near Paris not ten days past."

"H'mmn! Possibly you know Mendoza?"

"I know the Spanish ambassador intimately, sire!"

The old man stroked his gray beard reflectively. "Egad, Peter," he rumbled, eying Beckles who had relaxed against a chair back, "it appears we may owe your friend Moley an apology. What?" He turned his shrewd eyes back to the latter. "You sound well connected, my man. By the way, have you ever met Ambassador Mendoza's confessor, Frey Alonso de Cigales?"

It seemed to Magnus that Moley hesitated an instant before agreeing.

"On occasions too numerous to mention, sire!"

Sir Gregory smiled at Beckles. "That should clear up the doubt,

Peter. By my troth, if our esteemed friend Father Alonso sponsors him, Moley must be reliable!"

"Unquestionably," concurred Sir Peter.

Moley smiled the smile of a man at ease. "Unfortunately, gentlemen, I neglected to secure a recommendation from that esteemed Jesuit," he regretted.

"Pshaw! A small oversight we can soon correct," Duane assured him. Then rising, with the infinite caution of a man to whom every bodily movement is agony, he moved over to the fireplace. His bony fingers touched a hidden spring under the mantel. The back of the firebox rolled silently open.

"Father!" Duane called softly. "Will you come out to meet an old friend?"

Magnus' eyes bugged when, as though conjured by legerdemain, a black-garbed figure stepped out of the very bowels of the hearth. When the man moved into the radius of light, Magnus recognized the vulturine face he had seen in the mirror.

But Magnus' reaction was as nothing compared to Moley's. He gave a piteous bleat of terror as the priest crossed toward him, and would have fallen had not the burly retainer supported him.

Duane's grin was ghastly. "What?" he jeered. "No embrace between old comrades? What's wrong, Father Alonso? Don't you recognize Moley?"

As the Jesuit moved into the center of the room, Magnus had a clear look at him. He was thin to a point of emaciation, with a narrow fringe of black hair around his tonsure. His expression was so cold, Magnus was certain if he touched the flesh, it would feel the same way.

After a painful pause, Frey Alonso spoke (or, more aptly, made his pronouncement) with a strong Spanish accent, sounding each word as clearly as a striking bell.

"I . . . have . . . never . . . seen . . . him . . . before!"

It was a death sentence if Magnus ever heard one!

Duane stumbled into his chair, his manner changing from silk to steel.

"Now, by God, we're getting somewhere! Let's have an end to this comedy! Who are you, knave? Who sent you here?"

Moley made one last valiant attempt to bluster it through.

"Sire! Sire! Hear me! This man is not Alonso Cigales!" he cried desperately. "He is the impostor, not I! I swear it before our Sacred Virgin. . . ."

Duane nodded to the pock-marked giant in the leather jerkin. "Groswick—*get the truth!*"

The big man bared his teeth. "Aye, m'lud!" In a blur of motion

42

he looped a cord noose around Moley's neck and cinched it tight.

"Now *talk*, ye dog!"

The captive sank to his knees, clawing futilely at the garrote. Groswick merely gave it another turn, and Moley's face purpled.

With his head cocked, Beckles watched intently. "Not too hard," he advised lazily. "Give him sufficient air for voice."

When the torturer slackened the cord, Moley groveled on the rug. "Have mercy, sires!" he gasped. "Dear Jesus, have mercy!"

"Who sent you here?" Duane reiterated dispassionately.

Once again Moley babbled his innocence, but Groswick was plainly a man of experience. He rammed a knee against the victim's spine and drew his head far back, slowly twisting the garrote. Moley jerked and threshed convulsively and his eyes protruded from his blackening face.

Magnus flinched, and it took all his will power to keep from plunging out the window into the courtyard below. Only the certainty of death restrained him, for the men-at-arms were still fussing with their horses, and the bandogs were loose.

Meanwhile, Frey Alonso had moved around behind Sir Gregory to lean over the back of his chair. Beckles remained with one hip perched on the desk.

After an interminable time, Moley made a flutter of assent with his hands. Duane nodded at Groswick. When the pressure was released, Moley toppled onto his face.

The old man gave him no peace. "Your answer?" he barked.

"May God Almighty help me!" gagged Moley. "I was commanded here by Thomas Phelippes!"

Beckles sprang to his feet with an oath. "*Phelippes!* Mother of God, Phelippes is Walsingham's chief agent! Do you think he suspects . . ."

"We'll see, we'll see," Duane grunted coolly. "Now, *spy*, what were you assigned to steal here? The truth, mind you!"

Magnus caught his breath. What sort of a plot had he stumbled upon? Sir Francis Walsingham was Queen Elizabeth's Principal Secretary, an implacable enemy of papistry and Spain, a friend and ardent supporter of Drake, and perhaps more than any other loyal subject in the realm responsible for suppressing religious insurrection in England. For the time being, curiosity made Magnus forget his own plight.

Moley was coughing and massaging his lacerated throat. "A list of traitors," he panted at last, "and any other incriminating papers I could find. Phelippes suspects letters were passing through here between Mary Stuart and France. Before God, sires, I was only obeying . . ."

43

Beckles cursed furiously and bent over him. "Was my name involved? Did that swine Phelippes mention *me?* Speak, you treacherous dog!"

"No, Sir Peter, no! Your name was not spoken!"

"Thank God for that!" breathed Beckles, mopping his forehead.

Old Duane's short laugh sounded like a death rattle. "Bah, stop fretting, Peter!" he sneered. "We won't dirty your precious skirts. You're much too valuable to us as you are." He turned his attention to the wretch on the floor.

"Now give us back those papers you stole!"

Moley raised up on his hands. "I didn't get any papers, sire!"

"Bowels of God!" thundered Duane. "Am I to be kept up all night by these damnable lies! Search him, Peter! I know he's got them!"

Despite Moley's protestations, Groswick looped the garrote around his neck and stretched him on his back while Beckles went through his clothing methodically. Finally, Beckles straightened.

"He doesn't have them, Sir Gregory."

"He *must* have!" stormed the old man. "I myself locked that desk this morning! It is now empty!"

Beckles spread his hands resignedly. "There's nothing on him now."

Moley began to babble hysterically. "I swear before my Maker, I stole no papers, sire! The drawer was unlocked when I came in, and I . . ."

"You lying dog! Frey Alonso stood directly behind you and watched you pry open that drawer with a dagger!"

"No, sire, *no!* As God's my witness, I did not!"

"*Groswick!*"

As the garroter twisted his noose, the Jesuit touched the old knight's arm.

"One moment, sire! This man . . ."

Duane waved him aside. "Keep out of this, Father!" he commanded brusquely. "I know how to deal with a spy caught redhanded in my house!"

"But I'm trying to tell you . . ." persisted the priest, but the old man was beyond reasoning.

"Silence!" he roared at the priest. "Wring it out of him, Groswick!"

Frey Alonso sighed. "*Requiescat in pace!*" he mumbled softly.

Meanwhile, the realization that he would be forfeiting his own life to no avail was all that kept Magnus from springing out of hiding. Moley, he knew, was doomed; his confession, rather than the supposed theft, had sealed his death warrant. Yet as he stood transfixed in indecision, Magnus was suffocated by a sense of guilt. There was no way to help Moley. With the solar door locked, he

44

could not hope to fight his way past four desperate men. He turned to the window. The grooms had gone with the horses, but the mastiffs still roamed the quadrangle. He was debating whether to take his chances with them, when another thought occurred to him. If he could not go *down,* perhaps he could go *up!* As he remembered it, the vines interlaced the front of the wing from ground to eaves!

He took another look into the room. Groswick was going about his chore with enthusiasm, while Moley flopped on the rug like a beached fish. Inured as he was to violence, Magnus was revolted. He turned away, but before he could slip outside, there was a sudden quiet.

"A pipeful more air, Groswick," he heard Duane growl. "Methinks he'll talk now."

Magnus couldn't resist another peek through the drapes. Moley was hanging from the end of the garrote, and when released, dropped like a wet towel.

"Bring him to, bring him to!" rasped the old knight.

Groswick prodded the victim with his foot. That failing, Beckles knelt down and examined him.

"Sire!" he cried. "He's *dead!*"

Duane started to his feet, only to sink back cursing.

"You damned clumsy bungler!" he raged at the startled giant. "Don't you know your business?"

Groswick gaped stupidly at the body. "B-b-but, m'lud, I . . . I on'y gi' 'im a gentle twist er two! Ye saw it yersel'! 'Tweren't enough to 'urt a cat, I swear!"

Sir Gregory threw up his hands in temper. "God's death! Don't you fools understand—there's enough evidence in those letters of Mary Stuart to have us all hanged, drawn and quartered! They *have* to be in this room, for we caught him here! Doubtless he hid them after Father Alonso left his hiding place to summon us! Don't stand gawking—*search the place!*"

Fearing lest his sands would run out if he tarried longer, Magnus eased open the sash and slid one leg over the sill. He was groping for a hand-hold on the vines, when the friar's words froze him.

"You are wasting your time, Sir Gregory! Moley is *not* the man who stole the letters!"

This announcement was greeted by an ominous silence. Magnus was no less astounded than the others. He held rigid, lest the thumping of his heart betray him.

"What's that, what's that?" exploded Duane at last. "What are you saying? Didn't we catch him right after you reported seeing him pry . . ."

45

"Moley doubtless came after Mary Stuart's letters," Alonso interrupted. "He confessed as much. Nevertheless, I repeat—*he is not the man I saw open the drawer! I marked the other well!*"

"Bowels of God!" trumpeted Duane. "Why did you not say so before?"

The Jesuit regarded him stonily. "My attempts to tell you this were brutally shouted down!"

"Dear Jesus!" wailed Beckles in panic. "If her Majesty sees those letters, it will mean my . . ."

"A pox on that heretical Jezebel!" bellowed the old man. He jerked the key out of his pocket and flung it at Groswick. "The other dog must have been Moley's accomplice. Rouse up the men! Cover all the roads and scour the grounds! The knave cannot have gone far!"

Magnus shuddered, thinking of his own horse tethered in the woods near by.

"Aye, m'lud!" cried Groswick, striding for the door. " 'E won't get far, I trow! An' w'en I catch 'um, I'll slit 'is bloody gullet!"

"You'll do nothing of the kind!" screeched the old man. "You'll bring him here alive! *Alive,* you addle-pated oaf!"

Magnus had heard enough to last him a long time. Under cover of Groswick's noisy exit, he caught a sturdy vine and swung into the darkness.

Chapter 4

AFTER taking the precaution to close the window gently with his foot, Magnus started his perilous ascent. He had anticipated it would be as simple as scrambling up the ratlines of a ship, but he was quickly disillusioned. The main stem of the vine wandered tortuously over the face of the wall, first up and then down, as if in no hurry to reach the roof. Yet follow it he must, for the lesser branches were sometimes rotten and at all times untrustworthy. Twice within the first two yards, he came within a hair of crashing into the courtyard below.

He was barely halfway to the eaves when Groswick burst out of the house, followed by two link-bearers, and bellowed for the grooms. The rain had ceased, and the puddles pock-marking the flagstones acted as reflectors for the lights. In a matter of minutes, the quadrangle became an inferno of blazing torches, shouting men, nervous horses and eager hounds.

Under the circumstances, Magnus dared not continue, so with infinite caution, he wriggled in among the foliage to make himself as inconspicuous as possible, and hugged the wall. But after a time, the unnatural position affected his muscles until he doubted his ability to hang on much longer. His limbs grew cramped to a point of numbness, yet he clung stubbornly to his perch, more by sheer instinct of self-preservation than by strength, until the last rider clattered through the gate. Thereupon, he continued his laborious ascension and at long last his fingers touched the eaves.

At that point, he was confronted with a new difficulty—how to get onto the roof! To his horror, he discovered that the vines stopped just under the long overhang of the eaves. Frantic, he clawed his way under the protrusion, seeking a branch which might have had the tenacity to continue up onto the slate, but though he worked halfway along the front of the building, he found none.

His choice was a bitter one: he must either concede defeat and climb back down into the arms of his pursuers, or take the risk of making a flying grab for the ancient gutter and attempt to haul himself onto the sharply sloping roof. There was a third choice, he grimly conceded; he could release his grip and break his neck on the flagging far below. That appealed to him even less than the others.

Delay increased his danger, for his strength was ebbing, so he made his choice. Locating a spot where the gutter seemed most likely to support his weight, he let go his hold on the vine and launched into space.

His fingers closed over the rim, and for a few minutes he hung suspended in the air, trying to catch his breath. As he was about to lift himself, he heard a man yell excitedly.

"Master! Master! Come quick!"

In all his eventful life, Magnus Carter had never experienced such a sensation of pure terror. He was satisfied his end had come. That in itself was bad enough, but to be caught in such a helpless position and shot out of the air like a sitting bird was almost more than he could bear.

Sick with dread, he forced himself to look downward. A couple of grooms were leading his horse across the courtyard.

"Master!" one of them cried again. "We've found a strange 'orse!"

Magnus gasped with relief. It wasn't himself they had seen! That they had captured his nag was serious, but it wasn't fatal. The re-

47

action lent him strength, and he drew himself upward until he was able to hook one elbow in the gutter. Then swaying pendulum-like, he heaved a knee over the rim. Soon the rest of him followed and he lay on the slope, panting and quivering from exertion.

Overhead, the moon was quarreling with the storm clouds, and for once, Magnus favored the latter. When his pulse returned to normal, he drew himself to a sitting position and debated his next move. One fact was obvious: he had to be off the roof before daylight, but daylight was still hours away. He decided finally the wisest thing to do was to try and get into Rosalind's room and give her the letters from her father. As for the other letters, which had engendered so much turmoil and tragedy, he was at a loss. In a general way, he knew that Mary Stuart, the Queen of Scots and now a prisoner of Elizabeth, had been long conniving to incite the Catholic nobles of England to rebellion and enlist the armed intervention of either France or Spain. That Sir Gregory Duane should be involved in such treason seemed incredible. Yet Magnus had heard the old knight's frank admission, and now the evidence of this perfidy lay in his own doublet. The implications were staggering!

His ascent up the forty-five-degree slope was more difficult than he had expected, for the rain, after the long dry spell, had made the roof as slippery as if greased. He eased upward like an inchworm, keeping his body spread and as flat as possible, for he realized that if he once started to slip, nothing could save him.

Eventually the apex was attained and he sat astride it to steady his breathing. When the persistent moon dodged from behind a cloud, he was afforded a splendid panorama of the surrounding countryside. Far along the road and in the grounds below, the bobbing flambeaus of the searchers resembled a swarm of fireflies. Something of his old jauntiness returned. He was the fox, hiding comfortably atop the kennels while the hounds chased a false spoor. Chuckling, Magnus continued his hazardous journey.

He followed the ridge to the west wing, then headed north along that apex. His next problem was to judge when he was directly above Rosalind's window, but to a seasoned navigator trained in perspective, this gave scant concern. What tickled his sense of the dramatic was the amazement his unheralded appearance would be sure to occasion.

He calculated his distances carefully until, satisfied he was over her bedroom, he cautiously slithered down the slope to the gutter. Peering over the rim, he was delighted to find he had guessed within a couple of feet.

The sill of the window was nearly ten feet below the overhang of the eaves, but as the wall was thickly vined, he expected no diffi-

48

culty. The warm glow of candlelight behind the leaded glass made him reckless—and almost caused his undoing.

It was his plan to reverse the procedure used in mounting the roof. But in his eagerness to see his betrothed, he chose a spot too close to the window, where the grip of the vines was weakest. He eased his body over the rim until he was hanging by his hands in mid-air, then swinging back and forth to gain momentum, he let go the gutter and hurled himself at the vines.

He grasped a sturdy branch that checked his plunge—then to his horror, the vines began to pull away from the wall! It required all his self-control to suppress an involuntary scream. The process was agonizingly slow. One by one the smaller branches let go and the whole web leaned farther and farther away from the building.

Magnus could do nothing to help himself. Any movement on his part would merely hasten the disaster. When finally the vines steadied, he found himself dangling over the black abyss of the moat, a full six feet away from the wall.

Scarcely daring to breathe, he worked his way down the branches to a section where their grip was firm, then inching over to the far side of the window, he climbed up level with the sill.

Too shaken to announce his presence immediately, he clung there while his eyes devoured the scene within the room. Rosalind was sitting up in a huge bed, and to Magnus' hungry eyes, as lovely as a queen. He was slightly awed by the richness of the setting. The bedposts of imported wood were elaborately carved, and the spread, curtains and valance of the tester beautifully embroidered. It came to him abruptly that he was jealous of all this lavishness. He had never seen the like, and he wondered if, having grown accustomed to such luxury, Rosalind could readjust herself to his station. His chest of gold, which heretofore had seemed a veritable fountain-head of wealth, began now to shrink in his mind.

Suddenly, he realized that she was weeping, and immediately tenderness swept the disloyal doubt aside. He reached up and drummed his fingers on the pane.

He saw her start up in fright, and he feared she might cry out in alarm. He rapped again. This time she sprang out of bed and came running toward him. Grinning relievedly, Magnus heaved up and pressed his face against the pane.

She opened the window at once.

"Magnus! Merciful Heavens, how did you get here?"

"I guess it's the first time anyone ever climbed *down* from hell to heaven," he chuckled, crawling over the sill into the room.

When he put his arms around her waist, she arched her back and cupped his face in her hands, studying him anxiously.

49

"Oh, my sweet—what happened? I heard shouting below, then one of the servants come to warn me to keep the door locked because a thief was loose! I near died of fright!"

Magnus laughed ruefully. "I *almost died* too. But I got your letters!"

"Thank God!" She drew his face down and kissed him passionately, making little sounds of ecstasy. Then she broke away to close the window and draw the curtains. He saw her shiver slightly, so he put an arm about her shoulders and steered her toward the bed.

"Come, get under the covers, sweetheart. You're cold."

"I'm scared!" she confessed, smiling, but she slipped into bed as he suggested. When she had arranged her gown, she glanced up at him from under her long lashes. As the green flakes in her eyes caught the candlelight, Magnus felt his passions soar. Then he noticed that her face was smudged and her gown muddied. He spun around and surveyed himself in a full-length mirror.

He was appalled. His clothing, sodden by rain, was torn and plastered with mud and slime. His face was just as dirty, and even his red locks were lank and unflatteringly decorated with leaves and grime. Glancing downward, he saw a pool of muddy water forming around his feet.

He burst into laughter. "By my troth—is that scarecrow *me?* I'll swear it is the most perfect disguise I've ever worn! How in God's name did you ever recognize your Magnus?"

She gave him a knowing smile, "I'd know my Magnus anywhere, any time. Here, sit beside me and let us read Father's letters!"

"I'll make a mess of your bed, sweetheart!"

"Fiddle-dee! I'll tell the maid I got filthy leaning out the window. Hurry! I must know what he says!"

He fished the packets from his pocket, found the one addressed to her, and shoved the other back into his doublet. It seemed pointless to explain the truth about her uncle, or even the man he had wanted her to marry. That was, or would soon be, a closed chapter, and he did not want to hurt her unduly.

"Here it is, Roz!"

She seized it eagerly, and while she broke the seal, he moved a candle closer to the bed. He found himself holding his breath while she scanned the page, and exhaled relievedly when a smile illuminated her face.

"Oh, the angel!" she cried delightedly. "Read it, Magnus!"

His hands shook as he took the paper. "My blessed Daughter," Maynard had written in his fine, precise script. "I am very sorry Gregory hath distressed you by a proposal which runs counter to your wishes. Howbeit, I am writing him this night, sanctioning your

50

marriage to young Magnus Carter, since that is your desire. Magnus is a likely lad, and I have no doubt will acquire the necessary wherewithal to care for you in comfort. That is all I ask, for security is the all-important item in these troubled times, and I deeply regret my own inability to have done better by you, my dearest child.

"Our affairs here are progressing, but I will not burden you with details, since they are outside the ken of women. I myself am well enough, save for a touch of the flux, but low in spirit, for I cannot be completely happy until I know that you are. May God in His infinite wisdom hasten an early victory to our Cause so that you can soon be with, Your Loving Father."

Magnus' eyes misted—whether because of the pathos of the exiled father, or an overwhelming sense of relief, he did not know. He knelt beside the bed and pressed one small hand to his lips, unable to speak for the moment.

She fondled his damp curls with her free hand.

"Oh, Magnus, Magnus!" she whispered. "Now we can be truly married!"

"Aye," he agreed huskily.

Leaning down, she laid her check against his head. "I'll have no dowry to bring you, my love."

"*Dowry!* Good Lord—do you think I need pay for getting *you?*" He straightened cockily. "Wait until you see the chest of gold I have stored at the White Anchors! I'll make you the greatest lady in the land!"

"O-oo!" she cried, hugging him impulsively. "When can we be married? I grow impatient!"

The question tumbled him back to reality. "You had better let me have that letter," he said, after a thoughtful pause. "I'll get a few friends together, in case your uncle turns obstinate, and pay him a visit."

Her eyes widened. "Good heavens, *no!* He would have you seized as a thief!"

"He's the thief, Roz. That letter belonged to you as surely as you belong to me!"

She smiled that maternal little smile he adored so much. "I know you are not afraid of man nor devil, my sweet, but there are times when it is more practical to use guile. You leave the matter to me; I'll handle it!"

"How?"

Rosalind shrugged. "I'll have to think about it. However, now that we have Father's permission, there is nothing Uncle Gregory can do but bluster. I know! I'll tell him the letter arrived today when he was away. He hasn't actually seen the contents because the seal wasn't broken!"

Magnus frowned. "The old bear is no fool. He'll suspect the truth."

"Let him suspect! He can't *prove* me wrong. Anyhow, I have the letter, and that is all that matters." Seeing the dubious expression on his face, she chided softly: "Don't you trust my judgment, Magnus? I'm no longer a child, you know!"

He stared at her so hard, she colored. "Perhaps you had better go now!" she whispered.

He leaned toward her. "Do you want me to go, Roz?"

"I think you should."

"That is not what I asked you. Do you *want* me to go?"

Her eyes had dilated and her breasts rose and fell. She made a futile little gesture with her hands.

"Yes!" she faltered.

He brushed his cheek against hers. She closed her eyes, and he felt her body stiffen.

"Don't, lover! *Don't!* You are torturing me!"

"We are perfectly safe here!"

"No, Magnus, no! We'll be married soon, and then . . ."

"We are married now, Roz—in the sight of God!"

"*Please!* It is wrong. I want to be good! Help me, Magnus!"

"Why is it wrong? Because we lack the prattling of a priest? Is that what you mean?"

She began to cry softly. "Oh, God, I don't know what I mean!" She threw her arms around his neck and pressed her body tightly against his. Her teeth bit sharply into his lips. Then she tried to fling away.

"I'm bad, bad! I hate myself!" she sobbed.

"Egad, why?"

"Because I want you! No, it's stronger than that! It's lust!" Her arms wound around his neck and she was whispering in his ear. "My whole body lusts for you—for yours! Every inch of skin, all of me, aches for you!"

"I hunger, too, Roz!" He started to untie his points with his free hand. "I know the remedy."

She sank against the pillow, trembling, her eyes smoky now, her breathing spasmodic.

"I'm bewitched! Hurry, lover, before I come to my senses!"

He swung around and bent down to pull off his boots. Before he succeeded, footsteps came dragging along the corridor. Rosalind gave a startled gasp and snuffed out the candle.

"Lord help us! It's Uncle Gregory!"

52

Magnus cursed under his breath. "Damn him! Well, we'll settle the matter right now!"

She was out of bed and standing beside him. "Are you mad? Why, he'd take the letter away from us and have you killed! No, no—you must go at once! I'll deal with him!"

The steps had paused just beyond the door. Then came a sharp knock. In the darkness, Magnus could not see Rosalind's face, but he felt the tremor of her body.

"As you love me—go!" she entreated.

When the rap was repeated, she muffled her voice to simulate sleepiness.

"Who is it?"

"'Tis I," came Duane's choleric voice. "I want to talk with you."

"Just a moment, Uncle dear! I'll get up."

She shoved Magnus toward the window, and he went with reluctance. "As you love me, don't be stubborn now!" she pleaded. "You will ruin everything!"

"The old bear ruined one thing!" Magnus grumbled, half-facetiously. Then realizing the futility of further objection, he threw one leg over the sill.

Duane was growing impatient. "Hurry up, girl! What's keeping you?"

"I'm getting into my robe!" she lied.

Magnus kissed her ardently. "I'll always hate him for interrupting us, sweetheart!"

"It will be all the sweeter for the saving, my dear one. Now go!"

"When will I hear from you?"

"As soon as possible! I'll try to get a message to you tomorrow!" She fingered his face with tenderness, then backed away. "Take care of yourself, Magnus, and may God protect you!"

"Good luck! I'll be waiting at the inn!"

She blew him a kiss, not trusting herself to touch him again, and, with a short laugh, he swung out and caught the vines. As he started the descent, he heard her open the door. He was tempted to tarry until he heard what the old man had to say, but decided against it. Rosalind was a woman now, and he had complete faith that she could handle the affair.

Chapter 5

Having lost his horse, the long hike back to Plymouth was something of a nightmare to Magnus. Sometimes he floated along on the wings of fancy; more often he waded through English mud. Later, when he had time to consider the journey in retrospect, he never could piece it together into a clarified whole. Though the chase had quieted down, several times during the trip he saw searching parties, but the wind blew strongly across the moorlands, and by keeping to the leeward of the road, the dogs were unable to pick up his spoor.

In effect, his emotions were similar to the terrain, oscillating between heights of elation and low valleys of despair. He wondered how he could constrain himself until he heard from Rosalind. When would that be—tomorrow, the next day, possibly longer? Anxiety and doubts plagued him until he came nigh to turning back.

Suddenly a thought struck him as he remembered the second packet of letters, still in his doublet. By the powers, there was a weapon he had not considered! Old Duane himself had admitted there was enough evidence in that to hang them all!

On that note, his optimism soared until he laughed aloud. If Rosalind failed to turn the trick with her father's written consent, Magnus would bring his own broadside to bear! That would bend the treasonous old lion to his knees in short order! He cursed himself for not having thought of it before, and in the intoxication of his new found power, he even contemplated returning at once. Then the recollection of Moley's fate brought him to his senses. He would hold his weapon in reserve, to be used only when needed.

However, the knowledge shortened the weary road, and it was with some surprise when, on topping the crest of a hill, he saw the roofs of Plymouth shimmering before him in the gray light of dawn.

At this point, a new problem arose—his disguise had been seized with his horse. This portended trouble with Dame Prettyman, for the old biddy hated him, as she hated anyone favored by her un-

54

fortunate husband, and in her pique at having been fooled, she was almost certain to vent her spleen by notifying the bailiffs if Magnus appeared at White Anchors.

He tried to shrug aside the foreboding, but as he strode down the cobbled street, his misgiving increased until a knot formed in his stomach. It occurred to him that he had not eaten in four-and-twenty hours, nor slept in eight-and-forty. He pondered the advisability of seeking other lodgings until he could communicate with Tim, then he recalled that in his first flush of elation on seeing Rosalind, he had tossed all his gold to the little pageboy.

To his intense relief, on turning the corner near the inn, the first person he saw was Tim Prettyman himself. Magnus hailed him, and the old man hobbled to meet him.

"By Neptune, 'tis glad I am to see you, lad!" roared Tim. "W'ere's yer bloody nag?"

Magnus grinned wearily. "It's a long story, and I may have to buy you another horse. But at the moment, I'd like to get up to my room. Can you slip me in the back way without encountering your wife? *Don Ruster* was in my saddlebag."

Tim crowed with laughter and beat his brass-bound peg on the flagging.

"Aye, that I can! 'Tis a lucky star ye was born under, lad, fer the ol' termagant be away fer the nonce! One o' 'er nieces is big wi' child, an' since me ol' woman dabbles in midwifery, she's gone over to mishandle the cargo! There'll be no squalls in this anchorage 'til she returns, praise God!" He linked an arm through Magnus'. "Tell me—d'ye see yer lass?"

Magnus nodded, his tired eyes drinking in the fine old two-storied timbered building, with its carved gables and slate roof, which had become home to him. As they passed between the huge painted anchors that gave the place its salty name, he answered, "I'll tell you all about it, Tim, but first order me some food. On my oath, I haven't eaten since . . ."

"Well, damme, w'y didn't ye say so before!" cut in the old man. "Come, we'll victual yer 'olds an' put rum in yer casks, an' time enough fer gammin' later!" He limped toward the door, bellowing for Kate.

It was only when he crossed the threshold that Magnus realized how utterly exhausted he was. Dragging himself up the stairs, he collapsed into a chair, too weary to remove his mud-caked boots. The warmth of the room drugged him until he had to force himself to stay awake.

Tim hobbled in a few minutes later with two flagons of mulled rum, and before that was assimilated, Kate appeared with a tray loaded with food. She berated him profanely for sitting in his wet clothing, and despite the growls of the old man, insisted on taking off his boots herself and refusing him all food until he had changed his garments.

"You ain't got a lick of sense, I declare!" she scolded. "It is high time you found a wife!"

Magnus smiled. "I have that, Katie!"

The girl sniffed. "It's advice she'll be needing, you great hulking infant! I could tell her a thing or two!"

"Aye, no doubt," chuckled Magnus. "But I hope you won't."

Tim could not restrain his impatience. "Get out o' 'ere, Katie, before I lay stick to yer bottom! We uns want to talk."

Kate turned on him, her fists planted firmly on her ample hips.

"You'll be talking to a corpse, Master Timothy!" she retorted. "If this simple fool doesn't get some sleep. Look at him! Pouches big as saddlebags under his eyes!"

Tim spread his hands helplessly. "Mark that, lad! They be all alike! Screech at ye like a crazy parrot 'til yer seams open. An' ye want to *wed* one o' 'em! Bah, ye're balmy in the crumpet!" He banged his empty flagon on the table and reached for his stick. "By God, I'll larn ye to obey me, Katie!" he swore, starting to rise.

The girl made a face at him and flipped her skirts, then smiled gently at Magnus.

"Don't let the old gander poison your mind," she warned. "We are *not* all alike." As Magnus laughed, she stuck out her tongue at the old man and bustled out of the room.

Tim sank back with a chuckle. "I'm hag-ridden, so I am! Gimme a cut-throat crew o' jail-bait an' mutineers, an' I'll make lambs o' em wi'in a week. But a woman . . ." He shook his head despondently.

Tim's misogyny had developed into something akin to a game, and Magnus couldn't resist baiting him.

"Nonsense, Timothy! Your manner is wrong. Did you not see how easily your good wife was subdued by a little flattery? You must learn to gentle them!"

"Oh-ho! So 'tis a wizard wi' women ye be now, eh?"

"I merely understand them," Magnus said soberly.

Tim began to ruffle up belligerently, then deflated himself with a long sigh.

"Don Rooster was a fittin' name fer ye," he snorted disgustedly. " 'Tis the way o' a young cock to crow an' strut 'is fine feathers 'til the day 'is 'ead be lopped off an' 'e finds 'issel' on the spit, w'ilest the naggin' ol' 'ens squat comfortably in the nest. So crow now, ye block-'ead, fer by the signs, ye be close to the roastin' point!" He pounded his peg in exasperation. "Come, lad—I'm eager to 'ear o' yer voyage?"

56

With his stockinged feet propped comfortably on the bed, Magnus related all that had happened. Tim sat with his hands folded on his paunch and heard him out without interruption, save for a startled oath when Magnus described the treasonous letters and the death of Moley, the spy. At the conclusion, Magnus asked, "What do you make of it, Tim?"

" 'Tis plain enough," growled the old man. "Duane an' this bloody Beckles be mixin' in a papist plot to put Mary Stuart on the throne o' England. Ye say ye still 'ave the packet o' letters, lad?"

Magnus tossed the packet on the table between them. "Aye, here they are."

Tim scowled at them. "We'd better tyke 'em down to Cap'n 'Awkins. 'E'll know 'ow to get 'em to the Queen's ministers."

Magnus shook his head. "I'm not going to involve myself in a politico-religious dispute. That's what has caused all my troubles."

"*Involve?* Damme, ye're involved up to the gunnels already! 'Aven't ye the wit to see ol' Duane'll turn 'eaven an' 'ell to get back these letters?"

"No doubt. But he can have them back when I get Rosalind."

Tim was aghast. "D'ye mean to tell me ye'd put a wench afore yer Queen?"

"Would the Queen help me get Rosalind? Would John Hawkins lift a hand to help me?" Magnus countered hotly. When Tim did not reply, he went on: "You know bloody well he wouldn't. He'd give a song about 'England first.' Well, that's all right for Hawkins; he plucked enough Spanish tail-feathers to gild his own nest. But those letters are the only weapon I have against Duane, and I mean to use them if necessary!"

Tim picked up his wooden leg with both hands and moved it a couple of inches. When he spoke, it was with a soft earnestness that Magnus had never heard before.

"Aye, lad, 'tis true John 'Awkins singed King Philip's beard, times a-plenty. But 'e ain't rich, an' 'e ain't selfish. If we didn't 'ave men like 'Awkins an' Drake an' Francis Walsing'am, we wouldn't 'ave no England. If 'tis the wee wench ye desire, I 'opes ye get 'er, but this treason business be somethin' else again. Ye know me purty well, son, an' ye knows I ain't no Bible-back, yet it seems to me like the Lord's 'anded ye a great chance to 'elp yer country."

Magnus found himself too weary to argue. "Let it go, Tim," he begged. "I'll think it over. Right now all I want is sleep."

Tim clapped the arms of his chair and lumbered erect. "Mebbe a mite o' sleep'll 'elp yer thinkin'," he agreed. "Go to bed, an' w'en ye wake up—come below. Me ol' woman won't be back 'til tomorrer, so we kin broach a cask er two in peace."

When his host had gone, Magnus remained sprawled in his chair, strangely disturbed, for the very argument he had tried to avoid continued now in his consciousness. He was familiar enough with the political situation to know that many of the strongest nobles in England desired to get rid of Elizabeth and put Mary Stuart on the throne in order to bring back the Catholic religion and obliterate Protestantism. For himself, Magnus was indifferent as to which ritual was practiced, but he did not like the idea of the rebels' alliance with France and Spain. The weak voice of his little-used conscience warned him that civil war in England would bring tragedy and death to the Protestants—Protestants like old Tim and the staunch folk of Devon. Then he thought of Rosalind, and the voice was stilled. Was he to sacrifice *her* to play catchpoll for Whitehall? The Queen had ministers whose duty it was to handle plots. And hadn't Moley confessed that Walsingham's chief agent suspected Duane? It would be rank conceit to think that the Queen needed Magnus Carter to play the spy! No, he convinced himself, his first duty was to Rosalind and himself. That settled, he closed his eyes, to rest a moment before crawling into bed.

The morning sun streamed through the window, and he decided it would be wise to close the shutters. Yet when he opened his eyes, seemingly but an instant later, the sun had given way to a purple twilight. With a start, he realized he had slept throughout the day in his chair. He bounded, cursing, to his feet. Perchance a message had already arrived from Rosalind! Quivering with anticipation, he washed and hurried below.

Despite the early hour, there was a goodly crowd in the common-room. Kate was saucily serving ale and sack and exchanging banter with the patrons, while Tim hobbled from table to table playing host. Magnus paused in the doorway to see if he could recognize any of the drinkers, then satisfied there were no bailiffs among them, crossed over to where Tim awaited him.

"Ye look refreshed, lad, I trow!" greeted the old man.

"Aye, I didn't even dream. Any news for me?"

Tim shook his head. "Nary a word, though horsemen wearin' the Duane livery 'ave been thunderin' through the streets—the damn murderers!" His voice rose angrily.

"Murderers?"

"Aye!" bellowed Tim. "They trampled a wee boy to death this arternoon, not two squares from 'ere. Rode 'im down deliberate, say 'em as saw it!"

Magnus was about to comment when he noticed a man rise from one of the tables and slip furtively out the side door.

Magnus frowned thoughtfully. "You'd better keep your voice

58

down," he cautioned the innkeeper. "Some of these present may be Duane's men."

"Let 'em 'ear me, an' bad cess to 'em!" bawled the old man. "By God, this be my place, an' I want no truck wi' traitors like Gregory Duane an' 'at court pimp Peter Beckles! Tim Prettyman strikes 'is colors to no bloody Roman, an' ye can lay to 'at!"

His quarter-deck bellow had carried over the entire room, and the drinkers paused to stare at them. Magnus winced and pulled the old man into the near-by scullery.

"Stop caterwauling like a Billingsgate fishwife!" he snapped. "Can Kate fix me some supper?"

Undaunted, Tim summoned the girl, and stomped back to his patrons. Magnus followed Kate into the kitchen and lolled in the settle while she prepared the food. Watching her as she moved about the room, humming to herself, he marveled at her perpetual good humor. In spite of the everlasting nagging of Mistress Prettyman, the ofttimes grumpy moods of old Tim and the constant teasing of the patrons, Kate maintained her own unruffled poise. She was remarkably neat and clean for a serving girl, and though too robust to be termed "pretty," she was attractive in an earthy fashion. There was nothing subtle or mysterious about her, Magnus decided; her clear blue eyes and wide mouth spoke too revealingly of a frank directness. Perhaps in a different environment she might have learned some of the charming little mannerisms that made a woman so feminine and desirable—though, Lord knows, Magnus had to admit he had found her *desirable* enough! It came to him suddenly that he had never heard her called anything else but Katie, and he wondered if she had a family name. He concluded she had none, for as Tim had once told him, Kate was a foundling his wife had adopted, not out of charity, but simply because she would have a slave to work without pay.

The girl turned her head. "Did you hear about the accident, Magnus?"

He nodded. "You mean the boy who was run down? Tim tells me it was deliberate."

"Oh, I can't believe that!" she cried in quick sympathy. "Nobody could be so cruel to a poor homeless waif!" She crossed to the table and set a plate of steaming food before him. "It nigh breaks my heart to think of the wee mite laying in an old barn with nobody to bury him, and him not over twelve!"

Magnus had started to eat, when an appalling thought struck him. He dropped his fork with a clatter.

"Did you say a strange boy of *twelve* years?"

"Aye! Marry, Magnus, you're pale as a ghost!"

He was on his feet. "Tell me—where is he?"

She stared at him in amazement. "What's wrong with you, man? The child is dead, and . . ."

"Answer my question!" he cut her short. "*Where is he?*"

"Two squares west; in the old barn. Do you want me to show . . ."

Magnus crossed the kitchen in a bound. "No, no! I'll find it alone!" He slammed into the rear courtyard.

He covered the intervening distance at a dead run, yet when he reached the ramshackle old building, he hesitated, half afraid to put his suspicion to the test. Presently he brought his breathing under control and stepped into the dim interior.

By the wan light of a candle stub, he made out an old crone seated on a box. In front of her, a few planks had been set up across two trestles. On the planks lay a body.

Magnus forced himself closer. The old woman glanced up, a question in her rheumy eyes. Magnus shrugged, and in silence picked up the candle. He raised it slowly until the radius of light illumined the muddied features of the corpse.

As he feared, it was Donnie, the little page.

A cold hard knot settled in Magnus' stomach, as though his heart had suddenly petrified and dropped out of place. He stared dully at the battered face, dreading to accept the full implications. When the aged woman asked abruptly, "Ye know the bairn?" he jumped.

He waited until he could keep his voice steady. "I'm not sure," he muttered finally. He set the candle down on the planks and ran his fingers over the child's clothing.

"Ain't nuthin' on 'im now," whined the woman. "Them as run 'im down 'ave searched 'im already."

Magnus turned in her direction so sharply, she added hastily, "Wanted to find out 'oo 'e was, 'ey said!"

"Did they take anything away from him?"

She spread her hands. "Dunno! Mought be 'ey did. Four er more clustered 'round 'im so's I couldn't see. Then 'ey mounted their beasties an' galloped off, so 'ey did." She fixed Magnus with her watery eyes. "Ye know 'im?" she reiterated.

Magnus hesitated, then an innate wariness warned him against betraying himself. A wagging tongue might do him irreparable harm, and there was nothing he could do now for Donnie. Or, perhaps there was! Fortunately he had replenished the gold in his purse before leaving his room, so he extracted a coin and laid it beside the candle.

"I fear I was mistaken, yet the child reminded me of someone," he temporized. "I heard about the accident, and though a stranger,

60

I'd like to do something for the poor little fellow. Will you take this coin, mother, and see that he gets a decent burial?"

"Aye, master, that I will! An' God bless ye fer yer kindness!"

Magnus started away, then on an impulse, turned back and touched his lips to the child's brow.

"I'll pay the dogs back with interest for this, Donnie!" he vowed under his breath, then keeping his back to the old woman so she could not see his face, he hurried out.

Once beyond the paralyzing presence of the corpse, Magnus' grief turned to cold rage. What had happened was all too clear. Rosalind had sent Donnie to him with a message, and the Duane men-at-arms had intercepted him. That much was manifest. On the other hand, it was unlikely they would ride the boy down deliberately unless they had advance knowledge of his errand. Magnus' throat began to pulsate until his ruff threatened to choke him. If Duane had learned the child was seeking Magnus, it followed that the only person who could have given him the information was Rosalind herself! What in God's name had they done to her to force a confession?

The very thought sickened him, and a premonition of disaster almost overwhelmed him. He broke into a run. He would go to her at once!

Fortunately, Kate was not around to question him when he burst into the kitchen of the inn. She had probably gone to her cuddy over the stables to change for the evening's work. He went directly to his own room, and after refilling his pouch with gold, he buckled on his sword.

But in the act of leaving, he suddenly remembered the letters. His first impulse was to flaunt them in Duane's face, but a moment's reflection convinced him of the folly of such precipitation. Those letters, not his sword, were his power. With them, he could bend the old rebel to his will, but they would have to be safe from seizure.

He paced the room, trying to think coolly. Locking them in the chest with his gold would be so obvious that if Duane grabbed him and sent henchmen to search his room, it would be the first place they would examine. Then he considered giving them to either Tim or Kate, but promptly discarded the notion when he realized how seriously it would implicate them.

Finally, he decided the safest course was to hide them himself, and after a lengthy search, found a niche up under the gutter, just outside his window. By standing on the sill, he was able to slip the packet into the crevice and bend the drain back over it. Satisfied, he snuffed the candle and went downstairs.

To his relief, the common-room was empty, save for Tim, who was rearranging the flagons on their shelves. The old man opened his mouth to greet him, but Magnus cut in curtly.

"Tim—I want another horse!"

Tim's eyes widened at his tone. "Damme fer a lubber! Where away this time?"

"To Duane's again. And if peradventure I don't come back, the gold in my room belongs to you. Now hurry up. I want no argument!"

Tim squinted one eye like a quizzical rooster. "Thought ye was waitin' fer a message, lad?"

"It came," snapped Magnus impatiently, "though not in the form I expected. That boy—Rosalind sent him to see me. That's why they murdered him!"

Tim growled. "*No!* By God, 'tis the act o' a Spaniard! But hold, lad, else ye'll get the same dose! I warned ye ol' Duane 'ud not tyke it on 'is beam's end. 'E'll fight . . ."

"Aye, damn his soul, but he'll find he's not fighting a twelve-year-old child, nor a gentle woman! Now, will you get me a horse or must I . . ." Magnus paused when he saw that Tim was no longer listening to him, but was staring at the street door.

Irritated, Magnus glanced over his shoulder to see a tall, angry man with a riding crop in his hand come striding across the room toward them. The man was Sir Peter Beckles!

Astonishment left Magnus standing with his mouth open, but Beckles seemed oblivious of his presence. He walked directly up to the innkeeper and stopped short with his back to Magnus.

"Are you Tim Prettyman?" he demanded imperiously.

Tim eyed him. "Aye, that I am! An' 'oo might ye be to adopt that tone?"

Beckles towered threateningly above him. "I am Sir Peter Beckles, whom you publicly imputed to be a *court pimp* and a *papist traitor!*"

In the embarrassed silence which followed this charge, Magnus saw the blood flow into the old seaman's features, yet his eyes held unwaveringly on the courtier's face.

"If you were an equal, or even a gentleman," Beckles continued in a lethal voice, "I'd run you through, but since I cannot cross blades with a tavern lout, I've come to thrash you within an inch of your life!"

As he raised the whip above his head, Magnus caught the end and swung the man around until they faced each other.

"Not so fast, my lord!" he said softly. "If you prefer the sword, perchance I can oblige you."

Beckles regarded him coldly. "Pray who are *you?*"

62

Out of the corner of his eye, Magnus could see Tim frantically gesturing him to silence. He merely grimaced.

"An irrelevant matter," he told Beckles, "since my own opinion of you coincides with Prettyman's. To repeat—you are a pimp, a popish traitor, and on my own I'll add, a cowardly murderer!"

Beckles' swarthy skin lightened, but he covered his anger with a formal bow.

"You have said quite enough to warrant attention!"

"By my troth, I am honored!" jeered Magnus. "I feared you might deem a man with two legs too great an obstacle."

As the other made an impulsive motion toward his sword hilt, Tim bellowed his rage.

"Leave legs out o' this! By God, I can tyke care o' me own fights wi'out . . ."

"Silence, Tim!" interrupted Magnus shortly. "This *is* my fight." He returned Beckles' stiff-necked bow. "Your servant, my lord. Shall we have at it?"

Sir Peter had regained his poise. "As I explained," he remarked conversationally, "I do not engage in tavern brawls. Howbeit, despite the fact you are ashamed to give your name, if your courage is equal to your effrontery, I shall be most happy to kill you on the sward above the river tomorrow morning at one hour after dawn— if that is satisfactory?"

"Entirely, but can I depend on you to be there?" taunted Magnus.

Once again Sir Peter controlled himself with difficulty. He even managed a mirthless smile.

"You can, sir. We will bring one second each. Now, do you wish to measure the length of my blade?"

Magnus glanced down at the beautiful Spanish sword dangling from the other's doublet. He shook his head.

"The length of your blade is of small moment, Sir Peter. I'll be more interested to measure your blood."

Beckles bit his nether lip. "You are an insolent swine, sir!" he grated. "One hour after dawn then!" Without so much as a glance at Tim, he swung on his heel and stalked out.

When the door closed behind him, Tim waved his arms in rage.

"Oh, ye fool, ye bloody hot-headed fool! W'y didn't ye stand yer own course!"

Magnus laughed at him. "Bless you, Timothy, it was a perfect course! What a stroke of pure luck I happened to be here when . . ."

"Luck me arse!" fumed the old man. "Anybody save a dolt could 'a seen 'twas ye 'e was arter all the time, not me! 'E doubtless watched through the winder 'til ye came down!"

Magnus whistled thoughtfully. Such a possibility had completely escaped him. Yet now that it was pointed out to him, the timing did seem unnaturally fortuitous.

Tim was hopping about in anger. "Take a horse an' git out o' the country, lad, 'til this blows over! Ye're a marked man now! I would na' trust 'at viper no further . . ."

Magnus shook his head. "Beckles may be a viper, nevertheless, he's also a knight. A duel is a personal tryst he'll keep inviolate, depend on it. Will you be my second?"

"Ye know bloody well I'll be that, come hell er high water!" stormed the old man. "But, by Neptune, I like not the storm I see buildin'!"

Chapter 6

I⊤ WAS characteristic of Magnus that he should enjoy a deep, dreamless sleep from which he awakened clear-eyed and cheerful. Some of this might be attributed to mere youthfulness, yet in the main it was due to a healthy zest for living and an unbounded optimism which precluded the trespass of doubt. Having complete confidence in himself, he felt no concern about the outcome of the duel, for he viewed the affair not so much as a gamble but as a simple problem of arithmetic in which *one* subtracted from *three* leaves two. With Beckles removed from the stage, he had only Sir Gregory to deal with, and he was satisfied the treasonous letters would quell any further trouble from the old man. The future stretched rosily before him.

With Tim Prettyman, however, the question was not so easily resolved. He had spent a tortured night dreading the approach of dawn. He was all too aware of the complications which might ensue over the killing of a Royal favorite, and he was not by any means convinced that Magnus was a match for the courtier, for if the years had not dulled Tim's martial spirit, they had taught him that nothing in life is certain save death at the end. As a result of all this, he had arisen grumpy and sullen to cook their breakfast himself, it having been agreed to confide in no one, not even Kate.

It was still dark when they prodded their horses away from the White Anchors, but by the time they topped the hill above the town, a thin girdle of celestial steel lay along the eastern horizon. Magnus made a few abortive attempts at conversation only to give up finally when Tim limited his replies to surly grunts.

Thereafter, they continued in silence, each wrapped in his own mood. Though wispy streamers of land mist floated over the moors, there was a salty tang to the wind blowing in from the sea. Old Tim licked his lips, but there was not sufficient sustenance in air for such a hunger as his, and it only stirred up repressed memories. He appeared to age in the saddle.

But the flavor of the sea had a different effect on Magnus; it moved him with a singular restlessness he could not wholly understand. The terrain seemed to undulate beneath him and his gaze turned automatically toward the Channel where the molten sun hung suspended over the incoming rollers like a burnished temple gong.

A half hour later, they turned off the main road and wound down the hillside to the plateau above the bleak red cliffs. It was incredibly lonely at this hour and a brooding stillness blanketed the whole scene, which even the startled cries of jackdaws and thrush could not dissipate.

Tim reined in with a growl of disgust. "W'at did I tell ye? The ruddy bastard ain't come!"

Magnus laughed. "We're too early, man. Give him a chance."

Tim snorted his contempt, and despite the inconvenience of his wooden leg, tumbled unceremoniously from the saddle without assistance. Tethering their horses to the only tree on the plateau, they continued afoot toward the embankment. As far northward as the eye could reach stretched the jagged coastline, its blackness broken only by the feeble rays of a fisherman's shack perched on a rock in the middle distance. Fifty odd feet below where they stood, the swells crashed and thundered among the rocks with all the fury of angry beasts hurling themselves against the bars of a cage.

Magnus shuddered slightly. The stark beauty of this grandeur was lost to him, for like all deep-water seamen, he hated rocks with a deep and abiding hatred. Yet at the same time, they drew him with a terrible fascination that was almost hypnotic. He was staring at them intently when he heard Tim's startled oath.

"W'at the bloody 'ell!"

Magnus swung around to see half a dozen horsemen galloping across the sward toward them. They were all heavily armed, some with battle-axes, the rest with swords. As he stared incredulously, the riders fanned out in a semicircle to cut off their escape.

65

But even had he so elected, escape was impossible. Their own weary nags were secured a couple of hundred yards away, leaving them pinned against the rim of the cliffs. There was scant time for idle speculation; the intent of the horsemen was evident. When the leader of the group was a bare fifty paces away, Magnus was able to recognize the stained leather jerkin and the bestial features of Groswick, the garroter of Moley. Only then did he fully comprehend how treacherously he had been served.

His first reaction was of a blinding rage, but the imminence of danger steadied him. He whipped out his sword and squirmed his feet deeper in the damp sod.

"Boarders, by God!" bellowed Tim, drawing his cutlass.

"Aye! Back to back it is, Timothy!"

Had he been alone, Magnus might have taken his chances down the face of the cliff, but as the crippled condition of his friend precluded that, the thought of flight never crossed his mind. He kept his eyes on the onrushing Groswick, who appeared intent on personally running them down. When the bully was about fifteen paces away, he began to lean over the right-hand side of the saddle.

Magnus thought he understood. Groswick, a length ahead of his companions, intended to ride Tim down and at the same time get Magnus with his blade. Magnus leaped forward to meet the charge, slashed at the horse's head to deflect his course, and then hastily put himself on guard to block the other's steel.

The blow came with stunning force. Out of the corner of his eye, Magnus glimpsed old Tim jump nimbly aside, then he heard his own blade snap under the impact. Once again his temper soared out of hand, and as Groswick sought to recover his balance for another cut, Magnus caught the tail of his jerkin and yanked him out of the saddle.

They crashed to the ground, Magnus underneath. Groswick groped for his dagger, but Magnus wound his long legs around the man's waist and locked his arm. Both were veterans of too many death fights to waste breath on futile cursing, so they fought silently. Magnus rammed an elbow in his assailant's throat to force his head back. He managed to twist from underneath, but Groswick got a bear-hug around his chest and rolled on top again. In this wise, they moved toward the rim.

A wild scream, followed by Tim's triumphant bellow, assured Magnus that the old warrior was still alive. On the next roll, Magnus twisted around for a hurried glance. Tim was standing valiantly in the center of a ring of assailants, his slashing cutlass holding them momentarily at bay. But even as he watched, Magnus saw a rider throw himself out of the saddle full on the old man's back. Tim

66

vanished under the pack. Then Groswick stabbed two blunted fingers into Magnus' eyes, and he could see no more.

Magnus wriggled clear of the savage hold, and shifted his grip to the killer's throat. As his fingers tightened on the corded muscles, Groswick lunged backward, taking Magnus with him.

Abruptly the ground gave way, and Magnus felt himself falling through space. When he realized they had rolled over the cliff, he tightened his grip in a half-crazed desire to kill Groswick before the rocks ended them both. He heard one last clap of thunder as the surf hit the rocks, then oblivion. . . .

It was a good-humored rippling sound, like friendly laughter running through the audience at a play. Commencing softly, it gradually increased in volume and fullness of tone until it broke into a soft clapping noise. Magnus grew aware of it through a sense of *feeling* rather than by ear. He was puzzled. Then he became conscious that his whole body was a repository of pain; it even hurt him to think. He seemed to be poised on the brink of a longitudinal line which separated light from eternal darkness. When his senses inclined toward the black pit, he struggled to maintain his mental balance.

The laughter and the clapping continued with a measured cadence. There was something poignantly familiar about the sound, yet he could not recall having heard a crowd respond in that exact fashion. He sought to open his eyes, and to his amazement found them already open. A saffron haze floated overhead, a yellowish fog spotted with uncertain shadows. Out of this, a misted shape evolved to hover directly in front of him, and as the fuzzy outline began to assume substance, he recognized the head and shoulders of a man.

In a kind of mental explosion, Magnus was precipitated into full consciousness. He remembered the fight, his last hold on Groswick, and the fall from the cliff. So they had survived, and Groswick was still on top! Groaning involuntarily from the effort, Magnus made a grab for the throat above him.

But the form evaporated out of reach, like so much smoke, and Magnus was too spent to follow. Then a creaky, ancient voice said, "Here, here, matey, ye're snappish as a shark!"

Magnus rolled his head painfully in the direction of the voice. It took his eyes a long time to refocus, but eventually he distinguished the toothless head of a very old man. Surprise left him confused.

"Who are you?" he whispered.

"Now that be a moot question," chortled the old man, "but I didn't calculate I was no ruddy Saint Peter, the Fisherman o' men, yet when I hauled me seine, here's ye, neither fish n'r fowl n'r good red herrin'!"

Magnus closed his eyes and tried to make sense out of what had been told him. He heard the rippling laughter again, and this time he knew it for the lapping of waves around the rocks.

"You say you . . . you found me in your net?"

The ancient bared purple gums. "Aye, belly up, like a dead mackerel, but heavier than a ruddy whale. Couldn't bring ye aroun' so had to rig a tackle to drag ye in 'ere."

"Where's *here?*"

The fisherman scratched his head. "Naow that's a question I can't answer rightly. Three-an'-thuty year, come All Saints' Day, I been a-livin' in this 'ut, an' when I'm 'ere, I'm 'ere, an' w'en I'm someplace else, this 'ut's *there.* Now's I'm 'ere, it's 'ere, an' 'at's all I knows."

Magnus winced, and gave up, letting himself drift. As the fog cleared, patches of memory floated into juxtaposition. Finally, he tried again.

"Tell me, ancient, was there anyone . . . I mean . . . another man with me?"

The fisherman pondered the question. "Aye, an' nay. That is, they mought a been, er they mought not. Hard to tell. 'Ere's the way of it—'twas the mornin' I foun' ye, a mite after daylight. Some men was a-climbin' aroun' the rocks 'long shore, as if lookin 'fer some'at. I seen 'em through me door, but I didn't stir outside. No, sir, not me. I knows me place, I does, an' I don't want no truck with w'at goes on atop that bluff. W'en they left, I goes to me nets. There ye was. Naow, mebbe 'twas ye they sought, mebbe 'tweren't. 'Tain't fer me to meddle, say I." He cocked his head and eyed Magnus. "Mought they be friends o' your'n?"

Magnus ignored the direct question, for he was having sufficient difficulty fixing his attention on what had been told him. Suddenly the import filtered into his brain.

"My God, man! Did you say *the* morning you found me? You must have meant *this* morning!"

"There ye go ag'in!" complained the old man. "Trying to snarl up me words. *The* mornin' be w'at I said, an' *the* mornin' be w'at I meant. 'Twas the day afore yestiddy, rightly. Ye been kickin' an' squirmin' on yer back like a careened turtle these two days past."

Magnus sank back with a groan. *Two days!* Merciful God, what had happened to Rosalind? And old Tim? Suppose he himself had been reported dead? And all those priceless hours he had been lying here in this miserable shack—out of his head! By the powers, he'd waste no more time! He attempted to sit up. . . .

The agony was exquisite. Barbed splinters of pain flashed simultaneously through every muscle of his body until he had to fall back prone to catch his breath. There he lay, exhausted by the effort, his chest heaving spasmodically and globules of moisture dotting his forehead.

"A mite done in, ain't ye?" observed the fisherman philosophically. " 'Twill take a fortnight to bring ye 'roun'."

Magnus could have wept. A fortnight was an eternity, too timeless to contemplate. His whole life would be wasted! Rosalind, believing him dead, would be forced into marriage with the treacherous Sir Peter and spirited away to Spain, to be lost to him forever! The mere thought of it shattered Magnus more painfully than his injuries.

"I must get to Plymouth at once!" he shouted. "At *once,* you hear!"

The fisherman exposed his gums in what was meant to be a smile. "Aye, yer Majesty, I ain't deef. How d'ye choose to travel? Mebbe by yer royal coach an' four, though to speak true, I ain't seen yer master o' horse the nonce? Or peradventure ye'd ruther use yer imperial barge, yer Highness?"

Magnus shut his eyes against the nightmare of the toothless skull.

"By God!" he moaned. "It's a matter of life and death!"

That brought a cackle from the old man. "So I see, so I see! At yer age, everythin' 's a matter o' life an' death. Yet methinks a nip or two o' good white ale 'll tip the scales in favor o' life. Come, younker, drink this!"

Magnus did not want the drink, but was too distraught to resist. He had sampled once before the mystical Cornish ale which contained among other things a secret ingredient known as "grout," and tasted as nauseous as a physician's draught. The fisherman raised his head with one hand and poured the liquor down his throat with the other.

The stuff revolted him, then, miraculously, the pain evaporated and a tingling numbness stole over his mind and flowed with warm lassitude through his veins. The rough bunk became downy as a cloud. His urgency melted away, leaving him satisfied just to float tranquilly in a timeless vacuum. As from a distance, the croaking voice of the old man came to him.

"Ah-ha! Better, ain't ye? 'Tis the gift o' God, son. Ye may figger ye're drunk, but ye ain't; ye're really not, mebbe fer the first time. Ye kin see things as they should be seen. Me, I lives on the stuff. Without it, I'd be an ol', ol' man, but a nip o' the blessed nectar, an' I'm young agin. Two nips, an' I start dreamin' o' beauteous maidens —an' me past me three-score-ten!" He leaned closer. "Here, matey, wet t'other eye, as the sayin' be!"

This time, Magnus accepted without protest. The pleasing paralysis grew complete. He seemed to step out of his battered body as one would step out of a coach. No longer weary and sore, he moved with the winged feet of a Mercury, then abruptly, in one of those quick dissolving transitions of a dream, he discovered himself in velvety darkness, lying beside a girl!

The sheer magic of it made him incredulous, and he began to explore her young breasts with tremulous fingers. At his touch, they blossomed. She, too, came alive. Yet there was no talk. In some fashion, mystical by its very naturalness, he and she merged into one being. As two fagots entwined in a hearth, their flames united into a single column of clean white fire. Exalted by this miracle, he reposed serenely in her arms. Time hung in abeyance. There was no time; nothing save peace and contentment. He did not question who this girl might be. In some as-yet-unplumbed depths of his consciousness, he *knew*, even though he could not identify her. She was *him:* he was now completely whole. A gale-battered craft, he had finally limped into the safety and serenity of his own harbor. He was home.

How long he slept, Magnus never knew. The fisherman would not tell him. But when he awoke, though still weak, most of the pain had left him. He began once more to talk of getting to Plymouth. The fisherman enumerated the manifold difficulties, but in a flash of insight, often granted the very ill, Magnus sensed that the alleged difficulties were mostly emotional.

The ancient was not only a very old man, he was a very lonely man. His mind, like his teeth, had rotted away, doubtlessly abetted by the white ale. Of the tiny shack perched on the barren rocks, he had created an imaginary citadel against which the world laid siege. So far, the hosts of reality had not found it, and he did not mean to tempt Fate by going to Plymouth. His was a philosophy of self-sufficiency, which he attempted to pass along to the younger man. He urged him to lose himself in the white ale, and proceeded, forthwith, to demonstrate the efficacy of the potion.

Magnus argued, pleaded, threatened—in vain. His condition held him prisoner because he was too weak to consider tramping the long road. Time hurried now, as if trying to make up for the pleasant recess. The old man's toothless grin grew increasingly vacuous under the effect of the potent liquor, and when he finally nodded off into a Nirvana of its making, Magnus decided to steal his boat.

The moon was full when he crawled out of the hut. The boat was riding to a bow line secured to a stake in the rocks, its stern held off by a stone anchor. Magnus surveyed the craft in dismay. It resembled its owner—a piece of beaten flotsam sadly fallen into decay.

Magnus sighed and hauled himself aboard. The wreck floated, and the wind stood fair for Plymouth.

He cast off the bow line, but the stone anchor was too much for him, so he cut it adrift and let the tide sweep him away. In his depressed state of mind, he read a symbolism into the simple act—cutting adrift from security to ride with the whim of the tides.

Once under weigh, however, the venerable craft assumed a subtle nobility, like a decadent aristocrat who, faced with sudden responsibility, reacts to breeding. Magnus felt this, and reacted with it. If the ancient hull could stand it, why not he? The sea was his mother: she had rocked him, trounced him, shared her bounties and carried him on her breast to fabulous places. She, at least, had never betrayed him!

He crawled forward and made sail, and as the much-patched wings spread and filled with an eager slap, the last of his uncertainty vanished. He spared one quick glance at the dark silhouette of the fishing shack humped on the rocks, then turned forward. Anchoring the steering oar under his armpit, he set his course for Plymouth.

The restorative qualities of that night's sail were incalculable. Magnus had dragged himself into the rotten cockleshell, pain-wracked and despondent, yet when he made Plymouth seven hours later, he was imbued with energy and resolution. However, he soon discovered that most of this was mental, for by the time he had climbed the winding hill to the White Anchors, the refusal of his limbs to coordinate warned him that his body was not so easily revitalized.

On reaching the massive anchors which served as guideposts to the flagstone walk, he paused to quell the tremor in his legs. He had nurtured a feeble hope that he might see Tim bustling about, as was his wont, but the old man was not in evidence. Although Magnus had not really expected to find him, he had avoided facing the truth. Now he had to, for his heart told him old Tim was dead.

As he stumbled toward the kitchen door, he met Kate coming out. At sight of him, she gave a soft cry of compassion and, dropping the milk-pail she was carrying, ran to meet him.

"Dear God in Heaven, Magnus!" she cried, grabbing his arms to support him. "What's happened?"

"Enough—and to spare! Has . . . has Tim come back?"

From the inn came a rumble as of a dray horse champing in his stall. Kate glanced anxiously over her shoulder, then as the noise drew closer, she put an arm around Magnus and half carried him toward the stables. Not until they were safely within did she answer his query.

"Tim vanished three days ago! Oh, Magnus, tell me honestly—where is he?"

Magnus sank onto a bale of straw and took his head between his hands.

"God help me—I don't know!" he groaned.

A long-drawn wail from the inn shook them both.

"Kat-tie! Kat-tie!"

The girl shuddered. "Magnus, *she* knows you were here, and she knows that Master Tim left early that morning in your company! What else she may know, I cannot say, but she is telling everyone you lured Tim away from her and . . . and *murdered* him!"

Magnus raised his head to meet her eyes. "Peradventure I did, Katie," he faltered miserably. "Aye, 'twas I who murdered him!"

"*Magnus!*"

He swayed to his feet. "I must go to my room."

She tried to push him back. "No, Magnus! Oh, God, *no!* She'll turn you over to the bailiffs! I don't care what she says, or you say either, I know you wouldn't hurt dear old Timothy!"

"I'll buy her silence," he muttered grimly. "The old bitch cared naught for Tim, so gold will quiet her. Let me go!"

But she still clung to him. "Wait! You don't understand what has happened! Sir Gregory's men have been here. They claimed you killed their captain!"

"By my troth, I hope that is true, at least!" He took her hands in his own. "While I'm inside, have the hostler saddle me the fastest horse in the stables. There'll be more killing before the sun sinks, for I've an account to settle at Duane manor!"

He brushed her aside and strode toward the inn. The kitchen was empty, so he continued on into the common-room. He glimpsed the flabby hulk of Dame Prettyman hovering near a group of men at a table, but he ignored her and headed toward the staircase.

He had barely set foot on the lowest step when he heard her nasal squeal. Despite his urgency, the cry all but paralyzed him, like a blade thrust into his spine. Bracing himself against the newel post, he turned.

"*Pirate! Thief! Murderer!*" shrieked the old woman. " 'Ow dare ye sneak into the 'ouse o' a poor widder!"

"Hold your puling tongue!" he snapped at her. "I'm going to my room!"

She bore down on him like a water-logged galleon running free before a gale.

"*Yer* room? Ye ain't got no room 'ere, ye black-'earted knave!" She appealed to the patrons. "Seize 'im, b'ys! 'E murdered me poor dear 'usband!"

72

While the men hesitated, Magnus made one more attempt to reason with her.

"Listen, you old fool—it was I who came here dressed as the Spaniard, Don Ruster! You yourself rented me a room. So stop blatting, and hear what I have to say."

She didn't stop, and she didn't listen. "A gold piece to every kind man w'at 'elps seize 'im!" she screamed.

Too late, Magnus realized how wrongly he had underestimated the old shrew. Whether she had known all along that his masquerade had been false, or whether his present admission sufficed, her offer of gold to the loafers proved that she was aware of his hoard, if not in actual possession of it. The knowledge made him desperate, and when he saw the men rising to the bait, he sought to escape up the stairs. But for all her unwieldy bulk, the old woman could move with amazing rapidity. He gained but three steps before she plummeted on him like a bloated vulture and anchored his legs.

" 'Elp! 'Elp a poor widder woman!" she shrilled. "Gold for all w'at 'elps!"

Magnus fought, but in vain. With a Gargantuan heave, she dropped him flopping on the sanded floor and the men swarmed over him. When he attempted talk, she herself sat on his face, in the fashion of a hen sitting on a single egg. The flabby, pungent posterior had the effect of a sack of soured grain. Humiliated and unable to breathe, he was bound hand and foot. He felt his senses slipping away from him. When at long last she got up, he opened his mouth wide to gasp for air. Immediately a rag was thrust into his maw.

The old witch wiggled herself like a hen ruffling her feathers.

"Tyke 'im out to the stables!" she commanded. "I can't 'ave 'im interferin' wi' trade. 'Orace, run down to the Justice and tell 'is ludship I've caught the criminal w'at killed me dear departed 'usband! There's a good lad. 'Urry, an' I'll gi' ye a shillin'!"

For the time being Magnus was too soul-sick to care what they did with him. He closed his eyes to blot out the nightmare. Rough hands picked him up and trundled him through the kitchen. His head was used as a battering ram to bunt open the door. He felt the sunlight on his closed eyelids, then the smell of the stables closed around him and he was flung into a stall.

A voice said, "St'y wi' 'im, Jamie. We uns'll myke sure the ol' 'ag p'ys us!"

Grumbling, the man Jamie acquiesced, and the others went out. Magnus opened one eye. Jamie stood etched against the doorway.

It was not the nature of Magnus to concede defeat, and now the very desperateness of his plight calmed his nerves. He ceased his futile struggles and let his brain take charge. Reason warned him that if he hoped to escape at all, it would have to be before the bailiffs arrived.

His first thought was to buy Jamie to his side, so with that in mind, he worked methodically to void the gag. It had been used apparently for mopping greasy tables, and the flavor nauseated him. But as time passed and he failed to spew it out, he turned his attention to his bonds.

With them, his success was no better. His hands were secured behind his back and he was lying on them. He tried to roll over, but Jamie walked into the stall and kicked him.

"Lie still, ye dog!"

Magnus gave him a look pregnant with promise. Jamie drew back his foot for another kick, when the stable door opened and Kate sauntered in with a pewter tankard in her hand.

"Here, Jamie!" she called cheerfully. "The mistress sent this out to you!"

Jamie grinned and moved toward her. Kate smilingly extended the tankard, but as he reached for it, she abruptly hurled the contents in his face.

Jamie coughed a startled oath and pawed at his blinded eyes. Kate measured him calculatingly, then swung the heavy receptacle. The blow caught Jamie flush on the left temple. He fell back against the stall and began to slide down the timber to the floor.

Before he hit the ground, Kate was past him into the stall.

"Magnus!" she cried. "Are you all right?"

He could only nod. Kate wasted no time on talk. She jerked the rag from his mouth and rolled him onto his face. A slash of a knife severed the cord around his wrists.

"My poor Magnus! Have the swine hurt you bad?"

"Bless you!" he gulped. Even the fetid air of the stable tasted sweet. "I'm all right. Here—give me that knife!"

He freed his own legs, but when he attempted to spring erect, his knees buckled and he stumbled against the manger. Instantly, Kate was beside him, steadying him.

"You *are* hurt!"

"No, no! But I must get out of here!"

"You can't make it, Magnus!" she protested. "The bailiffs will be here any moment!"

"Well, by God, I'll not be taken!" swore Magnus. "I'll ride . . ."

"Which is exactly what they'll expect you to do," she cut him short. "Now listen to me! This is more serious than you think! Sir Gregory himself was here last night, and he was closeted with Mistress Prettyman for a long time. What was said, I don't know, save

74

that she's been waddling around all day like a goose full of golden eggs!"

Magnus winced. "Aye, and so she is—full of *my* golden eggs!"

"It is plain they have joined forces against you, though I can't imagine what they have in common. But the mere fact that he, a noble, should . . ."

She stopped with a gasp as a burst of voices from the inn broke around them like thunder. Magnus braced himself belligerently for a last stand, but Kate was more practical.

"Up into the loft! *Quick!*"

"It's no use. This carrion will report you hit . . ."

She scooped the tankard off the ground and hefted it threateningly. "Damn you, Magnus—*get up that ladder!*" she hissed. "Else before my God, I'll give you the same as him and drag you aloft myself!"

"But you . . . ?"

"I can take care of myself!"

The approaching tramp of men across the cobbled courtyard necessitated a quick decision. Still Magnus hesitated, appraising her. Aye, Katie could take care of herself, and more! He started to smile, when suddenly he was overwhelmed by an emotion that blinded him as completely as the beer had blinded Jamie. Through the smarting film, he saw Kate, not as a buxom wench, but as a female incarnate, ablaze with a protective ferocity which transcended anything a male animal could equal.

"*Quick!*" she spat.

"God bless you, Katie!"

This time it was a prayer, not a polite phrase. It came from a chamber of his being infrequently explored, and left him slightly bewildered, as in the presence of something mystical. He felt irresistibly drawn toward her, but as he bent forward, she straight-armed him toward the ladder. The contact jarred him back to reality. He scrambled upward, and as he passed through the trap into the loft, he heard a blow. Anxious, he looked downward. Kate had struck herself on the head with the tankard and was sinking slowly to the floor!

An instant later, the door burst open and men poured into the stable.

" 'Od's life!" shouted a man. "W'at's 'ere?"

Covered by the noise of milling and cursing, Magnus burrowed under the hay until he found a slit in the rough flooring. He peered below.

Seven or eight men crowded around the prostrate figures. Magnus couldn't help but recognize the two bailiffs in charge, for in

75

addition to their official staves, they wore the scars of their last meeting with Kate. It was equally evident they had not forgotten, since they remained a safe distance from her recumbent form.

One of the original captors was explaining: "'E was 'ere, in this werry stall, s'elp me! Trussed up syfe an' sound, 'e was! God's trufe!"

"Syfe an' sound!" sneered the pudgy bailiff. "Then w'ere the bloody 'ell be 'e *now*?"

"Aye, w'ere?" echoed his partner.

"'Oo knows! The De'il must 'a . . . *Ho!* Jamie's comin' aroun'!"

Magnus craned his neck for a better look. Jamie opened one eyelid experimentally, then seeing all the faces peering at him, closed it with a groan.

"Me 'ead! Ow, me 'ead!"

"Come alive, me man!" barked a bailiff briskly.

Jamie continued to moan. Then a bystander yelped excitedly: "The wench be stirrin'!"

Immediately, Kate became the cynosure of all eyes. Magnus was delighted with the way she handled the situation.

"Where am I?" she breathed, staring innocently about her.

The short bailiff had a long memory. He backed away a step. "No tricks this time, me fine strumpet! W'at 'appened 'ere?"

"I was hit on the noggin!" She fingered the fast-growing lump on her forehead. "Here!"

"The point is—'oo 'it ye?"

Kate glanced at Jamie who had guardedly raised his lids and was eying her reproachfully. He opened his mouth to say something, but she adroitly cut in ahead of him.

"Who did you expect hit me!" she snapped. "I had brought out a tankard of ale to Jamie here, and just as he reached for it, someone —and I'm not saying who—knocked the stuff into poor Jamie's face. Then they seized the tankard and struck him, then me, over the head."

"A likely tale, a likely tale!" jeered the short bailiff. "An' w'at was ye doin' all this time, me bad-tempered slut?"

Screeching in language too virulent even for a common-room, Kate came off the floor, and her tormentor leaped backward in alarm.

"'Ere, 'ere! Watch yersel', me girl!"

Kate restrained herself, then walked over and stood above Jamie. When she rested a hand on his shoulder, perilously close to his throat, the man blanched.

"Do you great fools think *I* did it?" she challenged. "If so, you insult Jamie!" Bending over the miserable oaf, she offered consolingly: "Imagine them thinking that a poor defenseless maid could beat

76

down a big powerful man like you, Jamie! Fie! *You* tell them what happened. Tell them, Jamie!" Her fingers, Magnus noticed, tightened slightly.

Jamie lowered his head into his hands. "'Tis as she tolt ye," he muttered. "There must 'ave been another man in 'idin' 'ere."

"At least one," Kate agreed. "Possibly two or three to drop Jamie the way they did."

"God's trufe!" acknowledged Jamie.

The tall bailiff stroked his jaw. He "Hummphed!" a couple of times, then heaved his shoulders.

"We uns ought to take the slut to the Justice!" suggested the short bailiff, from a safe position behind the crowd.

Kate marched majestically out of the stall toward him. The fellow cringed.

"A fine, brave hound you are!" she jeered. "You let the wolf get away and bay at the lambs. Phew, what a stinking, low-bred, misbegotten cross beween a rat and a snake! Come, stop hiding behind real men and crawl out where I can spit on you!"

Everybody laughed, except the bailiffs, and Magnus—he was too full of conflicting emotions. He knew now that if he escaped, he'd owe her his very life.

"That's enough o' yer lip!" admonished the tall bailiff. "Else, by God, we'll h'arrest ye fer h'obstructin' justice!"

Kate tilted her head back and crowed with laughter.

"*H'obstructin' justice!*" she mocked him. "Me? Am *I* detaining you fine catchpolls here while the one you seek may be galloping to safety? Good Heavens, if that be so, I release you at once, for in all truth, I prefer the smell of good fresh manure to your stinking presence! Be off with you!"

"The girl's right," grumbled Jamie, tired of his martyr's role. "The knave's gone, as any fool can plainly see."

"Not *some* fools, Jamie dear!" purred Kate.

The second round of laughter was too much for the short bailiff. He stalked out in an aura of his own profanity. After a moment's hesitation, his partner followed, and the others brought up the rear. Jamie wanted to tarry, but Kate laughingly helped him to his feet.

"Look 'ere, girl . . ." he began grimly, but she only wrinkled her nose at him.

"Go along with you, Jamie, and let well-enough alone!" she advised. "You're a hero for the nonce, but what I did once, I can do again—now, or later if need be. Don't forget that! Away with you."

Jamie sighed and sullenly led the way out of the barn. Kate never glanced backward, but she did put a hand behind her and motion for Magnus to remain where he was.

Magnus saw the door close, then reaction hit him like a poleaxe and he went to sleep.

Chapter 7

WHEN Kate managed to slip up into the loft, late in the afternoon, she found Magnus still asleep. He was lying on his right side, his cheek pillowed on his hands, after the fashion of a child who had drifted off while saying its prayers. The girl stole closer and knelt beside him, leaning over to study his features. Peculiarly enough, in spite of his obvious masculinity, in slumber the face appeared singularly feminine. Furtively, she lifted an unruly damp curl from his forehead and smoothed it into place. Magnus did not move. She smiled the kind of a smile she would never have let him witness, then touched her lips to his cheek. He stirred, and opened his eyes.

"Zounds!" he exclaimed, sitting up. "I must have dozed."

Kate's smile was conventional. "Dozed? Why, you've slept the livelong day!"

He yawned, then shook his head to clear it. Immediately the past crowded forward for attention. Creases marred his forehead.

"My God, I shouldn't have slept! Tell me—any news of Tim?" When she made a negative sign with her head, his fists clenched.

"Then it must be true! Duane's men killed him!"

"The old shrew insists you did it, Magnus!"

"You believe her?"

"Don't be daft! You loved him too much to do him harm. That I know. However, the whole town is aroused, and you must get away before . . ."

"I must get into my room first!"

Her eyes rounded. "That's absolutely impossible! Mistress Prettyman and Sir Gregory spent an hour or more up there. Later, your chest was taken out, and now four of Duane's men are waiting for you up there, as if they expect you're fool enough to come back, though Lord knows why!"

78

Magnus groaned, and rubbed one fist in the other palm. "*I know why.*" The furrows deepened between his eyes. "Katie, I'm not so sure now they did kill Tim. I've a growing hunch they're holding him, trying to make him talk!"

"*Talk?* What could Tim tell them? And why is Sir Gregory so interested in your room? What's it all about, Magnus?"

In his desire to unburden himself, he was sorely tempted to tell her about the packet of letters, then remembering the danger such knowledge implied, he decided against it.

"I can't tell you."

She settled back on her haunches, lost in thought. At first he feared he had hurt her feelings, but after a time, he sensed she had something else on her mind. He pressed her to explain.

"Well, it may be just another trick to catch you," she said finally. "But there's been a foreign-looking seaman hanging around all day. He was in there when you were captured, though to speak true, he took no part in that. Howbeit, after the hue-and-cry had quieted down, he drew me aside and offered me a shilling to get a message to you. I pretended to be indignant, and swore I hadn't the slightest notion where you were—God forgive the lie!—but he only smirked. He said for a gold piece he could tell you something you'd like very much to know."

Magnus whistled softly. "On my oath, there are many things I'd like to know! Where is he now?"

"Loafing about the common-room."

Magnus reached for his pouch—to discover it missing. So the old fisherman was a thief as well as a disciple of Bacchus! Kate interpreted the gesture.

"Would you really talk to him?"

"Aye, if I had gold."

"But it may be a trap!"

He shrugged impatiently. "I'm already trapped; they just haven't found me. But Duane knows I won't stray far from my room."

"I wish *I* knew why." After some hesitation, she drew a single gold piece out of her bodice and pressed it into his hand without comment. He stared at it a long time before raising his eyes.

"Where in God's name did you get gold?"

"That's a matter for my own conscience!" she snapped, then her manner quickly softened. "Oh, Magnus, I'm afraid for you! You're in terrible trouble, and foreigners are not to be trusted!"

He gestured her silent. His brain was taking fire. Why, the fellow might have a message from Rosalind! Or even Tim! *Aye,* cautioned an inner voice, *it might be from Duane!* Magnus silenced the voice as he had silenced Kate. This was no time to count risks—if the man

79

had a message, Magnus had to see him, cost what it may. His frown deepened. He could gamble with his own life, but he had to consider Kate. She might well be hanged for an accomplice if he wasn't careful to protect her.

"Look you," he told her severely. "Go to this man and assure him you know nothing, absolutely *nothing*, of my whereabouts! Make that plain! Then suggest that he prowl around the barns on the chance that I might, I just *might possibly* return to steal a horse. Advise him to come alone and unarmed. If he's smart, he'll perceive your meaning, yet won't be able to involve you. Is that clear?"

"Naturally! I'm not as stupid as you seem to think. But suppose . . ."

"Never mind supposing. Tell me what he looks like?"

"He resembles a little monkey a friend of Tim's once brought from the Indies: a small, dark creature with slit eyes that seem to have been punched into his round head with a knife blade. His thin mouth looks slashed. His ears are bat-shaped, and a golden ring hangs from the left one. A sow could run between his legs without touching his knees. He turns my stomach!"

The loft had grown dim and the sunset filled the cracks with scarlet light. Magnus tightened a hand on the girl's arm.

"As you love me—*hurry!*" he urged.

She searched his face intently, as if trying to read what lay behind it. Once again he felt himself irresistibly drawn toward her, impelled by a force beyond his control. Yet before he could take her into his arms, she scrambled out of reach and started down the ladder. When her head was even with the loft, she paused.

"I do love you, Magnus—*terribly!*" she whispered, and was gone.

Plagued by doubts and tortured by a hard lump in his diaphragm, he forced himself to remain burrowed in the hay until the scarlet chinks turned black. When finally the rats began to march boldly about him, he deemed it safe to go below.

He stepped outside, to find the night as dark as the loft, for the moon had not yet risen and a bank of high fog obscured the stars. The whole vast emptiness seemed to have weight and substance that settled heavily upon him, and his eyes unconsciously sought escape in the open waters of the harbor. Tiny lights dancing in the darkness marked the position of ships at anchor. Magnus sighed discouragedly. A ship meant peace, not necessarily of body, but a peace of soul. He wondered about his own stout little vessel. Where was she now? Doubtless prowling down the coast, hunting a Spaniard. What a bloody fool he had been to give her up; to trade her for *this!*

Immediately he became contrite. Such thoughts were disloyal to

80

Rosalind who was enduring just as much torment as he. Her safety and happiness were now paramount. Half-savagely, he turned toward the inn.

It loomed before him, blocky and solid. Like old Tim, he thought. Through the mullioned windows, he could see the reflection of the hearth-fire splashing on the beamed ceiling. Laughter and conversation filtered into the courtyard. Occasionally, a shadow moved across his vision. But no one came outside. Time passed.

Goaded by anxiety, Magnus slipped across the yard and warily raised his eyes level with the window sill. The long room appeared unusually crowded tonight. Mistress Prettyman waddled from table to table, grunting and simpering like a huge sow. As Magnus watched, Kate came out of the scullery with a trayful of tankards. The sight of that foaming ale reminded the fugitive that his throat seemed lined with linsey-woolsey, and when his glance wandered to the fat fowl revolving on the spit, his empty stomach rumbled complainingly.

Then, in a trice, Magnus forgot his hunger as he saw a lone figure detach itself from the crowd and saunter toward a side door, with the expression of a man about to relieve himself. His companions jeered at him, and he answered with a crooked smile. A moment later, he passed outside.

Magnus backed hastily away from the window. That was his man! The simian features, the barbarous earring, the bowed legs—aye, he was the messenger!

As Magnus rounded the corner of the inn, the other was padding toward the stables. The fellow's arms hung forward from the shoulders, but whether this apelike posture was natural, or whether assumed intentionally to prove his hands were empty, Magnus could not tell.

Upon reaching the stable door, the man hesitated, then peered inside. Magnus eased up silently behind him, and laid the point of his dagger against his spine.

"Not a sound!" he hissed. "Inside!"

"*Bon Dieu! Ne vous fachez pas!*" gasped the man.

Magnus prodded him through the doorway. "*Dépêchez-vous!*"

Once safely inside, Magnus turned the other so that the meager light touched his face, while he himself remained in the deeper shadows.

"Now talk!" he growled in French. "What do you want here?"

The monkey-man paused uncertainly, his slanted eyes oscillating between the blade pressed against his chest and the darkness which concealed his captor.

81

"I came seeking a friend," he stammered at last. From his accent, Magnus decided French was not his native tongue.

"You have a message for that friend?"

"*C'est selon!* That depends!"

Savage with impatience, Magnus handed him the gold piece. "Here's your pay! Now out with it, lout, before I slit your gullet!"

"*Mon Dieu!*" whined the seaman. "Do not press the blade so hard, *monsieur!* The point is sharp! I must know your name. To be certain, you comprehend."

"Carter. Magnus Carter! Speak, man! Who gave you the message?"

"He with the leg of wood!"

Magnus' heart jumped. "He's alive then! Thank God for that! Is he hurt? Where is he? Damn you, talk fast!"

"That I am trying to tell you, *monsieur!* No, he is not hurt. Ah, a swollen head, perhaps, but no damage save the loss of his temper. He is held aboard ship in . . ."

"A *ship?* Who holds him? By God's life, I'll . . ."

The seaman shrugged eloquently. "Ah, who holds him, I do not know, *monsieur.* I am but a common seaman. But I beg you—do not be rash! For the ship lies out of sight of the town, ready to slip her hawse and run for Spain at the first sign of trouble."

"*Spain?* What nonsense is this? Why should anyone take the old man to Spain? You are lying, you dog!"

The man heaved a sigh. "No, no, I speak only truth. Hear me—this is the way of it. Myself, I am a Portuguese, but my fishing boat being wrecked on the Spanish coast near Pontevedio, I was forced to take work on this accursed vessel. *Mon Dieu,* how I regret it! Why we came to England is not for me to know. I am an ignorant man. But we came, and last night, the one with the wooden leg was carried aboard. Because I speak the little English, I was set to feed the old man.

"But, by the Virgin, I have trouble comprehending, for he does not speak such English as I have ever heard. *Bon Dieu,* what oaths, what profanities! His speech is a garble of curses and the idiom of the sea!"

Despite his impatience, Magnus felt an urge to smile. Aye, there was no doubt the man had seen Tim!

"All right, all right!" he snapped. "Repeat what he told you!"

The other spread his hands in resignation. "Being English, perhaps you will make of it some sense. I cannot. This is what he said: some great noble, who is the male offspring of a canine (*monsieur,* that is impossible!) gave the master of the ship, who the old man declares to be a base-born illegitimate (ah, *monsieur, that* I can

82

believe!), much gold to carry him to Spain because of certain letters damned by the Deity. They were to leave on the evening tide."

Magnus groaned aloud. "Tonight? Then they have left already?"

"No, *monsieur*—not quite! True, that was the orders, but the captain moved the ship out behind St. Nicholas Island, where it cannot be seen from the land, and he and most of the men came ashore to get drunk. They leave early in the morning."

"Can you take me out to the ship?"

The man's eyes bugged. *"Me, monsieur?"* He shook his head decisively. *"C'est impossible!* Oh, I admit he has a small guard, but . . . no, no, it is impractical. He with the wooden leg told me to find you, who he said was an imbecile with the head of a pig (forgive me, *monsieur*, I can plainly see that is not so!) and you would find a way to release him. Doubtless, *monsieur*, you have many friends . . . ?"

"There is no time to gather friends!"

"That is too bad, and I am sorry. Spain is a wicked country."

Magnus was frantic. "You say he has a small guard. How many?"

"One, oh, possibly *two*. Not more. But, *monsieur*, you would not dare attempt it alone? Think of the risk! Ah, it might be accomplished if there was time, but the crew will return in a few hours and then there would be great danger!"

"Listen, man—I'll give you two gold pieces to help me!"

The seaman shuddered. "Two? *Bon Dieu*, I would not run the risk for five even!"

"I'll make it ten, with five additional if we succeed!"

"Fifteen pieces of gold!" The man whistled incredulously. *"Sacri!* It is a fortune!"

"We'll leave at once!"

The other's mouth flew open. "Just the two of us? *Monsieur*, I beg you! Consider? While I admit there is no time to get others, suppose the crew should return?"

"They won't if we move fast. Anyway, I know every inch of St. Nicholas, and we can get away in the darkness. Let's get started!"

The man hung back. "It is madness! But fifteen pieces of gold! *Mon Dieu, mon Dieu*, I am tempted!" He glanced obliquely at Magnus. "You pay me *now?*"

"No—later!"

"Ah, *monsieur*, then I regret . . ."

"Damn you, you're not dealing with a Spaniard! You have the word of an Englishman! Do you doubt *that?*" He lent emphasis to the argument with the knife point.

"Non, non, monsieur! You misunderstand! Only I am afraid! Will you hide me afterwards, for I cannot go back to the ship?"

83

"Agreed! Now in God's name stop haggling, and let us go!"

Despite his feverish urgency, he would have liked a word with Kate. But that was impractical; he couldn't go into the inn himself, and he did not trust the Portuguese out of his sight. The latter was highly nervous and his constant grumbling kept Magnus in a welter of anxiety. So keeping close together, they scurried through the back streets to the quay.

Fortune favored them. Pequeño—he told Magnus it was a native name for small—moved rapidly in a half-lope that furthered the simian illusion. It was Pequeño who located a small boat, unattended and having a lug sail loosely furled. Magnus gestured him into the stern-sheets while he himself made sail.

The overcast was an added blessing, for it concealed their movements without seriously cutting down the visibility. Off the Hoe, where the current of the Catwater met the southeast swells, they encountered a nasty chop, but by beating westerly until they made a lee of St. Nicholas Island, they worked out of it.

Magnus huddled amidships and tried to duck the spray flying over the blunt-nosed bow. Occasionally he was forced to bail, but his hardest chore was controlling his impatience.

He was fairly certain he knew what had happened. As Tim had been shrewd enough to foresee, Beckles—doubtless at the instigation of old Duane—had set a trap for them. The lackeys had taken Tim alive to be ruthlessly questioned about the letters. Magnus blessed his prudence in not confiding where he had hidden them. Unable to learn anything from Tim, Duane had sought the cooperation of Mistress Prettyman for a price—Magnus' gold! Magnus thanked God he hadn't left those incriminating documents in his chest!

But that they should take Tim to Spain didn't make sense. Magnus could understand why they might murder him—God forbid!—but why drag him all the way to Spain? And what, in Heaven's name, was a Spanish ship doing in Plymouth harbor?

His resolution began to waver. Was he even now following his usual practice of precipitancy? He recalled that Tim had roundly accused him of being selfish and self-centered, and the lurking suspicion that the charge was justified stung him. If he had taken Tim's advice and turned the treasonous letters over to John Hawkins in the first place, none of this tragedy would have happened.

It occurred to him suddenly that there might still be sufficient time to appeal to Admiral Hawkins. His was a name to conjure with—Hawkins of Plymouth, the dread *Achines de Plimua,* as the Spaniards called him! Even King Philip, who deemed himself master of the world, trembled at the name. Magnus cursed his own

84

stupidity. Why hadn't he thought of that before? If bluff old "Cap'n John," as he was affectionately known, suspected that an Englishman was held against his will aboard a Spanish ship in Plymouth Sound, he would rend the vessel apart, plank by plank! Aye, Magnus decided, he'd put back and appeal to Hawkins.

But even as he swung around to give the order, Pequeño pointed excitedly off to starboard.

"Praise the Virgin, *monsieur!* There she is!"

Magnus bent his head to peer under the foot of the sail. At first he could see nothing, then as the boat rose on a crest, through the flurry of spray he distinguished the loom of a ship broad off the bow.

Rearing out of the murk, she appeared immense, and unnaturally foreboding. There was no light aboard, and with her slab sides and lofty stern castle, she seemed impregnable. The foolhardiness of his scheme was sharply borne home to Magnus. Armed only with a dagger, and accompanied by a stranger he instinctively did not trust, his common sense warned him it was the height of folly to proceed.

Pequeño, however, seemed to have regained his courage.

"By the saints, *monsieur,* we are in luck!" he chortled softly. "Not so much as a stern lanthorn! That means none of the crew has returned and the watchmen are too drunk to light the lamps. *Gracias a Deus!* Maybe we find some gold? *Oui, amigo?*"

In his enthusiasm Pequeño was now leaping from one language to the other. The contrast with his own mood made Magnus savage.

"No!" he snarled. "We'll have all we can do to rescue the old man and get out alive! Where is the ladder?"

"*Puxa!*" chuckled the Portuguese. "These Spaniards are fools! We take the larboard side. *Oui?*"

"Very well, but for God's sake lay her alongside quietly! If you rouse the watch, we are undone!"

Pequeño knew his business. He put the boat on the other tack, smartly rounded the stern, and coasted up the lee. Meanwhile, Magnus doused the sail, slipped his poniard between his teeth, and stood ready with the painter. An instant later, the small boat veered alongside and Magnus could make out the rope ladder dangling above him. He caught it and made fast.

The little man sprang to his side. "I go first! I know the way!"

You're too damned eager, thought Magnus. Aloud, he growled, "You stay behind me!"

"*Oui, oui!* As you like it, *monsieur!*"

When the next roller lifted the boat, Magnus got his foot on the

lower rung and scrambled up the bluff topsides. From the jerk of
the ladder, he knew Pequeño was following.

Yet even as his head drew level with the rail, he had a premonition he should retreat. The huge ship was too silent. He must have
hesitated unconsciously, for he felt the Portuguese bump against
his leg. Cursing his own vacillation, he threw his legs over the rail
and dropped soundlessly to the deck.

Pequeño stopped at the head of the ladder.

"*Gracias a Deus!*" he bellowed loudly. "It is now in the hands of
God!"

Magnus spun around in temper, but no admonition passed his
lips. A great square of canvas dropped over his head and he was
borne heavily to the deck.

Chapter 8

WEIGHTED by a seeming score of men, the huge cloth effectively
enveloped Magnus, and made resistance impossible. Spanish oaths
and Spanish jibes filtered through, and once he thought he heard
a boastful cackle from Pequeño.

Yet his rage at the treachery was nothing compared to his bitter
disgust at his own gullibility. He writhed in self-contempt. He felt
himself picked up bodily and hurried across the deck. A few moments later, he was dropped unceremoniously on the planks and
the canvas removed.

The brilliance of a score of candles blinded him momentarily.
Before he could orient himself, he was pushed on his face while
his hands and feet were pinioned securely, then hauled erect.

When his blinking eyes accommodated to the light, he discovered
himself in the luxurious after-cabin of the galleon, standing between two armed seamen. He was aware of others present, but was
still too dazed by the twist of fortune to identify them—until a voice
remarked: "Catch one snake and its mate invariably appears."

Magnus went rigid and looked at the speaker. Sir Peter Beckles
sprawled in a red plush chair, silk-clad legs thrust forward, long

white fingers folded under his chin. Speechless, Magnus stared at the others. Standing on Beckles' right was a stocky arrogant Spaniard in half-armor, whom Magnus judged to be the ship's captain, and lurking in the background, his pallid features shaded by a black cowl, was the sinister figure of Frey Alonso de Cigales.

Magnus swung on Beckles. "You damned slimy bastard!" Then, forgetting his bonds, he tried to spring at the man, only to fall flat on his face.

One of the guards stamped on the back of his head and rammed his face into the thick carpet. Half smothered, he heard Beckles as from a distance.

"Confound it, what is the matter with your men, Captain Barahona? Have them remove this carrion and bring him in correctly!"

Then rattled a volley of Spanish too explosive for Magnus to follow. Rough hands scooped him off the carpet and he was hustled out of the cabin and carried forward of the mainmast. Sensing what was coming, he tried to fight, but a blow across the base of the skull paralyzed him.

The beating which followed was administered with diabolical precision. No single blow was sufficient to carry him into oblivion, yet painful enough to bring him close to the border. With boot and club they commenced at his head. His eyes were pounded closed, and he almost gagged from the blood of his lacerated mouth. When his upper extremities lost all feeling, they concentrated on his stomach. Time and again he vomited involuntarily, and only when he went limp on the very boundaries of consciousness did they finally pause.

By then, Magnus cared no longer what they did to him. Someone emptied a pail of salt water over him. He was hoisted erect and released abruptly. Unable to stand, he crashed over backwards, his head echoing hollowly on the planks.

"*Por Dios!*" laughed a seaman. "Truly, he's soft enough now to please the *magnifico!*"

"*Si!* Drag the dunghill aft!"

His feet were seized and he was dragged along the deck. Too sick to resist, he was set on his feet. This time, he made no attempt to stand, so supported by his guards, he was dragged into the cabin.

With his battered body slumped in the form of a rough S, he was brought to a halt. Although his left eye was completely closed, he could just distinguish the blurred outline of Sir Peter over the swelling of the other.

"My son, my son!" cried the Jesuit in his peculiar bell-like voice. "Why do you resist the will of God Almighty?"

Magnus did not reply, but Beckles gave a snort of impatience.

"Don't waste sympathy on the mongrel, Father," he advised. "Unless he submits, what he just went through will seem a loving caress." He raised his voice. "You hear that, Carter?"

Magnus heard, but gave no sign. He let his head sag forward against his chest while he fought to marshal his scattered wits.

Beckles grunted and went on in the same cold tone. "We have had enough preliminary passing and feinting, so I'll be perfectly frank with you, Carter. We know that you stole certain letters from the home of Sir Gregory Duane, and we mean to get them back. Pretended ignorance or obstinacy won't serve you now—make no mistake about that! There are methods of persuading the most stubborn to talk, and we shall take you apart, bone by bone, if the occasion warrants. Howbeit, for my own sake as well as yours, I trust you won't force us to that extremity. So—hear me now—*where are those letters?*"

The recollection of the unfortunate Moley in an almost identical predicament blurred across the screen of Magnus' confused mind. The vision sharpened his awareness. It was apparent now that if he should confess where the damning evidence was concealed, it would be tantamount to suicide. On the other hand, a flat refusal to answer meant torture. His plight seemed insoluble.

Beckles leaned toward him. "Don't be a fool, man! You must know this is beyond the personal. Come—we await your answer!"

Magnus managed to wag his head. "Don't know!" he mumbled.

Beckles spat an oath, then turned to the Spaniard. "Captain Barahona, see if your men cannot prod his memory!"

Before the surly Spaniard could give the order, the Jesuit swept majestically into the foreground.

"Hold!" he commanded. "Haven't you the wit to see that any more of this crass brutality will finish him?"

Beckles sniffed. "That is his misfortune. I want those letters!"

"And so does His Most Catholic Majesty!" the priest reminded him sternly. "If your blundering methods kill this man, we may never recover them! I warn you, Sir Peter, I will tolerate no repetition of the Moley incident aboard this ship!"

Beckles stiffened in anger, then the courtier in him prevailed, and he dissembled with a sly smile.

"Come now, Father, be practical. Didn't you assure me this is the thief you watched pry open the desk?"

"True, but also a sufficient reason for using circumspection!"

Somehow the innuendo hidden in the Jesuit's phrasing chilled Magnus more than any further ministrations from Barahona's men could have done. An icy wave coursed up his spine and he discovered he was holding his breath.

88

"Ah! Then you have something in mind, Frey Alonso?" observed Beckles.

"Possibly!" snapped the priest. "Meanwhile, I insist he be given an opportunity to make his peace with God!"

Beckles sighed resignedly. "So be it. Captain, be good enough to have this carrion removed."

Barahona thundered an order. Magnus was hauled bodily from the cabin, dragged along the deck, and unceremoniously flung down a darkened hold. The long fall was broken by the body of a man, and Magnus was rewarded by the welcome sound of salty English oaths.

"*Tim!*" croaked Magnus, and began to laugh hysterically.

There came a good-natured growl from the darkness. "Then 'tis you, Magnus? Why in the bloody three-masted 'ell don't ye watch yer course? Ye damned near sheared off me one good spar! So they took ye, too?" He waited for an answer, then crawled over and felt for the other.

"Speak, lad! Good God, ye're covered wi' blood! No, don't move. Lemme cast off those bonds! There—that's better."

Magnus groaned, and shifted to a less agonizing position. "Aye, they took me—with the help of that Portuguese rat Pequeño you bribed to come for me."

"*I bribed?* W'at are ye talkin' about?"

Though it was painful work forcing words through the bloody mess that had been his mouth, Magnus recounted his experience with Pequeño leading up to his capture.

Tim was furious. "As God's me life, I thought ye 'ad more sense! Why would *I* send somebody w'en I calculated ye was dead? Sure, they found Groswick at the foot of the cliff wi' 'is back broke, an' said ye must o' got the syme. Ye mean to s'y ye got clean away, an' then let 'em tyke ye?"

Magnus admitted as much, and sketched his adventures from the time they had been separated in the fight on the bluff. Tim listened in silence until Magnus told him about his return to the inn, then he could constrain himself no longer.

"But, God A'mighty, w'y didn't ye go straight to John 'Awkins?"

Magnus was ashamed to confess he had not thought of it in time.

"I figured Sir John wouldn't be interested in my personal problems."

"*Personal?*" thundered the old man. "Damn me for a lubber, I ne'er 'eard such guff! D'ye call it personal w'en ye stumble onto a pack o' traitors schemin' against yer Queen?"

"To tell the truth, Tim, I was chiefly concerned . . ."

Tim cut him short. "Ye was entirely concerned wi' yersel'—wi' none save Master Magnus Carter!"

"That's not so!" Magnus protested. "It was because of you I . . ."

"If ye'd a-thought o' me, ye'd 'ave gone to 'Awkins like I tolt ye in the fust place!" snapped Tim. "Howbeit, I care naught for mysel'. I've 'ad me 'eaven an' I've 'ad me 'ell, so death canna be much worse. But wi' ye, lad, 'tis different. I've allus liked ye, but s'elp me God, I ne'er seen so selfish, so cock-sure-'e-was-right a younker as ye be!"

Magnus was grateful for the darkness which hid his face. His beaten body which up to this moment had been numb now began to ache. He sought to better his position by shifting, and only succeeded in worsening it.

"I'm sorry you feel that way," he groaned finally. "I counted you my best friend."

"An' by God, ye can still count me yer bes' frien'!" barked the old man. "Am I less a frien' for speakin' the truth? Nay, more am I one!"

"I suppose you mean it is wrong to be ambitious. . . ." Magnus muttered, but again Tim interrupted heatedly.

"Ambitious? Self-seekin' be the better word!"

"Would you say that of Drake?"

"Sir Francis? Good God A'mighty, lad—would ye class yersel' wi' 'im?" He paused to laugh bitterly. "Aye, ye crazy cock, ye would! Well, I'll tell ye the difference: Frankie Drake was poor, aye, an' he started from scratch, true. An' ambitious 'e was, but on another tack. Sir Francis thought o' *England* fust, *'imself* second. 'E spread 'er fame, an' by so doin', made 'is own, but in that order. That I know, for the good Lord granted me the boon to serve under 'im! Ah, Magnus, Magnus, yer overweenin' vanity will be the death o' ye!"

As Tim had charged, all this was truth, and Magnus was sick enough to concede it. He felt as if Tim had poured raw salt into his wounds, wounds that went deep enough to touch his spirit. Crushed, he rolled over onto his face. He saw himself for what he was—a swaggering youth invested with overbearing conceit; a presumptuous cub who had attempted to wrest the kill from experienced old lions, only to blunder into a trap. For the first time in his active life, Magnus Carter examined his own soul—and found it wanting sadly.

Possibly the old man, out of his own experience, recognized what was taking place. He remained silent a long time, letting the bitter medicine purge the other, then he burst into a hearty laugh.

"Courage, lad, we ain't dead yet," he boomed genially. "An' 'tis a sorry day w'en two stout sons o' Devon be not equal to a few Spanish cutthroats! Courage, say I!"

"It's hopeless, Tim!" groaned Magnus.

"Bah!" sneered Tim. "I was wi' 'Awkins at St. John de Ulua w'en the plight was darker'n this. Did 'Awkins grovel on 'is belly an' w'ine? No, by God, 'e called fer beer, an' w'en the flagon was shot out o' 'is 'and by the Spaniards, 'e sang out to all o' us: 'Fear nothin', fer God, 'oo 'ath preserved me from this shot, will also preserve us from these traitors an' villains!' There spoke a *man,* lad—words to guide any true Englishman through a storm!"

Magnus forced his voice steady. "You've forgotten those letters! They'll do anything to recover them!"

"Aye, that they will, but I be not forgettin'. Question me they did, an' . . ."

"I hope to God you told them you knew nothing!"

The old man snorted. "Not I. 'Why, ye perfumed pimp,' says I to this fine courtier, 'I'll see ye in 'ell afore I'd 'and them letters o'er!' God, 'e was mad!"

"Oh, you magnificent fool!" groaned Magnus. "Now that they believe you know where the letters are, they'll put you to the torture!"

"Aye, yet if they thought I knew naught, they'd slit me throat an' feed me to the sharks!"

Magnus shuddered. "But *torture,* Tim! My God!"

Tim chuckled ruefully. "I won't lie to ye, lad—I'm scared pissless! The man 'oo says 'e ain't never afraid lies in 'is beard! But a mite o' fear be good fer a fightin' man, better'n a pint o' grog, I swear. W'y, I recolleck the time I lost me shank. I was scared, so 'elp me God, I was scared! It made me so mad, I hardly felt it w'en the Spaniard's axe took me knee aw'y. All I could think of was 'ow many Dons I could kill fust! I got me six, but if I'd been scareder, I might o' got more. So buck up, lad, we're still alive!"

"Only to prolong the agony."

"Nay, rather to serve God an' our Queen!"

Having touched the nadir of despair, Magnus' courage began to climb. "I'll try, old friend," he promised.

"Good lad! Be as scared as ye like but don't let these traitors know it. Remember, ye're a Devon sea-dog, same as Drake an' 'Awkins! Don't e'er forget that!"

Magnus opened his mouth to reply when the door in the bulkhead opened to reveal the baleful figure of Alonso de Cigales.

While the friar stood to one side holding a lanthorn high, two rugged seamen grabbed Magnus and hauled him erect. No word was spoken until he was dragged through the opening, then Tim bawled: "Take 'eart, lad, an' fear nothin' fer . . ."

A seaman viciously slammed the door and the voice was stilled. Yet the words were not lost, for Magnus soundlessly completed the charge: ". . . *for God will preserve us from these traitors and villains!*" In his mind he envisioned the original setting in which they were spoken, for he had heard the story many times: stout-hearted Hawkins braced on the shattered deck of the little warship, *Jesus of Lubeck*, her masts cut through by chain-shot and her decks awash with blood, outnumbered by Spaniards and trapped by Spanish treachery—calmly calling to his men: "*I trust in God the day shall be ours!*" The echo filled Magnus with resolve. He planted his feet firmly on the deck and stared at the Jesuit.

Frey Alonso read the look, and smiled thinly. "You . . . will . . . follow . . . me," he said, turning away.

Magnus shook off the hands of the seamen and stalked after the flowing black robe.

The friar led the way aft to a medium-sized cabin. As Magnus stood blinking in the light, Alonso ordered the guards to leave them.

One protested. "Devil take it, Father! You should not be alone with this violent heretic!"

The priest scowled. "Do you presume to advise a servant of God?"

"Heaven forbid!" gasped the seaman. "But the captain's express orders were . . ."

"Get out, you mongrel!" snapped the Jesuit peremptorily, striding toward the fellow. One of the pair was already moving out the companionway, and after hastily crossing himself, the other stumbled away.

Frey Alonso closed and locked the door. After a brief appraisal of Magnus, he crossed to a table already laden with food and drink. He poured a glass of wine and proffered it to the Englishman.

"Drink this, my son," he suggested quietly, "then eat your fill."

Magnus hesitated. He attempted to read the other's face, but found it inscrutable.

"After which . . . ?" he challenged.

"We will talk. But an empty belly aggravates the emotions, whereas food gives courage."

"Think you I need courage to face an enemy?" jeered Magnus.

Frey Alonso shook his head. "No, but you may require sanity."

The logic in that was irrefutable, Magnus admitted as his eyes strayed to the well-heaped serving dishes. He could hardly recall when last he had eaten, and the sight loosened the saliva in his mouth. Yet it was as much the need to gain time as it was his hunger that induced him finally to accept the wine.

The drink whetted his appetite, and at a gesture from the priest, he sat himself at the table. Avoiding the highly seasoned Spanish food, he ate heartily of fresh bread and beef which had obviously been brought aboard recently. Not until he had topped off the generous repast with a cluster of grapes, did he raise his eyes to the Jesuit.

From the shadow of the cowl, the bleak, feverish eyes burned into his own. Frey Alonso stood across the board as if carved out of ebony, his thin hands tucked into the opposite sleeves of his habit, his emaciated features as white and translucent as alabaster.

Magnus held his gaze steady with an effort, for there was an ominous quality in that peaked face which seemed not quite human.

"Now," he prompted, "I suppose we talk?"

The priest glided closer, which deepened the shadow on his face, yet by so doing appeared to intensify his eyes. Magnus drew back involuntarily, at the same time wondering whether the effect was natural, or premeditated play-acting. In either event, it was effective.

"My son," the friar intoned solemnly, "you stand on the very brink of disaster!"

Magnus had an insane desire to laugh. The Spaniard's English was stilted and excessively pedantic; in a more friendly setting, it would have been ridiculous.

"Thanks to you!" Magnus retorted.

Alonso shook his head. "Nay, rather it was the will of God that I witnessed your theft of those letters. Dare you deny it, and put an added lie to your sins?"

"For the meal—I thank you," Magnus said coldly, pushing back his chair to rise.

A gesture from the other gave him pause. "Hold! You pass through that door to your death!"

"So be it!" Magnus sniffed, yet he remained seated.

A ghost of a smile crossed the Jesuit's features. "I beg you to be sensible," he continued. "You are not an enemy of Christ, else I would not have interceded in your behalf. You merely blundered into something which does not concern you."

"Like Moley, perhaps?"

The cavernous eyes glittered. "Moley was a paid spy of that heretical Jezebel who usurped the throne of England. As a servant of Satan, he warranted his deserts. Your case is not comparable. We know the whole truth. You came to my lord's castle on personal business. That you chanced upon this other matter was a happenstance—at least I am charitable enough to believe so. Of course, you should not have been there; nevertheless, your offense was

93

secular, and therefore outside my province. But when you seized those documents, you served the Devil's own purpose. However, you can still escape the fruits of that folly by telling me where they are hidden!"

"And if I refuse?"

The friar shrugged his shoulders. "You will have tied my hands, and must reap the harvest you have unwittingly sown. But why throw your life away? That is what it amounts to, for it was only over Sir Peter's most vigorous protests that I am with you now. He insisted that you and your confederate be put to the question immediately. I disagreed. Knowing the Devil's own stubbornness which curses the English race, I argued that you would die rather than confess under the brutal mauling you would receive from those unskilled seamen."

Magnus scowled. He read a sinister import into the other's words though their meaning was obscure.

"In that, you spoke the truth," he conceded, "but the gist of your argument with me is a lie in itself! Suppose—without admitting it, of course—suppose I was either fool or coward enough to deliver those letters to you, would you liberate me? Do you expect me to believe such?"

Alonso flushed slightly. "I could liberate your soul, Magnus Carter!"

Magnus laughed without mirth. "My soul stays in my body, God willing! No, I'll not bargain with you. Let that pimp Beckles do his worst, and I'll show you how an Englishman can die!"

The priest was unimpressed. "I know that—I've seen Englishmen die," he said dryly. "An uncultured breed of beasts, they die sublimely in the heat of battle or sudden brutality. But there are other methods, slower methods, my son, when this grandiose valor wearies of posturing and slinks away, leaving them all too human. We more civilized peoples have given study to such problems."

Magnus felt his skin crawl. "I know your Spanish methods!" he snarled.

"That simplifies it. We understand each other."

"Call in this treasonous whoreson! Get it over with! I weary of mealy-mouthing!"

"Patience, my son, patience!" soothed the Jesuit. "There is no need to call anyone. You are now on a Spanish vessel, and I, and I alone, am the emissary of His Most Catholic Majesty, King Philip the Second. I give the orders here. Now the situation is this: I was sent to obtain certain documents; I cannot return empty-handed."

Magnus' nerves quieted slightly. "It appears you will have to, Frey Alonso."

94

"On the contrary, I must take, either the letters themselves, or . . ." He paused to let his words penetrate, ". . . or the living proof of what happened to them."

Magnus gasped. *"Me?"*

"The choice rests with you, my son. Naturally, I would prefer the letters. What will happen if you persist in your obstinacy, I cannot say, for it will then be a matter falling under the jurisdiction of the Holy Office. My responsibility ceases when we reach Spain."

Magnus was too appalled to speak. The gaunt face of the priest lengthened in sadness and the bell-like voice took on a note of supplication.

"Reflect well your answer, my son, I pray you! Let the Divine Grace of our Holy Father cleanse you of this false pride which is making you an unwitting instrument of Satan. Cast out his evil spirit and spare yourself unnecessary suffering in this world and eternal damnation in the next. Reflect, I beg you, before you close the door on mercy!"

Magnus lowered his lids to blot out the chilling black specter. The image of Rosalind passed across his mind then gave way before the recollection of one-legged Tim laughing in the face of death. *"We lives,"* he seemed to hear the old warrior whisper, *"to serve God an' our Queen!"*

Magnus opened his eyes to look Alonso de Cigales full in the face.

"No, damn you! Not even your Holy Office can make me betray my Queen! God bless her!"

For an instant the eyes of the other blazed in anger. He clapped his hands smartly, yet before the guards burst into the cabin in answer to his summons, the mask dropped back in place. Alonso's slim, transparent hand performed a benedictory gesticulation.

"Pax Domini sit tecum!" he intoned regretfully, and waved Magnus away.

Book Two

SPAIN

Chapter 9

THAT autumn of 1584 was a sorry period in England's history. Internally plagued by bitter religious strife skillfully abetted by fugitive Jesuits and the beautiful Mary Stuart, Queen of Scots; externally threatened by the menace of Spain, then spreading over Europe like a blight; boycotted and haunted by poverty, she was in addition ruled by a queen who dreaded to bring the issue to a head because she hated war. Precarious as was England's plight, Elizabeth continued to back and fill, and her policy, if policy it could be termed, was "the web of Penelope, woven in the day and unravelled during the night." Though she had no navy worthy of the name, she did have, in Hawkins, Frobisher and Drake, three of the greatest seamen of that or any other time. These, however, she kept on leash.

Meanwhile, Philip of Spain spread his nets. He fostered rebellion in England, connived with Mary Stuart and her adherents, and shipped over Jesuit agitators. His ministers intrigued, his generals planned, his spies plotted, while his shipyards hummed like giant hives building ships for the inevitable assault on England. English seamen were imprisoned, chained to galley sweeps, or tossed to the wolves of the Inquisition. Appeals to either monarch were futile: Philip merely shrugged and insisted he dared not offend the Holy Office; Elizabeth argued that she could not plunge her country into war to avenge the few.

Thus matters stood in 1584.

Magnus Carter had never troubled himself with these large problems, nor did he now, as he lay chained in the dank hold of the galleon. He had seen a deal of death in his short span, and he knew full well what to expect. Yet though he sought to reconcile himself to the inevitable, the suddenness of the disaster had caught him unawares. He found it difficult to conceive that the end of everything was actually at hand. Death, he began to realize, was too

99

serious an ordeal to face without due preparation, for there was so much, so tragically much, he wanted to accomplish before passing into oblivion.

Huddled in the darkness, he tried to talk it out with Tim. But the old shellback was a stoic; the root of his argument being that when you lived by the sword, you perforce died by the sword. Since death was unavoidable, why such a bother about it? Meet your God like a man!

During the endless nights of the voyage, asleep or awake, Magnus dreamed of Rosalind. Dallying in this treasure house of memories, he felt certain that could he but spend a year, aye, even a month, in her arms, he could meet death with fortitude. The realization that he would never see her again—worse, that the scoundrel most responsible for his plight would take her to wife—was almost more than he could bear. He felt that Fate had not played him fair.

He lost all count of time, but at last he heard the anchor cable scream through the hawse pipes. Spain—the beginning of the end! With the passage of time, suspense commenced to gnaw. Why didn't the hounds of hell come for them? Surely no torture could be worse than the uncertainty of waiting . . . waiting . . . !

A day or two later, the bulkhead opened and Magnus was hauled on deck. The blazing noonday sun seared his eyes, and when he could use them, he was appalled at his condition. His clothes were tattered and caked with filth; his face, a mat of hair. Anxiously staring over the rail, across the opalescent waters of the harbor, he saw a green hillside covered with terraced vineyards and small white houses. Several tall galleons lay close inshore under the protection of a circular fort high on the bluff, and in the opposite direction, out beyond the roadstead, a small fleet of galleys guarded the harbor entrance.

Then Magnus saw something else that all but congealed his blood. Six black-garbed figures skulked under the break of the poop, like a row of vultures. Too often had he heard of these creatures not to know them for what they were—the *alguaziles* of the Inquisition, the pursuivants of the dread Holy Office.

They appraised him with brooding eyes, yet made no move toward him. Magnus clamped his jaws tight. If they were waiting for him to show terror, they had a long wait ahead of them. He drew himself erect, despite his chains, and met their stares. This impasse was broken when his immediate guards prodded him into motion and steered him aft to the great cabin.

To Magnus' astonishment, he found himself face to face with Sir Peter Beckles.

100

Magnus was shoved forward until only the width of a long table separated them. On the other side, Beckles lounged in a crimson tapestried chair, his hands folded over the swept-hilted guard of a sword standing between his legs. He scanned the prisoner's bitter face for a moment, then turned to the guards.

"Wait beyond the door. I want to find out if time has brought this young cub to his senses."

While the guards backed out of the cabin and closed the door, Sir Peter leaned back in the chair.

"No doubt you wonder why I trouble to summon you," he observed, adding with a soft inflection, "especially when it is almost too late."

Magnus caught the inflection as it was intended he should, but was not lulled by it. Hope he had none; hate, plenty and some to spare. Beckles read his expression correctly.

"You do me wrong, Carter," he said with a short laugh. "I didn't bring you here to mock you, but to reason with you, if possible. It revolts me to see a fellow-countryman turned over to these crow-colored familiars of the Inquisition. After all, I, too, am an Englishman."

Magnus curled his lips in a sneer. "Are you so, *Ser Pedro?*"

Most of the mirth went out of Beckles' smile, but the grimace lingered. "It is not meet for a gentleman to lose patience with mean-born, gutter-mouthed brats," he went on slowly. "Though I confess you try me sorely." He straightened in his chair. "Look here, Carter, let us be sensible! If your intense animosity is predicated on personal jealousy, let me disabuse your mind—for both our sakes. In view of certain disclosures, I am definitely not a rival. This should prove it." He reached into his doublet and extracted a sealed letter which he slid across the table within easy reach of the other.

"It is addressed to you. From the writing, I assume it is from the hand of my lord Duane's niece."

Magnus could not believe his ears, nor, when he looked down, his eyes. Yet there it was, with the seals intact and his own name scrawled across the face of it. He almost feared to touch it, lest it vanish.

"Read it," Beckles urged, smiling. "It may clarify things."

Still Magnus hesitated. It seemed somehow profane to peruse a message from Rosalind in the presence of this man. Then the thought came to him that if he tarried too long, Beckles might retrieve it. He picked it up.

"How came you by this?" he demanded, turning the packet over in hands that for the life of him wouldn't stop trembling.

101

Without replying immediately, Beckles plucked a few grapes from a cluster on a near-by dish, and popped them into his mouth. Then he relaxed against the back of his chair.

" 'Od's death!" he chuckled. "Is it not enough to receive a letter from your lady love without questioning the circumstances of its delivery? Read it, man, and put your mind at ease."

Suspicious and distrustful, Magnus tore away the seal. He took a step backwards before unfolding the epistle, as if half-expecting Beckles to snatch it away. But Sir Peter was comfortably ensconced in his chair, studying him with lazy-lidded amusement. Magnus took a deep breath, as a diver about to enter deep water, and read:

My own beloved Magnus: Uncle has just now left me after a ghastly two hours' visit. By this time, with Our Lord's help, you should be safely on the road to Plymouth. I shall pray for you until dawn, whereupon I shall find some means of getting this note to you.

Well, dear one, as I promised you, I showed Uncle Gregory the letter from Father. I declare, I never saw anyone so angry! He raged about thieves in the house and vipers to his bosom, but I was adamant and insisted that Father's wishes be followed. At first, he flatly refused to heed me, claiming I was legally his ward. He even went so far as to threaten me with prison for breaking into his private desk. But when I assured him I could prove that I had not left my room, the goodness in him prevailed, and he surrendered to my wishes.

Howbeit, he made one stipulation. Without accusing you by name, he declared that certain valuable documents belonging to friends had been purloined from his desk. This loss is causing him grave concern. His final word was that we can be married as soon as the documents are returned to him, *but not before.* He was most emphatic about that.

What could I say, my sweet? Did you perhaps pick them up by mistake when you took the letters from Father? If so, by all means return them to me by the bearer of this note so I can slip them back in place.

So now, only that trifle stands between us, thank God! Oh, Magnus, Magnus, I love you so! *Hurry, hurry, hurry!* I'll be hungrily waiting for you if it takes forever!

Always, your own
Roz

The date on the letter was of the night he had visited the Duane castle.

102

Magnus slowly folded the paper and looked at Beckles. The latter was staring dreamily at the cross-beams overhead.

"You know the contents of this letter?" Magnus challenged.

Beckles lowered his eyes to meet the other's. "Only in a general way," he said with a shrug. "I was told it might change your attitude somewhat." His manner turned brisk. "Come, let's get down to business. The officers of the Holy House are already on board, and I dare not risk offending them by undue delay. These are busy days for them, and if they cannot secure a victim here, they'll have to look elsewhere. It is up to you."

"How so?"

A shadow of impatience darkened the other's face. "We are wasting time, Carter!" he snapped. "You know well what I want—those letters you stole! Give them to me, or tell me where they are, and you can have your wench and welcome."

"You'll take us back to England—Prettyman and me?"

"Yes, eventually."

"Ah! You qualify it, Ser Pedro?"

"God's death, you exasperate me with your sniveling mockery! Haven't you the wit to see I cannot turn you loose in England until . . . well, until certain matters take a turn for the better." He pointed toward the hillside, visible through the stern windows. "That castle you see there behind the town was placed at my disposal by the King of Spain. If you are reasonable, you and your foul-mouthed innkeeper can reside there until it is deemed safe to return you."

"Meanwhile, you will pay court to . . ."

Sir Peter interrupted tartly. "I take no used and soiled trulls to wife, Carter!"

Magnus started forward, but reined in his temper in time. After all, this reprieve, coming as it did at the eleventh hour, was more than he had hoped for. The unexpectedness of it dazed him. Peculiarly enough, it was the very deal he had planned originally; to trade the incriminating letters for the right to marry Rosalind. What more could he ask?

"It is your last chance!" warned Beckles.

Magnus was sorely tempted. He opened his mouth to agree, then closed it without speaking. Nor could he have explained his hesitancy, for at the moment, his mind was in a welter of confusion.

He said slowly, "You say you cannot return us to England *until certain matters take a turn for the better.'* Precisely what do you mean?"

Sir Peter smiled the smile of tolerance one might use on a child. "There's no harm telling you, I suppose," he drawled. "What I hinted at was that within a matter of weeks or, at the very most, months, the rightful Queen of England will replace that usurping whore Elizabeth. When that happens, you have my promise, you and your crippled friend shall be returned."

"But how can you be certain this will happen so soon?"

Beckles shook his head in irritation. "Confound it! Haven't I told you the plan is settled!"

"Then," sneered Magnus, "why are these letters so bloody important to you and your fellow traitors?"

Sir Peter sprang to his feet. "Enough! Do you tell where they are hidden, or not?"

Magnus drew himself to his full height. "No, by God, I don't! But what I will tell you, you murdering, treacherous whoreson, is that you stole this note from the body of a twelve-year-old child you assassinated!"

Sir Peter's face turned livid. With an inarticulate oath, he wrenched his sword from its scabbard, and started around the table.

Magnus scooped up a light chair and waited for him. "Come on, you half-Spanish mongrel!" he taunted. "You didn't show this kind of willingness when *I* had a sword in hand!"

Beckles had almost reached him when the door opened and Frey Alonso swept into the cabin.

"*Alto!*" he cried. "What goes on here? Stand back, Sir Peter!" He stepped in front of the irate knight.

"Out of my way, Frey Alonso!" stormed Beckles, completely out of temper. "This is a personal matter!"

The Jesuit raised an imperious hand. "Stop, I charge you! Dare you defy the will of the Holy Office? Do you presume to keep this heretic from God's justice? I warn you, Sir Peter, to interfere with the *Casa Santa* is a venial sin!"

Beckles' choleric color faded to a sickly paleness. With an obvious effort, he unlocked his muscles and let the sword arm sag to his side.

"The cur provoked me out of all reason!" he growled lamely.

"You were but the victim of passion," chided the priest, and turned to Magnus.

"My responsibility is ended, my son," he said sorrowfully. "May our Heavenly Father take pity on thee!"

Magnus understood him. "Call in your deputies of Satan!" he snorted.

Frey Alonso sighed, then glanced toward the open doorway and crooked his finger. An instant later, the black-garbed familiars closed around Magnus.

"*Dominus vobiscum!*" murmured the Jesuit as Magnus was led away.

104

On the deck, he found Tim, also in custody. Their eyes met briefly; Tim's held first question, then satisfaction. No word was spoken as they were prodded overside into the waiting barge, but as they huddled on the thwart, Tim growled, "By Neptune, lad, I figgered we'd parted company!"

Magnus sniffed. "We came damn close to it. That swine Beckles is aboard. He tried to run me through, but the priest stopped him."

"Aye, the devils won't be cheated o' their fun!"

As the barge neared the mole, they found the landing jammed with a gaping horde, drawn by the presence of the apparitors of the Holy Office. A guard of javelin-men cleared a path through the crowd as the landing was effected. Magnus and Tim were heaved onto a pair of mules, since their bonds prevented their helping themselves. Frey Alonso, who had accompanied them ashore, tucked up his gown and mounted a third mule. The *alguaziles* bestrode splendid black horses. A sharp command was barked, and with a trumpeter bearing the pennon of the Holy Office in the lead, the little cavalcade jangled into motion.

They traveled all that day over a road which was little more than a rutted mule-track. Magnus estimated they must have covered close to six leagues when, late in the afternoon, they saw ahead a town nestled in a green amphitheater, and dominated by the inevitable castle. To Magnus, there was something symbolic in the relationship of that castle towering above the simple white huts of the peasants; it seemed to embody the salient characteristics of an arrogant *hidalgo* lording it over his serfs. The Englishman's lip curled disdainfully. *Spain!* The very word was an epithet in his mouth.

When they entered the narrow streets, crowds formed quickly. Unlike the previous village where the people had been morbidly curious and mute, these spat and jeered at the human scarecrows reeling on the mules. Magnus was relieved when they turned at last into the courtyard of a long, squat, windowless building near the plaza. A gate was closed in the faces of the leering mob, and the prisoners were hauled to the ground.

Old Tim had trouble standing after the long hours in the saddle. His natal leg refused to support his weight, and he spun dizzily on his wooden peg, like a rundown top. His gyrations brought ribald laughter from the *alguaziles,* which was sharply squelched by their captain. The Englishmen were then half dragged, half carried toward the building.

Despite his exhaustion, Magnus appraised it carefully. They approached a large Gothic doorway, over which hung the green cross of the Holy Office, and beneath it, the motto: *Exsurge Domine et*

105

judica causam Tuam. The doors opened to admit them to a great stone hallway.

After the searing heat and dust of the journey, the cool gloom of the cloistered Holy House made it seem a haven of safety. Yet when the huge doors closed with ponderous inexorability, the sense of peace vanished, leaving Magnus with the suffocating sensation of being buried alive.

Two familiars, in the black-and-white robes of the Dominican order, took charge and the prisoners were herded down a winding stairway into the very bowels of the building. Here, the air was permeated with a contradictory blend of odors—wax and incense from a near-by chapel, excrement from the dungeons still below. A fitting stench, Magnus thought bitterly, for the den of the Inquisition.

His hope that he and Tim might remain together was soon blasted. On entering a long, dark tunnel, one of the lay brothers paused before an iron door embedded in the wall. Opening the door, he stood aside and gestured Magnus inside.

Magnus paused for Tim to precede him, but an *alguazile* gave him a shove that precipitated him headlong through the aperture. Freighted with chains, he tripped and fell down. Simultaneously, the door clanged shut with a crash that reverberated through the entire structure.

Stunned, Magnus lay where he had fallen and watched the light pass away. Soon he heard another door open, then close. The footfalls of the guards passed his cell once more, leaving only darkness and a sepulchral silence.

Chapter 10

Magnus dragged his weary body onto a pallet and sat huddled up with his head resting on his folded arms. He was haunted, as he had been all the day, by the letter from Rosalind. Why in God's name had he not agreed to the ultimatum Sir Peter had offered him? He was not the cloth from which martyrs were cut! Now he would die, and she, whom he loved more than life itself, would be abandoned to the will of Gregory Duane.

Judged by any standards that he knew, it just didn't make sense! Yet when he remembered the little page's body lying in the old barn in Plymouth, and the leering arrogance of Sir Peter, he realized that he could never have made his peace with such a knave. It was not love of his Queen, nor even country, which had guided his actions, so much as an innate love of justice. He could not have done otherwise. Better to die a score of times than survive in self-loathing and contempt.

Having made peace within himself, he stretched out on the hard pallet. What he needed now above all else was rest to prepare him for the ordeals ahead. . . .

Hours later, he was awakened by the grating of a key in the lock. He rose, stiff and sore, to face the familiars. They beckoned him without sound, and he stumbled out into the corridor where two men in sleeveless leather jerkins awaited him. The sight of their bruted faces, close-cropped skulls and naked hairy arms gave Magnus a hint of what was in store for him. He had seen hangmen's lackeys before this.

One of them gave him a shove that sent him reeling along the corridor. When he tripped over his chains and struck his head on the slime-covered wall, they laughed.

"These English dogs die hard," one chortled, not realizing, or caring perhaps, that Magnus understood Spanish.

"So much the better," gloated the other.

After a too-gentle admonition from the Dominican friars, they seized Magnus by the arms and hurried him up one flight of stairs into an austere whitewashed room where sat the ecclesiastic court in silent solemnity. Through a funnel-shaped opening high on the wall came a single shaft of daylight that made a square on the floor. The guards stood Magnus in the center of this, and retreated into the surrounding gloom.

Magnus absorbed the place in one apprehensive glance. Before him stretched a long table upon which stood a tall crucifix between a pair of candles, and near it, a vellum-bound copy of the Gospels. The tribunal, composed of four cowled and forbidding figures, sat on the other side of the table. At one end crouched a fifth Dominican, obviously the notary, from the quills, inkstand and tablets laid out before him. At the opposite end perched the black-robed Frey Alonso in the dual capacity of accuser and translator.

Through a vaulted arch was another chamber, dimly illumined by cressets—the torture room. In its center was the *garrucha,* or

107

hoist, which was nothing more than a rope rove through a pulley attached to the ceiling. To one side of it stood the dreaded *escalera*, used for the water-torture. Beyond it, dim and hideous in the fallow light, was the rack.

Magnus suppressed a shudder, and turned back to the tribunal.

The presiding Inquisitor was a heavy, black-visaged man with chill, pale eyes, who spoke in a rumbling growl that reverberated through the chamber.

"Como se llama usted?"

It came to Magnus that he would be well advised to plead ignorance of that tongue, for though he spoke it fluently enough for general conversation, he might well involve himself in fine shades of meaning before these masters of trickery.

"You will have to speak in English," he said.

The Inquisitor glanced questioningly at the Jesuit. Frey Alonso smiled faintly, as at a private joke, before translating Magnus' remark. Then he turned his strangely sad eyes on the prisoner.

"Hark now, my son, you have nothing to fear," he promised in a soft, confiding tone. "I pity you, and am anxious to help. Therefore, let us expedite this affair for the good of your body and your immortal soul." He repeated that in Spanish for the benefit of the notary, then turned back. "Now—what is your full name?"

"You know bloody well what it is!" snapped Magnus.

Frey Alonso chose to ignore the statement. To the others, he translated: "Magnus Carter, an English gentleman."

Again, to Magnus: "Do you confess you were reared in the Protestant heresy?"

"I confess nothing!" stormed Magnus. "I am an English subject, seized in English territory, and dragged here against my will! Therefore this damned Spanish mummery has no jurisdiction over me! I demand my immediate release!"

The Jesuit spread his thin hands in a gesture of helplessness and reiterated the outburst in his native language. The cowled figures stiffened and leaned forward in unison. The Chief Inquisitor spoke briefly, after which Frey Alonso reframed his comment into English.

"My son, my son, cease to employ this defiant attitude. It can gain you nothing but pain. We are all your friends, and realizing you have been trained in heresy from infancy, and therefore unable to tell right from wrong, we wish to help you for the glory of God Almighty. So do not attempt to conceal the truth from us!"

"I've had enough of this!" grated Magnus. "Come to the point!"

The Jesuit sighed. "You stand charged here with the heinous crime of heresy. Even an Englishman knows the penalty for that sin. That, and that alone, is all that interests my brethren of the

108

cloth. However, I sit here, not only as your friend, but as an envoy from His Most Catholic Majesty, our gracious and lenient Philip of Spain. Your cooperation might mitigate . . ."

"Philip of Spain is as much an enemy of God as he is to man!" Magnus cut him off. "I've witnessed his leniency and beneficence before this!"

Frey Alonso translated, and the answer was blunt.

"Let him be put to the question!"

The hairy-armed guards seized Magnus. For one mad instant, he was tempted to fight, but the utter futility of resistance and the sport it would afford these brutes constrained him. So with his chin held as proudly as his aching body would permit, he suffered himself to be led into the grisly antechamber. They moved past the brown ropes of the hoist, which dangled from the ceiling like the tentacles of a deep-sea monster, to the couch-like contrivance that was the *escalera*. It required all of Magnus' will power to stifle the panic threatening his sanity, for the curse of imagination is its ability to anticipate.

His chains were removed and he was slammed onto the narrow engine, shaped much like a ladder laid horizontally. His arms and legs were so tightly lashed to the sides of the machine that the circulation seemed cut off. After that, his head was bound rigidly in position by a leather strap across the forehead.

Not yet satisfied, the torturers wound a heavy cord across his chest and arms, then thrusting a spike into it to form a tourniquet, then began to tighten it until Magnus had to bite his lip to quell a scream. The tribunal meanwhile had gathered around the engine. The Inquisitor spoke, and the Jesuit interpreted.

"Reflect, my son, and spare yourself unnecessary suffering! By the mercy of our brethren, you are offered a last chance to confess. May Divine Grace soften your heart which sin has calloused. Speak now, I beseech you, Magnus Carter, else our duty is clear!"

Though it was agony to breath, let alone talk, Magnus managed one last sputter of defiance.

"Damn you all to eternal hell!"

At a nod from the Inquisitor, Magnus' mouth was pried open and held so by a metal prong. Wool was stuffed into his nostrils, and a strip of cloth laid across his open jaws. One of the torturers took up a vessel and commenced pouring water into his mouth. The weight of it pushed the cloth down Magnus' throat.

Never in his wildest imaginings had Magnus conceived such torment possible. As the water entered his mouth, instinct forced him to swallow, which in turn inched the strip of linen deeper and deeper. This brought on all the agony of suffocation, and when he writhed convulsively, the cords sank into his flesh. When he gulped frenziedly for air, just enough passed the saturated strip to maintain consciousness.

Twice the cloth was withdrawn, and he was exhorted to confess. On his second refusal, the executioners twisted the tourniquet about his chest until he was certain his end had come. This time he tried not to swallow, but let death bring him surcease from the incredible torment, yet the anguish of asphyxiation was more than he could endure, so he gulped in spite of his resolve.

Finally he reached the culmination of suffering, and a merciful darkness yawned before him. Gratefully, he began to descend . . .

In a trice the linen was jerked out and a pail of cold water sloshed over his face—recalling him to the immediate horrors. The thongs were slackened, and as he lay gasping for breath, the swarthy-visaged Inquisitor addressed him at length, but Magnus was in no condition to comprehend. It took the Jesuit's clear, bell-like translation to penetrate his consciousness.

"This is your final opportunity, Magnus Carter! Do you confess?" Magnus wagged his head weakly from side to side.

Frey Alonso exhaled in a lingering sigh. "My son, my son, you have scorned our mercy and tried our patience. By your obstinacy in refusing to confess, you have proven yourself a contumacious heretic, therefore the Holy Church of God can do nothing more for you. It now becomes our reluctant duty to abandon you to secular justice, and may God have mercy on your soul! *Gloria patri!*"

Flung back into his cell, Magnus had plenty of time for contemplation. He had no illusions about the meaning of his being *abandoned to secular justice;* this was merely an ecclesiastical euphemism for death by fire at the stake. Yet uninviting as that might be, he considered himself fortunate in having been sentenced after just one session of the torture, for he knew that few victims escaped the talons of the Inquisition so easily.

The explanation came later in the day when a lay brother entered the cell with a plate of food and a tabard of yellow sackcloth marked with a large red Saint Andrew's cross and decorated with dragons and devils.

No longer caring whether they knew he could speak Spanish, Magnus questioned the familiar in that language. After the first momentary start of surprise, the brother spoke freely, for he was very young, with the hunger of youth for conversation, an appetite not easily assuaged in the austere confines of the *Casa Santa.*

"Tomorrow is a Saint's Day, and there is to be a big *auto de fe,*"

110

he told Magnus. "You are to wear this *sanbenito*." He held up the cloak.

"Will my countryman wear one also?"

"*Sí!* Alas, he, too, rejected the loving mercy of the Church."

"Mercy?" scoffed Magnus. "You call torture *mercy?*"

The young novitiate seemed genuinely surprised at the outburst. "That borders on sacrilege!" he exclaimed. "How can you talk so? Is not the purpose of Divine Mercy the salvation of souls? Then it follows that the action of this Holy Tribunal is the administration of the medicine prescribed by that Divine Mercy for the curing of deadly sin! Consider, my son—would you defame the surgeon who purges his patient to eradicate a poison? Or censure a parent for punishing a delinquent child? Remember—the Holy Ghost sayeth: 'God punishes whom He loves.'"

Perceiving the futility of argument, Magnus took another tack. "Does the burning take long?"

"Only long enough to cleanse the soul. Yet there is a shorter way still. In its infinite tenderness, the Holy Office offers additional mercy to any heretic who will confess his guilt and make peace with the Church. For this kindly purpose, you will be accompanied to the stake by two of my brothers who will exhort you to save yourself."

Magnus seized at the straw. "Save myself? How?"

The younger brother smiled benignly. "If you accept this charity, you will then be strangled at the stake, thus saving your body from the temporal torment of physical fire and your soul from the everlasting suffering of spiritual flame. Is that not incontestable proof of Divine Mercy?"

In his overwrought condition, Magnus felt an insane urge to laugh. He took his head between his hands and sought to convince himself it wasn't all just a ghastly nightmare.

"Tomorrow is Sunday," the brother prattled on conversationally, "so there will be a goodly crowd. The Italians claim heretics should not be burned on the Lord's Day, but that is nonsense! Sunday assures the greatest multitudes, for the spectacle inspires attendance and presents an example which may turn them from evil practices. God Himself hath said: 'If man abide not in me, he is cast forth as a branch that is withered; and men gather them, and cast them into the fire, and they are burned.' Is that not logical?"

When he drew no reply, the familiar eventually padded away. Magnus remained huddled in the darkness, pondering what had been told him. One point was indisputable; he had closed the doors on life—his own, and Tim's. Even if he confessed now, his only

111

reward would be the strangler's garrote, and the opportunity to die, as it were, upon the loving bosom of the Church. His body would still be burned.

The macabre humor of the situation touched off hysteria, and Magnus Carter laughed himself to sleep.

Chapter 11

SHORTLY after five o'clock the following morning, Magnus was visited by two Dominican brothers. His chains were removed, and he was forced to don the grotesque *sanbenito*, which draped his big frame like an ill-fitting nightshirt. One of the familiars set a tall, pyramidal cap on his red head. This contraption was made of cardboard covered with yellow sackcloth, with a red cross and decorations of burning fagots, flecked with tongues of flame. The fact that the flames pointed upward signified that the wearer, as an impenitent heretic, was to die by fire.

Thus arrayed, a rope was tied around his neck and his wrists pinioned with the other end of it. An unlighted green candle was thrust into his hands, after which he was led into the courtyard of the *Casa Santa*. Though there were five or six other victims parading there, Magnus had eyes only for Tim Prettyman.

The sight of the stocky old seaman draped in the ridiculous gown, with its red cross and lurid little devils, his peg leg jutting under the hem, and his leathery old face glaring defiance from beneath the miter, brought an involuntary laugh from Magnus. The blasphemous sound intruding on the somber setting made Magnus the cynosure of every eye, including Tim's. Then Tim himself burst into an obscene cackle.

"Damn me, matey, ye look like ol' Nick hissel'! Ha' ye taken t' orders?"

Magnus grimaced. "Aye, the same orders as you have, Tim, though I swear the devils on that nightshirt suit you better than the cross!"

A friar sought to admonish the old man, but Tim ignored him. "'Tis us 'oo should be wearin' the crosses an' these bastards the

112

pitchers o' the Devil they serve!" As two angry *alguaziles* seized him and started for the gate, he bellowed over his shoulder: "To 'ell wi' Philip, an' God bless Queen Bess!"

The other prisoners were herded after him to the gateway where they remained in a group, waiting to take their places in the procession now forming. Magnus took the opportunity to scrutinize his fellow-sufferers.

Nearest him was a young girl, not over sixteen, with a dark tinge to her skin which suggested Moorish blood. From the unnatural twist to her body, Magnus decided her shoulders had been dislocated, either on the rack or the hellish drops of the hoist. Her sunken eyes had a metallic cast, a resignation to her fate. The flames on her costume pointed down, indicating she had chosen to be strangled at the stake.

Next to the girl stood a large, powerful-looking man whose shaven tonsure marked him for a priest, yet he wore the *sanbenito* of an impenitent heretic. Magnus was intrigued, for he could not imagine what twist of circumstances could have brought a priest to such a pass. The man's lips moved soundlessly as if in prayer, though he exhibited not the slightest evidence of fear.

Before Magnus could examine the other prisoners, the procession began to move.

Led by the great green cross of the Holy Office, now shrouded in black crepe, marched a column of chanting friars of the Order of Saint Peter the Martyr. Behind these Soldiers of the Faith came four acolytes bearing a canopy of scarlet and gold, to shade the priest who was to celebrate the Mass. He bore the Host, and was preceded by a bell-ringer. More Dominicans followed the canopy, and as they drew abreast the gate, the prisoners were prodded out to take their places in the line, each attended by two familiars.

The big fellow whom Magnus suspected of being a priest went first. His attitude was puzzling, for it was not actually defiant, it was exceedingly firm and determined. When the accompanying Dominicans commenced exhorting him to confess, he raised his voice in Latin prayers as if to drown out their whining supplications.

The young girl went next, moving in a pathetic crab-like motion and supported by the Soldiers of Christ, then out strode Tim Prettyman, his brass-bound peg rapping incongruously on the cobbles. Above the clamor of the bell-ringer, Magnus heard him bellow at the two monks beside him.

"Belay the talk, ye Spanish swabs. I don't savvy that Spanish gibberish!"

Magnus wagged his head in admiration and wondered if he himself could face the ordeal ahead with the same fortitude. Then at a nudge from his guards, he moved into the line shuffling ponderously through the crowded streets.

On reaching the town plaza, the procession circled it, affording Magnus a glimpse of the rest of the cortege. Directly behind the prisoners came a company of constables and men-at-arms with glistening halberts, then the official banner of the Inquisition followed by the sacred Inquisitors on mules draped in mourning. Lastly came the secular justiciary and his armed *alguaziles*. In this wise, the bizarre parade continued to the Cathedral Square where two immense scaffolds had been erected.

It reminded Magnus of a gigantic stage. On one side were tiers of benches, rising like steps, for the prisoners; the highest being reserved for those to be turned over to the tender mercies of the secular arm. As each victim took his assigned seat, his accompanying familiars sat on either side of him.

An altar had been raised on the opposite scaffold, and chairs arranged for the Inquisitors, who waited until all the prisoners had been settled before assuming their places. With theatrical pomp, the green cross was laid on the altar, tapers lighted, the thurible kindled, and as a pungent cloud of incense spiraled upward, Mass was said.

Magnus wished heartily that all this fol-de-rol would end so they could have over with the sordid business, but he soon learned that the Inquisition was not to be hurried. As the young novitiate had explained, this was a spectacle, a warning to the faithful not to stray from the path charted by the Church. No sooner had the Mass droned to a conclusion, than the Presiding Inquisitor delivered a lengthy sermon on the virtues of faith and the everlasting hell yawning for those lambs who wandered.

But at last it ended and the dignitaries turned their attentions to the human sacrifices broiling in the sun. As the ecclesiastic notary thundered the name of the accused, the victim was brought forward and seated on a stool in the center of the stage to receive sentence.

The young girl went first. She had to be carried to the stool and supported while the brass-lunged notary read a wearisome complaint. In essence, she was accused of an affair with a Jew, and of refusing to tell the familiars of the Holy House where her lover could be found. For this unpardonable sin, the Church had cast her out and abandoned her to the secular arm.

That seemed the end of it, but to Magnus' astonishment, there followed the farce of the *efficaciter*—an intercession in which the Inquisitor pleaded with the secular justice to so deal with the girl

114

that no blood would be shed and that she suffer no hurt in either body or limb. Having thus sidestepped the responsibility, the Inquisitor added that, because under the *question* she had confessed her sins and begged for mercy, the divine tenderness of the *Casa Santa* permitted that she be strangled at the stake.

Despite the support of the Soldiers of the Faith, the girl fainted on hearing her sentence, and slipped to the planks. She was quickly removed by the *alguaziles* and tied onto an ass to be transported to the burning place.

Before she was off the scaffold, the notary bellowed the name of one Diego Valesco. Magnus' interest quickened when the big ex-priest rose with dignity and strode down to the stool. He shrugged off the supporting hands of the guards and sat straight-spined and aloof, boldly eying his accuser.

The complaint revealed that Diego Valesco had been a Capuchin monk who had warranted canonical purgation because he had been suspected of harboring the thought that the Inquisition was over-zealous in its search for heretics. When charged with this mortal sin and exhorted to abjure his alliance with Satan, Diego Valesco had wantonly admitted the felonious thought, and gratuitously added other sacrilegious statements, proving his unrepentance. He had thereupon been unfrocked and degraded, and was now to be turned over to secular justice.

It was manifest that Diego Valesco was still unrepentant, for he nodded his complete agreement of the accusation, and at the conclusion, moved proudly from the platform.

Puzzled, Magnus watched him go. That the man was still a Christian was evident from his prayers, yet Magnus had assumed that all papist priests were of the same mind. How, then, this paradox?

His thoughts were interrupted by the summoning of Timothy Prettyman. Tim limped down from the benches but refused to sit on the stool until forced onto it by the *alguaziles*. The complaint was succinct: Prettyman was a violent and impenitent heretic; he had scorned the mercy of the Church; he had vilified the sacred name of Christ's Vicar, His Holiness the Pope; he had voiced scurrilous opinions of the Holy House; and emitted sundry other statements of a sacrilegious nature. He was an enemy of God, of the Church, and of Spain! Away with him!

Magnus prayed that his own sentence might be delayed a little while, for he couldn't bear the thought of seeing old Tim roasted alive. But even this boon was not granted, for Tim had barely mounted the ass before Magnus himself was summoned.

His charge might have been read from the same dossier, for the counts were identical. He tried to pretend ignorance of the language by staring blankly into space, but when the notary screamed that he had denied the existence of God, Magnus forgot himself.

"You're a bloody liar!" he roared in Spanish so that all might understand. "I serve God to the best of my ability. It is you fiends who make a mockery of His Name!"

A hand was clapped across his mouth and the charge hurriedly concluded. Magnus was loaded onto his donkey before Tim's had turned the first corner.

The burning grounds were in an open field, just beyond the city walls. Here the crowd was denser than around the scaffolds and the *alguaziles* had to force a path through them with horses. The heavy charred stakes were set in a semicircle against the ancient walls so that all could view the edifying spectacle. As Magnus rode up, he saw the young girl hanging limp against her blackened chains. The strangler had just stepped back as an ecclesiastic lackey plunged a blazing torch into the fagots. A delighted roar went up from the throng as the flames rose about the body.

Diego Valesco was already chained in place, and the guards were securing Tim to his stake. As Magnus rode past, the old man looked up.

"Now we'll show these black-'earted bastards 'ow an Englishman dies!" he sang out, adding with a wry grin, "Anyway, it can't be much 'otter'n this damn sun."

"Aye, we'll show 'em," returned Magnus with all the jauntiness he could muster.

A moment later, he was hauled from the donkey and thrust against the stake.

"There is still time to repent," coaxed one of the brothers. "Confess and save your soul!"

If Magnus had needed a stimulus to bolster his courage, that whining supplied it. He was almost overwhelmed with rage, and had his arms been free, he would have knocked the supplicator down. As it was, he could only shout, "Get away from me, you sniveling hypocrite! You have my body, but God willing, you'll not get my soul!"

Somehow, his glance caught the eye of Diego Valesco. Though the executioner was just shoving his torch into the ex-Capuchin's fagots, Valesco smiled, and in a soft, penetrating voice, called across the intervening space: "*Valor, señor, valor!*"

Magnus forced a grin. "*Gracias, amigo!*" he shouted back. "Go with God!"

Leaving the flames licking at Valesco, the executioner started to ignite Tim's fagots. Magnus couldn't stand the sight, so he turned

116

his head away, just as a horseman fought his way through the press of people and came galloping across the clearing.

"*Alto ahí!*" he commanded, flinging out of the saddle. The captain of the *alguaziles* sprang forward to stop him, but the courier whipped a folded document from his pouch and thrust it into the captain's hand.

As the latter scanned the message, his scowl deepened. With an oath, he barked an order to his henchmen. They gaped in open-mouthed astonishment until he snarled a second time; then they ran forward, and with their halberts, raked the burning fagots away from the stakes.

Having braced himself for the ordeal, Magnus was badly shaken. When the grumbling executioner unfastened his chains, he asked what had happened.

"You'll find out soon enough, *perro de inglés*—English dog!" spat the other. "And you'll be sorry you did not die peacefully here! *Vamos!*" He gave Magnus a shove that sent him reeling after the others.

In company with Diego Valesco and Tim, Magnus was loaded onto a cart. That the reprieve had not been general was demonstrated by a ghastly screech from the stakes. Magnus glanced back, and saw the flames rising about the torso of an old man. The young girl had long since lost human shape. Sickened, he turned away, whereupon the driver, cursing his misfortune in having to miss the show, lashed his horses into motion.

"W'at did I tell ye?" grunted Tim. "The swine daren't murder us 'til they find them letters!"

Magnus shrugged. The reaction from this eleventh-hour respite had almost unnerved him.

"It doubtless means more torture. I'd as soon had it over and done with."

It took a squad of pikemen to drive a crevice through the crowd who, seeing three of their victims escaping, cursed and pelted them with filth.

Tim refused to duck, bearing it with contemptuous stoicism. The Capuchin smiled.

"You are a very valorous man, *señor!*" he said in Spanish.

Tim looked at Magnus. "W'at's 'e blubberin' about?"

Magnus translated, then explained to the other that his compatriot spoke only English and a smattering of French.

"*Bon!* Then we shall speak French, for I, unfortunately, am ignorant of English." In the former tongue, he repeated his comment to Tim.

117

Tim grunted, not dissembling his distrust of all foreigners.

"I be English," he said brusquely. "These accursed papists can't scare me!"

Magnus was slightly embarrassed, but Diego Valesco only grinned.

"Say, rather, *misguided* papists, *monsieur*," he urged. "Not all good Catholics concur in these hellish methods, believe me."

Before Tim could widen the breech, Magnus put in: "Brother Diego is a Capuchin monk, Tim. He was condemned to death for openly disagreeing with the Inquisition."

Despite the jolting of the cart, Tim craned his head around for another look at the priest. But further discussion was postponed by their arrival at the gate tower. The prisoners were shoved into a small, airless guardroom and left alone.

"I don't understand this," Magnus mused aloud. "Why didn't they take us back to the *Casa Santa?*"

"That I can explain," offered Brother Diego, "for one of the pikemen whispered the news to me. It was an order from the King, forbidding the execution of any able-bodied men capable of serving in the galleys."

"The *galleys?*" cried Tim. "God's death! I'd rather be roasted alive!"

Magnus stroked his chin. "But I understood your King had no influence over the Holy Office! He himself wrote as much to our Queen when she protested the burning of Englishmen."

The Capuchin snorted. "The King is like a chameleon. When it is expedient, he hides behind the cassocks of the priests, as they, in turn, scuttle to him for protection when the Pope attempts to moderate their activities. It is a case of fellow thieves hanging together, or hanging separately."

Magnus gasped. "That from a Catholic priest and a Spaniard?"

"*Compañero,* you are too prone to categories," Valesco chided gently. "I am first of all a Christian, which means I love my fellow man. Secondly, I am a Spaniard, and so I love Spain. There is nothing contradictory in that. Being so does not mean I have to agree with those fanatics who corrupt the word of God and commit crimes in His Holy Name, nor with a King who uses the Church to further his political aspirations."

"You have to agree with them both to live," countered Magnus.

The Capuchin laughed. "In this short life, perhaps, but the true reckoning shall come in the everlasting life beyond. That, my son, is what matters to one who genuinely believes in God Almighty. This brief period of travail you call 'life' is relatively unimportant."

Not convinced, Magnus changed the subject.

"Isn't this reprieve unusual? What does it portend?"

118

"War!" admitted the monk. "Philip would not interfere with the Inquisition unless his plight was desperate. Spain is in a serious condition, *amigo*. This year the crops failed, with the result we face famine. Due to the ineptitude of the Colonial administrators, plus the depredations of your English pirates," he paused, smiling, "or *privateers*, if you prefer—the treasure galleons are not coming through as anticipated. Thus, man-power becomes of major importance: men to work the land, to build a mighty armada, to labor in the mines. Philip is no fool, my son; he knows the *Casa Santa* can drum up enough human torches for their *autos de fe* without destroying ablebodied men. So"—he spread his long hands in an eloquent gesture—"we go to the galleys."

Magnus frowned. "You accept it very casually, *padre*," he said with a touch of irritation. "Have you any conception of what it means to be a galley-slave?"

Brother Diego chuckled. "If I let myself get angry, then I have two troubles instead of one. But, yes, I know what it means. You see, my son, I was not born a priest. Perhaps you will forgive me if I speak of myself a moment? I was bred an *hidalgo*, with all the *hidalgo's* ingrown virtues and vices. As such, I fought in the Italian campaign, and again in the Low Countries. I have been in Hispaniola. I have seen men, women and children slaughtered by the thousands. For what? For gold, for politics, for the vanities of man. Ah, it is truly said the greatest humiliation for a man is to give proofs that he is a man! Finally a satiation point was reached when I decided to lay down my sword and raise the cross."

"You didn't gain much by that."

"Ah, well, a good hope is better than a poor possession. I was young, and the young all hope to change the world between the rise of a sun and its setting. I had to learn that haste is a fool's passion, and that this small world is but a toddling step into the Kingdom of God." He smiled ruefully. "Pardon, *amigo*, I do not mean to preach. I use words to try to clarify my own philosophy. I am no longer an idealist; my only effort is to walk in the path of Christ. I ask nothing more, for there *is* nothing more."

Magnus sank onto a bench and took his head in his hands.

"I wish I had some of your patience," he admitted.

The priest laughed. "Frankly, I could do with a bit more myself. However, we are three, and three men helping one another can accomplish more than six singly." He settled himself on the stone floor. "Let us rest, my friends."

"My very thought," growled Tim, bored by the discussion. "If we're 'eadin' fer the galleys, 'tis damn little rest we'll be gettin', I swear!"

119

Chapter 12

SHORTLY after dawn the following day, they were roused outside to find a score of other prisoners standing in a long queue. A great length of chain was stretched alongside the line, and each man was shackled to it. Thus it happened that Magnus, Tim, and Brother Diego—in that order—formed the tail of the human serpent which painfully squirmed its way across the province of Pontevedra. At each town, the prisons debouched additional fodder to swell the ranks. It was plain to Magnus that the term *able-bodied* had been loosely interpreted by the magistrates, for a shoddier collection of human riffraff he had never seen.

After an interminable march, they reached the Bay of Vigo, one of the best of the Galician fjords. Stumbling down toward the waterfront, Magnus was appalled by the number of vessels crowded into the spacious harbor. If proof were needed to substantiate the truth of the Capuchin's prophecy about Philip readying an armada, he found it here. In half a dozen shipyards reared gigantic skeletons which swarms of workmen were busily sheathing with timbered flesh.

"Just w'at 'Awkins and Drake 'a been sayin'!" fumed old Tim. "It means war, damme! I wish m'lud Burghley could see this wi' 'is blind eyes!"

In Vigo they were herded into a stockade with several hundred other victims, and in the days that followed, new recruits spewed in from the various ports of Spain. Fortunately, or unfortunately, death weeded out the weaker, until it seemed that for every wretch coming in through the gate, a dead one slid out the gutter.

During this period, Magnus and Brother Diego built up an enduring friendship. Tim was in it, too, with reservations, for he couldn't quite bring himself to trust a papist priest. But if the Capuchin was cognizant of the stiffness in the old salt's manner, he gave no sign.

As for Magnus, he was fascinated by the man. Heretofore, the

120

clergymen he had known had filled him with a sense of pitying tolerance that bordered on contempt. In Diego Valesco, he discovered a man whose piousness added to his masculinity, instead of detracting from it. His humility was not cringing, but direct and fearless, and he used Christianity, not as a shield to hide behind, but as a sword of offense.

This was demonstrated on the fifth day of their incarceration in Vigo, when a Catalan blacksmith of monstrous proportions attempted to wrest some food from a forlorn little Jew. There had been a deal of this, for the food was bad and the portions niggardly, and since the guards remained outside the stockade, the laws of the jungle prevailed inside.

On this occasion, the Jew resisted and came scurrying across the compound with the blacksmith at his heels. The three friends were seated against a wall, and it was over Tim's outstretched peg leg the Jew tripped, his plate miraculously skidding across the ground without spilling. It came to rest in front of Brother Diego.

The big Catalan kicked the wailing Jew out of the way and reached for the plate, but the monk laid his hand over it.

"Do not touch it, my son," he cautioned gently. "It belongs to . . ."

"It belongs to me!" snarled the Catalan. "Who says it don't?"

The fellow's manner was so offensive, Magnus rose bristling to his feet. Brother Diego beat him to it.

"*I* said so. Hast thou not heard?"

The blacksmith scowled, then broke into a raucous laugh. "Ah, the renegade shavelin', eh? I've heard of you! What are you going to do if I take it?"

"You will leave me no choice, but I pray you will desist. We are all comrades in travail and . . ."

"Bah!" spat the Catalan, shoving the priest aside. "Go peddle your prayers elsewhere!"

Magnus stepped forward, motivated by an instinctive sense of protection for a man of God, but Brother Diego waved him back.

"Please do not interfere, *amigo*. He knows not what he does. Nevertheless, this is an excellent time to teach him." With that, the monk moved in close and hit the Catalan a back-handed swipe across the face that sent him reeling.

The Catalan was not the only one surprised. A breathless silence settled over the stockade, a silence broken by the quiet voice of Brother Diego.

"Take your food, my son," he told the terrified Jew. "Go in peace."

As the little man scuttled away with his prize, Brother Diego faced the blacksmith. The latter was smiling now as he carefully peeled off his dirty leather smock. Bared to the waist, he swelled his chest and flexed his corded muscles for the edification of the crowd.

Magnus didn't like the appearance of things, yet he wondered what to do about it. That he should do something was evident; he couldn't see a friend beaten to death, and he was satisfied the saintly monk was no match for the giant. Tim must have had the same reaction, for he rose grimly and took his place beside Valesco.

"Ah, three, eh?" jeered the blacksmith. "Only three dirty, stinking little heretics?"

Brother Diego spread his arms so that they reached across the chests of Tim and Magnus, then firmly shoved them into the background. "Let me handle this in my own way, *monsieurs*," he begged in French. To the blacksmith, he said, "I weary of your posturing. Get you gone at once, or you will have cause to regret it. I warn you—I have no desire to wallow in the gutter with a *cabrón* of your stripe. So go while you are yet able."

The blacksmith put his hands to his hips, tilted his beard skyward and bellowed with mirth.

"Hear him, *amigos?* Hear the cawing of the little shaveling crow? He seeks to hide behind the cassock, forgetting the Church took it away from him!" His laughter ceased abruptly and he glared at the monk. "Now, you yellow cur, we'll see whether you wallow or not . . . !" And lowering his head, he charged.

Brother Diego eluded the rush as gracefully as a dancer, and as the blacksmith swept past, Brother Diego pirouetted and slashed him across the back of the neck with the heel of his hand. The bully sprawled on his face.

He rose bellowing and charged again, but with more circumspection. Instead of the expected retreat, however, the monk moved forward. In a blur of motion, he dropped his right arm around the blacksmith's head, clamping the throat in the crotch of his elbow. Simultaneously, he threw himself backward and kicked upward with his feet.

The Catalan's head struck the flagstones with their combined weight on it. Then his body followed in a flying somersault. When Brother Diego released him abruptly, he landed, groaning, a fathom's length away.

Brother Diego gave him no rest. Springing to his feet, he walked over, seized a palmful of the coarse black beard and hauled the shaken giant to his feet as if he had been a child. Holding him thus, he see-sawed him across the face with his free hand. When he finally let go, the Catalan sank into a blubbering mass.

"As I tried to tell you, we are all comrades in travail," the monk

122

said sternly, "so we cannot tolerate the presence of a bully who attempts to worsen it. Live and let live, or you may stop living. You have been punished, so now get out of my sight!"

As the blacksmith crawled away, Magnus half expected the monk to offer some pious apology for his violence, but Brother Diego merely stretched and resumed his seat. Magnus let it pass, but the forthright old seaman spoke his mind.

"By God, *padre,* that was as fine a piece o' manhandlin' as I ever laid eye to. But fer a minute there, I figgered . . ." He paused.

Brother Diego grinned. "I understand, my friend—you *figgered,* as did the Catalan, that I was but a poor helpless monk who could do no more than turn the other cheek. If you will forgive my saying so, you have an erroneous conception of Christianity. Did not Christ himself drive the money changers from the Temple? To my way of thinking, in true Christianity the strong protect the weak, and since the Lord made me strong, I do my duty as I see it."

Tim scratched his head a moment in puzzlement, then his leathery old face split into a wide smile.

"Brother," he growled, thrusting out his hand, "ye may be a Spaniard, ye may be a papist, an' ye may be a priest. But, by God, ye're a *man* fer a' that, an' Tim Prettyman 'ud be proud to shake yer 'and!"

The Capuchin accepted with alacrity. "Thank you, *monsieur,*" he said with twinkling eyes. "And may I add—you may be an Englishman, you may be a Protestant, you may even be a heretic, yet, by God, Diego Valesco is proud to be your friend!"

Thus, the pact was sealed.

Two days later, a foppish young officer came to the stockade to choose replacements for his galley. Naturally enough, he picked the strongest, which included Magnus, Tim, Brother Diego and the much-chastened Catalan, Francisco Trajan. In company of five others, they were ferried out to the galley.

Despite his apprehensions, Magnus was seaman enough to be interested in the vessel as such. She was a lovely thing, low in the water and as lean and graceful as a swan. He judged her length to be a hundred and fifty feet and her beam something under thirty. Her hull was black, her sails red and yellow—the colors of Spain— and as Magnus drew closer, he glimpsed the three bronze demi-cannon on the bow. He counted twenty-five oars on a side.

They were herded aboard and driven down into the row-chamber —a cavernous, ill-lighted hole about a hundred feet long, and packed with emaciated wretches. The new arrivals were promptly assigned to benches, but by dint of hovering in a group, without

seeming interested in each other, the three friends were lucky enough
to be placed close together; Magnus and Brother Diego on one
bench, and Tim and the Catalan directly in front of them. They
were forced to strip naked, whereupon guards riveted iron bands
around a leg of each prisoner and chained them to the thwarts.

When the guards retired, an overseer strode along the gangway,
or *coursier*, that ran above the full length of the row-chamber, and
threw down a rough shirt and pair of drawers to each man. The
drawers were made without legs, because of the chain, and were
to be donned over the head, like a woman's petticoat.

That was too much for Tim. "The damn dirty bastards!" he
fumed. "They can w'ip me er burn me on their bloody stakes, an'
I'll tyke it like a man. But, by Neptune, w'en they try to dress me
in a bleedin' female petticoat, they go too far! I been under a
petticoat too damned long as it is! I won't wear it!" He flung the
garment aside. "If the Lord calls me, like you say, *padre*, 'E can
'ave me bare-arsed or not at all!"

"Modesty," chuckled the priest, "is a specious virtue promulgated
by man to cover his own deficiencies. Since the Lord created you
the way you are, Tim, I'm sure He can stand it if you can."

"You might add," interjected Magnus, "the Lord also put splinters
in these benches."

Tim grumbled a little longer, then the humor of the situation
melted his wrath. "Ah, 'ell, like the *padre* says—it'll cover me defick-
ulties!" He retrieved the drawers and pulled them over his head.

Meanwhile, Magnus took stock of his new companions. He had
been assigned to the fourteenth bench on the larboard side, and as
Brother Diego had the place next to the gangway, Magnus found
four oarsmen on his left. Since they must live cheek by jowl for
only God knew how long, he appraised them intently.

His immediate seat-fellow was a Moor, a lithe, sinewy man who
might have been anywhere between thirty and fifty years of age.
Unlike most of the slaves, he sat straight and aloof, with a pride
and arrogance more fitting on a poop. The trio beyond him were
nondescript. One was a Huguenot, having the racking cough of a
consumptive, and the other two were aged Spaniards who looked
as if they had spent their lives over oars.

Shortly thereafter, sounds above warned them the galley was
making ready to get under weigh. Magnus stared grimly at the
huge oar sloping before him. The loom—the inboard section—was
about thirteen feet and of such a thickness that wooden handles had
been pegged into it for the slaves to grip. The entire oar, Magnus
estimated, must have been fifty feet. It seemed impossible that six

124

half-starved humans could manipulate this gigantic timber for hours on end.

Yet manipulate it they did, and instruction was served at the rope's-end. The overseer—or chief *comitre,* as Brother Diego called him in French—stood where he could hear the captain's orders, which he in turn passed on by blowing certain notes on a silver whistle suspended around his neck. Two half-naked under-*comitres* swaggered up and down the gangway above the rowers, lashing the bowed backs and screaming blasphemies on the laggards, for it was imperative the fifty oars should move in perfect unison.

Magnus was never to erase the memory of that first trial run around the Islas de Cies at the mouth of the Bay. At the *comitre's* signal, the fifty oars dipped into the water as one, and the three hundred slaves began to row.

The newcomers had trouble from the start. Whether it was due to their fresh strength, or to lack of experience, was not made clear, but hardly had the galley gained steerageway before their oar rose too soon. Thus, when they threw themselves backwards in a new stroke, they crashed their heads against the loom of the slower oar behind. Immediately the mates were above them, shrieking in rage, and the whips taught them a bloody lesson.

So it went—for eight long hours without surcease. Brother Diego bore it best of the trio, since he expended no energy on emotion. Tim, too, stood it well enough, for his powerful constitution was inured to hardships. But Magnus, consumed with hate, and not knowing how to husband his strength, was soon exhausted. Sweat and blood streamed over his body, as with one foot set on a bar of wood below, and the other braced against the thwart ahead, he reared his aching being off the seat to thrust the ponderous loom forward to arm's length, then haul back with all his might.

Push and pull, push and pull, push and pull! At first he was nauseated by the ghastly stenches churned out of the bilge and distracted by the wails of his fellow sufferers who fell under the fury of the mates. But as the hours passed, he lost the power to feel and from then on functioned automatically. When the galley finally returned to Vigo, he collapsed without a word to his fellows.

For a while, sleep evaded him. Paradoxically, in the completeness of his physical fatigue, his spirit was liberated. It soared above time and space, and like a homing pigeon, returned to England, where, by the wondrous alchemy of desire, he found his beloved, not as he had last seen her, virtually a prisoner, but as he had known her in other days—a happy maiden in her father's home.

125

She welcomed him with that eager tenderness he adored—her wide eyes misted, a shy smile dimpling the corners of her slightly parted lips. It was as if, having offered herself so fully, she almost feared lest he had changed in his feeling toward her. When he took her in his arms to prove his constancy, she made funny little sounds of ecstasy, hugging him so ardently he could feel the tips of her budding breasts.

By unspoken assent, they left the house and wandered down a cloistered lane to their secret trysting place beside a little waterfall. It was a very beautiful night, such as astronomers have never known. Although the moon was full and the stars brilliant, it was quite dark. Yet love needs no light. Nature had fashioned them a peerless bower and spread a bed of downy moss. To this they wandered in perfect communion.

Interlocked on the grass, they matched their rhythm to the beat of the waterfall, while above, the tall trees murmured approval and the wise old moon attested the rightness of it all.

Afterward, Rosalind lay on her back while Magnus combed her silky hair, an act that had become to them a part of the ritual. Meanwhile, two stars had fallen to take their stations in her eyes and the moon lent some of its warmth to clothe her lovely body. Yet, the very perfection of the setting was a drug, and Magnus felt his lids growing heavy. He tried to resist the drowsiness, but surrendered finally and nestled beside her, his cheek against her breast. He would sleep only a little while. . . .

For seven days the training continued. Occasionally, if the weather was fair, the seamen hoisted the sails, during which time the slaves hooked their oars out of water and rested. When the weather was rough or stormy, they worked in water to their waists. The food—a handful of weevily biscuits and sour beans—was barely enough to sustain life. To drink the putrid water, they had to hold their noses. On rare occasions, such as the time they rowed twenty-two hours without rest, the mates crawled into the hold and put into their mouths a piece of biscuit soaked in wine to keep them from fainting. Every day or two a man died, to be promptly thrown overboard, whereupon his place was taken by a fresh sampler of the mercy of the Holy Inquisition.

From the other slaves, the newcomers learned that this particular vessel, the *Santa Ana*, was used mainly for the entertainment of important visitors and Spanish officials. By the end of the week, she was put back into service.

But after that first bitter experience, Magnus was a different man. He grew impervious to fatigue, and though others died, he appeared to thrive; when they sobbed in self-pity, he laughed a laugh as mirthless as a hanging. The *comitres* noticed his spirit and tried to lash it out of him. Failing, they became afraid of him. He was crazy, they said. His sinews hardened, and the muscles bunched about his arms and shoulders like splices of heavy cable. For Magnus Carter was living for just one thing . . . *escape!*

Chapter 13

Escape! The word became to Magnus a bright polestar, and in the nightmarish months which followed, he thought of little else. It supplied the will to live; he burned with the purpose. Yet when he sought to arouse a similar spark in his two friends, he met with indifferent success.

Brother Diego counseled patience, arguing their destinies were in the hands of the Lord. Everything in life, including their present sufferings, was all part of a vast, inscrutable Master Plan. It was futile, therefore, to run counter to the will of God.

When Magnus retorted that "God helps those who help themselves," the Capuchin only smiled.

And though old Tim expounded his reasoning in somewhat different phraseology, the gist was much the same—let Fate take its course. He high-lighted the insurmountable difficulties. They were securely chained to the benches; they were sedulously guarded twenty-four hours a day. If, by some miracle, they were able to sever the chains and elude the guards, what then? For himself, Tim couldn't swim. And if—another impossible *if*—they were to get ashore, how could they exist in that hostile, priest-ridden land, or hope to get back to England?

"Ye know me, lad," he summarized his argument, "an' ye know I ain't afeered o' death, yet I can't see no pi'nt in givin' these bastards the pleasure o' killin' me fer nuthin'. W'ile I lives, I 'opes. Dead, I'm naught but shark-bait."

Impatient with this negative philosophy, Magnus decided to cultivate the Moor.

This posed a problem, however, for the Moor exhibited no inclination toward friendliness. In all the time Magnus had been chained beside him, the man had spoken no word to a living soul. Yet this very insular quality intrigued Magnus, for contrasted with his fellow slaves, the Moor stood out like a proud hawk chained among a flock of mangy fowl.

By English standards, he was not a big man—being, Magnus estimated, something under five foot six—but he bore himself with the carriage of a prince. Magnus deemed him ugly at first. His nose was exceedingly prominent and beaked, and, from an Englishman's point of view, his cheek bones absurdly high. But with the passage of time, Magnus began to modify his original opinion. In his own peculiar fashion, the Moor was a handsome man.

The day the Huguenot on the other side of the Moor died was the first time they spoke. As the guards dragged the emaciated corpse out of the pit, the Moor muttered a brief benediction in *lingua franca,* that strange dialect blended of many languages used by the different races who sail the Mediterranean.

"Great is the Almighty God, and Mohammed is his Holy Prophet! Go with Allah!"

During his past voyages, Magnus had picked up enough of this dialect to make himself understood, so he softly added: "Amen! And may either God or Allah show us how to avenge ourselves on these spawn of hell!"

The Moor gave him a quick, piercing glance, but made no retort at the time. However, late that night when all the others were asleep save Magnus, he spoke again.

"How camest thee hence?"

Magnus tried to tell him, but the dialect was unfamiliar and it was slow, tedious work. However, the one thing they had to spare was time, and by the end of another week, they could exchange confidences with reasonable fluency.

The Moor, Abu Ben Absedik—or *Rais* Ben Absedik, to give him his proper rank—had been a captain of a galley belonging to the Sultan of Morocco. While it was apparent he despised all Christians, his especial loathing for Spaniards was so virulent it taxed even the ample profanities of *lingua franca* to express it. He was at particular pains to assure Magnus that his capture resulted solely from being shipwrecked on the Spanish coast—the inscrutable will of an all-wise Allah—for he swore by the beard of Mohammed that while he, Rais Ben Absedik, was afloat, the Spaniard never lived who could make him strike his colors.

The ignominy of being taken alive on land had made him refuse to be ransomed, and though he had already served three years at

128

the sweeps, he insisted he would rather "rot seven times seven life-times" as a slave than go back to Islam in disgrace.

"Are you content to sit here and be beaten?" marveled Magnus.

Abu Ben Absedik shrugged. "It is kismet. When you are an anvil, be patient; when a hammer, *strike!*"

Magnus thought it a propitious moment to broach the subject of escape, but to his surprise, he found the Moor indifferent. Escape was not what he desired so much as revenge—a vengeance so terri-ble it would shake the very foundations of Spain.

"Allah does not pay in season," Ben Absedik said grimly, "he pays at the end!"

However, when Magnus hastily assured him that nothing would please him better than to pay off his own debt to the Spaniards, the Moor agreed to join in a conspiracy.

Delighted to find a kindred spirit, Magnus introduced him to Tim Prettyman, but since they could not communicate with each other, their distrust was mutual. As for the Capuchin, Ben Absedik flatly refused to acknowledge his presence.

"He is a Spaniard, is he not?"

Magnus was hard put to explain the situation. "Well, yes and no," he said. "For myself, I hate Spaniards, yet Brother Diego is different from the rest. He is . . . he is a sort of citizen of the world."

The Moor smiled bleakly. "It is truly said you English can find an excuse for anything. We of Islam never forget, and we never forgive. What is written is written!"

Magnus wisely dropped the matter and turned to the more im-portant question at hand. Ben Absedik admitted to having given the problem considerable thought, and while propounding much the same arguments advanced by Tim Prettyman relative to indi-vidual escapes, he conceded there might be other methods peculiar to galleys, a type of vessel about which Magnus knew very little.

So Rais Ben Absedik explained the basic principles of galley tac-tics as differentiated from orthodox sailing craft. It was the differ-ence between a terrier and a bull. Lighter, and carrying very little armament compared to a regulation ship of war, the galley de-pended largely on speed and maneuverability against the ponder-ous, slow-moving windships. Like the agile terrier leaping in to hamstring the bull, the row-galley usually sought to gain victory by ramming her adversaries in their high-pooped sterns where they were most vulnerable. That such an attack required perfect timing and coordination was axiomatic.

But—and here the Moor's voice began to vibrate—if the galley, at the precise moment before impact, was suddenly thrown off course . . . what would happen? The galley would swerve, all the oars on one side would be sheered off, and under full weigh she would slide helplessly along under the very muzzles of her enemy's guns. One broadside would finish her.

"Aye, and the row-gang, being chained to the lowest portion of the galley would be the first to drown," reasoned Magnus. "That sounds like fleeing from the rain to sit under the waterspout."

Ben Absedik sniffed. "Truly, the plan involves risk, yet when thy head is in the mortar, it is useless to dread the pestle. Wouldst thou rather endure the flatulencies of these Spanish camels than risk the prayers of fishes?"

"Nay!" protested Magnus. "But I have sworn a sacred oath to kill a certain man before I die!" He confided the story of his quarrel with Sir Peter Beckles.

The Moor nodded approvingly. "Verily it is said that a noble purpose is a shield against harm. May Allah guide thy arm, O Rais Carter!"

As Magnus anticipated, Tim and Brother Diego assented, though appalled by the obstacles. To have any remote chance of success, the venture would require the unflinching cooperation of at least fifty or sixty oarsmen, which immediately opened the plotters to betrayal. After considerable discussion, it was agreed to broach the scheme only to certain key men on the larboard side. Tim had discovered about a half-dozen Englishmen among the slaves, and perhaps twice that number of French Huguenots. There were also a few Moslem seamen who might be approached through the medium of *lingua franca*, since they were too far from Ben Absedik for him to address them in their own tongue.

"I think it advisable to sound out the Protestants first," Brother Diego counseled with a wry smile. "Unfortunately, their hatred is based on religious differences, and as they have everything to gain by cooperation and nothing to lose, we run less risk with them."

"Meanin'," Tim put in bluntly, "even ye don't trust a Spaniard?"

"We must judge men as they are, not as they should be," countered the priest. "It is neither a question of nationality nor of religion, but of personal advantage. You are attempting to deal with extremely desperate men. Now, if you supply a desperate man with the means of escaping his plight only by being faithful to you, he will be faithful to the end. On the other hand, if by betraying you, he can gain same advantage at no risk to himself, he will be a rare man indeed who will keep your secret. Granted that, it follows that a Spanish prisoner, nearing the end of his sentence in the galleys, would profit more by betrayal than by risking his life with you."

When Magnus translated this to Abu Ben Absedik, the latter

130

leaned forward and took a piercing look at the Capuchin as if seeing him for the first time.

"By the Seven Heavens of Islam!" he gasped. "I disbelieve my own ears! Such wisdom is worthy of a True Believer! Yet to Allah, all things are possible."

"Thou heardst correctly," observed Magnus. "But is it not also possible that we, Protestant, Catholic and Moslem, are as *one* in the sight of the Almighty?"

Ben Absedik considered. "What sayeth the Frankish priest to *that?*"

Brother Diego smiled when the question was passed on. "How can we doubt it? Though there are many prophets, there is only one God."

The Moor laughed for the first time. "Truly it is written that even the fly knows the face of the milk-seller. Peace be upon thee all, O my Christian brothers!"

Tim Prettyman sighed. "Damme fer a lubber, I ne'er expected to see the day when I'd be in ca'oots wi' a Spanish priest an' a Moorish pirate!"

Now welded into a unit by propinquity, they fell to work to perfect the conspiracy. It was a nerve-wracking task. Unable to leave their benches, they had to pass the word to those nearest them, and as each man had less than two feet of space allotted to him, it was impossible to speak without being overheard. In this chore, Tim's salty vocabulary was invaluable, as he was able to talk over the heads of the other slaves to the English prisoners in a vernacular which even an English landsman could not have understood. Two of the English seamen were versed in *lingua franca*, and undertook to approach the few Moslems scattered among them. Magnus dealt with the Huguenots.

By the end of a month—four terrible weeks haunted always by the fear of discovery or betrayal—they had the key men enlisted. Then Brother Diego began on the Spanish slaves. Herein lay the greatest danger, especially from Francisco Trajan, the Catalan blacksmith Brother Diego had chastised.

Ever since they had been aboard, Trajan had fawned over them like a whipped cur. Brother Diego had forgiven him, with characteristic gentleness, but neither Magnus nor Tim trusted him. Ben Absedik disliked him instinctively; when he heard about the previous trouble, he would have none of him.

"A harlot does not repent, and water in a jar does not become sour milk," he warned. "Tell him nothing."

But that was difficult, if not impossible, for though Brother Diego

131

avoided confiding in the blacksmith directly, it was a moot question whether or not he was aware of the plot. This circumvention took time, and it was another ten days before everything was ready—everything but the opportunity.

The weeks dragged by, but finally came the day when it seemed the Almighty had answered their prayers. The galley had lain in Santander for three days while a northwesterly gale had churned up the Bay of Biscay, but when the fourth dawned clear and windless, they were ordered out for a cruise. About mid-morning, the lookout shouted from the masthead that he had sighted a sail.

The course was altered to stand toward the stranger, and the chief *comitre's* whistle piped for double-time at the oars. A trumpet blared, and the soldiers began buckling on their corselets and readying their arms.

Although the slaves could see nothing, much could be gleaned from the orders and comments bandied around the deck. In this wise, they learned the stranger was a Dutch *cromsteven;* a hoy-rigged vessel of about one hundred and fifty tons. It was obvious, from the elation of the Spanish officers, that the Dutchman had been badly mauled by the recent storm. The captain gave the order to ram and board.

"Think ye this be it, lad?" Tim asked anxiously.

Magnus shook his head. "I fear not. These *cromstevens* are not powerful enough for our purpose. It would be fatal to make a mistake."

Brother Diego and Ben Absedik concurred, so word was passed along to the other conspirators that this was not the time.

Late in the afternoon, they overtook the Dutchman. Her sprit was shattered, her sails in tatters, and without wind, she rode the giant rollers like a derelict. It was apparent the Spaniard could have taken her by boarding alone, but the galley captain elected to ram. The galley was swung into a great arc that lined her up with the stern of the *cromsteven.* Then, while the guards plied their whips, the galley surged in for the kill.

At this point, Fate played her cruel trick! Worn out with fatigue and pain, two slaves fainted simultaneously on one of the oars ahead of Magnus. The remaining four on the fateful oar were not strong enough to maintain the double-pace alone. They missed a stroke, and when the following oar crashed into their heads, they let go. The ponderous sweep fouled others, which in turn disrupted the entire larboard bank.

Despite the fury of the *comitres,* the galley swerved. Then followed a sickening, rendering crash forward as the oars snapped

132

against the stern of the *cromsteven*. The entire row-chamber was thrown into confusion.

As Magnus had foreseen, the Dutchman was in no strength to seize the opportunity thrown into her lap. Her guns remained silent as the galley slid alongside and the Spaniards boarded her with only a token resistance.

Whether in anger at the accident, or natural viciousness on the part of the Spanish captain, the officers of the *cromsteven* were incontinently put to the sword, her crew battened below hatches, and a prize crew put aboard. Then while the galley still wallowed in the heavy swells, the two unfortunate wretches who had fainted were dragged on deck, revived, tied to the gangway in plain sight of all the row-gang, and lashed to death. After this, the galley headed for Santander.

Tim vented his spleen in curses, and Ben Absedik called on Allah to witness the charity of Christians. But Magnus was sick with hate.

"Don't tell me this was the will of God!" he snarled at Brother Diego. "There is no God, else He would not have permitted this!"

The priest shook his head. "Rather let us say it was a whim of Fortune, my son. Some claim God rules but half our destiny, Fortune the balance. Whether so or not, I cannot tell, yet this we do know—Fortune ebbs and flows like the tides in the affairs of man. Today, perchance, she is on the ebb, hence tomorrow she will flood. But I beg you—do not lose confidence in God!"

"God has cast us out!" Magnus fumed bitterly.

When the galley finally moored in Santander, the guards came down into the row-chamber and, unshackling half a dozen Spanish civil criminals, including Francisco Trajan, marched them aft to the poop.

Brother Diego was the first to sense the impending catastrophe. "I am afraid the captain suspects something," he warned.

"But it was an accident!" protested Magnus, alarmed.

"May God convince him of that!"

What questions were propounded to the witnesses, the conspirators had no way of knowing, but before long screams proved they were being put to the torture. Then about dusk, two of the under-*comitres* came for Brother Diego. Magnus would have resisted, despite the futility of it, but the priest sternly forbade him.

"Have no fear for me, my son," he said. "I go with God! Hold to your courage and your hope!"

Marveling, Magnus watched as they led him away. Going off to death, or worse, Diego Valesco had told *him* to have courage and hope. Magnus' admiration soared to reverence, but it remained for old Tim to sum it up in his pithy fashion.

133

"By the grace of Almighty God—there walks a saint!"

And the Moor echoed: "Truly, and may Allah who guards the good and the faithful protect him!"

Huddled miserably in the bowels of the row-chamber, the three friends passed a sleepless night. They could hear the cursing of the guards, the sound of blows, and though they waited tensely for the cries of Brother Diego, no such sound filtered down to the hold.

Sometime before dawn, they heard the clang of the armorer's anvil. This prompted a thousand conjectures, yet none so horrible as the truth. For with the first early light, they saw something dangling from the tip of the main-yard, which had been cock-billed to hang over the row-chamber. As their visibility increased, they saw it was a small cage fashioned of strap iron, permanently riveted together. Inside, was compressed the naked body of Brother Diego. Only the rise and fall of his chest showed he was still alive.

As they stared in horror, the chief-*comitre* strode down the gangway.

"He'll hang there until he rots and drips among you," he told the stricken slaves. "Let that be a lesson to any of you *cabrón* who hope to escape!"

Magnus was too shocked to speak until after the *comitre* strode away. Then he whispered to Tim, "How long can he survive?"

The old seaman groaned. "Not many days, but let's 'ope 'e goes soon, lad, fer the iron will 'eat in the sun an' fry the 'ide off'n 'im."

"Then, by God, we must get him out before that!"

Magnus discussed it with Ben Absedik. The Moor was fatalistic. "It is his kismet."

"You are willing to do nothing while our friend dies an unspeakable death?"

Ben Absedik shrugged. "Thou canst not hasten Fate, O my brother. She is like a fickle woman. If thou woo her, she skitters away. But when she comes within reach, seize her boldly, and beat her as a woman must be beaten to be properly mastered. Only then will she serve you well. That is the will of Allah!"

Magnus raised his eyes to the cage. The sun was nearing its zenith and the pale skin of the priest was turning pink. Suddenly Magnus realized Brother Diego was staring directly at him with eyes that were calm and reassuring. They seemed to plead with Magnus: "*Hold to your courage and your hope!*"

Magnus nodded slightly, then closed his eyes. For the first time since childhood, he really prayed.

"Almighty Father, show us the way to save him who art thy most faithful servant! Amen!"

134

Late that afternoon, the slaves who had been questioned about the accident were returned to their places—sorely battered and chastened. Hardly had the guards left after chaining Trajan to his bench before Magnus made a grab for him, but Ben Absedik interfered.

"Wait!" he hissed. "The thing is done, hence it is of little use to hammer cold iron."

"The swine betrayed us!"

"Which is no reason thou shouldst betray the rest of us. Allah will punish him!"

Magnus desisted grudgingly, promising him a fitting revenge at the first opportunity. But in the morning, the burly blacksmith was found dead on his bench. Though the *comitres* made a thorough examination, there was no evidence of violence. It was presumed Francisco Trajan died in his sleep.

When the excitement had subsided, Magnus turned accusing eyes on Abu Ben Absedik. The Moor smiled faintly.

"The ass went seeking horns and lost his ears," he observed.

Magnus felt cheated. "You told me Allah would punish him!"

"True," the Moor acknowledged blandly, "yet a judge is not his own executioner. God must have two classes of servants: one to preach His laws, another to enforce them. Every cobbler to his last, and I am no priest."

Chapter 14

As THE Moor had observed, Fate was indeed fickle. Swollen with success which begot arrogance, the Spanish captain ordered the galley out in search of more prey. The second day, they took a small Portuguese merchantman.

Meanwhile, Brother Diego sweltered and bobbled in his ghastly cage, and his friends suffered with him. Fortunately, it rained the third night to assuage his thirst, yet by the end of the fourth day, his condition was tragic.

On the fifth day, the galley cruised far out into the Bay of Biscay, and in mid-afternoon, the lookout descried a sail on the horizon. The captain ordered the course altered to stand toward her.

Two hours later, word was passed down that the stranger was a medium-sized hoy flying the Dutch flag.

Magnus' heart sank. Just another Dutchman! He had prayed she would be English, and powerful enough to fight. When his co-conspirators looked to him for orders, he started to shake his head. Suddenly he remembered what Ben Absedik had said about Fate: *Seize her boldly and beat her . . . she will serve you well!*

Hesitating, he raised sweat-dimmed eyes to the man in the cage. Brother Diego appeared conscious. He was staring off toward the other vessel. As Magnus watched him, he turned slowly and glanced down. Their eyes met, then Brother Diego nodded perceptibly.

Magnus caught his breath. He turned to Tim.

"This *is* it!"

"But a Dutchman?" panted Tim. "The last one wouldn't . . ."

"We'll take a chance!" Magnus cut him off.

Ben Absedik was in accord. "To Allah all is possible!"

Word was passed along to the others that the time had come. Magnus shot another quick glance aloft. Brother Diego was watching him with large brown eyes. Magnus nodded. Brother Diego smiled, then abruptly his head fell forward against his drawn-up knees.

Magnus almost missed a stroke. Had the tide of Fortune turned too late?

For once, Magnus and his fellow conspirators slaved with enthusiasm. Neither the stenches, the festers, nor the lash concerned them. They were skimming toward either salvation or doom, yet either seemed preferable to this man-made purgatory of the present.

On the deck above, all was bustle. Trumpets shrilled and drums rumbled. A company of arquebusiers took their stations in the fore-peak; the gunners kindled their linstocks. Amidships, seamen readied the grappling irons while aft the Spanish officers, in gleaming morion and corselet, swaggered back and forth. The boarders, armed with calivers and pikes, bunched on the foredeck.

At an order from the galley captain, a gunner touched off a demi-culverin and the thunder reverberated through the row-chamber. This imperious demand to lie-to was answered with a defiant roar from the other vessel. A groan went up from most of the slaves, for a sea fight meant death to some, if not all. But to Magnus and his cohorts, it augured well.

Yet the comments of the Spaniards were discouraging. The

Dutchman, they crowed among themselves, was undermanned. They sensed an easy victory. Magnus began to waver. Had he again permitted his emotions to rule his judgment? Was he, perhaps, jeopardizing the lives of his fellows by impetuosity? Then his eyes strayed to the body dangling aloft, and he knew he was right.

He felt the galley swerve, and surmised she was lining up to ram. Whispering a quick warning to the Moor to carry his load, he risked a glance over his shoulder. He could see the two masts of the *cromsteven* as one.

An under-*comitre* spotted his defection and came charging down the gangway, foaming blasphemies. But as he leaned down to ply his whip, Magnus shot out of his seat to the length of his chain, seized the startled guard by the wrist, and yanked him into the pit.

"Now! *Now!*" shouted Magnus at the top of his voice. "*Pronto! Pronto!*"

The Moor took up the cry, first in *lingua franca*, then in Moorish. "*Y'Allah!*"

At the signal, the conspirators shoved their oars deep in the water and hurled their strength against them. The effect was instantaneous and devastating. With the larboard oars thus dragging while the starboard still drew full, the galley swerved as on a pivot. The next moment, she crashed into the *cromsteven*.

"Down! Down!" thundered Magnus, and threw himself to the floor as the oars were sheered off against the hoy's side, and the looms flayed around the row-chamber like a broken log-jam.

The confusion above was just as bad. Half stunned by the unexpected crash, the Spaniards stood bunched when the enemy loosed a broadside across their decks. Grapnels thudded into the galley's gunwales, and through the haze, Magnus saw the enemy swarm aboard.

The Spaniards were caught unprepared. Two-thirds of their force had been concentrated forward, with all the officers on the poop. Thus, boarding amidships, the attackers split the Spaniards in twain. The frenzied officers tried to fight forward to their main body, but were hacked to pieces.

To Magnus and Tim, crouched under their benches, the jeers and curses of the boarders sounded unbelievable.

"God in heaven!" gasped Magnus. "They are *English!*"

Tim climbed into the open, roaring excitedly. "An' 'oo else! 'Oo but Englishmen laugh w'en fightin' odds?"

Like a summer squall, the storm was violent but of short duration. By the time Magnus and Tim crawled to their feet, a burly man, dripping sweat and blood, strode down the gangway above them.

"Ho, down there!" he bellowed. "Any Englishmen among you slaves?"

Tim's hungry ears caught the rich flavor of Cornwall in the voice.

" 'Oo the bloody 'ell d'ye think kept this Spaniard from rammin' the arse out o' yer 'ulk but real Devon lads, ye stupid Cornishman!"

The black-bearded seaman blinked momentarily, then burst into laughter. "Curse my buttocks, he must be from Devon with that much gall!" He beckoned to some of his men. "Climb down there an' release all the English. We'll decide what to do with the others later."

"Never mind us," interrupted Magnus. "For God's sake get that man out of that cage! He's responsible for saving all our lives!"

The order was given at once, and while seamen scrambled aloft to bring down Brother Diego, others climbed into the pit. However, when they came for Tim, he refused to be released until Ben Absedik was freed.

"We stays together!" he declared flatly.

As soon as his chains were struck off, Magnus hurried on deck to see Brother Diego. The priest was still alive, but in a pitiful condition. Magnus himself carried the sufferer aboard the *cromsteven,* then, when the Moor assured him that he knew how to deal with sunburn and starvation, Magnus left him in charge of the priest, and with Tim went to pay his respects to their deliverer, Captain Meek Smythe.

Seated in the *cromsteven's* after-cabin, with a flagon of ale beside him, Magnus told their story. Captain Smythe combed his black beard with knotty fingers and listened without interruption. At the conclusion, he exhaled slowly.

"By God, gentlemen, I see the debt is mine! Without wind enough to blow smoke out of our eyes, we could not have maneuvered out of that shark's way. Aye, he'd have sliced us in twain had you not veered him when you did, though I won't admit we wouldn't have given him a bonny fight for all that."

"They seemed to think you undermanned, Captain," remarked Magnus.

Smythe chuckled. "Well, sir, I've been fightin' the Dons for a good many years, an' I picked up a trick here and there. A Spaniard don't like to fight unless he's got all the advantage, an' when he thinks it's easy, he gets reckless. Had I shown my strength, the bastard might o' been more cautious. So that's the way of it, gentlemen."

"But has England declared war on Spain?"

Smythe spat in disgust. "Would I be flyin' the Dutch flag if she had? No, friend, our good Queen is still backin' an' fillin'."

"And Drake and Hawkins?"

138

"Sittin' on spanked arses writing notes to 'er Majesty which she tosses away. An' God knows, gentlemen, if there ever was a time to strike Spain, this is it! What with famine, her plight's so bad she's offered safe conduct to all shipping that will bring grain an' food to her ports."

"Safe conduct?" growled Magnus. "Why our galley has been combing the Bay for neutral shipping!"

"Aye, don't I know it! Ships are leaving England daily bound for Spain, an nobody hears of them again." Smythe sighed and drained his flagon. "If only something would happen to jolt Queen Bess out of her . . . ah . . . innocence!"

"Innocence!" snarled Tim. "It ain't innocence, it's . . ."

"Easy, now, easy, Master Prettyman!" cautioned Captain Smythe, with a broad smile. "We be all loyal Englishmen, though for my own part, I confess havin' taken an oath to stay out of England 'til she comes to her senses. Hence, I sail under letters o' marque from the Prince o' Orange. Which, gentlemen, brings up the question o' what to do with the galley. We're headed for Africy, an' there's no neutral port handy for the disposal of a prize. But, by God, rather than let one plank o' her get back in the clutches of that bastard son of Satan, Philip, I'll scuttle her!"

"There are nearly three hundred slaves aboard her," Magnus reminded him. "Though many are Spaniards, I doubt they hold much love for Philip."

Smythe tugged on his beard. "Curse my bottom, 'tis a quandary! We're overloaded as it is with men and victuals, an' while I'll welcome you on board, we'll be taxed with three, let alone three hundred."

Magnus leaned forward. "Captain Smythe—do I take it you don't want the prize?"

Smythe glanced at him sharply, intrigued by his tone. "Aye, my very words. She's naught to me so long as the Spaniards don't recover her."

"Splendid! Will you turn her over to me?"

"To *you?* Lor' love a duck, man, ain't you had enough o' galleys? What would you do with her?"

"Go back to Spain!"

Tim nearly fell out of his chair. "*Spain?*" He looked helplessly at the Cornishman. "By God, Cap'n, 'e's teched in the 'ead!"

Magnus grinned. "Brother Diego, the Moor and I have a score to settle that can only be settled in Spain. And I can promise you, Captain Smythe, the *Santa Ana* won't fall into Philip's hands."

"Hell and damnation, you're welcome to it!" growled Smythe. "But like Master Prettyman here says, 'tis madness!"

139

"I'm not forcing Master Prettyman to go with us," Magnus retorted. "He can sail with you to Africa."

Tim shot to his feet. "Oh, I kin, kin I? Ye ain't arskin' me, eh? Ye'd abandon an' ol' comrade, would ye?"

Magnus feigned surprise. "By my troth, Tim, you just said it was madness! I wouldn't coax a comrade to put himself in danger!"

The old man bellowed as if stabbed. "Danger, 'e s'ys!" He shook a fist in Magnus' face. "Ye got the gall to sit there an' tell *me* 'tis dangerous? Me, 'oo stood wi' 'Awkins at St. John de Ulua!" He whirled around and appealed to Smythe. "By God, Cap'n, don't gi' the pup the damned 'ulk 'less 'e tykes me wi' 'im!"

Captain Smythe lay back his head and howled with laughter. "On my honor, I'll swear I never saw a fish work harder to get himself hooked! Sobeit, Carter, the *Santa Ana* galley's yours an' welcome. May God bless your venture!"

Chapter 15

IN THE sparkling glory of a spring morning in May, 1585, the lookouts in the watchtower at the mouth of the River Nervión descried a galley standing in toward the harbor entrance leading to the town of Bilbao. Though long accustomed to Imperial vessels, this one appeared singular. Gleaming in fresh paint, she clove through the sun-dappled water with the grace of a swan, her fifty oars dipping in an almost happy cadence. Through their glasses, the lookouts could discern a figure in dress armor reclining on a divan beneath an awning on her poop and surrounded by morioned and corseleted attendants. The masts were a gay panoply of banners and she exhibited the proper signals. Recognizing a craft of unusual importance, they dispatched a courier with the news to his Excellency, Licentiate de Escober, *corregidor* of the *signoria* of Biscay.

Duly impressed, though somewhat disturbed that he had not received advance notice of honored guests, that worthy *hidalgo* hastily sent word to the other dignitaries of the town to meet him at the mole. By the time he arrived there, the galley was in sight, and one glance sufficed to convince him this was no ordinary visitor. He ordered out his barge, and attended by six local officials, fared forth to meet the galley.

However, in spite of his importance, his Excellency was ignored until the galley was anchored to please the finicky taste of her captain. Then, and not until then, was De Escober invited aboard. Nor, as his exalted station decreed, was he greeted at the gangway by the captain. Instead, he was met by a tall, half-sick priest in the scarlet robes of a cardinal, who introduced himself as Pedro de Aragon, confessor to his Magnificence, Don Laurenzo de Alva, lately appointed admiral to His Most Catholic Majesty, Philip the Second.

If De Escober was piqued, he was also embarrassed that he had never heard of so illustrious a courtier, but before he had time to compose himself, he and his awed dignitaries were ushered aft. The good *corregidor* was in for more surprises.

Never before in his not unextensive experience had he seen such Sybaritic luxury aboard a galley. Even the stench so identifying to such craft was absent, and—almost to his horror—he noted that the slaves wore soft cotton shirts and caps to shield them from the sun! But that was as nothing compared to the splendor of the poop. Under an awning, fringed with cloth of gold, sprawled a red-headed young man with the indolent arrogance of a prince. He wore a priceless suit of half-armor, etched and punched with gold, and behind him stood a sharp-faced Moorish slave, who seemed to hover over him like a protective hawk.

"Your Magnificence!" breathed De Escober, bowing as deeply as his paunch would permit. "We are honored!" Yet with his eyes momentarily free from the blinding splendor, De Escober marveled that his King would elevate such a youth to the dignity of admiral. *Santa Maria!* The stripling could be little over twenty summers!

Yet young or no, the admiral was the epitome of courtliness. He ordered chairs for his guests, and begged that they do him the honor to dine with him. Since even the dignitaries of Bilbao had felt the pinch of famine, they accepted with alacrity. At a wave of the admiral's hand, the Moor produced wine with the speed of a genie, and under its mellowing influence, the *corregidor* relaxed.

The dinner served in the admiral's cabin was another cause for amazement. De Escober stared at the English beef, beer and biscuits, and exclaimed aloud, "*Vive Dios! Meat*, your Magnificence!"

The admiral smiled whimsically. "Ah, *amigo mío*, we chanced upon a ship of England. They supplied our wants, though, I confess, not without some reluctance." His eyes narrowed questingly. "Or am I betraying a secret?"

141

The *corregidor* drained his glass, and as he stretched it toward the Moor for a refill, he lowered one lid in a wink.

"Not at all, your Eminence, not at all!" He tapped the breast of his doublet. "My own orders relative to the subject of English shipping arrived a week ago from Barcelona."

The admiral frowned slightly and glanced at the other officials before returning his attention to De Escober.

"Is it . . . ah . . . general knowledge, *señor?*" he asked pointedly.

"General, no, your Grace, but among us here there are no secrets."

"*Ojalá!*" sighed the admiral. "Then I can talk freely."

"As freely as you please, my Admiral."

The youthful admiral turned the matter over in his mind. "Truly, great things are afoot," he mused slowly. "Marvelous things for the glory of Spain." He hesitated, frowning. "Your pardon, *amigo mío,* but just how much *do* you know? I must be discreet, not, you understand, that I have any doubts of your loyalty, nevertheless . . ." His voice trailed away significantly.

The *corregidor* flushed, then pulled a document from his doublet.

"Sire! His Majesty gave me *his* complete confidence! Read it yourself!"

The admiral made a deprecatory gesture. "I have no wish to pry, *señor,*" he demurred. "Possibly his Majesty made some personal references too delicate for others."

"No, no, I insist!" babbled the *corregidor.* "I take great pride in his Majesty's trust! See for yourself, sire, I beseech you!"

"As you will, *señor,*" submitted the admiral, and accepted the paper with languid indifference. Scanning it, he smiled frequently and nodded his head.

It was given under Philip's hand.

"Licentiate de Escober, my *corregidor* of my *signoria* of Biscay, I have caused a great fleet to be put in readiness in the haven of Lisbon and the river of Seville. There is required for the soldiers, armor, victuals, and munition that are to be employed in the same great store of shipping of all sorts against the time of service and to the end that there may be a choice made of the best upon knowledge of their burden and goodness; I therefore do require you that presently upon the arrival of this carrier, and with as much dissimulation as may be (that the matter may not be known until it be put into execution), you take order for the staying and arresting (with great foresight) of all the shipping that may be found upon the coast, and in the ports of the said *signoria,* excepting none of Holland, Zeeland, Easterland, Germany, England, and other provinces

142

that are against me, saving those of France, being of little and small burden and weak, are thought unfit to serve the turn. And the stay being thus made, you shall have a special care that such merchandise as the said ships or hulks have brought, whether they be all or part unladen, may be taken out and that the armor, munition, tackle, sails and victuals may be safely bestowed, as it also may be well foreseen that none of the ships or men escape away. Which things thus being executed, you shall advise me by an express messenger of your proceedings therein: and send me a plain and distinct declaration of the number of ships that you shall have stayed in that coast and parts, whence everyone of them is, which belongs to my rebels, what burthen of goods they are and what number of men is in every of them and what quantity they have of armor, ordnance, munition, tacklings, and other necessaries to the end that on sight thereof, having made choice of such as shall be fit for the service, we may further direct you what you shall do. In the meantime you shall presently see this my commandment put into execution, and if there come hither any more ships you shall also cause them to be stayed and arrested after the same order, using therein such care and diligence as may answer the trust I repose in you wherein you shall do me great service."

The youthful admiral concluded his reading with a chuckle. "*Ay Dios mío*, what a sense of humor his Majesty has! A pity, gentlemen, that Machiavelli used Cesare Borgia as a model for *The Prince*. Borgia was a rank amateur at subtlety compared to our incomparable Philip!" He leaned back and passed the document to the gaunt priest.

"You are acquainted with the order, of course, Father," he drawled. "But feast your eyes again on the daintiness of expression, the exquisite delicacy of tone. I swear our master of chivalry could pluck diamonds from a cesspool without soiling his sacred fingers!" He saw the bewildered, shocked expressions on the faces of his guests, so fearing he had gone too far, he raised his glass.

"A toast, gentlemen! To the King of the World!"

The visitors emptied their oft-filled goblets. The cardinal carefully refolded the King's order and proffered it to the admiral, who shook his head indifferently and nodded toward De Escober.

The priest forced a warped smile. "You should guard this well, my son," he cautioned the *corregidor,* handing him the paper. "That strange, unpredictable woman who sits on the throne of England would pay dearly to possess this."

De Escober, mellowing under the influence of the wine, spat an obscenity which brought a peal of laughter from the admiral.

"*Por Dios,* how clever you are, *amigo!* And how she would like to know of the little picnic Philip is preparing for her in Cádiz! Tell me, De Escober, how long since you have been in Cádiz?"

"Two months, Magnificence."

The admiral smiled patronizingly. "Two months! A lifetime these days! How many ships did you see in preparation there, *señor?*"

"Thirty mighty galleons!"

"Only *thirty? Carai!* You should .travel more, *amigo,* to keep abreast! There must be double that number now in Cádiz alone! Where else have you been?"

Flustered, De Escober named several other harbors and the vast numbers of ships he had seen readying for war, but the arrogant young admiral continued to belittle him.

In desperation, De Escober leaned forward and his thickening voice lowered.

"Your Excellency, I am not the ignoramus you think me! I even know the date of the attack on England! What do you think of *that?*"

The admiral stopped smiling. "Holy Virgin, is it possible?" He gasped incredulously, then shook his head. "No, no! I cannot credit it, *amigo! Válgame Dios,* aside from his Majesty and myself, not ten men in the kingdom know that secret!" He stared at the smirking *corregidor* in something akin to respect. "No, it could not be possible!" he reiterated with less assurance.

De Escober settled back in his chair and folded his arms across his paunch.

"Nevertheless, your Grace, I am one of those ten men!"

The admiral frowned perplexedly, then his sharp features broke into a sly smile.

"Come now, *amigo,* I suspect you jest! Why, I'll wager twenty ducats you cannot come within thirty days of the correct date!"

"The sailing date of the Armada?" The *corregidor* laughed mockingly. "Taken, Magnificence! Twenty ducats it is, although you will have to give me time to send ashore to collect it."

The admiral made a gesture of impatience. "The word of a *hidalgo* is sufficient. Now then, *señor*—what is your guess?"

De Escober hesitated. "But, your Eminence, who will be the referee?"

The admiral stiffened haughtily. "*Señor!* Is a referee required between Spanish gentlemen of honor? *Por Dios,* dare you question . . . ?" He started up in anger.

"No, no! *Ay Dios mío,* that was not my meaning, Magnificence!

You misinterpreted! What I mean to say . . ." He floundered help-lessly.

The admiral sank back and rubbed his fingertips over his fore-head.

"I ask your pardon, *señor*. My hasty temper flares too easily. It is a family weakness. My esteemed father killed eleven men, and I have had to kill six—I confess it with shame. Once again, I beg you to forgive my nature." He managed a tired smile. "Look, *amigo mío* —you whisper your date in the ear of the cardinal; I will whisper mine in the other. Being a man of God, we can trust him. Will that satisfy you?"

"Oh, yes, yes, your Excellency! Yet there is no need. I will tell you directly."

"I insist!" smiled the admiral. He turned his head. "Ho, Father! Please step over here, if you will."

When the cardinal came over, the admiral explained that he and De Escober had a little wager about a certain date. If the dates were within one month of each other, De Escober was to be de-clared the winner.

The priest nodded his understanding, and bent close to the *corre-gidor,* who, after a momentary hesitation, whispered in his ear. The priest then repeated the procedure with the admiral.

He straightened, smiling. "Your Excellency! The dates are *identi-cal!*"

The admiral gaped in astonishment. "Mother of God! I did you an injustice, *señor,* by underestimating you! I confess it! You win, not only the twenty ducats, but my most abject apologies. Believe me, I was not jesting when I said that only the most intimate friends of his Majesty were in on the secret!"

De Escober flushed with pleasure. "You do me too much honor, your Grace! I am hardly an *intimate* friend of his Majesty, although I like to think he . . ."

"No modesty, please!" the admiral cut him off. "You are obvi-ously one of the most important men in Spain, and I am honored to have you aboard. Come now—we will cement our friendship. My purpose in coming here was to entertain distinguished guests. We will take a little cruise out into the Bay."

"Ah, your Excellency, much as I would enjoy it, my duties pre-vent . . ."

"*Basta!* Enough! No excuses! Philip would be offended if his hos-pitality was spurned. He specifically bid me tell you . . ."

The *corregidor* almost swooned with ecstasy. "*Ay Dios mío,* his Majesty deigned to mention *me?*"

145

The admiral nodded. "By name, *señor!* 'My good and loyal friend, the Licentiate de Escober' were his identical words. Believe me, *amigo*, you must be a worthy *hidalgo* to warrant such fervent approbation!"

"I am overwhelmed, Magnificence! Possibly my name was called to his attention because of the five English ships I seized last month."

The admiral pursed his lips. "H'mmn? Five, eh? Excellent, De Escober, excellent! I trust no word of the seizures was permitted to leak out?"

"Not a breath!" The *corregidor* grinned. "As his Majesty instructed in his order, we used dissimulation. The ships were taken without struggle." He shrugged significantly. "That is, without noise. The useless old men we dispatched . . ."

"Naturally, being of no use to Spain."

"My very own thought. The rest we sent to the galleys."

"Where they are sorely needed," agreed the admiral. He permitted himself a whimsy. "Personally, I dislike seeing the English at the oars. They are surly dogs, De Escober; everlastingly scheming against his Holiness and Spain—scheming to escape. It keeps me on edge."

"*Escape?*" gasped De Escober uneasily. "*Por Dios*, is escape possible?"

The admiral smiled sardonically. "All things are possible, my esteemed friend, but some are highly improbable." He pointed to a burly, one-legged *comitre* patroling the gangwalk above the rowchamber.

"You see why *I* do not worry about the English we have aboard. My overseer, Herr Uglyman, knows how to deal with Englishmen who believe in plotting against Spain."

The *corregidor* stared in amazement. "But, Magnificence—he is not a Spaniard! I understood all officers had to . . ."

"I am perfectly aware of the customary regulations, *señor*," the Admiral interrupted haughtily, "but my peculiar position elevates me above such mundane considerations. You must know, De Escober, that *I* issue orders; others obey them. The point is, our Spanish overseers have too much humanity, too much sentimentality, to maintain discipline aboard such a galley as this. Herr Uglyman knows his job. *Caramba*, you should have seen the violence he used on the Cornish captain of the last ship we boarded! On my oath, you would have been astounded!"

"I presume, then, his wooden leg does not lessen his worth?"

"On the contrary," chuckled the admiral, "it increases it. Confidentially, *señor*, that is the root of his grudge, for the loss of a leg

146

rankles in more ways than you might credit. Ah, yes—Herr Uglyman nurses a bitter hatred against his enemies. Perhaps you may have a demonstration of what I mean before you leave the galley." He made a languid gesture to indicate the subject was closed.

"Well, it is a beautiful day for a turn around the Bay. There is only one thing to delay us. And by the way, my friend, I have a very special treat for you. His Majesty sent along a couple of luscious lambs which I will have slaughtered for our feast this evening. Think of it, man—*lamb!*"

The *corregidor's* mouth drooled. "You mentioned delay, your Grace? Pray tell me—can I do anything to facilitate matters?"

"*Gracias!* It is possible. His Majesty mentioned a certain English envoy who has had a castle here in Bilbao placed at his disposal. A Sir Peter Beckles, I believe. Are you conversant with the . . . ah . . . *affair?*"

De Escober winked. "Quite, your Eminence. I am also well acquainted with Sir Peter. A remarkable man—for an Englishman."

"His Majesty spoke of him with unaccustomed warmth."

"Small wonder, your Grace."

The admiral grinned his understanding. "Then you understand, doubtless, why I was instructed to entertain him aboard."

The *corregidor* evinced surprise. "By whose order?"

"The King's, of course! Who else gives me, Don Laurenzo de Alva, orders?"

"I mean . . . I mean," stammered De Escober. "No doubt his Majesty has forgotten."

The younger man showed a flash af anxiety. "Forgotten? Forgotten *what?* Come, man, you talk in riddles!"

"Why, Magnificence, his Majesty recently granted Sir Peter a galleon in which to sail for England to return to his bride!"

The effect on the admiral was electrical. He shot out of his chair, his face drained of blood, then recovering himself with an effort, sank back.

"His *bride! Ay Dios mío*, then he is married?"

The *corregidor* squirmed in embarrassment. "What have I said, your Excellency! I thought perhaps you knew!"

The admiral forced a smile. "Ah, dear friend, forgive me! Once again it is the curse of the Alvas—the hot blood, the temper!" He laughed to prove he was no longer disturbed. "It was stupid of me to forget about Sir Peter's marriage. His Majesty will never forgive my reaching here too late. Well, it cannot be helped, and I will take an oath to make it up to Sir Peter in some other way. Now—I shall give the order to weigh anchor. I have some delightful surprises in store for you."

147

De Escober hesitated. "Pardon, Eminence, but with your permission, I will send a message to my wife. When shall I tell her to expect me?"

The admiral laughed. "When a man boards a vessel, *señor*, it is difficult to be precise about time, as I have found. The unexpected is always to be considered. However, if you inform your wife to expect you when she sees you"—he smiled again—"then she will not fret over a trifling delay."

The *corregidor* rose. "You do not know *my* wife, Magnificence," he said ruefully. "Nevertheless, I will attend to it."

The other guests retired along with De Escober to send messages to their homes, leaving the admiral alone with his Moslem slave. It was perhaps fortunate the Spanish visitors did not see the familiar wink that passed between master and slave. Then the former blew a note on his silver whistle, whereupon the peg-legged *comitre* coiled his whip and limped aft to the poop. He made an elaborate salute, then after a surreptitious glance over his shoulder at the Spaniards grouped above the barge, he whispered, "Well, lad, w'at luck?"

The admiral scowled. "Herr Uglyman!" he snapped in English. "Is that the proper fashion to address an admiral of Spain?"

The overseer glared back at him. "Herr Uglyman is it, ye damned mimic? Belay yer clownin' an' gimme the course! By Neptune, I been starin' down the gullets o' them guns on the forts so long I can see the balls! Tell me—w'at's 'appened?"

The admiral rolled his eyes to the cardinal, who had joined them. "Insolent dog, eh, Father?"

The priest smiled wanly. "I confess, my son, to sharing his trepidation. Need I remind you, we are still in the jackals' den?"

"Nonsense! A lion sharing meat with jackals has no cause for fear. Furthermore, I am enjoying the game. What thought you of Philip's letter?"

"As damning as the brand on the forehead of a criminal!" admitted the cardinal sadly. "It is a sample of the vile treachery that will make the very name of Spain a disgrace for centuries! God pity the creature who penned such a document of perfidy!"

The admiral smiled without mirth. "Agreed! I also approve of your earlier suggestion that we show it to Queen Elizabeth."

The priest paled slightly. "That was a comment, not a suggestion, my son," he amended.

"An excellent one, nevertheless. Herr Uglyman, we sail for England at once. Can you use a few fresh hands on the oars?"

The overseer started, then after a hasty glance at the Spaniards, now about to return to the poop, bowed ceremoniously.

"Aye, yer bloody worshipful! I've several nice berths recently vacated by certain characters best not mentioned by nyme. But 'ow about Beckles, lad?"

The red-headed young man styled Don Laurenzo de Alva went pale.

"He has returned to England," he said harshly. "I'll attend to him there."

The Moor bent over him. "Your guests return, O my brother!"

The admiral recovered his *sang-froid*. "Guests no longer, my friends. Prisoners now."

The Moor sighed softly. "May Allah continue to guide us!"

Chapter 16

I F THE Spanish lookouts had been somewhat surprised when they saw the *Santa Ana* galley standing in to their vicinity, the English watchmen stationed on Rame Head, which guards the approaches to Plymouth Sound, were even more dismayed on seeing it gliding toward their shores. Being in a state of perpetual apprehension regarding the intent of Spain, they dreaded lest it be one of the vanguard of Philip's long-expected Armada. Messengers galloped off to spread the news.

Meanwhile, the galley in question shifted along under sail alone to a quartering breeze, her oars canted out of the water. Though tedious, the voyage had been without incident, save for the untimely death of a slave, one-time *corregidor* of Biscay, who (it was believed) had died of humiliation. Paradoxically enough, his passing was more deeply mourned by the galley's red-headed young captain than by his companions in the row-chamber.

The galley requested no pilot on entering the Sound—a peculiar oversight in a foreign vessel—and skillfully evaded the outer shoals. By the time she had passed the eastern end of St. Nicholas Island, the Hoe was thronged with wondering people.

On the *Santa Ana's* poop, four men stood together and watched the shore draw closer. It would have been difficult to have con-

149

ceived a more incongruous group, for by all the rules of society, they were as disparate as possible. Race, religion, nationality, and age separated them, yet now they formed a close-knit unit welded by adversity.

When the citadel gun fired a warning ball, the young captain chuckled.

"Methinks we'll get a warm reception, Herr Uglyman," he commented to the one-legged *comitre* beside him.

"Methinks it'll get too bloody warm if you don't haul down that stinkin' Spanish rag an' run up our own!" growled the *comitre*.

Magnus Carter, abandoning his role as Don Laurenzo de Alva, laughed heartily.

"You may have a point, Timothy. See to it."

The old man bawled an order and the Spanish ensign floated down to be instantly replaced by the Cross of St. George. This brought a cheer like distant thunder from the crowd on the Hoe.

Magnus felt his pulse quicken. For months on end he had dreamed of such a moment, and now it was his. He was coming *home*. To his surprise, Tim Prettyman failed to share his elation.

"W'y should I?" he snorted when Magnus chided him. "'Tis but to exchange one form of slavery fer another."

Magnus grinned. "Cheer up, Timothy. At least the knout won't bite so deep."

"Say ye! Ye don't know me auld woman's tongue, lad!"

Magnus glanced at the other pair. Long association made it no longer necessary to converse in several languages, for by this time, all understood the blend of *lingua franca*.

"Well, my good friends," he enthused. "We're safe at last. What think you of England?"

Brother Diego shrugged. "It is a trifle premature to form an opinion, Magnus. Frankly, there is some question in my mind as to how your good Protestant countrymen will receive a Spanish priest and a disciple of Mohammed."

"Nonsense!" scoffed Magnus. "You'll be welcomed like heroes! Take my word for it, when the Queen sees this perfidious document penned by her treacherous brother-in-law, she'll fair ooze with gratitude. Trust me to handle things."

The Capuchin smiled. "With all due respect to you, my son, I'll repose my trust in God. What say you, friend Abu?"

"I go with Allah," muttered Ben Absedik, staring moodily at the stern bluffs ahead. "Where the mind inclines, the feet lead, Magnus-Rais. Thou hast desired to come home, therefore thou art content. But, truly, I am disappointed. It was not safety I sought, but venge-

150

ance. As I told thee long ago, I took a sacred oath. I have not fulfilled it."

"Look you—did we not deprive the 'master of the world' of one of his best galleys?"

The Moor spat overside in contempt. "Bah! I have deprived him of dozens! To steal a single galley is but the vengeance of a woman, Magnus-Rais! Hast thou forgotten thine own oath?"

Magnus stopped smiling. "That, I'll never forget!"

"My friends, my friends!" chided the priest. "Must you wallow in hate? Did not God himself say: 'Vengeance is mine!'? Why take unto yourselves His task?"

Ben Absedik glanced at him quizzically. "My brother, if thou peruse the Holy Works a little further, thou wilt also find written: 'Thou shalt tear out the dragon's teeth and shall trample the lions underfoot, sayeth the Lord!'"

Magnus roared with laughter and Brother Diego permitted himself a wry smile. "*Touché*, Abu! Howbeit, if I were not a man of God, I might be tempted to observe that His Holy Works are a trifle too extensive. They lend themselves to contradictory interpretations."

"What is written is written," the Moor insisted.

Tim nudged Magnus. "Look, lad, I know naught o' tearin' out dragons' teeth n'r tramplin' lions, but I got somethin' worser'n that waitin' fer me. I don't want to go home!"

Magnus sobered. "Are you serious, Tim?"

"So 'elp me God, I be serious!" The old man was trembling. "I be a mariner, lad, not no bloody chambermaid. Yet, damme, onc't I set foot on shore, I be whipped."

Brother Diego saw his evident distress and laid a kindly hand on his arm. "Timothy, what bothers you?" he asked gently. "Can I be of help?"

Tim wagged his head. "Methinks not, *padre*. I got wife trouble."

Despite his sympathy, Magnus couldn't help chuckling. "Isn't there a Spanish saying to the effect that 'he who marries a widow will have a dead man's head often thrown into his dish'?"

The priest colored slightly, so Magnus went on: "Don't embarrass Brother Diego, Tim. Perchance Ben Absedik can advise you. How about it, Abu—have you a wife?"

The Moor nodded. "I have seventeen, by the grace of Allah."

Tim took his head between his hands. "*Seventeen!* No bloody wonder ye tyke oaths not to go 'ome!"

Ben Absedik was not lacking in a sense of humor, but he did not comprehend English raillery. He looked bewilderedly at Magnus.

151

"What ails our brother?" he demanded. "He speaks words without meaning."

"Oh, it's only that his wife nags him constantly," explained Magnus.

"If that is all, why doth he not cut out her tongue if it offends him?"

Magnus winked at Brother Diego before turning soberly back to Tim. "By the powers, Timothy, there's advice from an experienced man!"

" 'Tis an ill time for jestin'."

"I heartily agree with Timothy," put in Brother Diego. "It is not a subject for banter, Magnus, my son! Marriage is a sacred institution."

"*Sacred,* me arse!" growled Tim. " 'Tis just plain 'ell!"

Ben Absedik stepped helpfully into the breach. "Calm thyself, O my brother! We art thy friends, and will help solve thy difficulty. Now tell me—how many wives hast thou in thy seraglio?"

"How many?" gasped Tim. "Bowels o' God! Ain't one too many?"

"*One?*" The Moor was incredulous. "By the Seven Heavens of Islam, there lies the trouble. Buy thyself six or seven more, and cast out the one who offends thee." He glanced questioningly at Magnus. "Let us make Timothy a gift of wives, Magnus-Rais. Are they expensive in England?"

"Very expensive," Magnus acknowledged. "And the law permits only one."

"By the Lord Mohammed, that is ridiculous! What can a man do with *one* woman? Thou canst not be serious, because all the Englishmen who settle in my country purchase many wives." He put an arm around the old man's shoulder. "Return to Islam with me, O brother, and thy problem will be resolved."

Brother Diego did not like the turn the conversation was taking, and it was with obvious relief that he interrupted them.

"Look—a boat is approaching from shore!"

Magnus turned grave. "It might be advisable for you and Abu to stay on board until I arrange things," he told the priest. "Tim will come with me and . . ."

"Beggin' yer pardon," Tim cut in, "I'm stayin' aboard, too. There's naught I can do ashore."

"As you will," Magnus conceded. "I'll have the galley declared a prize and, as agreed, we'll divide the profits among us."

"Thou wilt not forget," interposed the Moor, "of thy promise to obtain a ship for me that I may return Brother Diego and his countrymen to Spain."

"On my honor, I will not forget."

152

The shore boat was drawing alongside, so Tim and Magnus walked down to the gangway.

"Fer the luv o' God be careful, lad!" pleaded the old man. "Remember—ye left England an 'unted man, an' the law 'as a long memory. Also, ye may 'ave to journey to London to find Sir John 'Awkins, but on yer life, don't turn that letter ye took from the *corregidor* o'er to anyone else but Sir John."

"I'll be wary, Tim."

"An', lad, if ye run afoul me auld woman, tell 'er I was burnt at the stake, will ye?"

"If you wish it, Tim, but . . ."

"Afore God, I wish it."

"But what will you do for a living when your prize money runs out, Tim? You'll lose your business and . . ."

Tim made a gesture of finality. "I've made up me min'. I'm signin' on wi' the Moor."

Magnus whistled. "*You,* a staunch old West Country Puritan serving under a Moslem infidel?"

"Aye, 'tis a strange mixture, that I own," Tim admitted, "yet I've learned a few things this voyage. 'Eathen or no, 'e's a man, blast me! An' the way I reckon, 'eaven be about as close by water as it be by land."

Magnus nodded agreement. "Aye, Tim, both Abu and Diego are men, none finer. I sometimes wonder . . ."

What he wondered was never known, for at that instant, a stern voice bellowed: "Ahoy, galley! Put your hook down an' vayle your sails, else we'll blow you out of the water! What the bloody hell d'you mean comin' in here without a pilot?"

Savoring the rich Devonshire accent, Magnus grinned happily. "Hear him, Timothy? We're home, really home!" He stalked to the rail and with his hands cupped over his mouth shouted, "Hold your puling tongue, you mouthy bastard, and lay alongside!"

"Aye, we'll lay alongside fast enough, and you can lay to that!" retorted a stocky, bearded man in the stern sheets.

Tim grabbed the rail and his eyes bugged. "Oh, Mother o' Jesus!" he groaned shakily. "Now ye've done it, lad! *That's Sir John 'imself!*"

Magnus stood frozen in awe. To an English seaman, no name was more revered, more hallowed, than that of John Hawkins, unless it was that of Sir Francis Drake. Here was the man who had "singed King Philip's beard"; the *Achines de Plimua*—Hawkins of Plymouth—as the Spaniards shudderingly called him.

Meanwhile, Hawkins grabbed the ladder as the boat hove alongside and scrambled dextrously aboard, despite his years which

153

Magnus knew to be somewhere in the fifties. He was short and squat, but seemed taller because of his straight-spined bearing. Dropping to the deck, he scowled about him.

"Now, by God, who is in command here?" he demanded grimly.

Magnus bowed. "I am, sir. To shorten a long story, Master Prettyman and I were taken prisoners some months ago and served as slaves in this galley. We captured her eventually and brought her home as a prize."

Hawkins turned his cold eyes on the quaking Tim, then a half-smile softened his features.

"God's life—aren't you Prettyman the gunner who served me so well at St. John de Ulua?"

Tim gulped. "Aye, m'lud, I 'ad the honor!"

Hawkins clapped him on the shoulder. " 'Pon my soul, you always were too strong a dish for the Dons! 'Tis happy I am to see you still striking 'em. Now I want to hear the details of this feat." His shrewd eyes began to sweep over the galley.

Not wanting Sir John to see the Moor or the priest before he had heard a full account of the adventure, Magnus begged the great man to accompany him to the cabin. Hawkins gestured him to lead the way, and followed.

Once seated in his own quarters, Magnus felt slightly more at ease, although the penetrating eyes of the famed old warrior disconcerted him. Then he bethought himself of the letter he had taken from the *corregidor*. He fished it out of a chest and proffered it to Sir John.

"I believe, sir, this will interest you."

Hawkins moved closer to the ports and read slowly. Though his expression remained the same, Magnus noticed the veins on his temple pulsating. Hawkins perused it through twice before folding it carefully.

"How came you by this?"

"From the recipient—De Escober, the *corregidor* of Biscay, whom we took prisoner."

"Ah! Then you have him aboard?"

"Unfortunately, sir, he died at sea."

Hawkins frowned. "Well, let's hear the whole story," he said gruffly.

Magnus hesitated. Hawkins must have read his mind, for he growled, "Begin at the beginning."

In spite of the old man's brusqueness, there was something about him that gave Magnus a feeling of confidence, even of security. Aye, Sir John was hard, hard as rock, but he was also just. Seated now amidst the oriental luxuriousness of the galley's cabin, like a

154

truculent old lion, he seemed to Magnus the epitome of English courage. As long as England had men like John Hawkins, she had nothing to fear.

So Magnus began at the beginning: he told frankly about his visit to Duane's castle, the murder of Moley, the trampling to death of Donnie the page, Beckles' assault on Tim, the challenge, the attack on the bluff, his return to Plymouth, and his subsequent capture by the Spaniards in the harbor.

At that point he paused, expecting a bitter castigation for his stupidity, but Hawkins kept his mouth closed tightly and his eyes on Magnus' face.

Magnus continued with the tale of their adventure in the Holy House, the *auto de fe,* their eleventh-hour reprieve and the meeting with Brother Diego. At mention of the priest, Hawkins' eyes glinted slightly. Magnus ignored the look and truthfully recounted the part the Capuchin had played in their salvation. When he began to talk about the Moor, Hawkins again evinced surprise, and on hearing the details of the torture of Brother Diego, his jaw tightened.

Magnus felt an explanation was in order. "I was born and raised a Protestant, sir, yet I must confess—without the assistance of this Spanish priest and the Moslem infidel, neither Tim nor I would be here now. I've never known finer, braver men!"

"Go on with your story," Hawkins snapped.

Magnus told of the shipping he had seen in Vigo and the story of the famine in Spain. Hawkins made no interruption until he reached the point of his encounter with the privateer under Captain Smythe.

"Smythe? A Cornishman—Meek Smythe?" cut in Hawkins.

"Aye, sir. You know him?"

Hawkins nodded shortly. "Proceed, young man."

If Sir John did not smile when Magnus told of his voyage into Bilbao and the capture of the *corregidor,* at least his old eyes twinkled momentarily. Heartened, Magnus concluded: "And so, sir, I made certain promises to my comrades and the other slaves to induce them to bring the galley here to Plymouth."

"H'mmn! Promises are easier made than kept, you know."

Magnus colored. "But, my lord, it takes nearly three hundred men to row a galley! Without their help, the thing would have been impossible!"

Hawkins stopped him with a gesture. "Exactly what form did your promise take?"

Magnus felt his anger rising at what he deemed indifference. "At the very least," he cried impatiently, "I promised Ben Absedik a ship to return to his own land. Diego Valesco asks nothing but to

155

be set ashore in Spain with his fellow countrymen. Is that asking too much?"

"We'll see, we'll see," rumbled Hawkins, dismissing the matter. "Now—you have made some astounding statements against two knights of the realm. I presume you are prepared to substantiate these charges with the documents in question?"

"Certainly! I can deliver them to you within the hour! They are concealed in Tim Prettyman's own tavern."

Hawkins frowned. "You don't mean the White Anchors?"

"I do, sir. And only I know where they are."

"Young man," snapped Sir John, "the White Anchors tavern was burned to the ground four months agone."

Magnus started out of his chair. "Burned? Oh, my God!" He sank back trembling. "I'll swear it must have been deliberate! Duane suspected I hid the letters there, for his men ransacked my rooms on at least one occasion I know of."

Hawkins shrugged. "Possibly. Gossip had it that it was no accident, for Dame Prettyman, having come into a fortune shortly before the fire, was reputedly anxious to get away. She visited me about that time to ask if I knew anything of her husband."

Magnus balled his fist. "The old bitch came to find out if you knew about the letters, sir. I know her only too damn well!"

"Be that as it may, she left town soon afterwards. But we cannot concern ourselves with supposition and rumor. Did you note the contents of the letters?"

"No, sir. They were sealed."

Sir John's mouth curled. "For a knave who breaks into a man's castle and purloins his private papers, you seem to have an overly fine sense of honor. An unfortunate distinction in this case, I must say, for the loss of those letters may well be a national tragedy. Between us, I have long suspected Sir Gregory of papist plotting. Now you've let the proof elude us!"

"I can testify to what I heard, sir!"

"Bah! The word of a confessed thief would not bear against a knight, in court or out. As the matter stands, Duane has withdrawn the old charges against you and pressed no new ones, so you are not in jeopardy. But if you attempted to expose him, you would probably be hanged for your pains. No, we may as well forget the whole incident and see what can be done with the letter you seized from De Escober."

Magnus turned livid. "*Forget*, you say?" he shouted, pounding the table. "By God, you don't know what you are asking! Aye, I'll forget their treason, if that will satisfy you, but not the rest of it.

156

No, no! Those months of torture and hell which Duane and Beckles arranged for me can only be wiped out by the sword!"

Hawkins shook his head. "Cool down, young man! You bungled the affair when you did not bring those letters to me in . . ."

"That was a mistake, I grant you!" Magnus interrupted heatedly. "But it doesn't lessen my case against Peter Beckles!"

"On the contrary, you have no *case*. You played the part of a common thief when you broke into the castle. If either Duane or Beckles had slain you then, they would have been well within their legal rights. Since the treasonous letters which might have excused your action are lost, the less said about the affair the better for you. I think I can promise you a pardon for your past sins, but an attack on a knight of Beckles' standing would cost you your head. No matter what *you* think of him, remember this—Sir Peter Beckles holds high favor with the Queen."

Magnus was badly shaken. "Am I, then, *nothing?* Is this the gratitude of England?"

"Gratitude?"

"Aye! Didn't I bring you that damning order from Philip?"

"And, pray tell me," Hawkins demanded coldly, "what Englishman wouldn't have brought it, and gladly, given the like opportunity?"

Magnus went red to his ears, and for a moment he was nonplussed. Hawkins placed a kindly hand on his knee.

"I understand what you are driving at, lad, but you must have patience. I doubt not the Queen will be appreciative, but the gratitude of a nation is not manifested quite the same as the impulsive effusiveness of a grateful individual. I know whereof I speak, for when I was young, I, too, chafed at what I assumed was lack of appreciation for deeds in which I risked my life and the lives of my men. I grant you it is a bitter lesson. But the Queen has many, many aspects to consider before she can act, and the wheels of justice are ponderous things which require a deal of power to start momentum. Yet once they begin to move, they are inexorable. It is merely a question of time."

"Time—with that hell hound loose?" groaned Magnus. "Sir, time is the one thing I cannot spare! The only hope I held to during those months of torture was that I could avenge myself on Beckles before it was too late!"

"Too late? How so?"

"Philip loaned him a ship to sail here to England to force into marriage the girl promised to me! I must stop that above all else!"

Hawkins grunted. " 'Pon my honor, lad, I'm sorry to be the bearer

157

of bad news, for if that was your intent, you are already too late. Beckles married the Maynard girl a fortnight agone, and, a week later, sailed with her to Spain!"

Magnus dropped his head into his hands. "Oh, my God!"

"Come, come, man, pull yourself together!" growled the old man. "Are you a seaman or a sniveling poet to weep over a woman?"

Magnus gritted his teeth and stumbled erect. "You are right, sir! I'll keep my personal affairs to myself." Ignoring the quizzical glance of his famed guest, he went on: "While the Queen is making up her mind about Philip's document, will you declare this galley a prize and furnish a ship for my comrades? Surely, even this tardy justice of which you speak cannot expect them to twiddle their thumbs indefinitely!"

Hawkins' face clouded. "I have no such authority."

"Oh, Christ! You mean even *that* small boon can't be granted— that in addition to everything else, I must betray my friends as well?"

"Young man, you arrogate to yourself too much authority!" Hawkins said severely. "As a private citizen, you had no right to make promises in the name of your country! I concede you handled your escape and the subsequent action with considerable adroitness, but now the time has come to leave questions of policy to your betters. Let me give you a piece of friendly counsel—learn to discipline yourself before you attempt to discipline others!"

Sir John stood up. "Now—we'll consider all that has been said as confidential between ourselves. I'll leave for London tonight with this letter. If you will give me your word not to stir out of Plymouth, nor engage in any hostile acts toward Gregory Duane, I shall grant you and Prettyman permission to go ashore."

Magnus stared unbelievingly. Was he to be treated as a prisoner when he expected to be greeted as a hero! He could scarcely credit his hearing.

"Well, sir—do I have your promise?" barked Hawkins.

Magnus restrained himself with an effort. "Aye, since you leave me no alternative," he acknowledged bitterly. "Yet my promise holds only until your return. Are my comrades likewise to be treated as captives?"

"Your comrades will be well cared for," Hawkins said crisply, "yet they must remain on board. If the Queen makes this document public, the streets of Plymouth will not be safe for foreigners, especially Spaniards!"

Chapter 17

O<small>LD HAWKINS</small> had rightly gauged the temper of his countrymen. When Elizabeth released Philip's perfidious letter, the reaction was immediate. The people cried out for vengeance and made demonstrations; even the powerful City merchants, who heretofore had been selfishly pacifist, joined in the popular clamor. For once Lord Burghley swallowed his scruples and united with the aggressive Walsingham in a plea for retaliation. The thunderhead loomed dark and menacing.

However, no one knew better than Queen Elizabeth that England was not prepared to declare war against the allied might of Spain and the Roman Church. To do so would be to play into Philip's hand. She had at her command a much more potent method of dealing with her treacherous brother-in-law. She sent for Francis Drake!

Meanwhile, aboard the captured galley in Plymouth, Magnus Carter chafed and brooded. To lose Rosalind was a tragedy, but to learn she had been forced into marriage with Peter Beckles was almost more than he could bear. He tortured himself with recollections: their sacred night together . . . the fragrance of her lips when last they parted . . . that precious line in her letter: *I'll be waiting for you if it takes forever!*

In vain his comrades tried to cheer him, yet he felt they could not understand. Peculiarly enough, they accepted their own situation with almost irritating equanimity, according to their natures; the Moor took it stoically, Brother Diego was philosophic, and old Tim was as a man reborn.

"Damme, lad, we got a sound deck underfoot an' no shrews to nag us!" he reiterated time without number. "W'at more kin a man arsk fer?"

When Magnus ranted against the abysmal stupidity of governments, the priest tried to reason with him.

"Magnus, my son, I realize nothing tries the patience like stupidity, yet, truly, nothing is more stupid than impatience. Time will heal all wounds, so I pray you, have patience."

Magnus brushed the advice aside. "Patience," he sneered, "is the characteristic of cuckolds and donkeys!"

Ben Absedik simply could not comprehend Magnus' melancholy. "Merciful Allah, if it is only a woman thou cravest, come to Islam with me and I will present thee with a score of maidens!"

Brother Diego winced, but Tim slapped his wooden leg. "By Neptune, there's a fair offer, lad! 'Ow about it?"

The priest saw the pain this raillery was causing Magnus, so he sought to silence them.

"My friend, you do not understand. Magnus desires only one maid."

Ben Absedik shrugged. "Then why does he not take her?"

"She is wed to another."

The Moor snorted disdainfully. "Magnus-Rais hath a sword, hath he not? Then if he desires her, let him take her. By the beard of my father, I will help him, for he is my brother!"

Brother Diego commenced a solemn dissertation on the sanctity of Christian marriage, but Ben Absedik interrupted scoffingly.

"*Effendi,* thy Christian religion is a latticework which does not keep off wind. It sayeth Magnus-Rais cannot have his woman even if stolen by a traitor; that the old one cannot divorce his shrew though they hate each other; that thou, a very priest, canst have no woman at all, even though no man can be a good physician who has never been sick." He smiled cynically. "What can I think of thy virtues, O onion, since every bite draws tears?"

Bored with their quarreling, Magnus wandered away. Yet the Moor had planted seed in fertile soil. Why *not* take Rosalind away from Beckles? Surely, the Almighty could not be unjust enough to sanction such a union forced on a young girl! The seed began to germinate. . . .

The news that the Queen had unleashed her sea-dogs struck Plymouth like a bolt of lightning. All was fervor and excitement. Ships sailed into the harbor from a dozen ports; the docks were piled with mountains of supplies; eager recruits and seasoned veterans milled around the waterfront, and bonfires lighted the Hoe. Drake—the redoubtable Sir Francis—was going to teach King Philip that English ships were sacred and that English seamen were not his slaves!

Magnus viewed all this enthusiasm apathetically, and with the passage of time, he became restless. He found the confinement of the ship irksome; the calm acceptance of his friends an irritation. Though it was rumored Hawkins had returned from London, Magnus had no word from him. He felt abandoned and betrayed. Once or twice, he tried to induce Tim to go with him to visit the ruins of White Anchors, but the old man flatly refused, saying he never wanted to see the "bloody prison" again. Magnus was not in the mood to go alone.

By the end of a week, his nerves had frayed to the breaking-point, so, unable to stand it longer, he ordered a boat and had himself rowed ashore.

Plymouth appeared strange to him. Although the streets were crowded, he wandered for hours without once seeing a familiar face. For some inexplicable reason this disheartened him; he had the sensation of seeking someone without knowing who. This was puzzling in view of the fact that he had come ashore to be alone.

Disgusted, he strode into a dingy waterfront tavern to get a tot of rum before returning to the ship.

He seated himself in an isolated corner and waited for the barmaid. The place was well filled, and the patrons a motley lot—cargo loaders, common seamen, and fishermen. Since his own elegant raiment set him apart, he was left alone, which pleased him mightily, for he had no desire for convivial companionship.

Just as the serving wench was approaching, he heard a man at an adjacent table call for a mug of "Cornish ale." The name struck a responsive chord in Magnus' mind. It recalled the last time he had imbibed the mystical draught, so long ago in the fisherman's hut below the dueling grounds, and he remembered the surcease it had afforded him. On impulse, he ordered Cornish ale.

When it was placed before him, he sampled it gingerly. As before, he felt his nervousness give way to a pleasing lassitude. The gloomy tavern took on an aura of warmth and friendliness. Magnus chuckled ruefully. Perhaps the old fisherman had spoken the truth when he said, "Ye may figger ye're drunk, but ye're really not, mebbe fer the first time." Magnus finished the mug, and sat back, waiting for the barmaid to refill it. He wondered idly whether a second potion would have the effect it had had before; if he would again meet the girl of his dreams. He hoped so.

But the serving wench was busy with other patrons, and Magnus had to await his turn. He did not care. He was thoroughly relaxed and slightly bemused. It was very pleasant. His mind flitted unconcernedly from one thing to another. He was even able to contemplate the tragedy of the tavern without rancor.

What had happened there was all too obvious: Dame Prettyman, having made herself independent by the theft of his treasure, had

161

sold the place to Sir Gregory, who, in turn, had razed it to destroy the letters he suspected must have been cached inside. Such wholesale destruction was the one contingency Magnus had not foreseen; the one which defeated him completely. What a bloody shame he had not entrusted those precious documents to Kate!

Katie! What a staunch friend she had been! He wondered what had become of her. Lord, but it would be good to see her again! Somehow, Katie always seemed to understand his moods. He felt an overwhelming desire to talk to her. When the barmaid came up to the table, a moment later, Magnus waved her away and rose, a trifle unsteadily.

Once outside, however, he paused, hardly knowing which way to turn. It seemed futile to go to White Anchors; Kate would not be living in the ruins. Now that he stood in the fresh air, the whole notion of seeking her seemed futile, yet the wish persisted. Finally, he surrendered to the impulse, and tramping up the hill to the old neighborhood, he went from house to house making inquiry.

He met with failure. No one knew anything about Kate. She had left Plymouth about the same time as Dame Prettyman, so it was presumed the old harridan had taken the girl with her. One man, however, said Kate had been posted as a runaway servant.

Magnus found his anxiety increasing. In desperation, he offered a substantial reward for any information as to her whereabouts. Several of the neighbors made vague promises to locate her, but that was the best help he could obtain.

It was close to twilight when he started back to the mole. Halfway down the hill, he was astonished to meet a group of seamen headed by Tim Prettyman. At sight of him, Tim roared, "W'ere the bloody 'ell ye been, lad? We uns combed the town from truck to keelson wi'out seein' 'air ner 'ide o' ye!"

Magnus frowned. "Has something happened?"

"Plenty, by God! Sir John be tearin' 'is 'air out by the roots. 'E swears 'e'll 'ave ye 'ung, drawn an' quartered fer desertion!"

"Desertion? A pox on Sir John! I'm not in his bloody navy!"

The old man grimaced. "Ye think naught, eh? Well, come wi' us an' ye'll soon find out!" He saw Magnus bristle, so he shook his head. "No argyment, son. Sir John ordered me to fin' ye an' bring ye back under all canvas. Knowin' Sir John, I aims to do jes' that! Come along!"

Magnus was afforded no time to change or prepare himself, but was escorted to Hawkins' quarters just as he was, where he found the old warrior awaiting him in the hallway.

Sir John was stern and unfriendly. "For a young cub growling with impatience, you are damnably hard to locate when needed.

162

Follow me—the conference has already convened." He turned abruptly and stalked through a doorway.

They entered a long, high-ceilinged chamber wherein about twenty stern-visaged men sat grouped around a massive table. Puzzled, Magnus glanced over the company and recognized but three—John Rivers, Thomas Seely and Edward Gilman, adventurers and seamen like himself.

The rest were strangers, and from their appraising stares, he guessed they were weighing him shrewdly. Deciding they had assembled to hear his story, he let the actor in him take the ascendancy. He bowed with admirable *sang-froid*. Then, as if by some preternatural power, his eyes were drawn to the head of the table where sat a short, square-hulled figure with bright questing eyes, peculiarly arched brows, and a pointed beard. When Magnus felt the impact of those eyes, his composure was shaken. Somewhat dazed, he heard Hawkins rumble: "Francis, here's the slippery young devil who picked King Philip's pocket." Then, *sotto voce*, he growled at Magnus, "Don't gawk, man! Make your obeisance to Sir Francis Drake!"

Magnus was nonplussed. *Sir Francis Drake!* The most feared and respected man in the world; the idol of all British seamen! His poise abandoned him, and in a half-coma, he heard himself introduced to the others—famous, all. Frobisher, Knollys, Fenner, Carleill . . . ! But Magnus Carter had eyes only for Drake.

And Drake, who never forgot his own humble origin, smiled. "Welcome, young man," he said kindly. "Sir John has been regaling us with the story of your escapade. On my oath, it was well handled, and timely, too. We're going to hoist King Philip on his own petard. Now—it has amused her Majesty to declare she was turning her sea-dogs out to hunt, and she suggested I take along a few likely pups for experience. Sir John, to whom I'm indebted for my own start, has strongly recommended I give you command of a ship in my expedition. What say you to that?"

Magnus could not believe his ears. For a long moment, he just stared with his mouth agape. Hawkins cleared his throat impatiently.

"Dammel!" he barked in Magnus' ear. "Is your silence a refusal?"

Magnus spread his arms. "*Refusal*, Sir John? God forbid!" He addressed himself to Drake. "Sire, to serve under you in any capacity would be a privilege, but to command a ship in your fleet is an honor beyond my wildest dreams! My lord, I am . . . I am speechless with gratitude!"

The company all laughed. Dour old Frobisher grimaced. "For a speechless pup, he gives tongue glibly enough, I swear!"

163

Magnus swung on him. "Your pardon, Captain. That was my heart speaking, not me!"

Rear Admiral Knollys pounded his fist on the table. "Hear that, gentlemen?" he chuckled. "The lad's not only got the makings of a fighting man, but a courtier as well! By God, Raleigh better look to his laurels!"

Drake smiled, and gestured Magnus into an empty chair. "Very well, Carter, that is settled. You shall have the bark *Sparrow*. Hawkins tells me you have some men of your own."

"Aye, sir. Seasoned fighters with a debt to pay against Spain."

"Good enough. Now to business . . ."

Sir Francis briefly summarized the situation. The expedition was a private venture sponsored by wealthy men. It was to set out, ostensibly, to inquire at Spanish ports as to why English ships and English seamen were being detained, and to demand their immediate release. The Queen had sanctioned that much—officially.

However, in private, she had given Drake his verbal orders: King Philip was to be taught a lesson he would be a long time forgetting. How Drake chose to administer this curative was his sole responsibility. Chuckling, he confessed to the company that the Queen had warned him if it became expedient, she might have to disown him.

"I assured her Majesty," he laughed, "that I had no objection to being disowned if I could but teach the Spaniards to be more careful how they handled Englishmen in the future."

For the rest, the voyage was organized along conventional lines. While Elizabeth had loaned two ships from her navy, she had given no money to pay for officers, crews or supplies. The enterprise not only had to pay its own way, it had to show a profit as well. The expenses were to be charged to the account of King Philip, for the twenty-one ships were not going to be satisfied with the mere release of British vessels in Spain. They were going to attack the very source of Philip's power—the fabulous towns of the Spanish Main!

When the conference adjourned, Magnus again thanked Drake for the honor conferred on him, then sought out old Hawkins in private. He wanted Ben Absedik confirmed as his principal officer, and a place in the company found for Brother Diego. At first Hawkins was adamantly opposed to commissioning "heathens," but Magnus was in a persuasive mood, and when he reminded the old campaigner how much of his own success had been due to the "heathen" Cimaroons of the Indies, Sir John grumblingly submitted, and promised to see whether Drake would agree.

Satisfied, Magnus walked back to the mole. He was not only delighted with his fortune, he was pleased with himself. He had played his part well, and won the approval of the entire company. He felt a heretofore unknown sense of power. By the grace of God, he was a captain; more, he was a captain of the incomparable Drake! And he was going out to avenge himself on Spain!

His cup of happiness was almost full—almost, yet not quite, for he had a private score to settle. But he assured himself there was no clash of purpose in that.

On reaching the galley, he found Tim awaiting him anxiously.

"W'at 'appened, lad? Be it more trouble?"

"Aye," laughed Magnus, "but not for us. Ask Abu and Brother Diego to join us in the cabin. I have news."

When the four had seated themselves in the cabin, Magnus looked at his comrades with freshened interest. Old Tim sat hunched on the edge of his bench, his wooden leg stretched out before him, his small, shot-like eyes searching Magnus' face. Brother Diego leaned back against the bulkhead, waiting patiently for whatever explanation was to come. His tonsure had grown out an inch or so, yet with the heavy fringe of hair around his temples, it resembled a stand of wheat surrounded by brush. Ben Absedik waited like a hooded falcon.

Magnus recounted his amazing experience with Drake, and of his appointment to command a bark.

"And so," he concluded, "I must have officers whom I can trust, and I know of none better than you men." He sensed their surprise, so he tested his ground with Tim.

"Are you with me, Timothy? Do you want to pay off your debt to Philip, and reap a golden harvest at the same time?"

The old man had tears in his eyes. "Wi' ye, lad? God 'elp me, jus' try to slip yer cables wi'out me! 'Tis the dream o' me life to sail the southern seas onc't more afore I get the deep-six. Aye, I'm wi' ye to the very end!"

"And you, Rais Ben Absedik? It will be an excellent opportunity to carry out your oath to Allah."

The Moor smiled thinly. "It is said if the camel gets his nose in the tent, his body will soon follow. This may be the opening, so if it be the will of Allah I find it on a Frankish ship, then I go. What is to be, will be."

"Brother Diego . . . ?"

The priest toyed with the lobe of one ear. "Magnus, have you forgotten that I am a Spaniard?"

"I haven't forgotten that you are a man, Diego Valesco. Furthermore, we are not attacking Spaniards as such, but an evil system of oppression."

Brother Diego laughed ruefully. "My son, my son, what carnage

165

has been perpetrated under that aegis! Was ever a war started for any other reason than to quell a so-called 'system of oppression'?"

Magnus reddened. "Can you term the Inquisition or Philip's conduct aught else but oppression?" •

"Come now, we mustn't quibble over phrasing," smiled the priest. "Let us call a spade a spade. You are asking me to bear arms against my own country."

"Not exactly," hedged Magnus. "England is not at war with Spain, so it is not one country pitted against the other. This is simply a private enterprise, out to teach a merciless tyrant a lesson."

"And accomplish a bit of profitable piracy at the same time."

Tim Prettyman bristled. "Blast me eyes, *padre,* are ye callin' Francis Drake a *pirate?*"

"By the beard of the prophet, thy Drake is the greatest pirate alive!" Ben Absedik put in so admiringly that Magnus broke into laughter.

Tim smiled sourly. "Well, damme, so long's ye grant 'e's the greatest, I'll no quarrel wi' ye. But 'e 'oo damns Frankie Drake damns Timothy Prettyman, an' ye can set yer courses by that!"

Brother Diego slapped him on the shoulder. "Bravo, my friend! I, too, agree your Drake is a great seaman, possibly the greatest, yet that is not the point. I am a man of God."

"Ye was a man of God," snorted Tim. "But that damned 'Oly Office defrocked ye. Now ye're naught but a plain man, like the rest o' us."

"True, the *Casa Santa* excommunicated me," conceded Brother Diego. "However, since it was to God I made my vows, only God can abrogate them. I am still beholden to Him."

"How better can you serve God than by joining us?" countered Magnus. "Are we not out to fight God's enemies?"

Brother Diego shook his head sadly. "Let us not make a mockery of the Lord's name, nor deceive ourselves. Hold now—hear me out! As I once explained to you, I am a realist. Very well. As such, I have no scruples against liberating captives, whether they be Englishmen, Huguenots, or Moslems. Furthermore, my conscience is flexible enough to permit me to relieve Philip of treasure he has so ruthlessly pillaged from poor savages of America. But, look you . . ." His eyes bored searchingly into Magnus' face, "I suspect you have something else in mind, something even your Francis Drake doesn't know about. Am I not right, my son?"

Magnus colored furiously when he felt the others staring at him. Did this paradoxical priest dabble in Black Magic, or was he merely questing?

"What if I have?" he challenged. "I returned to England seeking

166

justice. Instead of receiving it, they buy me off with command of a ship. So if I can secure justice and serve Drake at the same time, who's to say me nay? Is it because of this you refuse to accompany us?"

"I have not refused," the priest protested gently. "Yet before I join an expedition, I want to know what is expected of me. I have been a soldier, Magnus, and I know that once a soldier enlists, he must follow his commander without question. He cannot serve two masters. Let it be clearly understood that while I am willing to fight against what you are pleased to term the 'enemies of God,' I will have no part of personal vengeance."

Magnus was angry enough to withdraw his invitation. He glared at the other two.

Tim met his eye. "Ye kin count on me, lad! A fight's a fight to Timothy Prettyman."

Ben Absedik was more tolerant. "Truly is it written that a man cannot run counter to his faith," he reasoned. "Likewise it is written that when a man beats his wife, his neighbors shalt not interfere. Therefore, if Magnus-Rais seeks vengeance, he should not demand his brothers go against their faith. They, on their part, should not interfere. That is the wisdom of Allah."

"I'm not asking any of you to fight my battles!" snapped Magnus.

The Moor smiled a twisted smile. "*Effendi,* there is nothing in *my* faith to prevent me from killing Spaniards—or Englishmen, if necessary—and since kismet hath made us brothers, thy quarrels are my quarrels. So, let us remain together, and if it becomes expedient to deviate momentarily from the main business to fulfill our sacred oaths, let the Frankish priest, whom Allah has also made our brother, stand by."

Brother Diego laughed heartily. "Bless you, friend Abu, I almost envy the pliancy of your faith. Howbeit, rigidity of conscience is futile, and the most we can hope for is that more good than harm will result from our actions. May the deviation, as you so subtly put it, never arise."

Old Tim scowled suspiciously. "Damme if I savvy all this gam about deviatin'," he grumbled. "W'at goes on? Ye ain't aimin' to cross up Sir Francis, be ye, lad? Remember w'at 'appened to Doughty w'en 'e tried it!"

"An excellent suggestion," agreed the priest. "In case you have forgotten—Doughty lost his head."

Magnus grinned. "Just let me worry about my own head. Well, is it agreed we sail together?"

They nodded their assent.

Chapter 18

Magnus now found himself in a squirrel-wheel of activity from which there was no escape. Drake was a tireless taskmaster who insisted his captains supervise every detail of the preparations. The bark *Sparrow* was both a delight and a headache. She was long and narrow, with a beautiful clean run, and, under fighting canvas, would be able to flit around a Spanish galleon like a porpoise. Yet this very litheness made her a devil to stow properly so as not to spoil her trim, hence Magnus was forced to proceed by trial and error.

By the same token, their success, their very lives, depended upon these things, for once they bade good-bye to England, they would be entirely on their own. There would be no rope-walks nor dock-yards; no source of neglected supplies. Even the very food they would need would have to be won by the sword.

Nearly every night, Drake summoned his commanders to a conference, and Magnus, though occasionally impatient, was deeply impressed by the admiral's meticulous attention to detail. "Something must be left to chance" was one of his maxims, but certainly nothing over which he had any control. From the beginning, he demonstrated unequivocally that he was master; his was the mailed fist in the velvet glove. He was a paradox. He asked for counsel, then did as he pleased; he kept his schemes and decisons to himself until it was too late to dispute them. He was vain, even arrogant, yet almost in the same breath, kindly and considerate. It was impossible to anticipate him. And above all else, he was astute.

The planning continued for weeks; nothing was overlooked. Drake was an ardent convert to the then novel art of tacking. In the past, no sailing ship had ever succeeded in sailing so much as a single foot against the wind, until Fletcher of Rye made his epoch-making discovery that by trimming his sails fore and aft, he could beat his way to windward if given a sufficiently strong breeze. This achievement was of incalculable value in a sea fight, and Drake insisted that his captains take advantage of it.

168

In addition, strategy was laid down, and tactics studied for every conceivable situation. Rendezvous were charted for the ensuing year; dispositions made for every man in the company in the event of a foundering or other disaster. Signals were agreed upon, courses laid out, fortifications surveyed for possible assault. *Yet not one word was placed on paper!* Francis Drake wanted no tangible evidence of his actions to crop up at the wrong time.

Unaccustomed to continuous study and memorizing, Magnus grew restive. The golden glitter of his captaincy dulled; he became dissatisfied. He still felt the Queen should have assisted him to recover his Rosalind. As he saw it, she had been kidnapped literally. The actual marriage, he ignored.

Too, he was concerned about Kate. It was now definitely established that she had not left with Mistress Prettyman, for she was sought as a runaway servant. Although he had canvassed the town on several occasions, and increased his proffered reward to ten guineas, her whereabouts remained a mystery.

Meanwhile, the adventurers neared the end of their labors. The gear was all stowed; the victuals piled on the decks. Only the water casks remained to be filled. Drake set the sailing date a week away to permit the crews a few days of much-needed relaxation.

Late in the afternoon of the day they started taking on water, a fisherman sculled out to the *Sparrow* and demanded ten guineas in exchange for a letter. Magnus took one glance at the handwriting on the outside of the packet and promptly paid the man. Then he hurried to the privacy of his cabin to read it.

> Deer frend: I aint much at spelling out letters but I herd you was back and asking after me. I have been away but came wen I herd you was asking. It would not be fitting fer me to come to your ship. I will be at the old stable if you still want to see me. I would like to see you. Yrs. Katie.

Magnus was delighted. Laughing, he reread the note. Aye, no one but Kate could write in such ingenuous fashion. He dressed in his best hose and doublet, and went on deck. Under the circumstances, he decided against telling the others where he was going, so leaving Tim in charge of the casks, he went ashore.

About sunset, he reached the ruins. It was a depressing sight. The massive anchors, now overgrown with weeds, marked the walk, but of the tavern itself little remained save a gaunt and blackened shell. Magnus felt a touch of melancholia. Several important milestones in his life had been passed within these walls—his first experience with the mystery of sexual union (Kate had been the girl);

his earliest decision to seek his fortune on the sea (Tim had abetted him in that). Aye, it was the nearest thing he had ever known to a home.

He shook off the feeling. The stables, thank God, were still standing, though the walls were badly charred. He hurried toward them. The rusted hinges groaned complainingly as he pushed inside.

To his dismay, he found no one. He stood silent, while the sight and smells of the place resurrected a host of memories, as exquisitely painful as a hairshirt. The stillness grew oppressive. He began to wonder if, perhaps, he had walked into a trap. He looked warily around him.

"*Katie!*" he shouted.

There was no immediate answer and his anxiety turned to alarm. He had started for the door, when a voice called softly: "Wait, Magnus! Don't go!" Then, in a billow of petticoats, Kate dropped down from the loft.

Laughing with relief, Magnus scooped her into his arms. " 'Pon my soul, girl, I'd begun to think this was a trick to catch me!"

Arching her back to shake the tousled hair out of her eyes, she smiled up into his face.

"Peradventure it is, Magnus!"

"In which event, I give myself up!"

"Without a struggle, Magnus?" Even in the semi-darkness, her eyes were bright.

"Aye, nary a struggle!" He kissed her willing mouth, which merely increased his hunger. It had been such a long time since he had possessed a woman. When she took her lips away to catch breath, he kissed her throat, while Kate leaned back, her eyes closed in rapture.

"Magnus! Magnus! Dear God, how I've missed you!"

Her body was warm, pliable and eager, yet when his hands sought her breasts, she straightened.

"Let's go up in the loft," she whispered. "It's not safe here!"

"Safe?" he laughed. "Nobody is seeking me these days!"

"But they are seeking me," Kate told him ruefully. "Mistress Prettyman has offered a reward for me."

"So did I, my girl. I paid ten guineas to find you!"

She smiled wistfully. "Was it worth so much to you, Magnus?"

"Every penny of it! You'll not escape me this time, my lush wench!"

She giggled. "Then, to use your own words, Magnus—I give myself up."

"I'll accept your surrender in the loft," he chuckled. "Lead the way."

170

Kate needed no urging. They climbed into the friendly darkness and settled close together in the hay. There were a thousand questions he wanted answered, yet this was not the time for talk. There was magic in the setting; a peculiar naturalness, a rightness, as if this was as it should be. He had the sensation of having lived this moment before. True, he had had Kate on other occasions, but somehow it had been different. Then, he had been overeager, questing, experimenting. Now, he felt a sense of controlled maturity. He could not analyze it, and he did not try to. Perhaps, as Ben Absedik would say, this was kismet.

Kate, too, seemed perfectly attuned, in spirit and in body. Her breasts budded to his touch; she came into full flower. He had not remembered such loveliness beneath her coarse garments; such grace of motion. It was an equal partnership in ecstasy. The ancient loft was renovated into an Eden of their own making. . . .

Magnus awakened to find sunlight winking through the chinks in the walls. He raised up on one elbow and glanced at Kate. She was lying on her back, her arms above her head, sleeping as a child sleeps. He looked at the lovely body, at the long lashes resting on her cheek bones. He bent and kissed the nearest eyelid. She wakened, and smiled.

"Then it wasn't a dream, Magnus?"

"I had to kiss you to make certain," he told her.

Abruptly, she became conscious of her nudity. She colored slightly, and reaching for her dress, laid it over her body as a covering.

"So you don't get any ideas," she said in answer to his questioning look.

Magnus laughed heartily. He propped himself up against a mound of hay and pulled her head onto his lap.

"Now, my girl—tell me every single thing that has happened since the night I went away."

"Marry! What a large order!" She took one of his hands between her own and folded them across her breasts, while she collected her thoughts.

"Well, let me see," she began pensively. "It was the day after you went off with the Portagee that Sir Gregory himself came to the tavern and was closeted a long time with the mistress. What passed betwixt them, I know naught, but after he left, she shooed away all the patrons and locked the common-room. That same afternoon, another crowd of Duane's men arrived with hammers and axes. They tore up the floor of your room and ripped open the walls. I could hear them cursing clear down in the scullery."

171

Magnus grunted. "The bastards! They were searching for something I hid up there."

"So I gathered. Was it very valuable—*to you?*"

"Priceless!"

She eyed him reproachfully. "Then why didn't you tell me about it, Magnus?"

He hesitated. "I . . . well, I didn't want to implicate you."

"Are you sure it was *me* you were worried about? Or because your sweetheart was involved?"

"England was involved, Katie! What they were after was a packet of letters proving high treason! I had stolen them from Duane."

She gasped. "Oh, my God! I wish I had known that before!"

"That's why I decided not to tell you. Even Tim didn't know where I hid them. It might have proved fatal. But go on with your story—what happened after the search? I'll wager they didn't find them."

After a lengthy pause, Kate continued: "No, they didn't find anything. They searched for two days, then Sir Gregory came again. The moment he left, the old woman began to pack. She took three trunks away in the dead of night. A week or so after that, we had the fire."

"It was deliberate, wasn't it?"

"I imagine so, as it started in several places at once. Your room had special treatment, for from the loft here, I could see into a corner of it. Chairs had been piled in the bed, like for a bonfire. It was gutted before the rest."

"The bitch!" grated Magnus. "The treacherous old bitch!"

"Aye, she's that all right," agreed the girl. "Knowing we used to be so close, she suspected I knew something. She questioned me about you, then accused me of lying when I told her I knew nothing of your activities. She cuffed me and beat me, and threatened to have me arrested. When that failed, she changed her tune and sought to be friendly. She said she was going to stay with her sister in the north, and would take me with her. I grew fearful she meant to have me killed, so—I ran away."

"Smart lass!"

Kate shuddered. "It was terrible, Magnus! She had me hunted, and it was like an awful game of hide-and-seek. I hung around the waterfront for a week or more, seeking word of you, then I tramped to Teignmouth, because I remembered you used to sail in there of yore. I found work enough to keep alive, for I knew you'd come someday. Two days ago, I heard you were back and asking after me. I came."

Magnus felt choked up with emotion. She had heard, and she

172

came. How typical of Kate! He stroked her hair with his free hand, and, for the first time in months, knew complete contentment.

She startled him suddenly with a question. "Magnus—what were you going to do with the . . . the stuff you hid?"

"Get Rosalind back," he said unthinkingly.

"But, 'tis said she is already wed to Sir Peter Beckles!"

"If I'd gotten hold of those letters she wouldn't have stayed married long! Beckles and old Duane would be drawn and quartered for treason!"

"Oh-o! So you still desire her, Magnus?"

"Aye, and I'll have her yet, mark me! I've taken a sacred oath to kill this *Pedro* Beckles!"

Kate sighed softly. "Peradventure she loves this man? Have you considered . . ."

Magnus interrupted with a snort. "Bah! She doesn't love him; she loves me! She only married him because she had to. But I'll cure that! I'm on my way now, Katie my girl! As a captain of Drake's, I'll have some influence and an opportunity to make my fortune. I can't tell you the plans, for they are secret, but I stand an excellent chance of becoming a rich man and possibly—now that my name had already been brought to the attention of the Queen—of knighthood!"

She released his hand, and he could feel her body stiffen. "*Knighthood?* God in heaven, Magnus, aren't you . . . ?" She paused.

"And why not?" he laughed. "Drake did it; Hawkins did it—why not me? Come that day, I'll need a well-bred woman like Rosalind for wife." He began to wax enthusiastic. "You know, Katie, there's nothing more important than the right sort of woman to help a man get ahead in this world. To make my meaning clear, take a man like . . ."

"You have made your meaning clear enough," she cut in quietly. "When are you leaving?"

Still drugged with contentment, he failed to heed the signs. "Oh, in a day or so. And while I think about it—how are you fixed for money? I'll leave you enough gold to last . . ."

"I don't want your old gold!" she said sharply, jerking out of his lap. "You'd best go, Magnus!"

"*Go?*" he gasped, bewildered. "What's the matter with you, Katie?" He reached for her shoulders, only to have her draw away. To his astonishment, he saw her eyes were filled with tears of anger. Man-like, he capped one verbal blunder with another.

"I'm not done loving you," he teased.

She fairly hissed at him. "Oh, you're not, eh? And you're willin' to pay for it in gold, as if I was a common whore? Meanwhile, you'll

173

entertain me about your well-bred wench! Get out of here! I hate you!"

Magnus was now completely confused. "In God's name, what brought that on? You asked a question, and I answered you. I can't see why . . ."

"You can't see *anything!*" she cried. "Well, I'm glad you can't! I'd die of shame if you could! So begone, *Sir Magnus;* go find this *right sort of woman* you prefer!"

Dismayed, and completely puzzled, he sought to reason with her, but Kate refused to listen. He felt somewhat ridiculous, sitting stark naked in a hay loft, arguing with a raging female, so when she finally threatened to kick him out, he pulled on his clothes and went down the ladder.

However, once safely below and out of reach of her claws, he made one more attempt at logic.

"You're acting like a fool, Kate!" he said aggrievedly. "You should have the wit to know I wouldn't deliberately say anything to hurt you." Under the circumstances, that sounded a trifle inadequate, so he appended: "If I did, it was unintentional!"

He waited a few minutes, expecting her to call him back, but when she did not even deign to answer, he wrapped his dignity around him like a cloak and strode out of the barn.

He was halfway to the waterfront before understanding dawned: *Kate was in love with him!* The realization provoked him. She had taken advantage of his kindliness. He had proffered friendship; she had demanded love. He wagged his head in irritation. Hadn't she the wit to see that marriage between them was impossible—even if he were not in love with Rosalind? But that was the way of women. What was it the Moor had said!—*Love is the companion of blindness!* Aye, that was the trouble: Kate was blind!

Despite this rationalization, he suffered a sense of guilt. He conceded it was barely possible he himself was in part responsible for the quarrel. After all, it *had* been rather tactless to dwell on Rosalind's good breeding to poor Kate, who didn't even know the name of her parents. And what had prompted him to make that asinine remark about knighthood, when he had never even considered the possibility? The recollection embarrassed him.

He shrugged it off. There was one thing about Katie—if she bruised easily, she healed quickly. By the morrow, he concluded, she would be contrite and apologetic, and he knew from experience that when the tides of passion changed, she could be incredibly tender and affectionate. He sighed contentedly. Aye, the making-up would be very pleasant.

174

It was mid-morning when he got back to the *Sparrow*—to find his friends in a fury of anxiety regarding his whereabouts. Urgent instructions had arrived from the admiral. Drake had received a warning from Walsingham that the Queen had again changed her mind and was sending a courier with orders to disband the expedition. Drake had taken the hint. He commanded his captains to put to sea immediately. Hawkins could be trusted to deal with the courier after they were gone.

Magnus had no choice save to obey. Fuming, he scrawled a hasty note to Kate and sent it, along with a pouch of gold, by a fisherman he could trust. By the time that was accomplished, Drake's flagship, the *Bonaventure,* was already standing out the channel, faithfully followed by the *Primrose* and the *Galleon Leicester.* They made a brave sight, etched against a blood-red sky, but Magnus was in no mood for beauty. He felt cheated again. Savagely, he ordered the topsails shaken out and the anchor weighed.

The voyage had begun.

Book Three

THE VOYAGE

Chapter 19

O NCE the shores of England had safely melted astern, Magnus had leisure to contemplate his personal problems. With a fair wind for Spain, the little *Sparrow* soared swiftly and had no difficulty maintaining her place in the formation. Her bottom was clean, her gear new, and the hands eager. Magnus had just cause for pride.

Yet instead of pride, he had resentment. The glamor was gone. Instead of an independent command, he was bound irrevocably by the iron will of Drake; instead of issuing orders, he was expected to obey them. In the womb of this discontent, the nebulous scheme he had conceived earlier began to gestate. By the time they reached the Bay of Biscay, it was born. He would sail into the harbor of Bilbao, raid the castle loaned to Beckles, settle his account with that knave and recover Rosalind.

Crazed as he might seem, Magnus was sane enough to recognize the enormous difficulties involved, but with characteristic impetuosity, he lined them up mentally, in order of precedence, and attacked them individually. His most vexatious problem was how to slip away from Drake, for the fleet was proceeding in close order, and any straggling would arouse suspicion. He had no illusions about the admiral's attitude toward insubordination; Drake had lopped off the head of Thomas Doughty on lesser grounds than Magnus meant to afford him. But the true actor is a mimic, and Magnus Carter was as absorbent as a sponge. He had learned a lot from Francis Drake, doubtless a deal more than Drake himself intended. "Something must be left to chance," was a favorite maxim of the latter. Thinking about it made Magnus smile. Aye, he would trust *chance* to furnish the opportunity, but when it came, he would be ready.

Meanwhile, he adopted another of Drake's traits—that of keeping his own counsel. He did not even confide in Tim Prettyman, for though he trusted him implicitly, he was only too aware of the old mariner's veneration for Drake. So he completed his plans in silence, and bided his opportunity.

It came suddenly, in the guise of a violent storm. In the face of their precipitate departure from England, the admiral had issued eleventh-hour commands to put in at Vigo, Spain, to replenish the partially filled water casks. So it was that they were skirting Cape Finisterre when the gale crashed out of the northwest. With a lee-shore so close his larboard, Drake signaled the fleet to stand out to sea. The ships obediently altered course, and when by nightfall the full fury descended on them, even the signal lamps were blotted from view.

Through it all, Magnus had remained on the poop, savoring the magnificent spectacle. When he could no longer see the other ships, he judged they must have hove-to, with all canvas furled, save a steadying sail. The little *Sparrow* was pitching violently, rising heroically to the summit of giant combers, then plummeting down their slopes. Magnus slyly began to rationalize: a captain had first to think of the safety of his vessel; who could question his right to seek shelter if he deemed it advisable? And if Francis Drake was so partial to sailing *on* the wind, by the Gods, Magnus would oblige him. He quietly ordered the topsails trimmed in, then began to beat his way to the northeast.

He held this course until it was too late for his friends to dispute him, after which he summoned them to his cabin and outlined his purpose. They received the news with varying emotions.

Old Tim was aghast. "Lord God, man, ye *can't* steal one o' Sir Francis's ships! 'E'll 'ave yer 'ead!"

Magnus grinned. "Heaven forbid! I'm not stealing it, Tim; I'm merely seeking a safe harbor."

"Aye! Two 'undred miles through a gale to find it!"

Ben Absedik smiled his twisted smile. "They said to the wolf, 'For what art thou following those poor little sheep.' He replied, 'The dust they raise is good for my poor little eyes.' Verily, Magnus-Rais, I accept your explanation, for it is a venture to my liking, yet have you considered how to get past the fortress?"

"Naturally," Magnus retorted cockily. "We'll use the secret signals from the galley's code-book which I had the foresight to bring with me."

"Any fool kin get into a cage," Tim grumbled. " 'Tis 'ow to get out w'at counts."

"That's simple. We'll take hostages, and send word to the commander at the fort, warning that if he so much as discharges one ball, we'll hang the lot from the yards. As for the castle, surprise should avail us there."

The Moor shrugged. "The very hopelessness of it is its only hope. May Allah be tolerant."

Throughout the discussion, Brother Diego had sat braced against the wild gyrations of the little vessel, his eyes fixed resolutely on Magnus' face. When it was his turn to express himself, he said, "I presume nothing I can say will dissuade you from this mad course of murder and violation of a marriage?"

"Nothing!"

"Very well," went on the priest. "Let me ask one question: suppose you succeed—what then?"

"We'll rejoin the fleet at Vigo, of course."

"With the woman?"

Magnus scowled. All his careful calculations had dealt with the physical aspects of the raid; beyond that, he had not gone. The query took him full aback, hence he could only resort to anger.

"That will be my worry, *padre!*"

"Aye, an' a pretty worry it'll be!" grumbled Tim. "Ye bloody well knows the admiral's standin' order about women on 'is ships. God 'elp us, onc't 'e 'ears about it, as 'e's sure to do."

Magnus stood up so abruptly his head banged against a beam. This did not improve his temper.

"We'll cross the shoals as we come to them," he said by way of dismissal. "Those of you who don't choose to go ashore with me can stay aboard, and welcome. That is all I have to say about the matter!"

Magnus drove on relentlessly, carrying sail until the masts bent like coachwhips, so that in the afternoon of the second day, the lookout finally descried the Basque fort crouched high on the hill which marked the mouth of the River Nervión. The weather had moderated somewhat by that time, yet the gigantic swell, aftermath of the gale, tossed the little bark unmercifully. Even with two stout hands at the whipstaff, it was impossible to keep her from yawing.

Magnus was on deck when the call came down from aloft; he had scarcely left the poop since slipping away from the fleet. He sighed relievedly. For his mad venture to have even a remote chance of success, it was necessary to reach Bilbao just after dark. At the moment, luck seemed to be with him.

He sent for his code-book and ordered the Spanish ensign made ready, then braced himself on the heaving deck to watch the fort through his telescope. The cry of "Land-Ho!" had brought the others to the poop, where they stood in a silent group to await his commands.

About an hour before sunset, they drove within cannon-shot of the fort. When Magnus saw a small white cloud mushroom from the ramparts, he told Tim, "Run up that accursed flag, then dip it thrice —at five-second intervals."

Tim hobbled off to obey, while the bark fled onward before a stern wind. When the signal was made, a flag from the fort replied in kind. Magnus sighed and lowered his glass. The first obstacle was overcome.

The sun was sinking when they slipped into the river, whereupon the high banks blanketed the wind. The *Sparrow* slowed until she barely made steerage way. Magnus bit his lip in impatience, for if darkness overtook them in the treacherous channel, they would be undone. Savagely, he ordered out the sweeps, and himself stood on the prow to con the vessel in the dimming twilight.

After the exhilarating dash through the Bay, this laborious pace was agonizing. It was eight miles from the mouth of the town, and though the rowers had learned well their task in the grueling galley school, even at double-time, it was dark before they rounded a bend to find the lights of Bilbao dead ahead.

The sight of the town revived Magnus' humor. As he had anticipated, the recent storm had driven dozens of ships into the harbor, and these were huddled in a group, swinging to anchor like nervous sheep. He surveyed them with grim contempt, then conning the bark to a position safely astern of them, he ordered a small anchor put down.

Pausing only long enough to appraise the tidal current, he strode aft. Two small boats were already lying off the quarter. He glanced questioningly at his comrades, but they merely nodded soundlessly. The plans were understood.

Tim—much against his will—was to remain aboard. Magnus had insisted, on two counts; he had to leave a man he could trust, and Tim wasn't fast enough on his one good leg to keep up on a lightning raid. Ben Absedik would accompany Magnus to the castle, his special task to be the recovery of Rosalind, a chore for which he was admirably suited by experience, having admittedly stolen many a female in his time. Magnus left himself free for the pleasurable task of hunting down Peter Beckles and killing him.

Brother Diego, having refused to participate in the raid, had taken on a job more acceptable to his conscience. Because he hated war, and was willing to go to desperate lengths to prevent it, he had agreed to the destruction of the Spanish warships lying in the harbor. He himself would see to that.

In the darkness, Magnus could not see the faces of the others, but he thrust out a hand toward the shadow he knew to be the priest.

"Will you wish me luck, *padre?*" he asked.

182

Brother Diego gripped his hand. "May God forgive and preserve you, my son," he temporized.

"For Christ's sake get goin'!" pleaded Tim. " 'Tis less than two hours 'til turn o' tide. If ye ain't back by then . . ."

"If we're not back, you have your orders," Magnus growled. "So stop wuzzling like an old woman." He glanced at the shadow of the Moor. "All ready, Abu?"

Ben Absedik chuckled wickedly. "Verily, I have been ready these three years, *effendi!* So now, peace to thy tongue, and may Allah the all-wise smile upon us as we drive this serpent, who hath defiled thy garden of paradise, into the arms of Shaitan! Come, my sword itches!"

Magnus swung overside and dropped lightly into the boat. The half-dozen men awaiting him were invisible, having, like the Moor and himself, blackened their faces and weapons with burnt cork and worn dark clothing.

They shoved off, with no sound from the muffled oars save the furtive trickling of water from the blades. From their small boat, the Spanish galleons loomed stark and formidable. Slowly, painfully, they crawled across the black water toward the old fourteenth-century town of Siete Calles, which lay on the right bank. There, they tied up at the mole, and leaving a former Spanish criminal—who had been well coached on his responsibility—in charge of the boat, the other seven scurried ashore.

For days, Magnus had studied a sketch of the ancient town until he felt he knew it almost as well as he knew Plymouth. Taking the lead, with his sword loose in its scabbard, and a naked poniard in his hand for emergencies, he skirted the central part of the town, and slipping up a narrow street, gained a path which coiled upward toward the castle.

Now, however, the moon, which had fitfully served them, ducked behind a lowering cloud bank and plunged the scene into opaque darkness. They were forced to slow their pace, and Magnus cursed in impatience. The rotted road degenerated until it was little more than a winding cow-path, over which they had to grope their way. But when the moon suddenly reappeared, they discovered the great mound of masonry directly ahead.

Magnus called a halt and surveyed it gloomily. From the deck of a ship, the place had looked merely picturesque and pastoral, but now that they stood under it, the difference was startling. The grim menacing tower, the high encircling walls and wide moat made it appear impregnable. Twenty alert men could hold this castle against a thousand—and Magnus Carter had hoped to raid it with six!

Bidding the others wait, he beckoned Ben Absedik to follow and,

183

with infinite caution, crept closer. As he feared, the drawbridge had been raised, but only partially. Beyond it was the great iron gate, flanked by turrets. Through a funnel-shaped slit in the right-hand turret gleamed the light of the guardroom.

Magnus was nonplussed and discouraged. He glanced back the way they had come. Far below, he could just distinguish the black outlines of the fleet, like water-bugs settled on a dark mirror. In his mind's eye, he visualized Brother Diego even now stealing toward the outermost warship, and old Tim anxiously pacing the poop of the bark. He shook his head. Once again, he had played the fool.

He turned back to the castle. A thin coil of mist spiraled out of the moat, to wind its tentacles around the half-raised drawbridge. Magnus accepted it as a sign, and suddenly, out of apparent hopelessness, an inspiration was born. He outlined the scheme to the Moor.

"By the Seven Heavens of Islam, it might be done!" swore Ben Absedik. "Let me attempt it?"

"No, Abu, this is my pleasure. Bring up the men whilest I make ready."

As the Moor glided away, Magnus peeled off his doublet. He was wearing a coat of mail beneath it which, though reluctant to discard, he knew to be too heavy for his purpose. Removing the armor, he replaced the doublet and took off his boots. He retained his sword.

He had barely accomplished all this when a faint scraping warned him his companions were at hand. Not knowing what conditions they might encounter, they had brought along a miscellany of gear from the ship. Magnus chose a small grappling hook from this collection, and wrapped the prong with cloth to deaden the sound when it touched masonry. Then securing a length of line to the grapnel, he tied the bitter end to his waist, and lowered himself cautiously into the water.

A few swift strokes carried him across the moat where the opaqueness against the dark sky told him he was directly under the drawbridge. He groped around until he encountered the rusted chain, then drew himself onto the bridge.

For a time, he lay flat against the timbers, fearful lest his exertions had attracted attention. All was silent. The shaft of light in the turret gleamed undisturbed. Breathing more easily, he peered back across the moat. He could see nothing of his companions, but a slight tug on the line brought an answering signal. He hauled the grapnel in, coiling the surplus line with infinite care.

However, all this took time, and Magnus was sick with impatience. He bitterly censured himself for allowing such a narrow

184

margin. If they were delayed here at the castle, Brother Diego's enterprise would alarm the entire countryside. When that happened, escape would be impossible.

Yet "something must be left to chance!" Dividing the coil of rope into two sections, he stepped back up the inclining bridge and hefted the grappling iron experimentally before heaving it upwards. In the interval between his throw and the instant it thudded into the masonry, his heart stood still. When it landed, he flattened himself against the iron-studded gate and waited to see if the sentry would take alarm.

No cry forthcoming, Magnus pulled gently on the rope. To his dismay, it came in freely for a while. He hesitated, wondering if, in falling downward, it would clatter on the bridge. He did not dare attempt to catch it, for the sharp prongs would pierce his arms like a lance-thrust.

But there was no turning back now—that he had vowed—so he gave the line a vicious tug, hoping to hurl it backward into the moat. To his unbounded delight, it tautened abruptly as the hooks lodged in a crevice. Gingerly, he tested the hold with his weight. It was secure. Thereupon, he clamped the poniard between his teeth, shoved his sword around to the middle of his back so that it would not rattle against the stone walls, and, sailor fashion, ascended the rope.

On reaching the top, he looked carefully in both directions for the silhouette of a possible sentry. He saw none, so he pulled himself over the rim and crouched between two merlons while he surveyed the darkened courtyard beyond.

There were a few lights winking in the windows of the chateau, but no stir of life on the outside. Obviously, the castle was not expecting an attack, and Magnus reasoned it was doubtless understaffed, since Philip required all fighting men for his armies. He began to breathe freely for the first time in an hour.

Magnus glanced briefly into the solid darkness where the Moor waited with his men. Then, holding his poniard in his right hand, he crept off in search of the inefficient sentry. After a short prowl, he found a flight of stone steps winding down into the inner bailie. Descending, he tried desperately to keep track of the turns so as not to lose his sense of direction in the absolute blackness, but that was impossible. The steps ended, and he seemed to be in a tunnel-like passage. He followed this a short distance, pausing every few steps to listen, yet all he heard was the pounding of his own heart.

An unexpected cough nearly tore a scream from his throat. He pressed against a wall, his knees gone weak. On conquering his terror, he realized the sound must have come from somewhere ahead.

With his pulse racing, he continued. A few steps brought him to a sharp bend in the passage, where just ahead, a square of light shone through a peep-hole in a door.

Once again, he stopped to consider. After mentally reviewing his course, he decided the door belonged to the guardroom in the turret. He edged forward with extreme caution and peered through the opening.

Two men sat on either side of a small table, playing at cards by the light of torches set in iron sconces on the walls. One was a dark, bearded fellow clad in leather, with a ring of keys dangling from his belt; his companion was a pimply-faced youth barely out of puberty and wearing a steel corselet. His morion lay beside him on the table and his halbert leaned against the wall close to hand. Magnus decided the former was the gate-keeper, the latter, the sentry. On the other side of the table from the door stood the heavy winch for raising and lowering the drawbridge.

Though the ease of his entry had been due to the sociability of the sentry, Magnus cursed the fellow. It would have been much simpler to have dealt with them separately. He pondered the problem. Unless the door was latched on the inside, which was unlikely, he might be able to dash in and settle them both. However, this could not be done simultaneously, and one scream would be sufficient to arouse the entire citadel. On the other hand, to wait patiently, until one or the other chose to step out into the corridor, was a luxury time would not afford. He decided to press the issue.

Stepping back, he contemplated his poniard. The blade was razor-sharp, yet from experience he knew a man seldom died silently from a knife thrust. He hefted it calculatingly. The weighted hilt might suffice if he could but lure them out singly.

He took the precaution to run his hand over the flagged flooring. It was amply smooth for fast footwork. A coarse oath stiffened him, then a chair scraped inside the room. He sprang erect and risked another look. The sentry had shoved back his chair, but only to stretch his legs. The bearded man was glowering at his cards and calling upon God to witness his bad luck.

Magnus smiled grimly. If his plan worked, the lout could tell his troubles to his Maker in person. He rapped smartly on the door.

The men straightened guiltily and, in the same motion, swept their cards out of sight. The sentry pawed for his halbert.

"Por Dios!" muttered the bearded one, *sotto voce*, then loudly: "Come in!"

Magnus ignored the invitation, and flattened himself against the wall. The keeper repeated his summons.

186

"Hola!" he growled on receiving no reply. "Who the devil can it be?"

As his heavy stride crossed the room, Magnus gripped the poniard by its blade and raised it. He heard the keeper tell the sentry to relax, then the door opened. . . .

Light flooded the corridor, but Magnus pinned his faith on the contrast between this semi-darkness and the brilliance of the room. Sure enough, the bearded man glanced casually around, then with another oath, stepped out into the passage.

The instant he moved away from the open doorway, Magnus clamped his left hand around the fellow's throat to stifle any outburst and at the same time, brought the loaded handle of the poniard down on his head. The keeper sank without sound.

After a tense moment of silence, the anxious voice of the young sentry piped: *"Caramba!* Who was it, Juan?"

Magnus gently lowered the inert body to the flagging and crouched for a spring. The youth in the guardroom repeated his query, his voice cracking in nervousness. Finally, with a puzzled whimper, he stuck his head through the doorway. The poniard descended once more and the convivial youth joined his companion in oblivion.

Dragging them into the room, Magnus sprang for the winch. He let the bridge down as slowly as possible, yet the chain rasped and clanged until he was sure the entire garrison would be aroused. That accomplished, he slashed the keeper's belt, retrieved the keys, then snatching a torch from its sconce, dashed out to unlock the main gate. Seconds later, Ben Absedik and his companions charged through the opening.

There was scant need for words since every man knew his part. Two stood aside to guard the portals, while the remainder swept across the quadrangle in the wake of Magnus and the Moor.

Thus far, things had gone almost too smoothly. They knew it could not last. The rattle of the drawbridge and the groaning of the gate had aroused the men-at-arms, who now, led by a blustering *castellan,* came running out of their quarters. The sight of a coal-black figure racing toward them with a flaming torch in his hand, and closely followed by four similar apparitions, was enough to set the *castellan* bellowing for action.

But though outnumbering the invaders more than two to one, the defenders were overwhelmed by surprise. Before they realized fully what was happening, they found themselves assaulted with utmost savagery. One agile Spaniard managed to loose a bolt from his crossbow which took a young Huguenot full in the throat, but before the visitor could tilt his head to crow, he lost it by a single stroke of the Moor's two-handed scimitar. Since no quarter was expected by the invaders, they gave none. Only the *castellan* was spared.

Magnus had singled him out for his personal prey. Sweeping aside the man's first cut, he speared him through the arm, forcing him to drop his sword. Then with his own point to the *castellan's* throat, he commanded him to lead them to the chateau.

There, they met another burst of opposition in the hallway, but this was quickly subdued. Leaving two begrimed seamen to maintain order, Magnus and Ben Absedik prodded the now-cowed *castellan* to the second story.

As they climbed the stairs, Magnus felt suffocated with excitement. His pulse raced until he was dizzy, and despite every effort to calm his nerves, he trembled like a schoolboy. When finally they reached the closed door of the bower, he had to hold up his hand for a pause.

"Remember," he warned Ben Absedik—more to gain time than for any actual need, "no matter how it goes, leave the man to me!"

The Moor gave him an eloquent glance. "Are we women that we must waste priceless time on prattle over what is already agreed? Whilest thou cast this camel-dung in the pit of Gehenna, I will snatch thy pearl! *Hola! Balak! Balak!*"

The *castellan* sobbed out an impassioned protest, but Magnus rapped him on the base of the skull, and leaving him floundering on his hands and knees, pushed open the door.

Rosalind—*his Rosalind!*—sat there before a dressing table, while an aged duenna brushed her luxuriant hair. At the sudden intrusion, she clutched the gown around her throat and sprang up in terror. In the mirror behind her, Magnus caught a glimpse of himself. He made a grisly spectacle with his blackened face and dripping sword.

"Rosalind!" he called to reassure her. "It's me—Magnus!"

Her eyes widened in disbelief, and she swayed weakly against the serving woman.

"Where is your husband?" Magnus demanded. "I've come to avenge you!"

It was then she seemed to recognize him. "Magnus!" she wailed. "Oh, dear Jesus . . . !" Her legs folded and she went down in a faint.

Magnus started toward her, but the Moor was quicker.

"This be my task!" he snapped, shoving Magnus aside. "Settle thy own!"

As Magnus turned to the old woman, who was now speechless with astonishment, a dull boom shook the castle. He glanced through a window. The entire harbor seemed ablaze.

188

"All praise to Allah the bountiful!" shouted Ben Absedik. "The Frankish priest has succeeded. We must hurry!"

The duenna recovered her voice in full volume. While Magnus sought vainly to silence her, Ben Absedik tore a silken covering from the bed and wrapped it around the unconscious girl. From the floor below came shouting and the ring of swords to warn them the men were hard-pressed. The Moor hoisted the girl across one shoulder and, with bared scimitar in his free hand, started for the door.

"Art rooted, *effendi*? In the name of Allah, let us go!"

"Go then!" snarled Magnus. "I'll follow when I have done here!" He slapped the old crone hard across the face, but it was impossible to stem the torrent of screams. Disgusted, he ran into the hallway and caught the *castellan* who had just managed to stagger erect. Slamming him against the wall, Magnus poised a sword before his face.

"Where is your master?" he thundered. "By the Almighty, if you don't tell me . . ."

It took the old soldier several moments to find his tongue.

"In . . . Barcelona!" he stammered finally. "He's gone to see the King!"

"You lie, *cabrón!*"

"By the Holy Virgin, I swear 'tis so, *señor!*" babbled the *castellan*. "He left three days agone!"

There was no point arguing; it was plain the fellow spoke the truth, yet Magnus could have killed him in sheer pique. He contented himself with knocking him on the head.

The Moor had vanished by this time, but now there were cries from below.

"Cap'n! Cap'n!" he heard a Cornishman bellow. "'Elp us, in God's nyme!"

Half crazed by frustration, Magnus charged down the winding staircase. An all-but-decapitated corpse at the foot indicated where the Moor had slashed his way through the press, but the two faithful seamen still on guard were being beset by five lackeys. With a paralyzing roar of defiance, Magnus fell on them from the rear and hacked a passage to his weary men.

"Get you gone, lads!" he commanded. "I'll cover your retreat! Protect the Moslem!"

They hesitated, dreading to leave him against such odds, but when he peremptorily repeated his order, they obeyed. Magnus sprang backwards to the doorway, where his opponents could not surround him. Jerking off his cloak, he wrapped it around his left arm, with the folds hanging loose. With this disconcerting shield, he worked back slowly through the passage.

189

Never was Magnus in better stomach for a fight. All the pent-up hatred he had generated for Sir Peter Beckles, he expended on Sir Peter's bravos. This savagery awed them. However, though mediocre swordsmen, their very numbers made them formidable. Had they rushed in unison, he would have been lost. Yet that would have inevitably caused the death of one or two, and none seemed anxious to make the sacrifice.

On his part, Magnus had no thought of perishing. His mind was occupied solely with the fight; to kill without being killed. He retreated a step at a time, spitting an arm here, slashing a cheek there, never daring to bury his sword too deep in a body. Thus he reached the great front door.

As he backed through it into the courtyard, a bold fellow sprang forward to end it—and ended himself instead. Magnus deflected the lunge, and sent his point through the bravo's throat. The man tried to scream, but succeeded only in a ghastly gurgling cough before toppling backward into the arms of his fellows.

Magnus seized this respite to dash across the courtyard. His men were gone. With the yelping lackeys pounding at his heels, he made for the gate, still guarded by the two trustworthy seamen he had left there. On reaching them, he pirouetted to face the Spaniards, whose numbers had been reinforced en route.

He fell on guard to receive the attack. One of the bravos was bellowing for a crossbow.

Magnus gasped at his men. "Is the petard ready?"

"Aye, Cap'n! It awaits yer signal!"

"Then let's have at them!" roared Magnus, and led the charge.

The unexpected counterattack threw the enemy into momentary confusion. They fell back a few paces to brace themselves. This was all Magnus needed. Barking a sharp order to his men, he turned tail and fled across the drawbridge. Giving tongue like a pack of hounds, the Spaniards started in pursuit, a dozen paces behind.

The instant Magnus cleared the far end of the bridge, he shouted: "*St. George!*" then threw himself full-length on the ground and buried his face in the dirt.

Almost simultaneously there was a terrific explosion, blended with the rendering of timbers and the shrieks of men. Magnus felt the powerful air-pressure wash over him before he risked a backward glance. Debris was settling in the moat where but a moment before the bridge had been. In the gateway beyond, too stunned to speak, huddled the few surviving Spaniards.

Magnus staggered to his feet and shook his fist at them. "Tell that yellow mongrel you serve that I shall call again!" he taunted them in Spanish.

190

A weary seaman tugged his arm. "Fer the luv o' God, sir, let's begone!" he begged. "The 'ole bloody 'arbor be in flames!"

Magnus nodded bitterly. It was pointless to tarry longer. Once again, his quarry had eluded him; there was nothing more for him here. Yet he was sorely disappointed. His was less than half a victory; for though he had rescued his beloved Rosalind, he had failed to remove her husband. Thus, before he could rightfully claim her for his own, Beckles would have to be slain.

Cursing softly, he followed his men down the hill.

Chapter 20

THEY reached the town without incident, to find it apparently deserted. With Ben Absedik in the lead, and Magnus bringing up the rear, they padded through the narrow cobbled streets. On nearing the waterfront, their way was lighted by an eerie saffron glow, and when they broke cover of the buildings, they saw the crowds jamming the mole.

Then another awe-inspiring spectacle greeted their jaded eyes. A dozen ships of war blazed until the flames seemed to spread over the very water itself. As they started out onto the mole, a galleon blew up with a thunderous roar that shook the ground underfoot. The crowd stampeded in terror.

Magnus ran to the head of his company to force a way through this human herd. At first, the mob fell apart to afford a passage, no doubt appalled at their black and bloody appearance. But the last twenty yards to the boat had to be won by dint of hard fighting, with barely room in the press to wield a blade. Ben Absedik wriggled through and, springing into the boat, laid his burden under the protection of the bow and shielded it with his body. Magnus waited until the last one of his men was aboard before he followed.

The mob rallied as they tried to shove off. Someone shouted: "*Perros ingleses!* English dogs!" At that, the crowd went wild. A shower of rocks descended on the boat.

191

Magnus slashed the shore-lines with his blade. "Shove off!" he yelled. "For Christ's sake, get to your oars!"

The men dropped their swords and grabbed the oars. A Spanish soldier leaned over the mole with a halbert and tried to spear Magnus, who was standing up in the sternsheets. Magnus caught the weapon by the handle and jerked the man into the water. When he stooped to finish him, he found the weight of the soldier's armor had spared him the trouble.

Just as he started erect again, a rock took him flush on the forehead. . . .

The next thing Magnus knew, he was lying on the *Sparrow's* poop, with Ben Absedik leaning over him. His first question was for Rosalind.

The Moor grinned wolfishly. "The peace of the Prophet be upon thee, O my brother. The peri-faced Frankish pearl rests safely below. Didst thou haply disembowel the offspring of Shaitan thou sought?"

Magnus groaned. His head felt swollen to twice its normal size. "No, damn him! He wasn't there!"

Ben Absedik accepted it fatalistically. "So it must have been written. May Allah the all-seeing rot his bones! Meanwhile, we are not yet out of this Gehenna." He moved away to help with the work.

By gripping the rail, Magnus managed to pull himself erect. His brain still whirled giddily, but he was aware that Tim had severed the anchor hawse and the bark was turning slowly with the current. Fortunately, the wind had veered into the east, which was fair for the river. But there was scant cause for elation, for already several row-galleys were converging on the *Sparrow*.

She seemed hardly to move, even with the sweeps out and all canvas set. Magnus couldn't understand it. He wondered if she might have fouled a shoal, or a submerged wreck. Then a sudden flare from a burning galleon showed him the *Sparrow* was towing a small hoy.

Bellowing in fury, he swayed aft to the taffrail to cut the hoy adrift. Brother Diego stepped out of the darkness and seized his arm.

"Wait, my son!"

"Wait . . . ! This is no time to seize a prize! It is slowing us down!"

"For the moment only," remonstrated the priest. "Soon it will slow the others. You are in no condition to command, so leave this to me."

Dazed and confused, Magnus held his peace. The *Sparrow* had

192

worked around by this time, and despite her drag, was moving into the channel. Nevertheless, the Spanish galleys were fast overtaking them. It was plain that before they could possibly get through the narrows just ahead, the nimble row-galleys would come abreast. The latter were loaded with soldiers, and once they sank their grappling irons into the bark, resistance would be futile.

Though Magnus was able to comprehend the danger, he could not tell why he did not assert his authority. Possibly, it was because of the calm self-assurance of the priest. Whatever the reason, Magnus stood mute beside him at the rail and watched the sharp prows of the galleys carve a phosphorescent furrow through the black water.

Soon the channel narrowed, and the banks rose sheerly on either hand. The galleys were racing forward in a triangle, one ahead, two behind. As they watched, the leading galley fired a bow culverin. The ball passed through the *Sparrow's* mainsail. Tim and Ben Absedik came running aft.

"It is Allah's will that we be boarded!" the Moor observed.

"Don't be too sure," retorted the priest. "Timothy, be good enough to hand me a lanthorn."

He took the light from the old seaman and, holding it aloft, waved it back and forth. Suddenly the shadowy outline of a man appeared on the bluff bow of the hoy, and began to wave his arms frantically.

"She's rigged, sor!" he called to them. "'Aul me aboard!" Then he slashed the tow-line where it passed through the chocks of the hoy, and grabbing that portion still secured to the *Sparrow*, flung himself into the water.

While Magnus stared stupidly, Brother Diego set down the lanthorn and, with Tim's help, hauled the dripping seaman aboard the bark.

He came over the rail, dripping and gasping, but on recognizing Magnus, he knuckled his forehead in salute.

"Praise God yer safe back, sor!" he panted. "D'ye mind if I tarry 'ere to watch me 'andiwuk? 'Twill be a right merry sight, I wean!" He bowed to the priest. "I done w'at ye ordered, *padre*. Four casks o' pitch an' a train o' gunpowder. I only 'opes to God we move out o' the way!"

Magnus began to understand. The *Sparrow* had picked up speed the moment she was relieved of the drag, whereas the hoy was drifting sideways, almost blocking the channel. He watched breathlessly as the galleys swerved to avoid the hulk.

The lead galley was close abreast the hoy's quarter when, with a tremendous *whoosh* of air, she burst into a cauldron of flame, hurl-

193

ing searing pitch in all directions. The endangered galley veered desperately to escape, and in so doing, stuck on a shoal. An instant later, the following galley crashed into her.

That ended the pursuit.

Magnus broke into a raucous cheer. "Bravo! Bravo!" he shouted, pounding Brother Diego on the back. "By my troth, for a squeamish, conscience-ridden parson, you're a damned intelligent warrior!"

Brother Diego grunted. "It doesn't require intelligence to destroy, my son," he chided. "Yet it is manifest you don't grant even that modicum to a priest."

Magnus chuckled. "Oh, come now, my friend, I ask your pardon. I forgot that before you took your vows you were a soldier."

Brother Diego shook his head. "You continue to make it worse," he said ruefully. "Magnus, when will you learn that the ability to fight is nothing but a low animal instinct; even a rat can do it proportionately better than a man. Martial courage is simply a defense, and certainly not a source for pride."

Magnus arched his brows. "H'mmn! Say you so? However, I thought it was agreed we would not argue religion between us!"

"This is not a question of religion, but of humanities. Well, let it pass—did you accomplish your nefarious purpose?"

Magnus shrugged. "In part. Beckles, damn his black soul, was away. But, as God's my witness, I'll never let up until I find him!"

"Meanwhile, you have stolen his wife."

"*His* wife? The dog had no right to her!"

"That is beside the point. She is a married woman!"

"Through no fault of mine," Magnus growled. "And, God willing, I'll make her a widow at the first opportunity."

"Leaving God out of this for the time being," rejoined the priest, "she is still a married woman, and therefore beyond you."

Magnus felt a hot flush of anger sweep over him. "What are you driving at?" he demanded. "That girl belongs to me, and me alone! So let's have no more sermonizing about it!" He turned abruptly and started for the companionway, but before he reached it, the priest sprang over and blocked the passage.

"Wait, my son! Consider what you do!"

Magnus stopped short in amazement. "By God!" he bellowed. "Do you dare dictate to me?"

Tim and Ben Absedik stood quite still, looking from one to the other. Yet when Tim started toward Magnus' side, the Moor restrained him. Tim paused in bewilderment.

"Magnus," the priest said firmly, "that woman remains in my cabin!"

"We'll bloody soon settle that! Do you want to fight me for her?"

194

Brother Diego shook his head. "Not *for* her, my son. I have neither desire nor designs. But so long as I am able, neither you nor any other man on this vessel shall violate her. If you honestly cherished her, you would have the wit to see the wisdom of this."

Always short of temper, and now keyed to a fever pitch by the events of the night, Magnus went for his sword. But before it cleared his scabbard, the Moor caught his arm.

"Stay thy wrath, O my brother!" he pleaded. "For the mistakes of a learned man are as a shipwreck which destroys others with it. By the beard of the Prophet, let us not shed blood over a mere woman. The friendship of men is above such trivia. Consider now: If the priest covets the maid, barter with him. That is the custom in my country!"

Ben Absedik's ingenuousness unconsciously released the tension. Tim broke into a too-loud guffaw, and Brother Diego smiled in spite of himself. Even Magnus felt an insane desire to laugh.

"The priest doesn't want the maid, Abu," he explained sourly to the Moor who was frowning in puzzlement at the effect of his well-meant suggestion. "He just doesn't want me to have her. He's playing dog in the manger."

Ben Absedik stroked his spare beard a moment, then spat in disgust. "Bah, then it is a game you play! By Allah, you unbelievers practice ridiculous customs!"

Tim tried his hand at peacemaking. "Hell, lad, the infidel's right: no woman's worth fighting with friends about! Anyhow, w'at the *padre* says be true enough. 'Twill but cause trouble wi' the 'ands if ye go sleepin' wi' the wench w'ilest they have naught but to twiddle their thumbs for'ard. Let be 'til we gits ashore, fer the riper the fruit, the better the flavor!"

Still quivering with rage, Magnus was loath to back down. Then a sudden call from the lookout broke the deadlock.

"*Ahoy the poop! We're comin' wi'in range o' the fort!*"

Magnus moved swiftly to the rail, the girl momentarily forgotten. He could just distinguish the dark mass of the fort, poised like a vulture on the high bluff. He did not need to see the cannon; doubtless their eager gunners were even now sighting his little craft along the long barrels. Fuming, he glanced aloft. The sails were drawing nicely under a freshening breeze that came over the quarter, but the moon which had aided them through the river channel was now their enemy. The white wings of the *Sparrow* would offer a perfect target—once they came within range.

Magnus turned to Tim, who stood at his side. "Let go a stern anchor," he ordered. "Then slacken the sheets."

The old man gasped. "Lord God, lad, ye can't anchor 'ere! 'Twill

195

be daylight wi'in four hours, an' then the river'll be swarmin' wi' Spanish ships, to say nuthin' o' the fort. Run for it, say I!"

Unaccustomed to having his commands questioned, Magnus started to bristle. But still ashamed of his recent outburst of temper, he held himself in leash.

"Tim, that fort commands the entire mouth, and her guns reach clear to the opposite shore. We wouldn't stand a chance in this moonlight."

"Better to take 'at chance than sit 'ere to be taken!" argued Tim. "Blast my keel, lad, I want no more Spanish tortures!"

"Nor I, Timothy, and by the same token, I do not mean to die just yet. Look you—" He pointed to the sky behind them. "See that cloud? The wind is inching it this way. It will soon obscure the moon."

Tim grunted. "It moves slow."

"So much the better. It will blanket the moon that much longer. Now do as I bid you, Tim."

As the old seaman moved to obey, Magnus walked into the waist. While not quite ready to resume relations with the Spanish priest, he was beginning to see the wisdom of his argument, albeit reluctantly. However, it wasn't the moral aspect that weighed with him —he had had Rosalind before, and he meant to have her again—but he realized the men would resent it. He wondered how many of them knew she was aboard. He called the Moor to his side.

"Did you caution the men who accompanied us to say nothing of the woman, Abu?"

Abu Ben Absedik smiled slyly. "Verily, I did better, *effendi*: I kept the maid wrapped up and let the men believe her to be the body of the man on whom thou plannedst to wreak vengeance." He saw the astonishment on Magnus' face and laughed softly. "By the grace of Allah, I have had much experience in the stealing of women. It is a rare sport indeed. Yet it is better thy men do not know, for nothing disturbs the harmony of a company so much as the presence of a female. Truly, she is as a serpent in Paradise."

"Well, they'll find out sooner or later."

Ben Absedik did not agree. "Why so? Listen, O my brother— years agone, when younger, I made a raid on an Arab settlement with a company of brave men. In the sheik's tent, I discovered a plump, desirable maid, barely used. I coveted her, but not being in charge of the raid, it was meet that I place her in the common pool that all might have an equal opportunity to barter for her. Yet there was something so soft and yielding about this delectable creature my loins were warmed, and I would not be thwarted. So—I

196

disguised her as a camel boy, and by this device got her to my harem without any of my companions suspecting."

Magnus grinned. "Was she worth the risk, Abu?"

"I swear it on the Koran! This veritable fount of delight beguiled me for almost a season before I had to sell her."

"*Sell* her?"

"Yea, for I was but young and foolish. I should have slit her throat."

"I understand. She betrayed you?"

"No, no! Allah forbid! I would have slain her for that. It was only that she learned I favored her above all others, and, woman-like, took advantage of the fact. Truly, the fault was mine. A woman is like a horse, *effendi,* never to be entirely trusted. So long as thou art completely master, thou canst keep her under control. But let her get the notion she is invaluable, and she becomes a tyrant."

Magnus sniffed. "That may be true of Moslem women, but our English . . ."

The Moor interrupted. "A woman is a woman, Magnus-Rais. Heed my warning!"

"Warning?"

Ben Absedik nodded solemnly. "Place no excess of faith in this woman, O my brother. Hear me—she is cunning and . . ."

Magnus went red to the ears. "You don't know what you are talk-ing about!" he cut in sharply. "I've known her all my life. I'll hear no word against her, Ben Absedik, even from you!"

The Moor drew himself erect. "What is written is written," he said haughtily. "Silence is the best answer to the stupid!" With that, he turned on his heel and strode aft.

Magnus cursed bitterly. Though the opposition of his comrades tended to increase his obstinacy, he was loath to lose their friend-ship, for despite the deep-rooted prejudices of his race, this Spanish priest and infidel Moslem had come to mean almost as much to him as did old Tim Prettyman. Their attitude toward Rosalind seemed inexplicable, yet when he attempted to attribute it solely to a difference in nationality, he came up against the fact that Tim felt precisely the same about her.

He stubbornly thrust the matter aside. No matter what they thought, Rosalind belonged to him, and when the time came, he would have her—whether they liked it or not.

Meanwhile, Tim had put out the stern anchor, and now, with the sheets well started, the *Sparrow* quivered like a race horse at the post. Magnus gave his attention to the dark thunderhead roll-ing closer. There was wind in that ominous sharp-edged cloud—perhaps too much, yet it was their only chance. He walked back to the compass and took bearings, for once the squall struck, there would be very little visibility.

Suddenly, what wind there was died away. A few drops of rain fell tentatively. Soundlessly, Magnus quoted the old sea rhyme:

> "If the wind before the rain,
> Hoist your tops'ls up again;
> But if the rain before the wind,
> Tops'l halliards you must mind!"

The rain increased, listlessly at first, then angrily. It *was* going to be a blow! Magnus ordered the lowers furled, after which he took an axe and stood beside the anchor rode. A few minutes later, he could hear the wind coming with the violence of a blinded bull.

"Stand by!" he shouted at the anxious seamen. "Man the tops'l sheets! Tend the braces! *Sheet home! Sheet home!*"

The instant he felt the first puff on his cheek, he severed the anchor rode. The squall struck! The *Sparrow* reeled under the impact; he heard the masts groan and the rigging twang like plucked harp-strings, then the little bark recovered her balance and fled before the fury like a thing possessed.

It was well Magnus had had the foresight to take bearings, for now he could see nothing. But the speed exhilarated him, and the wild tempest struck a sympathetic chord in his nature. He felt an overpowering impulse to sing, to join his own voice in the cacophony. The helmsman was having difficulty holding the bucking whipstaff, so Magnus seized the great timber in his own hands and ordered the man forward. The whipstaff was the pulse of the craft, and through the quivering shaft, he could feel her very heartbeat. Doubtless it was due to his superior strength, yet she seemed to grow more confident under his firm touch.

The fort ceased to be a problem. As they plunged past it, Magnus was tempted to loose a demi-culverin in defiance, but common sense told him he could do no damage, and even the spiteful bark of the gun would be unheard in the howling wind. So he contented himself with holding her to a compass course until he was certain they had at long last cleared the shoals and were safely out into the Bay, then he ordered two hands aft and turned the tiller over to them.

His friends having gone below, Magnus now went in search of them. The squall had blown away his distemper, and he felt in rare good humor. He found all three crowded in the starboard cabin. The reason was obvious.

Chuckling, Magnus opened the windows and let some air into the stuffy cuddy.

"Well, we're safe, my friends," he said genially, then added slyly, "A trifle crowded, are we not?"

Brother Diego matched his smile. "At least it is more comfortable than on the galley, my son."

"Aye, I'll grant you that!"

Tim stirred restlessly. He was accustomed to meeting problems head-on, and verbal fencing disturbed him.

"Blast me, stop backin' an' fillin'!" he grumbled. "Speak yer mind! Ha' ye come to yer senses?"

"That's a matter of opinion," Magnus rejoined. "Yet before I settle down, we're going to have a burial. Which one of you can scream the loudest?"

Tim's eyes started out of his head. "Jesus wept! The lad's teched in the 'ead!"

Magnus snorted. "Nonsense! I've made up my mind to square things. For a satisfactory burial, we require two essentials—a death and a corpse. I'll supply the death, Tim, but you must supply the body."

"Me?" howled the old man. "The 'ell I will! W'at 'ud I do to ye?"

"You're going to make a corpse," Magnus insisted soberly, then he turned to Ben Absedik.

"A little while ago, on deck, you made a remark that stuck in my mind, Abu. Can you scream loudly?"

The Moor's still-blackened face remained stoical, but his lithe fingers toyed with the hilt of his scimitar.

"I only scream in victory, Magnus-Rais," he said significantly.

Brother Diego leaned forward and rested his elbows on his knees. "Magnus, if this is a jest, I think you had better explain it!"

Sensing the tension, Magnus realized he had carried his humor too far. He laughed heartily.

"Faith, it is neither jest nor insanity, but a device I learned from the Holy Fathers of the Inquisition, when I saw them burning heretics in effigy. I'm going to kill my old enemy, Ser Pedro Beckles, in like fashion for the edification of the crew. If they hear convincing screams emanating from here, and then see us heave a *body* overboard, they'll ask no questions about who we brought aboard. That's why I want Tim to crawl into the lazarette and find me a coil of old rope and a small pig of iron ballast to serve for a corpse."

Tim exhaled relievedly. "For God's sake, w'y didn't ye say so in the fust place?" he stormed. "Damme, I figgered ye was goin' to . . ."

The laughter of the others drowned out his tirade, so shaking his head, he hobbled off to assemble the gear.

"By Allah," chuckled Ben Absedik, when Tim had gone, "our brother hath the cunning of a fox! May the angels smile upon thee,

199

for I shall supply such a scream as has not been heard in all Christendom since my ancestors stormed Granada! Art ready, Magnus-Rais?"

Magnus nodded, smiling, but he was totally unprepared for the blood-chilling shriek which followed. He felt the hair stiffen along his nape, and even Brother Diego flinched. As the ghastly sound vibrated through the timbers, Magnus could hear men pounding across the deck.

"Mother of God!" he gasped. "That's enough, Abu! *Padre,* you'd better stick your head out the hatch and pacify the crew. They'll be coming in here if you don't stop them!"

The priest nodded and hurried into the companionway. A moment later, Tim Prettyman staggered in with his load.

"God's death!" he panted. "I figgered the powder magazine 'ad blown sky-'igh! Ye near shivered the treenails out o' 'er, I swear!"

Laughing, Magnus and Ben Absedik fashioned the rope into a reasonable facsimile of a human body, and wrapped it in canvas. Then each taking an end, they carried it up onto the heaving deck. The startled hand at the whipstaff gaped in wordless wonder as they dragged their burden past him to the taffrail. Tim, braced against the vessel's roll, bellowed stridently: "Toss the dirty swine overboard, lads! Killin's too good fer the likes. By Neptune, if ye'd 'a let me 'ave my way wi' 'im, I'd a torn 'im . . .'"

Magnus and the Moor swung their burden back and forth until Magnus shouted "*Heave!*" whereupon it went over with a splash. Magnus then swung on the helmsman.

"Keep your mouth shut about this, my man!" he commanded sternly. "This is a personal affair!"

"Aye, aye, sor!" mumbled the man nervously. "I'm blind, I am, sor! Blinder'n a ruddy bat, I be, so 'elp me God!"

"Vengeance is a terrible thing!" observed the priest clearly. "I trust you are completely satisfied now, my son."

Magnus kept a straight face with difficulty. "Not entirely, but at least that particular object will trouble me no more," he growled, and strode below.

"That I'll also grant," acceded Tim, and with a nod to the others, followed Magnus.

But once they were gathered in the privacy of the cuddy, Brother Diego shook his head.

"While that act had an element of macabre humor, Magnus, exactly what did it accomplish? After all, the woman is still on board."

Magnus grimaced in mock horror. "What woman, *padre?*"

"The woman in my cabin!" snapped the priest.

"Oh-ho! You are confused about my new cabin boy! By my troth, *padre*, you can't think that *I* would sail back to join my admiral with a wench on board? God forbid! No, no, my friend, thanks to a timely suggestion by our wily Moslem, we have traded the troublesome woman for a cabin boy!"

Ben Absedik's sharp face broke into a smile. "All praise to Allah, who art the mighty, it is well conceived."

Brother Diego sighed. "Deception is the blood-brother of lies. Howbeit, so long as you practice the deception on yourself, my son, I will not object."

Magnus laughed at him. "Thank you. And now, my guardian of morals, I trust you will not object if I have a few words with my guest?"

The priest smiled wearily. "A few words are doubtless in order. If I read her temper correctly, it will require more than your glibness to pacify her. So go to her, my son, and may God forgive what you have done, for I don't think she will."

"And I," sneered Magnus, "think you had better stick to your saints and gospels, and leave earthly women to those of us who understand them." He walked out.

Chapter 21

Having washed off the blood and grime as best he could, Magnus went down to Rosalind's cuddy. Though trembling with anticipation, he lingered in the companionway outside her door. After all the insurmountable obstacles which had stood between them, the months of agony and the audacious escapades, it seemed incredible that now only a flimsy panel kept them apart. He was tempted to crush it with his fist, as a kind of symbolism, but he feared such violence might startle her unduly. This was an occasion for tenderness, not play-acting, he assured himself, so he knocked gently, and opened the door.

The tiny cabin was lighted by a candle pronged to a sconce on the bulkhead, and by its wavering glow, he saw her slender body

201

stretched on the lower bunk, her face buried in the cushion. It was apparent she had not heard him. He stood silent, his throat constricting. After a long pause, he found his tongue.

"Roz!"

She pressed her palms against the hard mattress and raised her shoulders clear of the bed. For a few moments, she stared as if he were a total stranger, then with an obvious effort, swung herself into a sitting position. Her eyes were dull and tear-streaked. It came to him abruptly that she was suffering from shock.

All contrition, he dropped to one knee before her and took a limp hand in his own.

"It's all right now, sweetheart!" he said soothingly. "You are safe."

She looked uncomprehendingly into his up-turned face. Then she reached out with her free hand and tentatively touched his features, feeling over them one by one as the blind do when attempting to identify someone they know. Her silence terrified him.

"Rosalind! Speak to me, my love! Are you hurt?"

She shook her head apathetically. "Is it truly you, Magnus?" she whispered.

"Aye, to be sure! But what ails you, Roz?"

"Ails? I don't know." She fingered his red curls. "Yes, it *is* you, Magnus! Oh, my dear, my dear . . . !" And she burst into tears.

Magnus was badly shaken. He sat on the edge of the bunk and took her into his arms.

"Don't cry like that!" he pleaded. "Everything is all right now, sweetheart!"

She shuddered violently. "Oh, merciful God, it was ghastly!" she sobbed. "That terrible black creature, jibbering like an animal! The screams, the fighting, the tossing about! Then I was thrown in here and unwrapped by that begrimed monster who babbled in Spanish as though he were a priest! I didn't believe them when they said you had ordered it!"

Magnus smiled. "They are my friends, sweet—Abu the Moor and Brother Diego. Old Tim Prettyman is here, too."

"But, God in heavens, what does it all mean, Magnus? Why was I treated so?"

"There was no other way to save you! I tried to explain at the castle, but you fainted!"

"Then you were there? I thought I heard your voice, but your appearance—I couldn't believe it was you! Magnus, whatever possessed you to do it? Didn't you know I was wed?"

Unconsciously, he had anticipated the question. He stiffened.

"Aye, I know. Does it make any difference to you?"

"Dear Lord, doesn't it to us both?"

"Not to me. We were betrothed—you yourself said we were already married in the sight of God—then through the machinations of this blow-fly Beckles and your traitorous uncle, I was turned over to the Inquisition while you were forced into a marriage which, in my eyes at least, has no validity!"

She looked at him in amazement. "Inquisition? Uncle traitorous? Magnus—what are you talking about?"

Briefly he reviewed his experiences. She was incredulous and distraught.

"Oh, it can't be true!" she wept. "It can't be!"

"It is easily proven," he assured her grimly. "Tim, Abu or the priest will substantiate every word of it."

She sat quite still, staring into space, as if trying to adjust her mind to something too large to grasp. Waiting, he suffered.

"Well?" he demanded. "Do you want me to call witnesses?"

She flung herself into his arms. "No, no! Don't leave me, lover! I'll go mad if you do! Where are we, and what are we going to do?"

He explained about the *Sparrow*. "We'll have to rejoin the fleet," he admitted. "There will be complications, but"—he paused to kiss her cheek—"nothing matters so long as we are together."

"*Together!*" she repeated. "And I had given up all hope!"

"You should know me better than that, Roz! I told you I'd never quit until I got you!"

"Oh, yes, but, but . . ." She hesitated. "What about Peter?"

"Leave him to me." Magnus said harshly.

She shuddered once, then lay quietly against his chest for a time. Finally she sat up, composed.

"Magnus, I must think this out. Will you leave me for a little while?" When she saw the anxiety spring into his eyes, she leaned over and kissed him tenderly. "Now—please go, sweetheart!"

He obeyed reluctantly, and went up on deck. The squall having passed, the bark soared along before a fresh, clean breeze. Overhead, a tenuous line of black clouds kept pace, breaking occasionally to permit a glimpse of a few pale stars shivering in the cold. Magnus moved aft as far as possible from the silhouette of the helmsman and leaned over the rail to watch the silvery wound of the wake heal swiftly in the night.

There was a gnawing ache in his diaphragm which made him half sick. He dreaded the possibility that Rosalind had had a change of heart. It filled him with panic. He reviewed his conversation with her, and began to find hidden innuendoes in her words. What he had accepted a little while ago as shock, he now interpreted as evasion. He had expected her to be delighted; instead she was revolted. The enormity of his blunder numbed him. He stopped thinking.

How long he huddled there, he neither knew nor cared. In a vague fashion, he was aware the bell had clanged, for he heard the helmsman turn over the whipstaff to the relief. Yet he did not hear the approach of Brother Diego until the latter laid a kindly arm around his shoulder.

"Courage, Magnus," he said gently.

Magnus didn't have the courage to face him. He kept his elbows braced on the rail and his eyes on the long white scar.

"You were right, *padre*," he confessed. "I am awakening from a fool's dream."

The priest's grip tightened in affection. "No, Magnus, such dreams as yours come not from fools, but from idealists. True, perhaps, in your eagerness to reach the summit, you may have taken the wrong path and stumbled momentarily, but that is not defeat. Do not let the twilight and shadows dismay you, my son. Yours is an intensity that transcends mere daydreaming. Cast off despair, for it is but a weighty, useless burden that holds you back."

Magnus looked at him in wonder. "And you called yourself a realist?"

Brother Diego smiled wistfully. "I am," he conceded, "but then, so is a horse. The realist, like the horse, is a beast of burden necessary to maintain the *status quo*. He accepts things as they are. It is the idealists who fashion the universe to their own vision and lift it to a higher, better plane. Alas, I have no such capacity! You have, Magnus! Be not embittered."

Magnus wagged his head in bewilderment. "You are a paradox. I thought you were opposed to all I did."

"I am opposed to your methods, Magnus, but not to your ideals. The paradox, if it exists, is within you. True love is one thing; a hot, animal desire to gratify your senses, quite another."

"Are you so sure they are not the same?" mused Magnus.

"Frankly, I do not know," the priest confessed, "but I am sure of this—you cannot gain the heights by theft and murder. The Church calls them the Laws of God. Possibly—yet they are also the laws of nature itself, for without some guideposts, society would be lost in chaos. Can't you see that, Magnus?"

"Laws, like the spider's web, catch the flies and let the hawks go free," grumbled Magnus. "You claim to be a realist: when others violate the laws—what then?"

"Then," sighed Brother Diego, "the realist is trapped by his own lack of faith. He retaliates, and the original crime multiplies as it

204

gains momentum. Thus wars start, and civilization regresses. Only the true idealist, treading the cleaner air above, can save it."

"I think you have our roles reversed, my friend. You are the idealist. What have I ever said or done to lead you to believe I share such visions?"

The priest laughed. "Very little, I admit, yet it is revealed in the flash of your eyes, the timbre of your voice, aye, even in the lilt of your stride. Magnus, to one who has studied his fellow man, you are easily read."

Despite his skepticism, Magnus felt as though some of the weight had been taken from his shoulders. However, he was still confused about Rosalind. He turned impulsively to ask advice, then restrained himself. He knew the priest would tell him to set the girl ashore and give up his quest for Beckles, and he was prepared to do neither. While he was brooding about it, old Tim limped over and joined them.

"Ho, lad, the chit's seekin' ye," he announced. "Wanted to come topside arter ye, but I forbade 'er. W'at'll I tell 'er?"

"Tell her? Why, you imbecile, I'll go at once!"

Tim stamped his wooden peg and cursed in three languages. "Damme, the Moor was right!" he concluded bitterly. "An' I lose arf a crown. 'E said ye'd run to 'er the instant she snapped 'er fingers, but I wagered ye 'ad more sense. The bigger fool, I!"

Magnus did not know whether to laugh or swear. "I'll thank you two old women to keep your noses out of my affair!" he snapped.

"Oh-ho! So now it becomes *your* affair, eh? 'Oo guarded this bloody cockleshell in the 'arbor? 'Oo burnt the Spanish warships? 'Oo carried the wench out o' the castle an' aboard ship? Tell me 'oo, ye young cockerel?"

Brother Diego drew the irate old seaman against the rail. "Let be, Timothy," he placated him, then to Magnus: "Go along, my son!"

"Aye, trot along!" Tim jeered belligerently. "But, by Neptune, don't go callin' me no *ol' woman* agin!"

He found Rosalind perfectly composed. By some strange feminine alchemy, she had eradicated the circles under her eyes, and the eyes themselves were clear and bright. He closed the door and stood with his back against it. He was anxious and uncertain. She stared at him a moment, then smiled suddenly. It was like stepping out of a dark cavern into the full radiance of sunlight. Automatically, he opened his arms. She sprang off the bed and came over. His arms tightened about her.

"Magnus," she said, so simply it hurt him, "I'm glad!"

205

"Roz! Roz!" was all he could mutter.

She led him over to the bunk and they sat down. He was astounded by her self-possession, for his had abandoned him. He had never felt this way before. The realization that she was now his, that she was *glad* of it, was almost more than he could bear. It seemed to stun him.

She must have sensed this. She gave a warm maternal laugh and ran her fingers through his hair.

"Tell me that you love me," she urged softly.

"God Almighty, don't you know that?"

"Yes, yes, but I want to hear you say it. I want to see your lips form the words."

"I love you!" he said, as solemnly as an oath. "I have always loved you, and I'll love you till the day I die!"

"And after that, my darling?" she laughed.

"All through eternity!"

She sighed, and buried her nose in the turn of his neck. "And I, Magnus, have always been, and always will be . . . yours!" She lay silent a while, then straightened. "Magnus, let us agree to bury the past—never to mention it again between us?"

"We'll never mention it between us," he agreed.

She bit her lower lip. "But you mean we . . . you . . . won't forget?"

"We won't mention it between us," he repeated grimly.

She laughed nervously. "All right, my sweet, but you'll have to help me. We'll be outcasts—you know that, of course."

"I've always been an outcast, Roz. Will it matter to you?"

"I don't think so; I'm sure it won't. Only I wish my marriage . . ."

He interrupted brusquely. "We weren't going to mention that!"

"Let me finish," she pleaded. "Even though I was forced into it, it did happen. There's no sense pretending it didn't, sweetheart! No matter what you or I may think about it, others will regard . . ."

"I don't give a damn what *others* think!" he cut in heatedly. "We have a right to our happiness and our lives. As Brother Diego says —it is idealists who fashion the universe."

Her eyes widened. "Does he, a priest, agree to . . . well . . . to us?"

"No, he doesn't; you couldn't expect a Catholic priest to go that far. However, when I . . ." He paused. He was going to say when he killed her husband it might alter things, but delicacy forbade his putting it into words.

She swept the whole subject aside. "I don't care! I don't care about anything! I tried to do what was right, and they wouldn't let me! I'm yours, Magnus—right or wrong! Now . . ." Her voice trailed away so softly he had to bend his ear to her lips to hear. "Help me forget, my darling!"

Breathless, he lowered her gently to the bed. He was almost blinded by the smoky fires smoldering in her slanted eyes, and when he saw her hands stray to the fastenings of her bodice, his knees turned weak with desire. He leaned down to draw off his jack-boots, when the door opened, and Brother Diego walked in.

Magnus turned white with temper. "Get out!" he snarled.

The priest yawned wearily. "Come, my son," he urged mildly, "it is time for rest." He shucked off his sea-coat and tossed it casually onto the upper bunk. "Have you given the helmsman his course for the night?"

Magnus trembled. He wanted to hurl himself at the priest's throat, and it was only the knowledge that the others had agreed with Valesco that restrained him.

"You can't sleep *here!*" he growled.

Brother Diego laughed. "Not trusting yourself, you don't trust anyone else, do you, my son? Bless you, have no fears for the maid." He drew a poniard from his belt and proffered it, hilt-first, to Rosalind, who accepted it in embarrassment. "If any man aboard this vessel molests you, *señora,* use this. It has been agreed among us all that you are to be kept inviolate." He glanced obliquely at Magnus.

Magnus went red to the ears. He glanced at Rosalind. She gave him a wistful little smile.

"Perchance it is best, sweetheart," she whispered tenderly. "We have a long time ahead of us. Go then."

Defeated, Magnus glowered at the priest. "We'll settle this to-morrow! Meanwhile, remember—if you dare . . ."

Brother Diego smiled and pushed him gently toward the door. "You should know by this time, Magnus, that I do not forget my vows. Go now, and sleep in peace."

Later, when Magnus was making a pallet on the floor of the other cabin, Tim Prettyman lay chuckling in the lower bunk.

"Blast my scuppers, if this ain't the damndest situation!" he observed. "Magnus steals another man's wife, an' a priest sleeps wi' 'er!"

"You lie!" snapped Magnus. "He's not sleeping *with* her!"

"Aye, I kin believe that," grunted Tim. "A skinny, boney bit o' fluff. 'Ell, I wouldn't touch 'er me own sel', nor would the Moor. Ain't that so, Abu?"

From the upper bunk, Ben Absedik, ever literal of mind, disagreed.

207

"It is true the Frankish priest won't touch her, for it runs counter to his faith, yet there are no faults in the thing we want badly enough. To me, my peg-legged brother, a woman is a woman. As thou sayeth, this one is skin and bone. For mine own loins, I prefer spacious hips and well-fleshed thighs, with breasts that . . ."

"Silence—both of you!" raged Magnus. "Else on my oath, I'll . . ."

His threat was drowned by a feigned but raucous snore from Tim Prettyman. Cursing, he snuffed out the light.

Chapter 22

THE *Sparrow* flew as best she could against contrary winds and, by dint of skillful handling, soared into the Vigo River four days later. There she found the English fleet anchored above the town, the crews busily engaged in filling their water casks. The bark's arrival was greeted by acclaim, yet the instant Magnus got his hook down, he hurried aboard the *Bonaventure* to make his excuses to the admiral.

He was fortunate to find Sir Francis in rare good humor. For nearly a week now, Drake had made himself master of Galicia. In addition to liberating English prisoners, he had forced the governor of the province to supply him with victuals, and by his very presence, had humbled and embarrassed the King of Spain. He could afford, therefore, to be lenient to this young cub who argued that, having believed the storm too violent to weather, he had deemed it expedient to seek out a safe anchorage. So after a stern lecture on the necessity of obeying orders explicitly, he commanded Magnus to hasten the replenishing of his water casks and be ready to sail the following day, and dismissed him.

Magnus was delighted to escape so easily, and promptly dispatched his entire crew about the business. On their return, they learned, in the devious fashion seamen learn the doings of their superiors, that their captain had acquired in Vigo a young cabin boy who had been released by the Spaniards. Aside from a few ribald comments among themselves, the matter caused scant attention.

However, this only resolved the problem in part. The *Sparrow* was less than seventy feet in length, and with sixty men crowded before the mast, it was inevitable they would encounter the new "cabin boy." Magnus took what precautions he could. In Vigo, he secured two pageboy suits; one of scarlet velvet, the other of white silk. Though the hands might smirk, the most they could charge him with was emulating Drake, who had a taste for swank, and carried a page to stand behind his chair while he dined, and musicians to amuse him.

Rosalind accepted the masquerade with glee, but protested tearfully when Magnus decreed her lovely hair be cropped. For his part, he would have surrendered to her pleas, but Tim and Brother Diego insisted it be done, so he compromised by cutting it off at shoulder length. Rosalind submitted with good grace, and tried on the suits. When Magnus saw her slim young body sheathed in white silk, with her glossy waves of black hair touching the starched ruff, only the presence of the other men kept him from taking her in his arms.

The next morning, the fleet weighed anchor and stood a course for Las Palmas.

The days that followed were idyllic. To Magnus, it was as a voyage to heaven. He spent every possible moment in Rosalind's company and on several occasions, when the priest was safely out of the way, he would have consummated his love if Rosalind herself had not prevented him.

"No, lover!" she pleaded. "Remember your promise."

"I made no promise to the old duenna," Magnus protested. "He appointed himself to the post."

Rosalind snuggled, laughing, in his arms. "Yet methinks he is right, darling. Oh, God knows I yearn for you, yet it might spoil everything if we . . . I want everything to be beautiful, Magnus. Help me to be good, won't you?"

Despite his ardor, a deep-rooted puritanical strain in him forced him to agree. He, too, wanted "everything to be beautiful." He restrained himself.

On reaching Las Palmas, Drake attempted a landing, but the shore batteries opened on him with round shot. That in itself would not have deterred him, but a boiling surf made it impracticable, so he continued for the coast of Barbary in the hope of intercepting the Spanish treasure fleet, reputedly homeward bound. He tarried a long time in these waters and every few days put into Capo Blanco with his ships to buy fresh fish. The second of these excursions came near to being Magnus' undoing.

It was the admiral's custom to pay surprise visits to the various ships of his fleet; a practice of which Magnus was not aware. Officially designated *inspection* trips, the real purpose was to buoy the spirits of the men and cement the loyalty of the officers. So it came about that one afternoon when they were anchored in Capo Blanco, and Magnus was below decks with Rosalind, Tim burst in on them.

The old seaman was bug-eyed. "God 'elp us, lad—Sir Frankie's 'ere!"

Magnus shot to his feet. "*Here?*"

"Aye!" panted Tim. "'Is barge be comin' alongside this very minute! 'E's got Frobisher, Carleill, Fenner an' Winters wi' 'im. They'll nose into every cranny o' the ship!" He glowered resentfully at the girl.

Magnus forced a bitter laugh. "Sobeit. It had to happen sooner or later. Tim, you break out some wine and biscuits for Rosalind to serve."

Rosalind collapsed into a chair. "Oh, Lord, Magnus—I *couldn't!*"

He patted her arm reassuringly. "There's no help for it, darling. They are bound to discover you, and it would arouse immediate suspicion if you didn't fulfill the duties of a cabin boy. Now hurry into your costume."

"Aye, it'll be all our necks if ye fail!" Tim growled at her. "An' mind—I said *all!* Sir Frankie be gallant enough in Court, but 'e's a Tartar afloat. God 'elp ye if 'e guesses the trufe!"

Magnus silenced him with a gesture. "Don't be alarmed, sweetheart! I'll hold their attention while you're serving them. They'll never notice you."

He went out smiling, but once the door closed, his smile vanished. Tim was savage.

"They won't notice ye!" he mimicked sarcastically. "The hell they won't! Ye'd be smart to tie the anchor 'round yer neck an' jump . . ."

"Silence, damn you!" Magnus commanded. "It's my head, not yours, that's in jeopardy!"

"Aye, but 'tis your 'ead I'm thinkin' of!" retorted the old man, and scuttled away after the wine.

The boatswain's pipes were already twittering the guests aboard when Magnus dodged on deck, and he barely reached the rail in time to greet his admiral. His intuition told him that Drake was in good humor, but it was evident his companions were not. The reason for this last was easy to guess: Sir Francis rarely divulged his plans, even to his intimates, and rough old campaigners like Frobisher would quite naturally be impatient to get their hands on some of Philip's gold.

As Tim Prettyman had forewarned, Drake insisted on a thorough

210

inspection, which started forward and continued aft. Nothing missed the keen eyes of Francis Drake—a leak in the deck, a loose fastening, a split block. He went over the vessel with the thoroughness of a surveyor.

To Magnus, the ordeal was unmitigated agony, and the ghost of Thomas Doughty, who had been summarily executed for crossing Drake, stalked beside him during the wearisome tour. If Rosalind failed in her act, there might be *two* ghosts to haunt some future captain instead of one.

Finally, Drake was satisfied. "The bark is in good shape," he told Magnus. "See that you keep her so, for it will be a long haul back to Plymouth."

Magnus' pulse began to pound. The crisis was at hand. He felt suffocated by suspense.

"Thank you, sir," he managed. "I'll do my best. And now . . ." He clenched his fists behind his back. "And now, if you gentlemen will do me the honor, we'll broach some wine on the poop."

"Blast me, that has a welcome sound!" boomed Frobisher. "My throat's rustier than an old cutlass!"

At Drake's nod, they climbed to the poop, where an awning had been stretched for their comfort. The sun was abdicating its majesty in the west and above them towered the purpling bluffs of the cape. When all were seated, Magnus tinkled a bell to summon Rosalind, then held his breath.

He heard the movement of the hatch and it required all his self-control to keep from turning to look at her. He knew she was approaching the table. He wondered if the thumping of his heart would betray him. It became difficult to breathe.

Fortunately, Carleill was telling a long story about the Irish campaign and Drake was listening with the fine attention he invariably gave to a speaker, but, for the life of him, Magnus couldn't comprehend a word. Out of the corner of his eye, he saw Rosalind deftly fill the goblets. She was wearing the suit of red velvet, it being less likely to draw attention to her figure than the revealing silk, yet to him she looked appallingly feminine. However, her *savoir-faire* was magnificent, with just the proper shade of obsequiousness. No one appeared conscious of her presence and Magnus was beginning to relax when there came a loud guffaw from Frobisher.

"As God's my life!" he bellowed, interrupting Carleill's tedious tale. "Seems our good Queen ain't the only one who likes pretty lads around 'em!"

The conversation ceased abruptly as every eye turned to where Frobisher sat with a brawny arm thrown around Rosalind's waist.

"Soft as a wench, by God!" he laughed, as Rosalind struggled silently to escape him. "Come, lad, let's hear if your voice be as soft as your body?"

The stem of the goblet snapped in Magnus' hand. Before he realized what he was doing, he had leaped around the table and struck Frobisher's arm away.

"Keep your damn hands off my page!" he thundered.

There was a moment of utter silence. Frobisher blinked in astonishment, then the half-drunken smile faded and his expression grew ominous as a thunderhead. The others shared his surprise, for his jest was commonplace among rough seamen. As Frobisher reared out of his chair, Magnus barked at the terrified girl.

"Go below immediately!"

When she had gone, he turned to face the irate vice-admiral. He knew he was in for it. He had not only insulted a guest, he had laid violent hands on a superior officer. Yet the realization did nothing to assuage his fury.

"You had no right to molest one of my crew!" he said doggedly.

Frobisher flung his chair out of the way. "You damned pup!" he roared. "I'll teach you your manners!" He drew back his heavy gauntlet to swipe Magnus across the face.

But the blow did not fall. Drake's sharp voice crackled like musket shot.

"*Martin! Sit down!* You—Carter—get back to your place!"

Frobisher flattened his massive palms on the table and scowled at the admiral.

"By God, I won't take insults from this cub!"

Drake eyed him bleakly. "You will both apologize and shake hands! You, Carter, for an unseemly display of bad manners and temper, and you, Martin, for an equally boorish piece of conduct."

"Now see here," blustered Frobisher. "He can bugger the page all he likes, but by God, he can't knock me around!"

Winters eased the tension with a short laugh. "Oh, come now, Martin!" he said placatingly. "You seemed interested in the boy yourself!"

Fenner joined in the peacemaking. "Damme if he didn't! A bit of jealousy on both sides, I'd say."

Drake did not smile. "I am not accustomed to repeating an order, gentlemen!" he reminded them coldly.

Frobisher grumbled under his breath and glowered at Magnus. Though still pale and trembling, Magnus recovered his poise first.

"My lord," he said, bowing to Drake, "I must humbly beg your forgiveness, and that of the other gentlemen present. This being my first inspection, I fear my nerves were a trifle frayed." He straightened and looked grimly at the scowling Frobisher.

"As for you, sir, in obedience to my admiral—I apologize." He offered a tentative hand.

Frobisher stared at the outstretched hand a moment before bursting into laughter. He clamped the hand in his own.

"As I said before, you're a glib young pup, Carter, but, by God, you'd better save your temper for the Spaniards!"

Magnus grinned. "That's why I have such difficulty keeping it on the leash, sir!"

Frobisher groped around for his chair, but before he could sit down, Drake rose, and the others followed suit.

"It is time we were getting back, gentlemen," he said crisply.

As the others moved toward the gangway, Magnus saw Drake hesitate and glance toward the companionway hatch, as if about to say something. Magnus felt his heart skip a beat, but an instant later, Drake turned away.

"You got out of that easier than your offense warranted, young man," he said in a stern, low voice. "This makes the second time you have strayed out of bounds. Let me warn you—and heed this most diligently—any further lapses will be summarily dealt with."

Without waiting for a reply, he quickened his stride and joined the others at the rail.

Himself shaken to the marrow by the ordeal, Magnus expected the others to share his trepidation. True, Tim Prettyman exhibited considerable agitation, but when he went below, Magnus found Rosalind almost hysterical from laughter. Abu and Brother Diego were with her, both smiling broadly.

At sight of his stricken expression, Rosalind giggled. "Oh, Magnus, you were so funny! I thought I'd die!"

"I damn near did," Magnus said sourly. "I'm glad someone found it amusing."

The Moor grinned his wolfish grin. "By the Koran, when thou went for the camel, I thought the hour had struck! I had my scimitar bared when thine infidel admiral stopped the fight."

Brother Diego smiled ruefully. "Truly, Magnus, I, too, feared our sins had caught up with us. But God was merciful!"

Magnus sat down with a weary sigh. "You mean—Drake was merciful. I'm afraid he suspects."

Rosalind stopped laughing. "Oh, dear God! Did he say so, Magnus?"

"It wasn't what he said—it was what he *didn't* say," conceded Magnus. "I don't quite understand him."

"If he suspected, ye'll be danglin' from a yardarm!" swore Tim.

Brother Diego disagreed. "I think you err, my friend. Your great

213

admiral is a many-sided man, and he has doubtless learned that in war patience is more often of service than force. He is like a player at chess, who plans his moves far in advance."

"Then you think as Magnus does, Father?" gasped Rosalind. "That he *knows*?"

"It would be folly to prognosticate, my daughter. My only contention is that Drake is too wise to endanger the success of his expedition by precipitation. As for knowing of your presence—if he doesn't suspect now, it is inevitable that he will eventually. You cannot live a lie without discovery."

"I've a notion to run for Africa!" growled Magnus.

"That would be rank folly!" protested the priest. "Will you fly from ills which may have no real existence? That would avail you nothing, my son, for you would be taking your troubles with you. They are in your conscience, Magnus!"

"Verily, *effendi*, our comrade's words are wise," Ben Absedik concurred. "Flight is a confession of cowardice and guilt. Also, we have our sacred oaths to fulfill."

"But where will it all end?" asked Rosalind.

The Moor shrugged eloquently. "Only Allah the all-seeing can answer that. But what is written is written."

Tim stomped his wooden leg in impatience. "Let's stow the gab!" he growled. "I jus' want to know one thing—w'at are we goin' to do?"

Brother Diego laughed. "Tim's directness is always refreshing. What is it to be, Magnus?"

"We'll stay with the fleet—for the present," Magnus said grimly.

"*Ameen!*" echoed the Moor.

Chapter 23

Convinced, finally, that he had missed the plate ships from Panama, Drake continued on to the Cape Verde Islands, and on the sixteenth of November, brought his fleet to anchor in the Bay of Santiago. It was here their bad luck began. First the Spaniards refused to deal with him, then barbarously mutilated and murdered one of his ship's boys. Drake promptly retaliated by burning the city of Santiago to the ground, and on the twenty-sixth, stood away for the West Indies.

But a week later, while running before the Trades, the indirect vengeance of the Spaniards caught up with them in the form of the deadly Yellow Jack which had been picked up at Santiago. Not one ship in the fleet was spared.

When the dread fever appeared aboard the *Sparrow*, Magnus was distraught for fear Rosalind might contract it. He quarantined the infected men in the forecastle and fumigated the entire ship with vinegar poured over hot shot. But death would not be cheated. In the first three days of the epidemic, seven men died on the little bark; two hundred in the fleet. A school of sharks appeared, and as if by some diabolical arrangement, divided the ships between them. Two monsters trailed the *Sparrow* a hundred feet astern.

Magnus did everything he could to save his company. On the advice of Brother Diego, he doled out purgatives and urged the hands to drink copious quantities of salt water, but the disease continued to spread.

For a while it seemed as if the horror might stay forward of the mast, but the loss of so many hands put a strain upon the others. The men went about in terror of their lives. Rank was forgotten, and Magnus, Tim and Abu worked with the survivors. Brother Diego wanted to help, but Magnus forced him to remain isolated in the cabin with Rosalind, with orders to keep his pipe going steadily, for it was believed that tobacco was a preventive against infection. The priest merged his smoking with his prayers.

While Magnus refused to spare himself, he did urge Tim and Ben Absedik to guard their health, but they, being fatalists, ignored the advice.

"I will only die when Allah wills it," insisted the Moor.

Tim's brusque comment was equally characteristic. "If ye're born to swing on the gallows, ye'll ne'er drown in the sea."

However, the Yellow Jack played no favorites and two days later, Tim succumbed. Magnus was shaken. Despite his warning, he had come to believe the tough old mariner was somehow indestructible, and the sight of him reduced to agonized helplessness wrung his heart. The priest volunteered to nurse him, but Magnus would not agree. He had an awning stretched amidships and a pallet brought on deck, then he took charge of Tim himself.

While still able to talk, Tim argued against it. "Get aw'y from me!" he fussed. "There's no sense o' us both goin'!"

"You'll pull through."

215

"Sharks still there, ain't they?"

Magnus glanced over the quarter to where the black dorsal fins clove the water.

"Suppose they are; that means nothing."

Tim snorted. "The 'ell it don't! Ye can't fool a shark, boy. They knows I'm comin'. I 'opes the bastards choke on me wooden shank!"

Soon after that, the fever snatched his mind away, and the sturdy frame appeared to dissolve before Magnus' anxious eyes. From a man, Tim degenerated into something more grisly than a corpse. As the fever mounted, it threatened to burst out of the shell. The pain was excruciating. His tongue and mouth turned black. At first he vomited quantities of putrid black bile, then the discharges were forced from every vent in his body. The stench carried over the entire deck until the hands wailed for him to be taken below. Magnus was adamant. Tim remained on deck.

Magnus bore it for a day and a half before fatigue struck him down. He wasn't even aware that Ben Absedik had carried him below until he awakened, twelve hours later, to find himself in his bunk. Cursing his own weakness, he hurried on deck.

To his horror, he discovered Rosalind ministering to the old man. He ordered her away peremptorily, but she refused to heed him.

"Stop bellowing like a madman, Magnus! I'm not going! I'm needed right here. Lord knows, there's little enough I can do, without shirking below decks like a coward."

"Damn it, you'll catch the fever!"

She smiled at him. "Nonsense! Am I more likely to catch it than you? And what would I do if you caught it?"

Strangely enough, the Moor agreed with her. "Truly, *effendi*, we cannot escape our kismet." Then, more practically, he added with a shrug, "She hath been with him these twelve hours past. If she hath not contracted it now, she will not."

Because the logic in that was irrefutable, Magnus gave in. He had more than enough to occupy him with the vessel. Over half the crew were sick, and the rest overworked. Magnus expected momentarily that Drake would signal the ships to heave-to for a rest, but Drake elected to drive on for the islands. The voyage became a nightmare.

Old Tim grew steadily worse, and on the third night, the crisis reached its apex. Then it became a hand-to-hand struggle with death, like dogs fighting over a bone. Time and again, the old man toppled over the very threshold, but each time Magnus and Rosalind dragged him back. Slowly, painfully, they coaxed life into the harrowed body. Finally death surrendered, and Tim began to mend.

Completely exhausted, Magnus turned the sick man over to

216

Brother Diego and ushered Rosalind to her cabin. Neither spoke. Rosalind stretched out wearily on the bunk while Magnus opened the stern windows. The wind had freshened, and it filled the cabin with the scented air of the tropics. Magnus had never seen the stars so brilliant. The very night itself seemed unreal—a sort of *special* night such as had never happened before, nor could ever happen again.

He turned away from the window and sat down on the edge of the bunk. The ship seemed to soar through a vast silence. He stared at the girl. Her eyes had captured the quality of the stars.

"Sleepy, sweetheart?" he asked softly.

She shook her head. Her lips parted slightly to form an invitation. He listened briefly to the celestial song of the night, then bent to claim them.

When she could speak, she whispered, "*Magnus!* Oh, my God!"

He rose just long enough to bolt the door. . . .

Once during the night, they heard someone try the door, then go away. They knew it was Brother Diego.

In the morning, Magnus sought out the priest and told him the truth. "I just wanted you to know it wasn't premeditated," he concluded. "It just happened. You must not blame Rosalind."

The priest shrugged. "Though I tried to prevent it, my son, it is not for me to sit in judgment. That is God's prerogative. Perchance the Moor is right in saying 'What is to be, will be.' I do not know. Like you, Magnus, she could be superb if she is only strong enough."

"She *is* superb!"

"Aye, my son, I grant that," smiled Brother Diego. "The way she nursed old Timothy was heroic. Yet you must remember that all of us are a blend of goodness and evil, of virtue and sin. There are no all blacks and all whites."

"Have it your own way, *padre*, but I don't feel we have done wrong."

"Then why argue about it?" said the priest, and dropped the subject.

That afternoon, he moved his gear into the other cabin.

About the middle of December, Drake brought his weary fleet to anchor off the uninhabited island of St. Kitts. Here the sick were taken ashore and housed in tents while the ships were aired and cleaned. Fresh fruits were served in abundance, and in this tropical paradise, the sick recovered and hope was revived. Christmas was celebrated by giving thanks to God for those who had survived,

217

and Drake chose the occasion to announce his great plan—to attack San Domingo, the very heart of Philip's western empire!

On the evening of December twenty-eighth—the day before the fleet was to sail from St. Kitts—Magnus was loafing on the poop with Tim, watching the weather. The glass had been dropping steadily since noon, and by this time the sky was streaked with mares' tails and low, greasy-edged clouds hovered along the horizon. Even Tim opined "as 'ow we're in for a mite o' weather."

The old man's fever was long gone, but as yet he had not recovered sufficiently to navigate under his own power for any appreciable length of time. Now, mellowed by the breathless lull which precedes a storm, he began to grow garrulous about the bygone days when he had sailed these same waters with John Hawkins.

Magnus listened absently. For him, too, the hands of time had turned backward, though not so far as for Tim. He was content to remember England, and all she had meant to him.

When a pause presented itself, he spoke his thoughts.

"I wonder what became of your wife, Timothy? And Kate?"

The old man grunted. "Me auld woman'll take care o' herself, never fear. Like as not she's found another 'usband, figgerin' I've jined 'er precious 'Erman in 'ell. Yet, I own I ofttimes think o' little Katie." He sucked on the pipe in his mouth and blew a spiral of smoke upward. "There was a lass fer ye! Damme, I wish I 'ad 'er 'ere now!"

Magnus grinned. "I thought you were through with women?"

"Aye! That I be. 'Tis summat more'n a peg-legged ol' derelict our Katie needs. Tell me, lad—d'ye find no trace o' 'er in Plymouth?"

"I found her."

Tim looked startled. "Ye never told me that!" he chided.

"There wasn't much to tell," yawned Magnus. "She asked after you, of course."

"Did she so? Bless 'er!" Tim sighed softly. "Ye got a fine lass in Rosalind. I ain't sayin' a word against 'er, mind ye, an' I be mighty grateful fer w'at she done fer me. 'Twas more'n I expected, aye, an' more'n I deserved. Yet if I was a young buck . . ."

"Which you are not," chuckled Magnus.

"True, but the p'int I'm tryin' to make is . . ."

Magnus laughed him to silence. "I know exactly the point you're trying to make, Timothy. But you're a poor Cupid." When he saw Tim's jaw begin to jut, he rose from his chair and strolled forward. The idea of comparing Rosalind and Kate was too ridiculous to contemplate.

218

Yet, before he had taken three strides, he heard a startled oath.

"*Mother o' God!*"

Magnus ran back, fearing the old man had had another attack of the fever, but Tim was staring wide-eyed over the rail toward the mouth of the harbor.

"Look!" he gasped. "D'ye see w'at I see?"

Magnus looked and saw a sight no Englishman of that era ever expected to witness: two large ships-of-the-line rounding the point; one flying the ensign of England, the other, the flag of Spain!

While he stood gaping, the crash of a signal gun proved the rest of the fleet had sighted the strangers, now standing into the bay in peaceful company. The effect was electrical! The first thought that occurred to every man was that Queen Elizabeth had changed her mind and joined with King Philip to stop Drake!

The oncoming English ship fired a friendly salute, then dropped her hook just inside the cove. A moment later, the Spaniard anchored beside her.

"What can it mean?" wondered Magnus. "What is an English ship doing in these waters with a Don?"

"God knows! Yet methinks we'll find out afore long. They both be puttin' their boats o'er."

It was so. The two boats glided across the water toward Drake's ship, the *Bonaventure*, and, through his glass, Magnus saw the officers climb aboard the flagship. Shortly thereafter, the *Bonaventure* signaled for all the captains of the fleet to attend the admiral at once.

Tim groaned. " 'Tis the end o' the venture! The Queen—God bless 'er!—'as changed 'er mind agin. Like I tolt ye, lad, nobody knows w'ich way a woman's goin' to jump!"

Magnus hurried below to prepare himself. His mind was in a contradictory state; he would be disappointed at missing a chance at the wealth of San Domingo, yet at the same time, relieved that Rosalind's life would not be placed in jeopardy.

He encountered her in the companionway. She ran into his arms, trembling with excitement.

"What are those ships doing here, darling?"

He gave her a quick squeeze. "I can't say. Peradventure we're going home."

"Home? You mean England?"

He suffered a twinge of jealousy. "Where else is *home?*"

"Wherever you are, my sweet!" she laughed, kissing away his frown. "Do hurry back! I will be most anxious to know what it means!"

219

Magnus sent Ben Absedik topside to order him a boat, and Rosalind helped him lay out his best clothes, then curled up contentedly on the bunk to watch him dress. When he had completed his toilet, he appraised the result in the mirror. Despite a similar daily survey, he could not get accustomed to the change in his appearance brought on by his experiences in the past months. The endless drudgery in the galleys had developed his shoulders to nearly twice their former size and slimmed his waist until his body approximated a huge wedge. Responsibility had etched mature lines about his mouth and eyes and strengthened his jaw muscles. Wind and tropical sun had dyed his skin the shade of saddle-leather and bleached his hair. Like most of the captains, he had affected a "Drake-trimmed" beard, but unlike the others, it suited his picaresque features.

Buckling on his sword, he took Rosalind briefly into his arms.

"God speed you, darling!" she whispered.

He left her with regret, and hurried on deck to find the boat waiting. The weather looked worse, and although it lacked an hour of sunset, the sky was dark. Unfortunately, he had anchored the *Sparrow* on the seaward side of the fleet, in order to secure the coolest air, which meant he now had the furthest distance to row to reach the flagship. When he did arrive, he found the other captains already aboard so, ordering his boat to await him, he climbed on deck.

A master's mate was stationed at the head of the gangway to escort him to the cabin, and as they tramped aft, Magnus tried to glean an inkling of what was behind the summons. The mate knew little enough.

"Damme, sor, I dunno w'at's in the wind. Some 'oighty-toity blueblood from 'ome came aboard wi' the two cap'ns, bringin' orders from both 'er 'Ighness an' 'at bastard Philip—beggin' yer pardon fer sayin' so, sor! Threw the admiral into a ruddy 'uff, it did, sor."

"I suppose it means the end of San Domingo," Magnus commented.

"Gor' blime, I 'opes not, sor! I been countin' on me share to buy a wee pub back 'ome."

They had reached the door of the great cabin, so Magnus thanked the man and gave him a piece of gold.

"Well, if you can't buy the pub, at least you can get a drink."

The master's mate knuckled his forelock. "Thankee, sor, an' God bless ye!" He opened the door and stood aside for Magnus to enter.

The cabin was jammed. Under the feeble light of a hanging lanthorn, Drake and his immediate staff sat around the table with the guests, while the captains crowded into the remaining space.

220

Magnus doffed his hat and took two steps into the smoke-filled cabin—to stop short, his heart jerking convulsively.

Seated directly opposite the door sat the man he hated most in this world, and the last he expected to see—*Sir Peter Beckles!*

Chapter 24

A RED haze filmed Magnus' eyes. The blood in his veins turned icy cold so that his whole body shook as from a chill. If there was any sound in the cabin, he did not hear it. For him, the silence had substance and texture; it closed about him like a shroud. He tried to convince himself it was merely a figment of his imagination: Peter Beckles could not be sitting here, aboard Drake's flagship. More likely he had caught the fever, and all this was a delusion. As from a distance, he heard Drake's voice: "Find yourself a place, Captain. We must get to the bottom of this ugly affair."

So it was not an hallucination! Beckles was flesh and blood! Then in a flash of insight, Magnus understood what had brought this ill-assorted pair of warships to the Spanish Main: they had come in search of Rosalind and himself! He kept his eyes on the suave, handsome face across the cabin, undecided whether to plunge his poniard into the man's heart, or dash out of the cabin in a desperate effort to escape. He held his breath, awaiting the inevitable denunciation.

Beckles, too, had been staring at Magnus, but soon he turned and spoke to the portly, red-faced Englishman beside him. Magnus was puzzled. It had not yet dawned on him that his guilt was not common knowledge, and he wondered why Beckles did not accuse him openly. Was the devil playing another of his devious tricks, or could it be . . . was it barely possible, the scoundrel had failed to recognize him? Magnus gathered his scattered wits and stumbled into a vacant corner, his fingers toying restlessly with his sword hilt.

Drake was speaking in his calm, perfectly controlled voice: "Gentlemen, as there is a storm making and you are doubtless anxious to get back to your ships, I'll make this brief for the nonce.

221

Tomorrow we will go into the matter in detail. Suffice to say now that Captain Sir Chester Hardy, of her Majesty's ship *Triumph*, and Admiral Don Alvarado Perrez, of the *San Philip*, representing His Most Christian Majesty,"—he bowed respectfully to the two uniformed guests—"have brought disquieting intelligence. It appears men from an English vessel raided a castle at Bilbao which the King of Spain had placed at the disposal of this gentleman, Sir Peter Beckles"—he bowed in turn to the latter—"our Queen's envoy, and carried off his bride.

"That in itself would be heinous enough to arouse all loyal Englishmen, but, to make the matter even more serious, rumors reached their Majesties that the perpetrator of this foul act was a member of *this* company, with the result their Majesties saw fit to join hands in sending out a searching squadron to round up the culprit."

During the grim silence which followed this announcement, Drake's alert eyes shifted significantly from face to face of his captains. As plainly as the spoken word that look said: *"If this be true, God help the wretch, for it means the termination of our venture!"* Yet when he spoke again, his voice remained unruffled.

"I have assured these gentlemen that the charge against my company is unfounded. At the time this crime took place, we were all in the harbor of Vigo." His glance strayed with studied casualness to Magnus' tense face. "I have also told them what you all well know—of my emphatic orders against the molestation of women, which I regard as a capital offense. Unfortunately, the perpetrators are not known, so . . ."

At this point, Sir Peter interrupted. "Your pardon, Sir Francis, but we do have several clues. The ship in question was an English bark, and though the dastards who raided the castle were disguised, we know that one was an oriental of some kind; a Turk or a Moor . . ."

Frobisher burst into an explosive grunt. "God's death, man, d'ye think we carry Turks and Moors in our company?"

"That remains to be seen!" snapped Beckles, then he controlled himself and bowed to Drake. "You realize, Sir Francis, that our visit in no wise intimates that you personally were involved in this ghastly crime, or had any knowledge of it."

"Thank you," Drake said dryly, "but what concerns my men concerns me."

"Well, we're here to clear up doubts," put in Captain Hardy.

A rumbling crash of thunder sounded in the east, and a moment later, one of the stern windows was blown open by a gust of wind. The officers stirred restlessly.

"Aye, we'll resolve your doubts," Drake went on. "Meanwhile,

222

gentlemen, you will retire to your ships and be prepared for a thorough inspection at ten of the clock in the morning. During the interim, it is my express command that no boat be permitted to leave your ships. Patrols will see that this order is obeyed. Is that perfectly understood, gentlemen?"

Once again his eyes touched Magnus briefly, but whether by accident or design, Magnus could not tell. Yet one thing was obvious: Francis Drake was in no temper to be crossed. As the others moved toward the door, Magnus did likewise. He felt Beckles' stare, but forced himself to avoid meeting it. He was certain that if he looked his arch enemy squarely in the face, he would be unable to control himself. Somehow, he managed to make his *adieu* and escape from the paralyzing atmosphere of the cabin.

However, huddled in the sternsheets of the long boat on his way back to the *Sparrow*, Magnus had an opportunity to ponder his predicament. It still seemed incredible that Sir Peter had failed to recognize him! No doubt it was because of the dim and smoky light of the cabin and the tension engendered by the threatening storm. But whatever the reason, it could at best be only a respite, and in the cold sunlight of tomorrow, the truth would out. What then? The politic term "inspection" had been merely a synonym for "search." Rosalind would be discovered and returned to Beckles. For Magnus there could be but one end. He would hang!

The more he considered, the surer he was that Beckles, if not actually recognizing him, at least suspected him. He knew Frobisher did; the gruff old mariner's kindly effort to discount the presence of the Moor proved that. But what of Drake? Drake had eyed him significantly several times. Magnus sighed gloomily. Doubtless he, too, guessed the truth.

The instant the long boat pulled alongside the *Sparrow*, Magnus swung aboard and hurried aft. Fortunately, Rosalind had retired to her cuddy. He hadn't the courage to face her just yet. Brother Diego was playing at cards with Tim and Ben Absedik in the larboard cabin when Magnus stalked in.

"Blast my buttocks!" hooted the old man. "Ye look blacker'n a thunder'ead, lad! D'ye learn w'at brought them bloody warships out 'ere?"

Magnus closed the door and tossed his sodden cloak into a corner. "Aye! They came after *me!*"

There was a moment of stunned silence, broken finally by a raucous cackle from Tim.

"Ho! Now there's conceit fer ye, *padre!* 'E thinks 'e's important enough fer two nations to send nyvy ships arter 'im!"

Magnus sank onto a bench. "It's not me who's important; it's Peter Beckles. The bastard's aboard the *Bonaventure* now. He's coming to search the *Sparrow* in the morning!"

Tim tried to stagger to his feet, but the roll of the vessel was too much for him. He sank back weakly.

"Jesus God! Ye seen 'im fyce to fyce?"

"Aye, but he didn't recognize me. At least he didn't say so."

Tim sighed. "Then 'e don't know the wench be 'ere."

"He'll know in the morning!" Magnus groaned, clenching and unclenching his fists. "That is—if he lives 'til morning!"

Brother Diego laid a restraining hand on his arm. "Steady, my son! This all sounds incredible! I agree with Timothy, Magnus; two nations as embittered as England and Spain would not send navy ships halfway across the world to seek a girl. You should know that."

"You saw those ships, didn't you?" Magnus cried angrily. "And I saw Beckles! I'll never forgive myself for not killing him when I had the opportunity!"

"An 'ell of an opportunity in a cabin full o' men!" scoffed Tim. "Come now—cool down. We'll row the lass ashore 'til the search be o'er."

Magnus shook his head. "It's no use. Drake has ordered out patrols to prevent that very thing. He said so. Furthermore, Beckles' bravos marked Abu as a Moor. We're in for it, but I'll not run from *Ser Pedro*, the traitor! By God, I wish I had those letters with me now!"

"Well, ye ain't!"

"Granted. But I still have my sword. I'll go aboard Beckles' ship tonight and carry out my oath!"

"Fair enough," Tim agreed sarcastically. "But afore ye leave—tell us w'at to do wi' the maid. We can draw lots fer 'er, I reckon, yet none o' us want 'er, poor mite. One thing be sure: if ye pull a fool trick like that, ye'll not be aroun' to enjoy 'er."

"True," said the priest. "Every word of it!"

Ben Absedik leaned forward. "May Allah rot the bones of thy enemy, *effendi!* Yet, verily, it would be folly to sacrifice thyself to no cause. Why not drift alongside this ship the evil one is on, and sink her with a broadside. Since she is Spanish, it would be doubly delectable to . . ."

"I doubt Beckles is on the Spanish ship, Abu," Magnus interrupted. "But whether or no, it would not do. He might be saved, and I must be certain he is dead." He rose to his feet. "No, I'm going to see him tonight and end this suspense."

The others tried to reason with him, but Magnus was beyond

224

reason. Finally, rather than permit him to commit suicide, an alternate plan was grudgingly agreed upon: they would ready the bark for instant flight—Tim was sufficiently recovered to see to that—while Magnus and Abu Ben Absedik, with a hand-picked boat crew, would row over to the *Triumph* in search of Beckles. Magnus was not happy about the scheme, since he preferred to go alone. Brother Diego argued against it to the bitter end, but eventually agreed to assist Tim.

Magnus debated the advisability of discussing the problem with Rosalind. His companions were set against it.

"Don't see 'er, lad," pleaded Tim. "It'll on'y rile ye, an' ye'll need all yer wits to 'andle Beckles."

"It would be utter madness!" warned the priest. "No matter how casually *you* regard the marriage, this man is still her husband. Such ties are not easily pushed aside."

"Aai! The tongue is the neck's enemy. Say nothing, *effendi!*"

Magnus acquiesced. While he hungered to see Rosalind again, he felt an aversion to confiding his plan to kill the man she had married, willingly or not. Furthermore, he dreaded lest the revelation of Beckles' arrival might terrify her unduly.

The rain had let up when he stepped on deck, but the wind was strong and gusty, and the bay alive with chop. Amidships, he met the priest, who had been assisting in the lowering of the long boat.

"By the saints!" the priest remarked conversationally. "It is a nasty night for murder."

Magnus winced. "Not as nasty as some of the nights I've endured because of this dog!" he growled. "Is the boat ready?"

"Aye! The infidel awaits you."

Magnus smiled ruefully at that. Brother Diego only referred to Ben Absedik as "the infidel" when the latter was engaged in matters antipathetic to his own faith.

Drawing his cloak around his body, Magnus continued to the waist. Somewhere in the darkness below, Ben Absedik and the oarsmen were trying to fend off the long boat to prevent her crashing into the bark. Magnus announced his coming and threw one leg over the rail. . . .

At that moment, another boat with muffled oars slipped out of the darkness and hove alongside. A voice called: "Clear the gangway! I'm coming aboard!"

That voice, though distorted out of recognition by the wind, was vaguely familiar. Tim groaned.

"Damme! We've been discovered!"

Magnus hesitated, then shouted down to the Moor, "Give way! Let them aboard!"

225

When he heard the boat thump against the *Sparrow's* side, he dropped back on deck and faced Tim, who held a hooded lanthorn.

"It's the guard!" he told the old seaman. "When he hits the deck, shine your light in his face. I'll handle him."

They listened grimly to the retch of straining rope, and then saw the silhouette of a man heave himself over the rail. Magnus whipped out his poniard and when the visitor landed on deck, barked: "Let's have a look at him!"

Tim jerked back the hood and a flood of yellow light splashed across the round, bearded face of—*Sir Francis Drake!*

"Oh, Jesus Christ!" breathed Tim, and nearly dropped the lanthorn.

"No, merely your admiral," snapped Drake. "Now be good enough to take that damned light out of my eyes!"

If the Devil himself had appeared, Magnus could not have been more astounded. He stood rooted, his eyes and mouth wide open. The blood throbbed against his temples until he was dizzy.

"Forgive me if I seem to be interfering with your exercises, Captain Carter," Drake observed with precise sarcasm, "howbeit, I decided a visit was in order. *Privately,* if you don't object?"

The rigidity went out of Magnus, leaving him limp and shaken.

"Certainly, my lord!" he stammered. "Mr. Prettyman, light us to the larboard cabin."

"Thank you. Under the circumstances, I'll appreciate your sheathing that poniard and preceding me."

Magnus had forgotten the bare blade in his hand, and in a welter of confusion, fumbled it into its scabbard and stumbled after Tim. At the entrance of the companionway, Drake paused.

"It is blustery weather to trail a small boat, Captain," he said pointedly. "I recommend you have it hoisted aboard."

Magnus felt the blood rush to his features, and he was grateful for the darkness.

"Very good, sir! See to it, Mr. Prettyman."

"Aye, aye, sir!" croaked the old man, and hobbled away.

Magnus led the way into the cabin, and Drake followed, carefully closing the door behind him. He glanced around the cuddy, then dropped into a chair. For a long time he appraised Magnus without speaking. The effect on the other was devastating, and he felt that if the silence lasted much longer, he would topple over.

"Sit down!" Drake commanded abruptly.

Magnus lowered himself gingerly to the edge of the bunk. The reaction he suffered was awe, not fear. Never before had he been alone with this legendary man who gambled with the whims of queens and defied the might of Spain. It was an overpowering sensation.

Then Francis Drake began to talk in the casual tone he might use to an equal in a drawing room, and the effect was more appalling than if he had raged in a temper.

"I presume, Carter, you have some intimation of the embarrassment the arrival of these ships has caused me?"

Magnus nodded, unable to speak. Drake tugged reflectively on the point of his beard.

"Yet I wonder if you comprehend it fully. Frankly, the whole expedition hangs in jeopardy, and with it, my own personal fortune, not to mention the fortunes of the friends who so graciously backed me. Aye, it means ruin to us all, *unless* . . ." He paused with his eyes fixed speculatively on Magnus' face.

The latter turned scarlet. "Unless the guilty man is found, sir?"

To his surprise, Drake shook his head. "That would not be sufficient at this juncture. If I believed for an instant it would, I'd hunt the blackguard down tonight and kill him with my own hands, instead of waiting to hang him in the morning—which I will surely do, if found. No, the problem is far more complex. While the search for the woman may be paramount with this man Beckles, Philip of Spain doesn't sent his ships across the seas simply to seek an English girl. Nor does our good Queen, for that matter. The girl is merely a convenient pretext, and I believe I recognize the hand of my lord Burghley behind the voyage of the *Triumph*. He was bitterly opposed to our expedition proceeding beyond Spain. I have every reason to suspect that Captain Hardy carries secret orders, and that, *after the hanging*"—Drake studiously emphasized the words—"he will hand me my recall home. The presence of the *San Philip* supports this assumption. Philip intends to make sure I obey."

Magnus was nauseated with suspense. He felt that Drake was torturing him deliberately. Unable to bear it, he blurted: "I understand! You want me to tell you . . ."

Drake interrupted hastily: "I'll ask the questions, if you please! Just tell me what you know of Beckles!"

"He is a double-dealing papist traitor!"

"Ah! So you know him personally?"

Magnus realized he had trapped himself, but he was past caring. "Aye, sir, I know him—much too well! It was he who delivered Tim Prettyman and myself into the hands of the Holy Office!"

Drake's peculiar eyebrows arched upward. "Incredible!"

"You can ask Prettyman, sir!"

"I'm asking *you*," Drake reiterated with numbing calmness. "Why do you call him a traitor?"

227

Leaving out all reference to Rosalind, Magnus explained that certain treasonous letters had "fallen into his hands." He told of the efforts of Duane and Beckles to recover them, the quarrel at the tavern, the debacle on the bluffs, his capture, and subsequent conversations with Beckles during the voyage to Spain.

Throughout the discourse, Drake listened in rapt attention, never taking his eyes from Magnus' white face. Magnus was in a mood to confess the whole thing, but when he brought the story up to the point of sailing from England, Drake held up a restraining hand.

"That's quite sufficient," he cut in. "It answers several perplexing questions—such as why Philip is so concerned with the affair—yet does not tax my conscience with . . . ah . . . shall we say *needless* information." He rose and took a slow turn around the cabin, his head bowed in thought.

After an uncomfortable pause, he began to muse aloud in the fashion of a man talking to himself.

"Men do strange things under emotional stress; thoughtless things, selfish things. Unfortunately, others have to suffer for these blunders. It seems inconceivable that one of my own captains would be so derelict in duty and respect as to imperil this expedition because of a personal vendetta. That alone makes the crime unforgivable. Such a self-centered scoundrel should be hanged." He recrossed the cabin twice before continuing.

"Yet, tragically enough, hanging *him* will not solve *my* problem, but only worsen it. There's only *one* thing that could salvage the expedition at this juncture and that is—if the knave had sense enough to run away!"

Magnus swallowed nervously. "How could that help you, sir?" he stammered. "A"—he was about to say *bark*, but caught himself in time—"an ordinary vessel could not hope to outrun a ship of the line!"

"Too true," Drake agreed moodily. "Yet a shallow-draft craft, bearing southeast of here to the tip of the island, could cut through the shoal water channel there." He sighed and shook his head. "It would be a difficult feat of seamanship, demanding the utmost courage and skill, for if he grounded, he'd be taken off in long boats. No, I fear this is the end of our hopes. The wretch will have to hang."

"My question, sir," said Magnus, "was not concerned with the culprit, but with *you!* How could his escape benefit you and the company?"

Drake reared his head in surprise. "*Me?* God's life, Carter, you don't think I'd sit idly here while the *Triumph* and the *San Philip* wander around the islands on a wild-goose chase! God forbid! Unless I receive *written* instructions from my Queen to the contrary, I sail for San Domingo tomorrow as scheduled. However, I can't sail with these accursed warships blocking my path!"

Magnus rose unsteadily to his feet. "Sire, I know not why you singled me out from among your captains to honor me with your confidence," he said, bowing. "Yet I believe I can promise you the problem will resolve itself this night."

Drake smiled thinly. "I suspected you could, Captain; you seem a man of parts. I congratulate us both that you are not the man I have to hang in the morning! Good luck to you." He clapped his hat to his head. "Now, I must return to my ship."

Somehow, Magnus managed to escort him to the gangway. Drake clambered over the rail, but as he fitted his boot onto the ladder, he paused, and in the lanthorn's glow, his eyes twinkled mischievously.

"Just one thing more, Carter," he said gruffly. "Take good care of that pretty *cabin boy*."

And then he was gone.

Chapter 25

M AGNUS made his way aft and leaned on the taffrail. He wanted a little time alone to pull himself together. He was still in a state of shock as a result of the interview, and a tumult of thoughts crowded into his mind for attention, but he resolutely ejected them to concentrate on the more pressing problem of escape.

In such matters of physical action, where his emotions were not involved, Magnus Carter was at his best. Danger, laced with chance, was heady stuff. It stimulated his brain and cooled his nerves. His perceptions grew so keen, he seemed almost to have the gift of second sight.

Now he stared into the blustery darkness. Little could be seen save the phosphorescent beards of the rollers sweeping in from the sea and, occasionally, the dancing lights of the fleet. Yet in the mirror of his mind, he saw much more. The tide was flooding, at the moment, and as a result, the anchored ships all lay in unison, their bows seaward. Within two glasses, the tide would change, and on the ebb, the fleet would stream to anchor in the opposite direction. Magnus smiled cannily, and glanced at the sky.

A few stars shone through the murk, despite the driving cavalcade of clouds. The wind was fair and though violent, not unmanageable. He shrugged. This was no time to weigh risks; to tarry meant disgrace and death. Flight could offer nothing worse.

He was still pondering his course when his three friends came trooping aft to join him.

"Lor' luv ye, lad!" panted Tim. "W'at 'appened? W'en I seen it was Sir Frankie, I reckoned 'e'd guessed the trufe!"

"He did," Magnus admitted. "The hanging is scheduled for the morning."

Tim groaned miserably. Brother Diego peered skeptically at Magnus.

"You appear to accept it with unnatural fortitude, my son," he observed.

"It is written that life, like a fire, begins in smoke and ends in ashes," offered Ben Absedik. "Truly, this may be thy kismet. Yet by the Seven Heavens of Islam, if thou choose to resist, O my brother, I place my sword by thy side!"

"Aye, an' me cutlass on yer other side!" roared Tim excitedly. "Though methinks 'twill be a short fight an' merry!"

Magnus laughed and put his arms around the shoulders of Tim and Abu.

"Bless you, my friends! It is not swords I need this night, but your help to form a plan. To speak plain—I have small intention of attending my own hanging."

Tim's eyes narrowed. "Hold, lad! Sir Francis would not 'ave left wi'out takin' yer pledge," he said slowly. "If ye gave him yer promise, ye can't break it."

"My very own thought," chuckled Magnus. "And for that reason, we must set to work, for I gave Francis Drake my solemn promise I'd not be here to embarrass him in the morning."

"Blast my buttocks! I don't ken ye!"

"It is too involved a tale for now," Magnus cut him off. "Rouse up the hands, and to work! I want a stout line bent to the bight in the anchor rode, then secured aft. When you've done that, cast off the rode forward, and we'll lay by the stern."

"But, God A'mighty, that'll leave us 'eaded fer the beach!" protested the old man. "If ye plan to run for it—as ye plainly do—ye'll 'ave to round-to, whereas right now we're 'eaded fer the open sea!"

"Exactly! But I don't intend to buck this tide. When it turns, however, we'll be the one craft headed seaward, while all the others will be facing the beach."

"Clever enough," conceded the priest. "Yet haven't you overlooked the element of *time?* If you wait for the ebb, you will not clear the gut ere daylight!"

"That is correct, *padre.*"

"Are ye daft?" demanded Tim. "Them two warships'll tyke arter us like 'ounds arter an 'are!"

"Oh, let be, Timothy!" Brother Diego said wearily. "Magnus prefers to work like the mole—underground and in the dark."

"On the contrary, I'm trying to get my orders obeyed. Unless we lure those plagued ships away from this anchorage, Drake will be undone. Now—enough talk. *Padre,* will you and Abu attend to the hawse? I want Tim at the whipstaff when we make sail."

When they left him, he tried to clarify his plan. His reluctance to discuss it had not been due to lack of trust, but rather because it was still in a formative state. The one thing he had to fear was discovery. While the howling wind would drown the noise of the work, there was a possibility that in shifting the anchor hawse from bow to stern, they might lengthen their scope sufficiently to alarm near-by vessels. Yet this was a risk they would have to take, for to shorten scope would necessitate using the winch, and the clank of the pawl would doubtless carry above the wind.

But once again the arduous experience of the Moor stood them in good stead. By putting a spring on the hawse, he was able to ease her about without commotion. All this took time, and before the evolution was completed, the tide was slack. Yet when the ebb began, the little *Sparrow* lay poised for flight with her head pointed seaward.

Then came the most painful part—the waiting! Magnus took his station in the bow and peered into the darkness. The preparatory work was finished; he was cursed with time to think. His resolution wavered. Should he leave without finishing Beckles? Deep in his heart, he was beginning to suspect that he could never completely enjoy Rosalind so long as her husband lived. Was he not, then, defeating his own purpose by flight? Yet the alternative, if not certain death for him, meant the betrayal and ruin of Drake. Drake had afforded this one honorable chance to make partial amends. Could he fail him again?

He felt Tim touch his arm. "Lad, 'twill be daylight wi'in the glass!"

Magnus exhaled heavily and turned to find the hands grouped about him for orders. They knew their tasks, for there was to be no shouting of commands.

"Sail-loosers lay aloft on the fore tops'l," he said quietly. "The rest of you man the tops'l sheets and halliard! Tend the braces! Move lively, lads, if you want to see another sunset."

As the men sprang to their stations, Magnus turned to Tim and Ben Absedik. "Abu, take an ax and sever the anchor hawse. You, Tim, take the helm, and for God's sake, don't foul any cables on your way out!"

"All we've done be sever anchors," grumbled the old man. "D'ye realize we got but a small bower left?"

"Aye, but we'll have no use for anchors if you shilly-shally longer! Bestir yourself, man!"

Somewhere in the darkness overhead, he heard the topsail rumble down, followed by the creak of blocks as it was sheeted home. The *Sparrow* tensed, as if suddenly awakened, and tautened against the hawse astern. Then came the sharp *chunk* of an ax, the fiddle-string twang of the parted line, and the bark started forward as an arrow loosed from a bow.

To Magnus, no music was sweeter than the sounds of a ship getting under weigh. The crack of filling sails reminded him of the start of a great musical theme. The harps of rigging began softly under the fingers of the wind, while the sheets and brace strummed a somber bass. The swells rumbled around the cutwater, growing into a rhythmic drumming. Now a living thing, the *Sparrow* soared from crest to crest. The song increased in volume.

The priest, standing beside Magnus, felt the grandeur. "Verily, Magnus, I believe that God is with us!" he breathed softly, as if reluctant to break the spell. "I do not infer that He approves, exactly, yet somehow I am conscious of His presence."

Magnus did not scoff this time. "It is a strange sensation," he agreed.

It *was* strange, for Magnus. He felt exalted. All doubt left him. He was, he assured himself, doing the right thing. It was peculiarly satisfying to consider someone other than himself.

Abruptly, a black shape loomed up in the murk ahead. Magnus cupped his hands to shout a warning aft, but at that instant, Tim forced the whipstaff down and the bark veered smartly aside. Magnus marveled. It seemed incredible that old Tim could have seen the obstruction from the stern. Was it possible some unseen hand was giving guidance?

The silvery heralds of the sun appeared on the horizon. The sleeping fleet stirred uneasily, like tethered cattle, their tall horns black against the sky. The *Sparrow* gained speed. The land stretched forth a long dark arm to seize her, but the nimble bark avoided it, and soared toward the sea. As she passed the bony fingers of sand, the sun lifted its blinding face. . . .

The crash of a gun shattered the mood. Magnus was jerked back to reality. He glanced ahead to make sure they would clear the bar, then hurried aft. The fleet lay silhouetted against the still dark western sky, but when he focused his glass on the two warships, he saw the seamen swarming up their rigging. Seconds later, their fore topsails blossomed in unison, then their headsails. They got under weigh so swiftly, he judged they must have slipped their cables, but because they were lying bow-on to the beach, he knew they would have to circle through Drake's fleet to come about. Before they had completed that revolution, the *Sparrow* had rounded the spit and was soaring southward.

Yet all too soon they came driving through the gut, the *Triumph* in the lead, and the high-castled *San Philip* bludgeoning along behind her. In spite of a natural apprehension, Magnus was not impervious to the beauty of the scene. Birds of prey they might be, yet the loveliest creations of the hand of man! The *Triumph* swooped down swiftly, her acres of snowy canvas billowing forward, the long pennon of St. George streaming from her main truck, and her gilded beak-head flaming in the sunlight. Her bluff stem seemed to part the water just where depth changed its color from royal blue to the line of green which marked the shoal. When she loosed her bow-chasers, however, Magnus forgot the beauty.

"Station a leadsman in the starboard chains, Abu! Tim, keep her in as close as you dare."

"We be in a bloody lot closer'n I *dare* right now! Ain't enough water betwixt sand an' keel for a crab!"

"That's sufficient. At least those damn galleons won't venture in here."

In that he was correct, for when next he glanced astern, the *Triumph* had veered offshore. Nevertheless, running free before the half-gale, she gained rapidly, and Tim Prettyman but voiced the common thought when he grumbled: "Afore midday, she'll pass us to seaward, leavin' us pinned against the beach, with that accursed Don followin' to prevent us comin' about! Damnation, lad, can't ye see 'ow that peninsula arcs out ahead? We be runnin' into a trap!"

Magnus laughed at him. "That's no peninsula; it's another island, and there's a shoal-water channel between. With luck, we'll make it, and from what the admiral assured me, the *Triumph* won't find water enough to follow."

Tim's eyes widened. "Sir Francis? Ye mean 'e advised . . . ?"

"He advised nothing," interrupted Magnus. "It was mentioned in conversation."

233

"Magnus!"

He turned to find Rosalind coming out of the hatch. "I heard gun-fire!" she cried in alarm. "What is going on? Why are we at sea?"

After a warning glance at Tim, Magnus took her arm to steady her against the pitch of the vessel.

"Don't get excited, sweetheart," he said lightly. "We're just shifting our anchorage."

But Rosalind had eyes, and the pursuing ships were close enough to show their colors.

"That's an English ship firing at us! And, look—there is a Spaniard following! Where is Drake's fleet?" She caught his arm. "Magnus! You are keeping something from me! As you love me—speak!"

Magnus hesitated, conscious of the presence of his friends. Ben Absedik wore his habitual cynical smile and Brother Diego's eyes were compassionate. Tim also watched him quizzically, as if curious to learn how he was going to explain the situation.

"Well," began Magnus carefully, "to speak true, these two ships came in search of . . . us."

"Us? Merciful God, Magnus, do you mean Spain and England sent warships after *me?*"

He shrugged. "Aye, you chiefly, although *I* was not to be neglected. It was to avoid the unpleasantness of hanging that induced me to leave so precipitately."

She was aghast. "Is Peter . . . is my husband . . . ?" She faltered, unable to continue.

He frowned, not fully comprehending what she was driving at.

"Alive? Aye, unfortunately he is, or was when I saw him last night."

She sank terrified to the deck. "Then he is here! Oh, no, no, no!" She covered her face with her hands. "Mother of God, we are undone! What will he do to me when he catches us?"

Glimpsing the curled lip of the Moor, Magnus flushed in embarrassment.

"For heaven's sake, Roz, pull yourself together! He isn't going to catch us!"

"Oh, he will, he will!" moaned the girl. "With the ships of two nations after us, we cannot possibly escape!"

Magnus was torn between sympathy and impatience, but before he could speak again, the priest gestured him to silence and gently lifted the girl to her feet.

"Come now, my daughter. You have nothing to fear."

Rosalind clung to him. "My husband will kill me, Father!"

"Nonsense, child!" soothed the priest. "We do not know what God has in store for us, yet if we should be taken, you cannot be held

234

responsible for what has happened. After all, my daughter, you were seized against your will."

"Do you think he would believe that?"

"I doubt if he would have voyaged this far if he did not already believe it," reasoned Brother Diego.

"You won't let him harm me, Father?"

Magnus was furious, and when he heard a startled bleat from the leadsman, he said sharply, "*Padre,* take Rosalind below! The *Triumph* will be within range!" Without waiting to see his order obeyed, he sprang into the lower shrouds.

The *Triumph* was abeam now and steadily crowding the bark against the shoals.

"By the mark three!" shouted the leadsman in desperation.

Magnus flinched. The *Sparrow* drew over two fathoms, which meant they had less than six feet of water under the keel.

"Larboard a point, Tim!" As the bark veered, he called to the man in the chains: "What do you get now?"

"Mark under water three, sor!"

They had gained a foot or two. Not enough. Magnus glanced aft, weighing his chances of coming about, but the *San Philip* was driving up under all sail. If he rounded-to, he would put himself directly under her guns.

"And a *quarter two,* God 'elp us!" screamed the leadsman.

Magnus bit his lip. Ahead, he could see the surf breaking between the islands. It looked hopeless, yet Drake had assured him there was a passage there. Doubt assailed him momentarily. Had Drake told him that to trap him? Magnus wouldn't believe it.

"Steady as she goes, Tim!" he ordered, and climbed to the cross-tree.

At first the boiling surf appeared to form a solid wall across the bar, but when he studied it awhile, Magnus finally spotted a dark patch near the smaller island. He bellowed the course to Tim, and the *Sparrow* stood inshore.

Looking aft, Magnus could see the consternation of Captain Hardy reflected in the maneuvers of the *Triumph.* She appeared to falter, then a series of signal flags blossomed from her truck. The *San Philip* answered in kind, after which she rounded up into the wind. The *Triumph,* meanwhile, altered course and stood in after the *Sparrow.*

Magnus smiled grimly. The courage of a fool! The *Triumph* must draw at least three fathoms, probably four! Then he saw the white mushrooms spout from her bow-chasers. The balls dropped uncomfortably close. Five minutes later, the *Triumph* grounded and came to a shuddering stop.

A wild tumult of cheering broke out on the *Sparrow*. Now they were safe! A short dash through the cut and all would be well! The cheers still echoed when the *Sparrow* herself struck with such force that Magnus was nearly thrown from his perch!

Cursing bitterly, he grabbed a brace and slid to the deck. The crew seemed paralyzed as they crowded into the waist to stare at the grounded warship.

"We be lost, Cap'n!" groaned the bos'n. "They be 'oistin' out their boardin' boats!"

"To hell with them!" thundered Magnus. "Jettison these guns! Leave only one to a side! Jump, my hearties, unless you want to decorate the *Triumph's* yardarms!" He grabbed a gun and spiked the nearest culverin. Ben Absedik followed suit, and soon all the hands were working desperately.

Old Tim wept like a child to see his beloved guns go by the board, but the little bark seemed relieved and tried to stagger erect.

"Broach the water casks!" Magnus commanded.

While the hands emptied their precious water, Magnus stole an anxious glance aft. Two long boats, loaded with armed seamen, clove through the swells less than a chain's length astern. If those boats came alongside, Magnus knew he was finished.

He thought of all the conventional methods of floating a stranded ship—kedging, rigging floats, erecting sheers, altering trim. Any one of these required time, and Magnus Carter had no time. Then, out of desperation, a scheme was born.

"All hands to the sheets and braces!" he shouted.

When the bewildered seamen took their stations, Magnus ordered the sails hauled around until they were squared with the wind. Tim winced when he grasped Magnus' intention.

"God A'mighty, man! Look at that mast bend! It'll carry aw'y!"

"*It* will, or *we* will," Magnus agreed grimly.

Under the full pressure of the wind on the stationary sails, the little bark began to heel. Yet, though she canted until the lee rail vanished under water, she held fast.

Magnus grimaced. The *Triumph's* long boats were now barely a hundred yards astern, and he could see the marksmen readying their muskets. He found it difficult to accept defeat when he had been so close. . . .

"Jesus Christ!" shrieked a hand. "She *moved!*"

Magnus scarcely dared believe it. He jumped into the windward rigging. Aye, by the powers, she *was* moving—slowly, painfully! He could hear the timbers groan in protest, feel her quiver from truck to keelson.

"Up helm, Tim!" he yelled. "For God's sake, get her higher!"

236

Brother Diego had returned to the deck, and he rushed to help the sweating Tim. Between them, they forced the whipstaff up.

The *Sparrow* strained and struggled to extricate herself, like a horse fighting out of quicksand, then with a suddenness that knocked half the crew off their feet, she slewed around on the sandy bottom and skidded sideways on her beam. On finding deep water a moment later, she lurched upright and began to run out of control.

"To the braces, on your lives!" bellowed Magnus.

The men needed no urging, for the marksmen in the boats had begun firing. But now Magnus could laugh at them. They soon passed out of range.

The Moor sheathed the scimitar he had expected to use. "I prostrate myself before thee, *effendi!*" he said with a smile. "Thou art a worthy enough mariner to serve Allah!"

Tim chortled. " 'E's worthy enough to serve Timothy Prettyman, damme if else! The *Triumph* won't 'ave no decorations fer 'er yards this trip!"

"May God grant you are correct," put in Brother Diego. "Howbeit, we still have this gut to navigate before we can relax our vigil."

"All too true," Magnus concurred. "Hold her steady, Tim. I'll con you from the trees."

He beckoned the priest aside. "Is Rosalind all right, *padre?*" he asked.

"Of course she is. But, if you'll permit a word of counsel, you will be a bit more considerate of her."

"Considerate? What do you expect me to do—turn her over to Beckles?"

Brother Diego chuckled. "I'd hardly expect *that* from you, Magnus. Nevertheless, you should be able to realize she cannot share your murderous hatred of her husband."

"By God, are you implying . . . ?"

"I'm simply stating the obvious, my son. I have no doubts that the child loves you, but she is a creature of convention. At the moment, she is appalled at what has happened, and"—Brother Diego smiled ruefully—"perhaps her conscience troubles her somewhat. Be gentle, and say no more in her presence about killing Peter Beckles."

Half angry, Magnus climbed aloft and settled himself above the hounds. The pass was plainly visible now, and with any luck at all, they could make it. He looked behind. The long boats were returning disconsolately to the stranded *Triumph*, and the *San Philip* was groping her way in close to lend assistance.

Magnus leaned back contentedly. He had eluded the warships of two nations; he had squared himself with Francis Drake, who doubtless by this time was merrily on his way to San Domingo. Meanwhile, the very most the *Triumph* could hope for would be to float off on the next high tide. Long before she accomplished that, Magnus Carter would be leagues away, safe among the islands.

Another hour put them safely through the gut and the *Sparrow* glided into a deep and lonely bay. Magnus exhaled relievedly. His immediate troubles were over.

True, he still had problems: he must replenish his water casks and, somehow, replace the guns he had been forced to jettison; he was a long, long way from home. On the other hand, he was his own master once again, for Drake, in his anxiety to be rid of the warships, had kissed him off without qualification.

Yes, the more he considered his position, the better he liked it. A stout little vessel under his command, loyal comrades to support him, and the treasures of Spain lying ripe for plucking. And, most important of all, he had Rosalind!

He couldn't help smiling when he thought of what Brother Diego had said about her. "A creature of convention . . . her conscience troubles her . . ." How little the good priest knew about women!

With startling abruptness, his reverie was shattered by a frantic shout from below.

"Cap'n! Cap'n! She's bilged! We're sinkin' fast!"

When he hit the deck, he found the men crowded around the main hold wherein the boatswain was sounding the bilge. Magnus shouldered his way through the press and dropped into the rank darkness, to land in water up to his waist.

"It's bad, sor!" groaned the bos'n. "I fear she sprang 'er garboard w'en she grounded."

"Will the pumps handle it?"

"I doubt it, sor. The most we could 'ope fer would be to keep 'er from takin' more." The old seaman shrugged. "If we could careen 'er in some quiet cove, mebbe . . ."

"With those two warships combing the islands for us!"

"As well 'ang as drown, sor," muttered the bos'n.

Leaving him with curt orders to find and pack the open seams, Magnus climbed on deck. The hands stared at him with anxious eyes, but he forced a confident grin.

"Man the pumps, lads! We'll keep afloat."

"Cap'n!" whimpered a ship's boy. "Beggin' yer pardon—wouldn't it be better to beach 'er w'ilest we can?"

Magnus opened his mouth to give him a tongue-lashing, but when he saw the same fear on all their faces, he brought himself under control. It was in such crises as this that men like Drake and Haw-

238

kins made themselves immortal. Once again, the actor in him cropped out.

"Beach her on a Spanish island, laddie?" he said, laughingly. "Have you grown so weary of life you want to burn on the stake, or be flayed alive in the mines of the Dons? Come now—to the pumps, I say, and before many moons, I'll get you back to England with more gold than you'll be able to spend in a lifetime!"

He saw them start the pumps, then beckoning his three companions, he sauntered aft to the poop. But once beyond the hearing of his men, he dropped his pose.

"It's bad," he told them bluntly, "very bad. A thousand leagues from home, in the heart of Spanish territory, only two guns and a sinking boat."

"And our vows unfulfilled," appended Ben Absedik.

"A bloody mess," agreed Tim. "We daren't tarry 'ere, fer as I recolleck—I syled this w'y wi' 'Awkins in sixty-five—we be 'ard by the Spanish town of Punta Arenas, w'ich maintains a considerable garrison."

Magnus tugged his beard reflectively. "How far is this Punta Arenas, Tim?"

"Methinks about ten leagues nor'ard, more or less, yet their ruddy boats scour these isles in search o' game an' fish. We'd better stand south."

"And run into the *Triumph* and the *San Philip*, if we don't sink meanwhile?"

Tim heaved his shoulders. "'Tis a rum choice, I grant ye!"

"The choice of Odysseus between Scylla and Charybdis," observed Brother Diego.

"Hold a moment, my hearts," said Magnus. "We're not yet dead. Tell me, Tim, didn't Hawkins sail into Punta Arenas?"

"Aye, that 'e did," Tim agreed proudly. "An' in open defiance o' the monster Philip. Sir John cared naught fer the laws o' the Dons; 'e insisted on tradin', did 'e, an' 'e 'ad goods to sell. 'E gi' the Spanish guv'ner a soft-spoke song about bein' a lost mariner in need o' necessities, an' since the Spaniards was eager enough to get 'is goods, 'e out-bluffed 'em, to the glory o' our Queen an' the rage o' King Philip."

Magnus laughed at the old man's reverence. "Well, what Hawkins can do, I can do!"

Tim's eyes rounded at this heresy. "God A'mighty, boy, 'tweren't the syme! John 'Awkins 'ad a nyme w'at struck terror into the craven 'eart o' every Don, even their King!"

"Granted! Yet Hawkins wasn't born with that reputation; he had to make it, as I'll make mine."

"Avast, ye crazy cockerel!" roared Tim. "'Awkins 'ad more 'n a nyme; 'e 'ad a sound ship o' fightin' men w'at bristled wi' cannon! 'Twas those guns w'at backed 'is words an' cowed the Spaniards!"

Magnus clapped him on the back. "Oh, come now, Timothy! Sir John never had half so fine an after-guard as I have! And as for guns —why I'll show these mangy dogs a set of teeth that would intimidate Philip himself!"

"Bah, ye're daft!" snorted Tim. "Will ye make guns out of salt water?"

"No, out of wood! True, they won't have much bark, but the sight of them will fool a Spaniard. Hear me out, my friends!"

As he started to unfold his hastily conceived plan, Rosalind came up on deck. Though smiling bravely, she looked tired and wan, so Magnus put an arm around her and drew her down beside him while he talked.

Under less desperate circumstances, the men would have laughed the mad scheme away, but now they listened in attentive silence. Magnus improvised as he went along, calling up all the half-forgotten lore of illusion he had learned as a strolling player. They would fashion cannons out of spare spars, black painted, with voiceless muzzles jutting out the ports. They would warn the Spanish governor that they were but the vanguard of a great fleet of English galleons bringing black slaves and other goods for sale. They would talk him out of guns and victuals, or perhaps even seize a merchantman lying at anchor. The possibilities, as Magnus viewed it, were unlimited.

Under the spell of his oratory, they were enthralled, but when he concluded, silence dissolved the illusion.

"If the governor comes aboard," Brother Diego objected, "he'll see the deception at once."

"No doubt, but he'll never get ashore to recount it."

"Have ye forgotten the warships?" growled Tim. "Punta Arenas be the only port 'ereabouts, so they're sure to call wi'in a week."

"A week will put us safely on our way."

"But, darling," interposed Rosalind, "he may know the warships are in the vicinity and send word to them! Wouldn't that be a simple matter?"

He patted her hand reassuringly. "You just leave the governor to your Magnus. I'll handle him as easily as I handled the *corregidor* of Bilbao." He instantly regretted mentioning Bilbao when he saw her wince.

The Moor alone was enthusiastic. "By the beard of the Prophet, it is well conceived! What if the guns cannot speak? Does not the

240

sword inspire dread, even in the scabbard? To Allah the merciful, all things are possible!"

"Sobeit!" surrendered Tim. " 'Twon't be no worse than drownin', an' mebbe we can take along a few Spanish dogs to keep us company in 'ell! 'Ow about it, *padre?* Ye'll jine us?"

The priest laughed good-naturedly. "I can hardly refuse, Timothy. But in your fierce desire to spill *Spaniards'* blood, kindly remember that the blood in my veins is Spanish and, incredible as it may seem to you, I cherish it quite as much as if it were English."

Tim flushed under the laughter of the others. " 'Twas but a manner o' speakin', *padre,*" he apologized.

Brother Diego slapped him on the shoulder. "Aye, Timothy, I understand. You merely use the word 'Spaniard' as a synonym for enemy. We shan't quibble about it. I'm with you, Magnus—say what's to be done."

Rosalind bit her lip. "I'm afraid I do not have that kind of courage," she said, with a wry smile. "I'll get out of the way."

Chapter 26

To the weary mariners, Punta Arenas seemed as alluring as a sea-nymph. The town nestled on the slope of a hill, a collection of white buildings dominated by a fort and the governor's palace. Above and behind it loomed the jungle; below, a small, snug harbor.

It was mid-January, 1587, when the tired little *Sparrow* wallowed into this paradise and folded her wings within three cable-lengths of the mole. Long before she set her hook, the crowds had collected at the waterfront. Even the governor, from his lofty perch, had watched the bark boldly enter his sacred precincts, and when through his perspective-glass, he saw the pennon of St. George flat from her masthead, he hastily donned his armor and hurried down to the landing to ward off the shore-boat the unbidden guest had lowered.

From that same boat's bow, old Tim Prettyman glimpsed the flash of armor, and looked significantly at Magnus, who shared the stern-sheets with Abu Ben Absedik.

"The mongrel be barin' 'is teeth, lad!" he called aft.

Magnus smiled. He, too, was arrayed in armor; an exquisite back-and-breast of black steel damascened with golden arabesques. He inclined his head in the direction of the bark.

"We show a fair set of molars ourselves, Tim," he laughed.

Tim glanced back, and even though he had helped set the stage, the illusion from this distance astonished him. The *Sparrow's* gunports were open to exhibit a formidable row of black muzzles. No wonder she appeared to sink so low in the water!

Tim chuckled. "Damme, 'tis enough to gi' a Spaniard apoplexy, I swear!"

By the time they came within hailing distance, a company of infantry, bristling with pikes and halberts, was drawn up across the mole. Magnus signaled his oarsmen to pause, then standing erect, addressed the governor in Spanish.

"Greeting, Excellency! Have I your permission to come ashore?"

His Excellency strode to the end of the mole and called through his cupped, gauntleted hands.

"Are you English?"

"We are."

The governor gestured them away imperiously. "You cannot land here!" he warned. "It is against the law!"

Magnus feigned amazement. "How now? What law is this you quote, sire? Surely not the law of hospitality which the Spanish revere! Nor can it be the law of the sea, by which succor is granted impartially to all mariners in difficulty! Are not our blessed sovereigns at peace? Come, your Magnificence—bid us welcome!"

The long boat had drifted close enough for them to see the governor's scowl. Once again, he motioned them away.

"Depart as you came!" he commanded. "My orders are explicit. We will fire upon you if you attempt to set foot on Spanish soil!"

Magnus wagged his hand regretfully and, turning his back on the governor, looked out into the harbor, where the changing tide had swung the *Sparrow* broadside to the town. Sighing audibly, he faced the governor.

"Your Excellency," he said grimly, "you compel me to be blunt. Despite the obvious fact—as you can plainly see—that my ship is too heavily laden with guns and soldiers, it is not my purpose, and certainly not my wish, to sack this town. To speak true, we had not meant to sail this way at all, being bound for the Guineas, but were driven hence by wind and weather. We are in dire need of victuals

242

and water for our large contingent, yet I would obtain them by peaceful means—*if possible.*"

The governor shot an apprehensive glance at the black muzzles protruding from the bark, then squared his jaw.

"My orders, *señor* . . ." he began, but Magnus cut him short.

"Surely, your Grace, your orders leave you room for discretion! Why, barely a month agone, the *corregidor* of Vigo supplied our fleet at Drake's request."

"*Drake!*" gasped the governor incredulously. "*Valgame Dios!* Are you with Drake?"

"I was," Magnus admitted, "before the storm blew me thither." When he sensed the consternation caused by the mere mention of Sir Francis, he added a bit more fuel to the fire. "But, come, sire, that need not concern you. As I stated, our destination is the Guineas, and my only purpose here is to re-water and overtake my admiral. However, I cannot continue in my present condition, and it would embarrass me greatly to have him come in search of me. That would be awkward for both you and me, for I know he would resent it."

It became apparent his Excellency did not desire a visitation by Francis Drake.

"Precisely what do you require?" he temporized.

"To come ashore," snapped Magnus, "and not stand here shrieking back and forth like a fish peddler!"

The governor capitulated, and when Magnus and Ben Absedik stepped ashore, he greeted them with strained courtesy, and introduced himself as Don Sanchez de Oquendo. Having disposed of that formality, he curtly repeated his question as to their requirements.

Magnus was not to be hurried. He ignored the hauteur and talked genially about his general need for victuals and water. But while chatting, he maneuvered around so that Don Sanchez could not help facing the harbor.

"*Ay Dios mío*, Magnificence, it has been a fatiguing voyage!" he remarked conversationally. "Due to the foundering of another bark, which we had to abandon, I am sorely overloaded with men and guns. Believe me, sire, if you have any use for such ponderous artillery, I'd be tempted to exchange the whole batch for a half-dozen small bronze culverins or the like."

It was irresistible bait, for no island fortress in Spain's fast-growing western empire ever had sufficient guns of heavy caliber. Magnus saw Don Sanchez' eyes glitter momentarily, then veil.

"Now it is barely possible I can oblige you in that," said the governor with studied casualness. "By a coincidence, we have a surplus of artillery."

243

"In which case, we should both profit," laughed Magnus. "And by the way, your Excellency, forgive me if I do not invite you and your staff aboard. These soldiers my admiral foisted on me are a surly, undisciplined lot, spoiling for trouble. Another reason for making my stay as brief as possible."

Don Sanchez bowed to cover his surprise at the temerity of this English cub who even dreamed that a grandee of Spain would set foot on his accursed ship.

"I understand," he purred suavely. "An incident would be unfortunate."

"Most unfortunate, sire! And while I have threatened to hang the first man who makes a hostile move during our visit, I would be most grateful if your Grace would instruct your subjects not to take their boats within pistol-shot of the bark. I find it advisable to use precautions before an event rather than punishment afterward."

The governor appraised Magnus with growing respect. "I shall attend the matter at once. We also wish to avoid unpleasantness." He barked an order to an officer near by, then turned back to Magnus.

"You speak excellent Spanish for a foreigner," he observed.

Magnus smiled. "Your Grace flatters me! Howbeit, I have spent considerable time in Spain. As a matter of fact, I recently had as a guest on my ship, the Licentiate de Escober. We voyaged to England together. A true Spaniard, that De Escober. I enjoyed having him aboard. You know him, perhaps?"

Oquendo was impressed. "By name only. But ten thousand pardons for keeping you standing here, sir! If you will do me the honor of accompanying me to the palace, we can discuss our business in comfort."

His manner indicated plainly he expected Magnus to refuse to stray from the protection of his men and ship, but the latter accepted with alacrity.

"Gladly, your Magnificence! Just give me leave to dispatch my boat back to the ship, and my aide and I shall be at your service." Up to this moment, Don Sanchez had pointedly ignored the presence of the Moor. "As a commander, sire," Magnus continued, smiling, "you can understand it was prudent to make certain arrangements in case . . . well, until I could ascertain the manner of my reception. My officers will be happy to learn of your reasonableness, and so release the gunners from their stations."

Leaving the governor to swallow this audacity, Magnus strolled to the edge of the mole. He gave Tim a significant wink, then in a clear voice commanded: "Return to the ship, Mr. Prettyman, and have the gunners close their ports. I am going to the palace with his Excellency. You may return for me here in two hours."

"Aye, aye, sor!" Tim answered briskly, pulling his forelock. "An' if ye ain't back in two hours, sor? Does we raze the town accordin' to plan?"

Out of the corner of his eye, Magnus saw Oquendo pale slightly. So—the dog understood English, did he? Magnus chuckled inwardly, but his voice was stern.

"I am satisfied that extremity will not be necessary, Mr. Pretty-man. His Grace has shown himself an honorable gentleman, in which case, we will transact our business in peace and amity and leave him richer than before. Now, away with you, man!"

As the long boat pulled away, Magnus rejoined his host and, for the first time, became conscious of the silent coterie of officers surrounding them, mute and shadowy as painted figures on a drop curtain. Even Don Sanchez appeared slightly ludicrous in his desperate effort to maintain the dignity of rank in this lonely outpost. He was personally unprepossessing. He looked to Magnus like a puppet made from scraps in the Lord's workshop. His long, mulish face belonged to a very tall man, whereas his Excellency was short and squat, with bowed, spindly legs which were not designed to carry so much weight. He had small boar's eyes, and a ridiculous beak of a nose which the Creator must have intended for a giant breed of parrot. The total effect was almost pathetic, and perhaps it was owing to a conscious effort to offset this grim jest of Nature that Don Sanchez surrounded himself with all the panoply he could muster. His manner was haughty and cold (at least as far as he dared under the present circumstances) and his clothes and armor were of the best. He maintained an official staff, like a conquering Caesar, but these, too, were caricatures, being mostly ancient pensioners, too feeble for active service.

Magnus bowed. "We are at your service, your Grace."

Don Sanchez rapped an order to his aide-de-camp, and horses were led up. Abu Ben Absedik grimaced at the old nag allotted him, but mounted without a word. Magnus did likewise, but his Excellency required assistance to get his grotesque body into the saddle of his richly caparisoned stallion. As soon as he was settled, a drum commenced to roll. Officers bellowed commands, a trumpet let go a blast that sent several hundred tropical birds wailing into the air, then the little procession moved pompously through the press of awed citizenry. Something about the setting reminded Magnus of the *auto de fe*—the pomp, the trumpets and drums, the glitter and clanking accouterments. This was the kind of pageantry the Spaniards loved.

When they cleared the main portion of the town, Magnus found himself riding beside the Moor. He leaned over and whispered, "What do you make of this clown, Abu?"

Ben Absedik's eyes frosted as he stared at the governor's stiff spine jolting just ahead.

"A jackal with the courage of a dove and the heart of an adder. The venom sac shows plainly through his eyes."

Magnus laughed. "You overrate him. He's just a common garden snake. I could crush his slimy head with my heel."

The Moor's thin mouth curled. "Do not attempt it with bare feet, O my brother. He hath many fangs!" Abu inclined his head toward the soldiery behind.

However, on reaching the pillared portico of the palace, whereupon the guard was dismissed, Don Sanchez seemed to abandon his haughty, stiff-necked role and became the perfect host. Chairs were placed in the patio so that Magnus and Ben Absedik could savor the incomparable panorama while savoring equally incomparable wine.

All the latent sensitivity and artistry in Magnus was awakened by the commanding beauty. Truly, this must be the legendary *Siren's Isle!* Far, far below, the little *Sparrow* nested on the water, like a black onyx set in a silver crest. Out beyond the protecting arms of sand, the eternal swells of the Main rolled in from hazy horizons. A profusion of strange flowers made of the land a palette fit for the painting of rainbows. It was a setting to drug the senses.

Yet when Magnus, drunk with beauty, turned to his companion, he found Abu staring speculatively at a huge black vulture wheeling in the sky. Don Sanchez having left them momentarily, the Moor nodded at the bird of prey.

"Allah hath sent us an omen!" he said softly. "Mark it well!"

Magnus laughed. His ruse had succeeded, and he was in no mood for omens. Before he could reply, Don Sanchez returned with his wife and presented them. It was soon manifest that the good woman did not share her husband's antipathy for strangers, for she was embarrassingly effusive in her welcome. The dykes of loneliness burst under the impact of guests, and she inundated them with her story of isolation, her anguish at being parted from family and friends, her yearning for her native land, and, above all else, her insatiable hunger to see a gentlewoman. When she begged to know if Magnus had a wife aboard, he was tempted to answer affirmatively. But he kept his wits and told her that, deeply as he regretted it, he had no wife aboard.

Don Sanchez seized upon the disappointed pause to usher out his wife, and when he returned, the men settled down to business.

246

Having sensed that the governor's chief interest was in the guns, Magnus brought up the subject first. He proposed to rid himself of eight demi-cannon and three culverins—if Don Sanchez could use them. Don Sanchez could, and in return, he promised a bronze falcon, three sacres and two demi-culverins, with ample shot for all. In addition, he agreed to furnish them with twelve prime bullocks and all the fresh water they could carry away.

Magnus appeared well satisfied until Don Sanchez betrayed his own eagerness, then Magnus hesitated. After some reflection, he admitted the deal hinged largely on whether he could careen his bark in the vicinity. Her bottom was foul, he confessed candidly, and unless he had her cleaned, he doubted he could overtake Francis Drake. Could Don Sanchez grant him the sanctuary of a convenient cove?

It was Don Sanchez' turn to hesitate. He rested his bearded chin on his fingertips and considered. Watching him, Magnus imagined he could see the idea revolving in the Spaniard's mind, like a fowl turning on a spit. Finally, Don Sanchez nodded. As it happened, there was a nearly landlocked cove within three miles of Punta Arenas which Magnus might use to careen. Regarding the delicate question of privacy during this operation, Don Sanchez suggested that Magnus station a few soldiers on the bluffs overlooking the cove, as the only conceivable danger might be from the Cimaroons—former Negro slaves who had run away from their Spanish masters and mated with native Indians. Occasionally, these renegades caused trouble, but it was nothing to worry about.

Magnus accepted the offer, and the governor sketched out the details of the cove. The latter had grown increasingly affable during the discussion, and Magnus found the change more offensive than the earlier hauteur. He was puzzled how to solve the problem of getting the Spanish guns without having any of his own to produce, when Don Sanchez volunteered a suggestion: if *Señor* Carter wished to facilitate matters, he might debark his heavy guns on the mole at once, and then take his lightened bark around to the cove for careening and repairs. This would save time and labor, and when the job was completed, the bark could then return to the mole at Punta Arenas to pick up the small guns and victuals which Don Sanchez would have waiting. It was admirably simple!

Magnus restrained his impatience with difficulty. How typically Spanish! He forced a smile, and offered a counter-suggestion: rather than put his benefactor to the inconvenience of dragging the heavy guns through the town and up the hill to the fort, Magnus would take them around to the cove in his own ship and have his men hoist them to the bluffs. This would be better for everyone, he insisted; it would give his accursed extra soldiers something with which to occupy themselves while the sailors were working on the ship, the guns would protect the bark against any chance ship stumbling into the cove while she was careened and therefore helpless, and at the same time, leave the guns in a convenient spot to be transported over comparatively level ground to the fort when Magnus sailed.

Before Don Sanchez could catch his breath, Magnus proposed that, in order to speed his own departure and avoid the necessity of bringing the bark back to Punta Arenas—and, of course, risk a possible incident—his men could pick up the light bronze guns in the long boat, while the bark was being careened, and ferry them back to the cove.

Don Sanchez balked at first, for the plan was as crude as his own. But since he had been the first to ask trust, he could not now exhibit distrust without giving offense. He sparred as long as he dared, then covered his chagrin with a bow of assent. Thus the conference ended.

Magnus had no opportunity to speak privately to Ben Absedik until they were ensconced finally in the long boat and clear of the mole. Then he burst into laughter.

"How now, my gloomy friend? Did we not gull the jackal?"

The Moor shrugged. "In any battle of wits there is room for error. Do not forget that treachery is instinctive in a Spaniard, whereas with thy English, it is a game of chance. The wise man sticks to his own way, my brother. The hawk does not attempt to out-dig the mole; he uses the wings Allah gave him to swoop in for a quick kill and flees."

Magnus grinned. "Still seeing omens, eh?"

"What is written is written!" warned the Moor.

Tim was itching with curiosity, but Magnus had signaled him to ask no questions in front of the hands, so he had to be satisfied with the smug smile on Magnus' face. As soon as they climbed aboard the *Sparrow*, they were met by Brother Diego and Rosalind, equally hungry for news.

Leaving Ben Absedik in charge of the deck, Magnus took the others below.

"Well," he announced to the anxious trio, "his Excellency is going to supply us with fine bronze guns, plenty of shot, twelve prime bullocks and a safe place to careen!"

They all stared, wide-eyed. "Say you so?" gasped Tim. "An' w'at miracle d'ye perform to induce such kindness from a Spaniard? A poniard to 'is gullet, perchance?"

248

Magnus assumed an expression of pain. "You do me wrong, Timothy! It was a fair trade. Because Don Sanchez was so strongly impressed by those fine black cannon leering at him from our ports, I gallantly agreed to give him the lot in return for his bounty."

Tim howled with mirth. "Blast my buttocks! Ain't ye the one!" He banged his wooden leg on the floor. "Damme, I'd like to a-seen it! Can the men go ashore now? They be grumblin' about . . ."

Magnus cut him short. "Absolutely *not!* There will be other ports and other women, but we cannot risk it here. If Don Sanchez so much as guessed we had no guns, he'd pounce on us immediately!"

Rosalind shuddered. "Good Lord, Magnus! Could he do that?"

"Aye, if he suspected the truth. As matters stand now, he is only too anxious to help us get away without ado."

Brother Diego wagged his head in bewilderment. "It strikes me, Magnus, that this Don Sanchez is either a complete imbecile, or . . . a very dangerous man."

" 'Pon my soul! You don't give me much credit!" complained Magnus.

The priest smiled. "That was unworthy of you, my son! Are we not good friends who can speak candidly, or do you prefer flattery to frankness?"

"I'm sorry, *padre.* Speak your mind."

"Very well then. It appears to me the thing went off too easily."

"How so? I offered him too good a bargain to resist. His avarice made him leap at the opportunity."

Brother Diego held up a warning finger. "The very point I do not like. A Spaniard does not *leap* in any business matter. That is an English trait, for trade being their primary source of income, they are trained to quick decisions. But Spaniards are not traders, and therefore difficult to hurry. Remember, my son, I am Spanish, and I know my countrymen's characteristics."

Magnus shrugged indifferently. "What else could he do? I had him pinned against the wall!"

"Precisely! And, having no choice, he agreed to everything you suggested. However, that does not mean he will abide by what he said. To a *hidalgo,* a promise is little more than a polite phrase, made for the sake of courtesy or expediency, but carrying no moral obligation. You English lay great stress on your word; it becomes a point of honor. But you err sadly when you expect other peoples to govern themselves by your native codes."

Magnus scowled. This was a facet he had not considered. The priest did not wait for an answer.

"Don Sanchez, by Spanish standards, could trap you without impairing his honor. In fact, my son, in the eyes of his King, he would

249

be derelict in honor if he failed to do just that. And do not overlook this point—you are not only the instigator of the matter, but also the main deceiver. For no matter what Don Sanchez may do about his promises, you cannot keep your word because you have no cannon to give him!"

Magnus grinned sourly. "*Padre*, you have the happy faculty of making even the Almighty appear in the wrong! Perhaps you should have tackled Don Sanchez?"

"Heaven forbid!" laughed the priest. "Nay, lad, you misunderstand me. Who more than I have reason to hope for your complete success, for though I am in orders, I do not wish for martyrdom. All I seek to do is put you on your guard against treachery, certainly not discourage you. Tell me—have you worked out the details of this astounding trade?"

Magnus glanced at Rosalind, who watched him with eager, curious eyes. She smiled when she met his look and slipped a small cool hand over his.

Thus encouraged, Magnus outlined his plan: they would haul around to the cove as soon as possible. The men would be divided into three groups; one, under Tim Prettyman, would take the long boat and row around to the mole to pick up the guns; a second group, commanded by the wily Moor, would patrol the cliffs above the cove to guard against Cimaroons or any treachery of the Spaniards; the remainder of the men would careen and repair the *Sparrow*.

Brother Diego pursed his lips. "Perchance it is the only course, yet by splitting up our small force so drastically, we leave ourselves almost defenseless if the governor attempts an assault."

"Granted. But with the *Sparrow* high and dry on the beach, we'd be comparatively helpless in any case."

"Would it not be wiser to wait until we get the guns *before* careening? You realize, Magnus, we have only two demi-culverins at the moment!"

"I know, but to wait for the guns would cost us at least a full day. I can't waste that much time. The *Triumph* and the *San Philip* will doubtless sail this way within the week."

"Why are you so certain, my sweet?" asked Rosalind.

Magnus chuckled. "Because it is so obvious, Roz. Having let Drake's fleet slip through their fingers, those noble minions of our hand-holding Majesties won't dare show their faces at home without you. And with so few harbors in these waters, it is inevitable they stop in Punta Arenas. Don Sanchez will supply them with a fresh spoor to follow."

250

Rosalind frowned thoughtfully. "You say they won't dare go home without *me!* I thought they were looking for you, as well?"

"I'm merely secondary," laughed Magnus. "They'll just hang me out of hand."

"If they catch you," observed Brother Diego.

"*If* they catch me. And since I can't proceed without repairs and guns, I intend to get them as expeditiously as possible."

Brother Diego spread his hands in resignation. "Sobeit! As your Drake says—something must be left to chance. Let us hope Don Sanchez de Oquendo does not learn the truth until we are gone."

Book Four

THE TRAP

Chapter 27

Dawn found the *Sparrow* hovering off the beach, awaiting sufficient light to discover the tortuous passage. Though the cove itself was visible from the sea, the entrance was concealed by two prongs of land which overlapped each other in such a fashion that a vessel had to make the course of a tight S to gain admittance. With the first light, the long boat, guided by Tim, crept in to sound the channel. The bark followed at a safe distance.

Magnus had climbed the masthead so that he could survey the conformation of the bottom. He distrusted his information, yet somewhat to his surprise, he found the details Don Sanchez had given him were accurate, and on the north shore, as the sketch showed, he saw the patch of corn-colored sand which indicated a formation of rock-free shelving. He signaled the long boat to explore it.

Once through the crooked passage, the steep bluffs cut off the wind, and the *Sparrow's* graying wings fluttered helplessly. Magnus called back the long boat and had a line passed for her to tow the bark onto the ledge, as the tide was high. When she grounded, he ordered the towing hawser secured to a giant ceiba tree ashore and an anchor carried out astern to hold her in position.

By the time all this had been accomplished, the sun had spied them over the rim of forest. There was no escape from her overpowering attentions, for not a breath of wind entered the bowl-like cove. The bark soon became unbearable, so when Rosalind begged to go ashore, Magnus detailed two men to protect her and set up an awning on the beach. At the same time, he called off ten of his best fighters to accompany Ben Absedik to patrol the bluffs. The rest were set to lightening the vessel.

It was grueling labor in the insufferable heat, yet by midday the *Sparrow* lay over on her side on the golden sands, her starboard bottom naked and exposed by the receding tide. Magnus waded into the shallow to examine the damage. The bottom was thick with grass and barnacles, and there was evidence of worms, yet the actual damage from grounding was relatively slight. The garboard was badly sprung, but the carpenter was already starting to refasten it and his mates were scrubbing the hull preparatory to recaulking. Magnus went over the planking inch by inch. He found a few tender spots and realized, as the carpenter had forewarned, it would take a week to do a thorough job, but he could not spare the time. The important thing now was to stop the leaks and get away as soon as possible. He summoned Tim.

"You'd best be on your way," he told the old man. "I reckon you should make Punta Arenas by four bells. The governor promised the guns would be waiting on the mole. Don't tarry, and for God's sake don't let a single man out of your sight! I doubt not Don Sanchez will be there in person to sound you out. Keep your conversation to a minimum and warn the men to hold their tongues, for the dog understands English, though he pretends he does not. Our very lives depend on your caution, my friend."

Tim nodded his understanding. "Aye, lad, I'll 'old a straight course. It shouldn't take long fer stowin' the guns."

"In which case, you should be back here by the second dog watch. And remember, Tim, darkness falls swiftly in these latitudes. If there is any delay or argument about the guns, return at once. Is that clear?"

Tim agreed, and hurried off with his crew. But as Magnus watched the long boat flit across the water, he was seized with a momentary touch of panic, for nothing is more nerve-wracking to a seaman than having his vessel helpless on the beach. When the long boat had disappeared around the headland, he glanced toward the strip of sand where Rosalind lay beneath her canvas shelter like an oriental princess. He smiled and shed his worries. Perhaps he would camp there with her tonight. The thought buoyed him, so peeling off his shirt, he went to work with a caulking iron.

A forge had been set up on shore, and under Brother Diego, new iron bands were fashioned for the water casks. Ben Absedik had discovered a spring close by, and his men brought down bunches of wild fruit to refresh the laborers. All the long afternoon, the cove echoed to the noise of hammers and the cheerful jests of the hands until the incoming tide made work impossible. Magnus kept at it until the water reached his chest, then gave up.

After scraping the tar off his arms and face, he donned his shirt and walked down the beach. He did not share in the general optimism; he felt nervous and restless. Behind him, the *Sparrow* was trying to right herself, like a horse staggering to its feet after a fall. He couldn't bear to watch her, for it only heightened his awareness of her vulnerability. He shuddered to think that on the morrow the whole procedure would have to be repeated on the larboard side, and he vowed inwardly he would never put himself to such torture again.

He found Brother Diego with Rosalind under the awning, while the two guards were attempting to make a smudge fire against the sudden influx of insects. As he settled himself in the shade beside them, Ben Absedik strode up.

"By the beard of the Prophet!" fumed the Moor. "This is indeed a veritable Gehenna on earth! The whole place stinks as of molten brimstone and these accursed bugs must carry spears!"

Magnus grinned ruefully. "Aye, it is that, Abu, yet methinks another day will see the end. With any luck at all, we should leave on the second morning. Did you see any Spaniards?"

The Moor shrugged. "Nay, yet I did discover a mule road that leads to Punta Arenas. I followed it to within sight of the fort—a distance of a league or so."

The priest looked concerned. "Did Oquendo speak of such a road, Magnus?"

"No, damn him, he did not! You'd better keep it under sharp surveillance, Abu!"

"That has been done, *effendi!*"

A sudden cry from a lookout startled them. "*Ahoy, Cap'n! Long boat's returnin'!*"

Magnus sprang to his feet in alarm. The others followed suit.

"Tim certainly made a quick trip," remarked Brother Diego.

"Too bloody quick!" growled Magnus. "He wasn't expected for another two hours!"

They walked out onto the spit to watch the boat come in. She was literally soaring through the water, and old Tim could be seen braced in the sternsheets, gesturing the oarsmen to added effort. The instant the boat grounded, the old man hobbled ashore.

"The *San Philip's* come!" he announced cryptically.

"*Where?* Is she in Punta Arenas?"

Tim gulped for breath. "I didn't wait to fin' out," he panted. "Jes' as we rounded the point to go into the 'arbor, I spotted 'er comin' up from the south! I near broke me arse gettin' back 'ere. We better get under weigh right smart."

The others looked at Magnus, but he was staring at the *Sparrow*, securely embedded in the sand. The present tide was already ebbing, and it would be morning before there was any possibility of floating her. And morning would be too late.

Tim had already grasped the situation. "Ye could get aw'y in the long boat, lad," he suggested.

"And leave some of my men? You know damn well the long boat won't carry us all!"

"It might be the best solution," the priest said. "After all, Magnus, your position is the most hazardous."

"Don't talk nonsense!" Magnus snapped impatiently. "If they didn't find me, they'd wreak their vengeance on the others. We've had a taste of Spanish justice. I'm staying with my ship."

"An 'ell of a ship!" observed Tim. "More like a ruddy barn, she be, set solid on land."

Magnus ignored that. "Did you sight the *Triumph?*"

"No, lad. Belike she's still stuck on the shoal, fer she grounded under full canvas. Mebbe the *San Philip* is on'y after assistance fer 'er."

"That may be her reason for coming to Punta Arenas," admitted Magnus, "but Oquendo is certain to report our visit. Then . . ." He shrugged. "If I thought it would do any good, I'd walk into town and give myself up."

"Now 'oo's talkin' nonsense!" stormed Tim. "By God, I'd knock ye on the 'ead an' truss ye up like a bullock if ye tried it!" He shook a ponderous fist in Magnus' face. "Blast my buttocks, we started this bloody cruise together an' we'll finish it together, else me nyme's not Timothy Prettyman!"

Tim's vehemence broke the tension, and the men all laughed. Rosalind, however, was white with fear.

"Don't you worry, sweetheart," Magnus told her, putting his arm around her shoulder. "We'll see that nothing happens to you."

"Aye," growled Tim. "The worst ye got to look for'ard to is goin' back to that bastard Beckles. The rest o' us'll swing!"

"By Allah!" jeered the Moor. "Why fill in the graves before the bodies are buried? Truly, O my brothers, I never felt more alive than at this moment!"

"Well said, Abu!" laughed Brother Diego. "We have still twelve hours' grace, at least, for the *San Philip* cannot reach us tonight. And if the wind dies with the sun, she may not get here in the morning. Be assured, Magnus, we will finish the cruise with you, as Timothy puts it."

A warm glow of pride stole over Magnus. Here were true friends indeed! He felt slightly ashamed of his indecision.

"Good enough," he said, grinning. "Abu, dispatch some scouts to cover the Punta Arenas road, for Don Sanchez may try to flank us. Station a couple of lookouts on the headland to watch for the *San Philip*. Tim, you and the *padre* . . ."

"Please, Magnus!" protested Rosalind. "Let Father Diego stay with me! I'm terrified."

258

To this, Magnus acceded willingly. Brother Diego, being of her faith, could comfort her and leave Magnus free.

"By all means, *padre*, stay with Roz. Tim, take some men and re-water. Don't waste time with containers—just fill the long boat and bail her into the casks. We haven't time to be squeamish. But first, take me aboard."

He started for the boat when, to his embarrassment, Rosalind threw herself into his arms.

"Oh, Magnus, Magnus!" she sobbed. "I've brought you nothing but trouble!"

He kissed her tears away. "*Trouble*, sweetheart? Bless you, you've brought me the only happiness I've ever known!" He glanced over her shoulder at the priest. "Make her comfortable, *padre*."

As Brother Diego led her down the spit, Magnus climbed into the long boat.

During the time Tim and his crew were ferrying water aboard, Magnus remained perched on the masthead, studying the approaches to the cove. It seemed improbable the *San Philip* would attempt to negotiate the narrow channel, since Oquendo would tell her captain that the *Sparrow* was heavily armed. On the other hand, the warship could lay off the entrance and fire her salvos into the bark without danger to herself, or she might elect to guard the passage and make the assault with shore boats. What was obvious to Magnus was the fact that the choice of action lay with the *San Philip*, not with the *Sparrow*.

By eight of the clock, the water casks were filled and the ship readied. It only remained for the morning tide to float her. Magnus sent Tim ashore with the boat to bring Rosalind and Brother Diego aboard.

Meanwhile, he loitered on deck, savoring the night. The moon had not yet risen, yet the stars were so bright it seemed like twilight. Before a faint offshore breeze came the tantalizing scent of the jungle. The whole ship was redolent with the pungent odor of warm pitch and oakum. All his senses were attuned to the setting.

When he saw the silhouette of the boat crossing the cove, he sauntered down to the gangway to await it. He was a trifle surprised when the priest came over the rail first, but when Tim Prettyman came next, his surprise turned to alarm.

"Where's Rosalind?" he demanded.

For a moment, he received no answer. He could not see their faces in the semi-darkness, yet their manner bespoke trouble. The big frame of Brother Diego appeared bowed. Tim, after a silent pause, turned away.

259

"Answer me!" roared Magnus. "Where is she?"

The oarsmen were climbing over the rail, so the priest took Magnus by the arm.

"Let us go to the cabin," he suggested quietly.

Magnus jerked away in fury, then controlled himself. Brother Diego was already stalking aft, so Magnus followed him down to the cabin. Once inside, the priest set his back against the bulkhead and stared sadly at the other.

"Magnus—she's gone!" he announced.

"*Gone?* Gone where?"

"To Punta Arenas!"

Magnus stared incredulously. "What are you talking about?" he gasped. "How could she go to Punta Arenas?"

Brother Diego exhaled wearily. "She walked. She wanted to return to her husband!"

"She wanted . . . ?" Magnus' legs gave way and he dropped into a chair. "You let her go? *You*, whom I trusted as a friend!"

The priest started across the room, then thought better of it and remained where he was.

"I had no choice, my son!"

Magnus staggered erect. "By God, I'll settle with you later!" Magnus stormed. "Right now, I'll overtake her. . . ." He started for the companionway, but the other's calm voice gave him pause.

"You can't overtake her, Magnus! She left several hours ago, and is there long ere this."

Magnus turned slowly into the cabin. He stared at the priest, his fingers twitching on the hilt of his poniard. Brother Diego read the look correctly, and shrugged.

"Suppose you hear me out," he counseled.

"Talk!"

Brother Diego sat down. "Fortunately, I can tell you the whole story," he said. "Rosalind granted me that."

"Really? Am I supposed to be grateful?" sneered Magnus.

"*I* am, at least. As you are painfully aware, Magnus, I am a priest, and, as such, obligated to receive confessions and bound never to divulge them. Well, Rosalind, being a Catholic, wanted to confess. I had no choice. She told me she had grown increasingly unhappy under these conditions and desired to return to the security of her marriage."

"You lie, Valesco! You talked her into it!"

The priest sighed. "You don't believe that, Magnus. What you mean, I think, is that I didn't talk her *out* of it. That much—I concede. You cannot force a woman to love you. People are what they are. Rosalind had . . ."

260

"Just tell me one thing—*did she tell you she did not love me?*"

"She told me she loved wealth and position more."

"I can't believe it! Oh, the bitch, the treacherous bitch!"

"My son, my son!" pleaded the priest. "You are not being realistic. Love blinded you to things you should have seen! Do not blame the child for things over which she had no control! She was raised to revere wealth, position, affluence. Her whole outlook was colored by those views. You yourself admitted her father set a minimum limit on the gold you had first to acquire before possessing her. How could you expect her to judge life by any other standards than the ones she was taught? We all—you, me, Tim and the Moor—are products of our early environment! We all differ in our philosophy of life."

"But we don't lie about it!" fumed Magnus. "Why, damme, she ran into my arms and kissed me when we parted! From what you tell me—she knew even then she was going to betray me!"

"Betray you, Magnus?"

"What else? She will tell the Spaniards we have practically no guns, that we are still aground and helpless!"

Brother Diego sighed again. "I doubt not they'll get the truth out of her, yet such was not her intent. That I know. She had a romantic notion that her husband would abandon his search for you if he got her back. She said she was going to tell him your ship had already sailed."

"You shouldn't have let her go, Valesco!"

"Frankly, I considered stopping her," the priest admitted, "but I was bound by my vows. I did beg of her one boon—that I might tell you the truth. She granted that, and I gave her absolution."

"Better you had slit her throat!"

Brother Diego smiled ruefully. "Magnus, you accuse her of changeability, yet five minutes ago you thought you loved her with all your power, now you think you hate her. Does not that prove my contention that we all have devious sides to our natures, unpredictable qualities that crop out when least expected."

"I weary of your philosophy," Magnus growled. "God's life! Do you defend a treachery that may cause the death of all these men of ours?"

"You are unreasonable. Her conduct is no more responsible for their plight than yours in bringing them in here. It is a matter of whose ox is being gored, Magnus. When it was your pleasure, no risk was too great. Now that Rosalind has suffered a change in heart, you want to blame the whole thing on her."

Magnus, despite his shock, was struck by the logic of this. Yet he wasn't prepared to admit it.

"Well, I'm glad somebody can find an excuse for her."

"It is not my privilege to excuse or accuse," the other retorted. "My only reaction is one of sympathy. The child is to be pitied. She will never know real happiness, because she lacks the capacity for it. Transient pleasures, possibly, for these can be purchased with gold and affluence. But the enjoyment of life is an art she cannot acquire. That is the tragedy—not what she may have done to you."

"She's certainly ruined any chance of happiness for me!"

Brother Diego laughed gently. "Oh, come now, my son; it is not as serious as all that. At the risk of being brutal, I think you are very fortunate."

Magnus started out of his chair in temper, then sank back.

"You cannot see it," continued the priest. "But, consider—since she is so beset by fear is it not infinitely better that she return to her husband now, while she has the opportunity of doing it gracefully, than that she should stay with you against her judgment and have her discontent turn into loathing? Had such a thing occurred, Magnus, you would suffer tenfold what you suffer now."

Magnus made no reply. His mind was in a tumult. Unable to face the bald truth, he sought desperately to shift the blame on someone else. He scowled up into the face of the priest. That did not help him. The wide, frank eyes were like mirrors which reflected his own weakness. The scowl faded.

"I'm sorry, *padre*," he acknowledged wearily. "You are right—as usual."

Brother Diego laid a big hand on his knee. "Nay, lad, let me beg your forgiveness. There is scant satisfaction in being right when it causes hurt to others. I confess—had I believed it would have assured you lasting happiness—I would have ignored my vows and dragged her back here."

Magnus shook his head. "Under the circumstances, I'm glad you didn't." He rubbed his hands over his eyes, as if to clear his vision. "I guess I just don't understand people. I was confounded when Drake, with his reputation for hardness, acted the way he did toward me, and now Rosalind . . . ! I'm confused."

The priest smiled. "That's because you are an idealist, Magnus; you attempt to fit everyone into the particular niche you have prepared for him. Unfortunately, human nature is too complex for that. Only a very few are what might be termed single-purposed. Good old Timothy belongs in that category; loyal to a fault, dependable, aye, even predictable. But most people, like Francis Drake and Rosalind—and you yourself, my son—are many-sided, presenting different faces to different circumstances. Hence, saints become sinners, and sinners, saints. As I observed once before, we are made up of

262

our pasts, thus all our actions are results of previous happenings. Only God can foretell how each of us will react to a given circumstance."

The brisk tap-tapping of Tim's peg along the companionway broke up the discussion. The old man entered self-consciously.

"Yer pardon, lad," he announced himself gruffly, "but word's come from the Moor. The lookout 'e posted down the coast reports the *San Philip* 'eadin' this w'y!"

Magnus stared at him, but the old man avoided his eyes. Magnus felt ashamed.

"Thank you, Tim. We'll give them a merry welcome!"

"A right bloody welcome, wi' our arses caught in the mud!"

Magnus recalled what Brother Diego had said about Tim but a moment before—*single-purposed, loyal, dependable, even predictable*. Aye, how true; how blessedly true! The knowledge warmed him like wine.

He stood up, revivified. "To work, my friends! We're not whipped yet! Summon the Moor!"

Chapter 28

W̲HEN Ben Absedik arrived, they held a council of war. Magnus reviewed briefly the situation. They had a total of less than fifty men; the *San Philip* would doubtless carry over two hundred, and, in addition, Don Sanchez was almost certain to send a foot company overland to flank them. They had two medium-sized guns; the Spanish warship would have at least twenty, and of large caliber. The *Sparrow*, being still aground, was useless, therefore they would have to fight on land. However, land, in this case, meant an island on which, without food, their little company would inevitably be starved, if not taken. Hence, as Magnus saw it, their only salvation lay in offense. They would seize the *San Philip* when she came through the passage!

The sheer audacity of this left the others speechless, but Magnus afforded them no time to recover. He quickly outlined his plan of action. Though reckless in the extreme, they had no counter suggestions, and as desperation is the mistress of the impossible, they went busily to work.

At the narrowest point of the passage into the cove, the two fingers of land formed a bottleneck. Here the banks were high enough to look down upon the decks of a passing ship, and here they placed their guns. In the darkness, it was dangerous, man-killing labor, and before the guns were set up and concealed with brush, the *San Philip* was visible, ghosting up the coast in the light airs. Magnus ordered enough food, powder and shot to last two days removed from the *Sparrow,* after which she was abandoned, with a few lights left aboard so as to appear occupied.

Dispatching Ben Absedik to guard the Punta Arenas road, and leaving Tim in charge of the guns, Magnus and Brother Diego climbed the cliff that commanded a full view of the scene. They watched the Spanish warship approach with mixed emotions. In the dim light, she seemed to ride the track of the stars with a sort of dainty majesty; proud, queenly, viciously beautiful. When Magnus' eyes strayed to the little *Sparrow,* his heart constricted. She was irrevocably doomed.

"Why doesn't she hurry it up!" groaned Magnus. "I wish it was over!"

The priest chuckled. "Steady, my son! The enemy will not be guided by your wishes, depend on it."

Magnus laughed ruefully. "*Padre,* you are getting to be a visible conscience!"

"God forbid!"

"No, I am eternally grateful. I've learned much from you, and the Moor."

"You learn easily, Magnus. The important thing is to learn to know thyself."

"That's what I meant. Tell me—if we get out of this alive, what are you going to do? Will you come back to England with me?"

The priest draped a comradely arm about his shoulder. "What man can foresee the future? Only God knows the answers."

"Peradventure that is so. Yet plan we must, else we should never reach a destination. Is that not true?"

"I wonder?" mused the priest. "Did you plan to come to this spot?"

"Ah, but that was circumstance!"

"Exactly! As someone has said: Man proposes, God disposes. No, my son, I plot no courses, but accept **my** lot with as much grace as possible."

"Nevertheless, you must have a goal," Magnus persisted.

264

"A goal, aye; to fight evil where I find it. You forget, perhaps, that I am a soldier, Magnus, in the service of the Lord. I go where He commands." He laughed softly. "Now don't accuse me of talking religion; I am merely trying to answer your question. I thank you kindly for the invitation, but I'm afraid the peace and tranquility of England are not for me."

"Where then?"

Brother Diego shrugged. "I cannot tell you. Of late, I have had a peculiar feeling that God has chosen an especial task for me. I thought perhaps it was in Punta Arenas, for the sensation of destiny seemed overpowering there. It was as though I had reached the end of a long, long voyage."

Magnus grinned. "In all truth—you had."

"You are an irresistible pagan, Magnus!" Brother Diego straightened abruptly. "*Hola!* The *San Philip* is already off the entrance!"

Magnus, who had been comfortably ensconced against a tree, sprang to his feet. The speed of the warship had been deceptive; she was much closer than he had thought possible. He was about to hurry down to his post, when the priest caught his arm.

"Stay a moment! I'm afraid she's not going into the cove!"

It was so. As they watched, the *San Philip* glided past the mouth of the narrow channel, then gracefully came up into the wind to stop, almost directly under the cliff on which they stood. Her hook went down with a clatter and men swarmed into the rigging to furl her sails.

Magnus stared unbelievingly. Once again he had demonstrated his ignorance of Spanish psychology, and now his desperate scheme to turn defeat into victory had misfired. He had baited his own trap.

He dropped limply to the ground, half sick with frustration. Why hadn't he foreseen that Admiral Perrez would be too wary to risk running a perilous channel in the dark, when, by anchoring off the beach, he could sink the English bark at long range whenever he chose? Magnus cursed bitterly. Would he never learn not to judge the actions of others by his own impetuosity?

"I suspect this necessitates some change in our plans," Brother Diego observed mildly.

Magnus grunted. In his present state of mind, he found the priest's calmness irritating.

"There's only one thing to do," he growled. "I'll give myself up on the condition they permit my men to leave in peace."

Brother Diego laughed dryly. "Magnus, my friend, can't you see you are not in a position to dictate *conditions?* Come now, put aside this desire for sackcloth-and-ashes; the martyr's role ill becomes you. I've always heard that you English are at your best in adversity. Don't lose heart!"

The gentle rebuke conjured in Magnus' mind a remembrance of the talk he had had with Tim, lying in the hold of the ship on the way to Spain, when the old man had told him about Hawkins at St. John de Ulua: *"W'en the plight was darker'n this.* Did 'Awkins grovel an' w'ine?" old Tim had asked him. "No, by God, 'e called fer beer . . . an' sang out to all o' us: 'Fear nuthin', fer God, 'oo 'ath preserved me from this shot, will preserve us from these traitors an' villains!'" With a flush of shame, he recalled his later boast: "What Hawkins can do, I can do!" Dear Lord, how ill-chosen words could return to haunt one!

Because he could not face the priest, Magnus kept his eyes on the *San Philip,* and because he stared so long and hard, the new scheme was conceived. It did not come full-born this time; it was merely the sum of a long list of contributing factors—the wind, the tides, the darkness, and the probable maneuvers of the Spanish admiral.

It was obvious the latter was waiting for daylight before commencing the action. That was just good sense, for his quarry could not escape him. Perrez had anchored as close to the beach as he dared to get under the lee of the cliff in case of a violent offshore squall; at the same time, his guns covered the entrance to the cove, and he had taken the precaution to buoy his anchor hawse so he could slip it easily in an emergency. At the moment, the tide was ebbing, and the *San Philip* streamed away from the shore, but in a few hours, the tide would flood, and swing her close to the beach. He would then be in a position to finish the *Sparrow* with a couple of salvos. Doubtless, Don Sanchez' soldiers could be depended upon to capture any survivors. It was beautifully simple!

"*Padre,*" Magnus asked abruptly, "do you think it possible to drag our guns up here in the darkness?"

Brother Diego whistled softly. "Possible? Aye, anything is *possible,* my son! Yet it would be a herculean task, I confess. You have an idea?"

"Of a kind, aye!" He began falteringly, for his confidence in himself was badly shaken, but as he talked, his enthusiasm returned. They would mount their artillery on the bluff, and when the tide changed, Magnus would swim out to the *San Philip* and cut her anchor line. Once adrift, even if an alarm was raised, it would be impossible for Perrez to get out a second anchor quickly enough to prevent grounding—directly under the bluff. Then, Magnus' guns could sweep the decks at will, for the Spaniards would be unable to elevate their guns sufficiently high to return the fire. By making the decks untenable, the English gunners could control the situation until a boarding party took over.

Brother Diego heard him out in silence, but at the conclusion, he broke into soft laughter.

"Bless you, Magnus, this scheme is much superior to the other! It may have flaws, and God knows it borders on madness, yet at least you are taking advantage of your opponent's weaknesses, rather than your own, which, if not a Christian virtue, is admittedly practical."

"If we want to stay alive."

"Precisely. In which case, we had better get to work."

Dragging the heavy, awkward cannon up to the cliff was an inhuman task, yet, as the priest had remarked, the English are at their best in adversity. It was a choice between accomplishing the impossible or being slaughtered, and they chose the former. It was also a race with time, and Magnus kept an anxious eye on the eastern horizon, dreading the first approach of dawn.

The moment the guns topped the summit, Magnus sent for Ben Absedik. The Moor's depressing news acted as an additional spur, for he reported that a large company of soldiers had left Punta Arenas and was advancing slowly to reach the cove about daylight.

While the guns were being planted, Magnus gave his orders. Tim would remain in charge of the gunnery and choose sufficient men to assist him. The moment the *San Philip* drifted within range, he was to open fire with small shot and, if possible, pin the Spaniards below decks until the boarders took her. When that happened, Tim was to spike his guns over the cliff (so that Don Sanchez' men could not emulate their own action) and, with his men, make his way to the beach, where the long boat would return for them.

Meanwhile, the remaining hands, under Ben Absedik, would ready the long boat and move her as quickly as possible to the mouth of the cove, where they would wait until the barrage had taken effect. Their conduct from that point on was obvious.

Brother Diego would serve as liaison officer between the gun crew and the boarding party. Magnus would see to the cutting of the warship's hawse.

The priest disagreed flatly. "It would be utter folly for you to hazard that alone, Magnus! I am a powerful swimmer; let me accompany you?"

Magnus refused. He had no illusions about the risks involved, but when he gave voice to his objections, Brother Diego laughed at him.

267

"Your reasoning is illogical, my son," he returned. "The success of the whole matter depends on setting the *San Philip* adrift, hence it follows that, if you fail, the rest of us are doomed. Is it fair, then, to insist dogmatically on assuming the responsibility alone?"

Tim and Ben Absedik supported him. "Truly, *effendi*, Allah has put wisdom into the mouth of our unbelieving brother," argued the Moor. "The mouse that hath only one hole is soon caught. Since the risk is so great, it is better that it be divided between two of us, then if one be killed, the other may succeed."

Magnus grudgingly acquiesced, following which, a search was made among the company for the two sharpest knives. The tide had long since turned, and now it was the time for parting. Magnus dreaded this; he had a growing premonition that this was the last time the four would stand together, and the thought left him mute. Tim growled a gruff "Good luck, lads!" to cover his emotions, but the Moor clasped each by the hand in turn.

"May Allah the merciful guard and prosper thee both, my brothers!"

"God go with you also, Abu," said Brother Diego. He touched Magnus' arm. "Come, my son!"

Managing a brief farewell, Magnus followed the priest down to the beach.

The swells were rolling in, increasing in size as the tide flooded. Here, on the water's edge, the warship seemed an appalling distance away. The thought of sharks flashed into Magnus' mind, but he hastily rejected it and shucked off his boots.

They stripped to the skin, and after securing their knives around their waists, entered the water. The sand sloped sharply. Before they started to swim, Brother Diego made a suggestion.

"You go around the starboard, Magnus, and I'll take the larboard. We will then converge on the buoy. Let us agree that if either one of us is wounded, the other will not pause, but continue with the important task. It would mean death to all if we should fail."

"Sobeit!" Magnus agreed. "But . . . for God's sake, take care of yourself, Diego!"

The priest laughed softly. "I fear nothing, Magnus, for I go with God!" He slid into the water as smoothly as a seal.

Magnus followed suit. In the darkness, the priest was soon out of sight, but not out of mind. For as he forged through the swells, Magnus thought about this strange character, with his seeming-contradictory qualities of honesty and shrewdness, his gentleness and courage; a man who could say "I fear nothing, for I go with God," and mean it. If, as he believed, everyone's actions are the result of previous happenings, what kind of a background had pro-

268

duced Diego Valesco? It would be enlightening to know. Magnus vowed he would ask Diego—if they got out of this scrape alive.

He began to wonder if they would, for he was growing tired. He had not spared himself in the moving of the guns, and his strength was spent. The water, too, was warm and enervating. He paused, treading water, to orient himself. At first he could see nothing and he felt a touch of panic, then a swell lifted him, and he saw the black loom of the *San Philip* just ahead.

The imminence of danger stimulated him. He swam swiftly, warily, keeping close to the great hull. Now his other senses aided to guide him. He could smell the tar and oakum; his ears picked up the slap of lines against the masts, the retch of spars. Once he thought he heard the tread of a sentry. A loose gun-port banged just above his head, and sent him into a startled dive.

Finally, he saw the straight line of the taut anchor hawse. Its size dismayed him! Could he possibly hack through that monstrous rope without arousing the guard? He felt his resolution waver.

He was past the cutwater when he glimpsed a movement in the water near by. For an instant, his heart stopped beating. He thought it was a shark. Then to his intense relief, he realized it was Brother Diego.

They reached the buoy at the same time, and hung there, drawing air into their lungs. After a brief rest, Magnus chose a place in the line close to the surface, and drew his knife.

Unfortunately, the giant rope was new and therefore tough. Magnus straddled the underwater section and began to saw desperately. It parted slowly, thread by thread. Brother Diego wrapped his left arm around the upper portion to work opposite him.

The knives dulled rapidly, yet the end was in sight. Two great plys had parted; only one remained. Three more minutes would finish that. . . .

"*Hola! Alto ahí!*" bellowed a voice above them.

Magnus was so startled he almost dropped his knife. He looked up. A sentry was leaning over the bow, holding a lanthorn and staring in their direction. Then a musket thundered, and a ball *chunked* the water close by.

"They see us!" whispered Magnus.

"Then hurry, lad, hurry!" urged the priest. "Our work is not yet done!"

Magnus swore savagely and continued cutting. On the warship, men were shouting and collecting on the bow and lights were brought up. More threads parted, twanging like tiny fiddle-strings. Another minute . . .

By now, the *San Philip* was ablaze with lanthorns, yet the light

269

did not quite reach the men struggling in the water. The musket balls drew closer. Once Magnus felt a faint tug on his hair, and realized vaguely he had come within a fraction of an inch of death.

Just a few more seconds . . .

In his concentration, he was not aware that Brother Diego had climbed astride the upper section of the hawser to shield him. His first intimation came when he heard the priest's involuntary grunt as a ball plowed into his exposed back. Magnus paused in alarm, but the priest commanded him to continue.

"Finish, Magnus, for God's sake . . . *finish!*"

Magnus hacked the last strands, and the hawser parted like a whiplash. As the priest was thrown into the water, Magnus caught him in his arms.

"Go, my son," pleaded the priest. "Save yourself that you may save the others!"

"I won't leave you alone, Diego!" vowed Magnus.

Brother Diego chuckled. "Bless you, my son, I am not alone; God is here!" His voice grew weak suddenly. "Go now! *Dominus vobiscum!*"

Before Magnus realized what was happening, the priest slipped out of his embrace and disappeared.

Frantic, Magnus dived repeatedly in an effort to find him, but to no avail. There was no evidence of Diego Valesco, save what remained in Magnus' own heart. The knowledge numbed him. When he finally controlled his grief, he found himself tragically alone. He reared out of the water and stared about him. The *San Philip* was fast nearing the beach, and even as he watched, she bumped a couple of times, then struck hard. The swells broke against her larboard beam and canted her decks toward the shore. A moment later, Tim's guns opened up on her from the bluff.

Still, Magnus hesitated. He was tired and spent. He thought how pleasant it would be to sink quietly below the surface of the warm water, as Brother Diego had done. Then, abruptly, the priest's charge echoed in his brain: *Save yourself that you may save the others!* Brother Diego had deliberately sacrificed his own life to that end. Magnus could not betray him.

"*Adios, amigo!*" he murmured aloud. "You followed your destiny and died fighting evil. Priest, Catholic, Spaniard, you remain the finest man I ever knew. May the Lord of Hosts cherish and reward you. *Alleluia!*"

Then he struck out for the *San Philip.*

The Spaniards tried valiantly to return the lethal hail falling from the cliff, but as Magnus had foreseen, they were unable to elevate

270

their cannon so high, and their musketry was ineffective. Their only recourse was to extinguish all lights and lay below decks.

With the warship plunged in darkness, Magnus could no longer see her, but as he had the wit to take a bearing on a star, he held his direction. Finally she loomed up dead ahead. He proceeded cautiously to avoid the rain of small shot, and worked his way around to the stern, where he rested against the massive rudder.

Shortly thereafter, he make out the silhouette of the long boat surging through the swells. He swam to meet it. At his cautious hail, the boat slowed, and he was hauled aboard.

Ben Absedik gathered him into his arms in the first burst of emotion he had ever shown.

"All praise to our Lord Mahomet the merciful that thou art returned to us alive!" he breathed ardently. "Where is our brother?"

Magnus buried his face in his hands. "Dead, Abu! He gave his life for us."

Ben Absedik drew his breath sharply. "It was kismet! When the tapestry is completed, the threads, however bright, are parted. May the peace of the Almighty be upon him, for though he wert an unbeliever, I loved him as a brother!" He gestured the rowers to continue. "By Allah, he shall be avenged seven times seven!"

A light was kindled and a signal made. Immediately, the guns of the bluff were silenced, and the long boat glided alongside the warship. Magnus and Ben Absedik sprang into the chains and swung themselves aboard, closely followed by a swarm of howling seamen.

At the cessation of gunfire, the Spaniards tried a double sortie from both the stern and forecastles. But Spaniards have never been at their best in close-quarter, hand-to-hand fighting, and they were demoralized by the punishing rain of shot which had seemed almost to have come from heaven. Their half-hearted attack was beaten back, and when two demi-culverins were hauled around and emptied into their closed ranks, they took to cover.

Now in complete mastery of the waist, Magnus shouted for Admiral Don Alvarado Perrez to come forth and surrender. His request was ignored. Ben Absedik wanted to turn a cannon around and blast the forecastle off the ship, but Magnus shook his head.

"Don Alvarado!" he bellowed in a voice that carried clearly throughout the warship. "Unless you put in an appearance by the time I count five, we will light a fuse to your powder magazine and send you all to hell! *One . . . two . . . three . . . !*"

At the count of *four*, a door in the stern-castle opened and the Spanish admiral stepped into the circle of light. He stared at Magnus in a haughty silence.

271

Magnus bowed. "Your Grace arrived at an opportune moment. We were about to leave."

Don Alvarado glanced at the handful of English grouped around him and, no doubt, thought of his own two hundred odd seamen cowering behind bulkheads and below decks. Some of this was reflected in the sudden hardening of his sharp features.

Magnus anticipated him. "Be not deceived, my Admiral," he cautioned. "Up to now, my gunners on the cliff have used only small shot, for I have use for this ship. However, at the slightest show of resistance, they will blow it . . . *and* you, also, my Admiral . . . out of existence. I beg you, sire, do not be a fool!"

The Spaniard flushed. "Be good enough to dispense with this mockery. What is your proposal?"

"Proposal is hardly the word," smiled Magnus. "But we shan't quibble over phrases. As I remarked, I require this ship, so I must respectfully request that you and your men depart quietly."

Don Alvarado stroked his beard. "You demand much, *señor*," he said slowly. "I must have time to reflect and consult my officers. Give me a few hours . . ."

Magnus laughed. "You ask me to dispense with mockery, my Admiral, yet you continue to invite it; I realize quite as well as you do that a *few hours*, as you so delicately put it, will bring, not only daylight, but the reinforcements his Excellency, Don Sanchez, had the foresight to start on the march. Therefore, at the risk of seeming unreasonable, I must ask your immediate surrender."

"On what terms?"

Magnus feigned astonishment. "Terms, your Grace? Why none—that is, to speak of. Having appropriated this ship, I merely ask you to get off my property. Ah, yes, there is one other stipulation. I require an honest answer to two questions?"

The Spaniard arched his brows. "And those are . . . ?"

"The present whereabouts of a certain Englishwoman?"

Don Alvarado stiffened. "Lady Beckles is a guest of Governor Oquendo," he said haughtily. "If you expect me to include her in the terms . . ."

"She is not included," Magnus cut him off. "I desired to know only that she is safe."

"She is quite safe," retorted the Spaniard with a sneer.

"That disposes of one question. The other—where is the English traitor?"

"I do not comprehend, *señor!*"

Magnus dropped his mocking pose. "Don't equivocate! You well know I'm talking about that treasonous lackey in the pay of your master—Peter Beckles. *Where is he?*"

272

The Spaniard hesitated a fraction of time, then spread his long white hands. "I regret, *señor,* I am unable to answer that!"

Ben Absedik, standing beside Magnus, understood the drift, if not the words.

"The infidel dog lies in his beard!" he warned Magnus in *lingua franca.* "Let me straighten his crooked tongue, *effendi!*"

Magnus shook his head. "It is of no importance." He eyed the admiral. "You will now instruct your men to lay down their arms and come out singly. While they are being loaded into the shore boats, you will remain at my side as a hostage. I am sure it is unnecessary to caution you that if so much as a hand is raised . . ."

"The insinuation is offensive, *señor!*"

Magnus smiled thinly. "In that case, I shall reframe my statement. Let us say, I will be deeply regretful if the conduct of your men makes it necessary to kill you."

"So will I," snapped Don Alvarado. "It might prevent me from hanging you later."

"It might," laughed Magnus. "But in the meantime, my Admiral, will you be kind enough to get on with the landings. Unfortunately, time is passing."

Under the watchful eyes of the English seamen, enough Spaniards were released to hoist out two long boats. These were quickly filled with common seamen and, with a strong guard, rowed ashore. On their return, the boats brought back Tim and his gunners.

Don Alvarado was left in the charge of the Moor, while Magnus conferred with the new arrivals. Tim, as usual, was pessimistic.

"I spiked the guns over the cliff, likes ye tolt me," he reported, "but Oquendo's forces was only a hop-skip-an'-a-jump be'ind me. True, we got the ship, yet w'at good is she—'ard agroun'?"

Magnus chuckled. "She won't be aground long. 'Tis a couple of hours before the full of the tide. If you bestir yourself and carry out a kedge anchor to hold us, we will float off in that time."

Tim sighed. "Ef ye ain't the bloody one for throwin' aw'y anchors!" he groaned. "Tell me—where's the *padre.* I ain't seed 'im since I came aboard?"

"He was killed, Tim!"

"*No!* By God, I'm sorry to 'ear it, lad! Ye ought to slaughter every dirty Spaniard on this . . ."

Magnus shook his head. "No, Tim. Diego would not want it that way. He, too, was Spanish."

"He was a *man!*" raged old Tim. "I'd not let the swine responsible . . ."

"We were the responsible ones," Magnus interrupted him. "Diego deliberately sacrificed himself for us."

Tim wilted. "Aye, 'twas the way o' 'im. As the good book says: 'Greater love hath no man than . . .' Well, whatever it said, the *padre* was that way. God rest 'im!"

"Amen!" agreed Magnus, and turned away.

Magnus had deemed it best to get the common seamen ashore first, for he reasoned that without officers to goad them into action, they would give scant trouble. When the last of these was landed, he ordered Don Alvarado to summon his officers. As they trooped out sullenly, the admiral turned to Magnus.

"Will you permit me to get my papers before debarking, *señor?*"

Magnus nodded. "Certainly, my Admiral." When he saw the Spaniard hesitate, as if waiting for a guard to accompany him, Magnus waved him away.

"I have complete confidence in your honor, Don Alvarado."

The Spaniard bowed stiffly, then without speaking, turned toward the companionway. He moved with bowed head, yet his step was firm.

Waiting, Magnus stared eastward. A gray, steely band had appeared above the trees. Somewhere on the island, a trumpet pealed a thin blast that sent a shiver up his spine. He moved to the rail. Below him, the Spanish long boats crowded with officers bumped against the slab sides of the *San Philip*. He could just distinguish Tim's boat returning from carrying out the kedge. A moment later, the winch began to creak as the hands took up the scope.

Magnus scowled impatiently at the companionway. Don Alvarado was taking an unconscionably long time to gather his papers. Magnus took a nervous turn around the waist, then decided to go aft to the great cabin himself. But as he started toward it, the door opened and he saw the beautiful brocaded cloak of Don Alvarado appear.

The admiral did not approach him this time, but moved swiftly toward the rail with bent head buried in the notch of his cloak. Magnus felt a quick pang of sympathy; he had tasted defeat too many times to be impervious. He stepped aside, watching silently.

Suddenly, he crossed the deck in a bound. The other was in the act of climbing onto the high bulwark, when Magnus grabbed the cloak and ripped it from his shoulder. The motion jerked the man around, flattening him against the rail. The feeble light of the lanthorns revealed the sallow features of . . . *Peter Beckles!*

Beckles tried to draw his rapier, but Magnus caught him by the throat and threw him to the deck, where Ben Absedik and three or four seamen pounced on him.

274

The Moor had his knife out, but Magnus stopped him.

"No, Abu—he's mine! Take him into the cabin, and we'll face Don Alvarado with his treachery!"

While they were dragging Beckles aft, Magnus leaned over the rail to shout at the men in the waiting boats. There was no English amongst them this time, for it was to be the last trip.

"Shove off!" Magnus ordered in Spanish.

One of the officers stood up. "But, señor—our admiral . . . ?"

"Your admiral has violated his parole!" roared Magnus. "Now shove off, else, by God, I'll sink you!"

As the boat pulled away with obvious reluctance, he strode aft. He encountered a strange scene in the cabin. At the opposite side of the room, Beckles was pinioned against the bulkhead by two seamen, while in the foreground, the Moor was on his knees beside the prone body of Admiral Perrez. Don Alvarado was quite dead, and a poniard jutting from his shoulder blades plainly indicated the manner of his passing.

Magnus leaned against the door jamb. "'Pon my soul, Ser Pedro, you are consistent to the last!"

Beckles started visibly. "My God! Then it really is you, Carter?"

"Aye, Magnus Carter! It has been a long time, I own, and though I've aged considerably, my memory is as sound as ever."

Beckles' features paled. "In the darkness and confusion—I didn't recognize you! I thought we were beset by pirates! In the name of God—what are you doing here?"

Magnus grinned. "*Doing* here? Come, my lord, you're a poor actor, so drop this ludicrous role. I am quite aware that your faithful wife told you that I was awaiting you here. I appreciate your promptness—*this time*."

"I . . . I don't understand you, man!"

Magnus feigned surprise. "Am I so obscure? Why, sire, have you forgotten the challenge you so bravely put to me in Plymouth, months agone? Oh, I confess to being somewhat tardy in keeping our appointment, due to circumstances not to my liking. Howbeit, we meet at last, and though the setting may not be quite as you desired it, nevertheless I am prepared now to give you the satisfaction you demanded." He gestured his men to release the prisoner. "Now, sir, since you have a sword, shall we have at it?"

"Good lord, Carter, you can't be serious!" Beckles protested. "I did not come here of my own free will; I was a Spanish prisoner! Don Alvarado forced me . . ."

"You're a liar!" Magnus cut him off. "When the *Triumph* grounded, you shifted your berth to the *San Philip* as casually

275

as you shifted your allegiance to Spain in the past. Then you murdered Don Alvarado so that you could escape in his place. But enough talk! Raise your sword, for though I've no stomach to run through a man too cowardly to fight, I've taken my oath to kill you!"

Sir Peter's face colored with a flush of hot anger, yet, miraculously, he kept himself under control. His mouth curled disdainfully.

"So—this is the great *Magnus the Magnificent*, who aspires to nobility?" he sneered. "Very well, it shall be as you say. But do not dignify your murder by calling it a *duel*, when you stand protected by henchmen!"

Magnus bowed. "I stand *corrected*, rather, my lord," he amended. "God forbid that I should emulate traitors who have henchmen—as you term them—do their killing." He turned to the others.

"Abu, you and the men await me on deck. And understand this clearly—if peradventure I am slain, Sir Peter is to be set ashore *unharmed*. Is that plain enough?"

Ben Absedik started to object, then shrugged. "Thy word is law, *effendi*," he agreed. "What is written is written."

When his men had gone, Magnus turned back to his old enemy. Beckles stood with his back against the bulkhead, his long face jaundiced in the wan light. Magnus knew that he would have his way with the man, so he dallied to savor the full flavor of his revenge. Yet, strangely enough, it lacked the spice he had anticipated. Peter Beckles no longer appeared the suave, menacing courtier Magnus had remembered, but a vain, weak-willed fop who was attempting (not too successfully) to compose himself to the inevitable. Magnus discovered his own hatred was diluted with contempt.

Provoked, he tried to shake off the reaction. "You don't seem singularly happy about our meeting, Ser Pedro?" he taunted.

"No happier than you were when the situation was reversed," Beckles conceded. "And on that occasion, I, at least, was motivated by something better than personal vindictiveness."

"Aye, by *treason!*"

The other shrugged. "A matter of opinion, that. However, if it affords you any satisfaction—your blundering interference ruined our plans. So now that you have baited me sufficiently, suppose you get on with your slaughter."

Magnus sneered and raised his blade. This was the moment of which he had dreamed for nearly two long years; the fulfillment of his oath. Then as he opened his mouth to call *"En Garde!"*, he heard the voice of Brother Diego speak to him: *Must you wallow*

276

*in hate, Magnus? And for what purpose? Did not God himself say:
"Vengeance is mine!"?*

Magnus hesitated. For what purpose, indeed? Rosalind was gone,
and he was reconciled to it. The treasonous plot was broken up.
True, he had reason a-plenty to avenge himself on this knave who
had caused him so much suffering, yet it was in the depths of this
very travail he had found himself. He thought of his oath, and of
a sudden, it seemed pathetically childish.

The cold note of a trumpet jerked him back to the present. He
glanced through the open stern windows to the beach, now glistening in the early light. He took a step backward and lowered his
point.

"Beckles—can you swim?" he asked abruptly.

Sir Peter frowned. "Certainly. But what sarcasm is this?"

"Only that I've changed my mind," growled Magnus. "You're not
worth killing. To let you live with your rotten conscience is all the
vengeance I require. So get you through those windows and join
your Spanish friends on the beach."

Beckles' eyes widened. "Dear God—do you mean it?" he gasped.

Magnus snorted. "You should know by this time I always mean
what I say. Tell Rosalind I bequeath you to her with my blessing.
But—remember this: *Stay out of England!* Your treason shall be
reported to the Queen, and if we ever meet again, so help me God,
I'll kill you for the treacherous mongrel you are! Now get out of
my sight!"

Peter Beckles needed no urging. He hastily shed his boots and
backed nervously toward the windows. When he saw Magnus
sheathe his sword, he scrambled onto the sill and sprang out of
sight.

Magnus spat in disgust and wiped his hands, as though he had
touched something unclean, then turned toward the door. A great
weight seemed lifted from his shoulders. He chuckled ruefully. He
still had to explain his conduct to old Tim and the Moor, and he
was not at all sure he could do it successfully.

He found the pair awaiting him on the poop. With the combined
help of the kedge and tide, the *San Philip* had been refloated, and
was ready to sail. Tim greeted him with obvious relief.

"Praise the Lord!" crowed the old man. "Ye be alive, lad, an'
we're rich!"

Magnus grinned. "Aye, in all truth, I'm alive! But what's this
about being rich?"

"Hog-rich, I swear! I was soundin' the bilges, to see if she'd
strained in the groundin', w'en I found fourteen large iron chests

o' minted gold Philip 'ad sent to pay 'is dirty 'enchmen in the Colonies! Abu says we kin set ourselves up like princes in 'is country, since 'tis sure we can't go 'ome to England."

Ben Absedik nodded agreement. "Verily, thou wilt find it a veritable garden of paradise, *effendi!* But, tell me—did thine enemy die hard?"

Magnus looked toward the east. He could see the figure of a man wading weakly through the breaking surf. He sighed softly.

"He didn't die, Abu. His life was of no value to me, so I gave it back to him."

Tim's mouth flew open, and he gaped at the Moor. But Ben Absedik couldn't help him, for he was equally astounded.

"In the sacred name of Allah the all-wise—what weakness possessed thee, my brother? Hast thou lost thy senses?"

"Aye, be ye daft?" echoed Tim.

Magnus shook his head. "Diego talked me out of it, lads."

"Ye're balmy!" roared Tim. "The *padre's* dead!"

"Nay, Tim, you're wrong. Men like the *padre* never die. Come now—let us get under weigh, for we sail to England."

"England?" bleated the old man. "Why, man, they'll 'ang ye!"

"Peradventure they will. Yet 'tis a risk I have to take, for the Queen must have the truth about Beckles and Duane."

The Moor was staring at him quizzically. "Hast thou forgotten thy sacred oath, *effendi?*"

"No, Abu, I haven't forgotten. But the circumstances have altered, and to continue the grudge would have been the act of a willful child. It is a thing of the past."

Ben Absedik accepted this fatalistically. "Truly, the way of the unbeliever passeth all understanding! May the peace of Allah be upon you!" He walked away.

Tim groaned. "Lad, ye ain't drunk, be ye?"

Magnus chuckled. "No, Timothy, I'm not drunk." Then, out of the limbo of his mind, a phrase came back to him. "I'm not drunk— *perhaps for the first time.*"

Who had said that? The fisherman in his rockbound hut the night Magnus had imbibed the Cornish ale! With startling abruptness, the veil was torn from his mind—he knew now who was the girl of his dream! In his blindness, he had believed it was Rosalind. It was not! Why had he not had the wit to recognize the truth the second time he had taken the stuff in Plymouth, when his senses had directed him, unknowingly, to Kate!

He broke into a wild laughter. "Rouse yourself, man!" he bellowed at the astounded old Tim. "I've a too-long delayed rendezvous in England!"

278

Chapter 29

Early one April morning, in the year 1587, a fisherman—whose name history neglected to record—was groping his way through the drifting fog off Plymouth Sound, when the mist cleared sufficiently to reveal a great galleon towering above his cockleshell. Recognizing it as Spanish, he veered off in terror, which gave way to amazement when an English voice hailed to ask:

"Ahoy, friend! Is our Queen alive?"

The fisherman gasped out that she was alive and well, then asked what ship it was.

The tall, red-headed captain leaning over the rail laughed heartily.

"Why, 'tis the galleon *Queen's Gift!*" he shouted, and tossed a leather sack of gold into the fishing boat. "Take this, fellow, and hurry into Plymouth. Report to Sir John Hawkins that Magnus Carter is bringing home another prize—if God sends enough wind to move us into the harbor!"

The fisherman hefted the purse, then yelled with enthusiasm.

"Aye, aye, an' God bless ye, sor!"

The little smack drifted nimbly before the feeble air and was soon lost in the fog, leaving the heavy galleon floundering helplessly. Tim, standing beside Magnus, grunted sourly, "Ye'll need God's blessin', else I'm a lubber!"

Magnus grinned, and turned to look for the Moor. He saw him by the taffrail, staring moodily to the south, where the shores of France lay shrouded in infinity. Somehow, he resembled a chained and lonely falcon.

Magnus crossed swiftly to his side and laid a comradely arm about his shoulder.

"What now, old friend? Are you not glad to be home?"

Ben Absedik sighed. "For thy sake, yes, since it is thy desire. Yet for me, *home* is still as far away as ever."

"Say not so! My home is your home, Abu. And, peradventure I

279

should live, someday we'll sail the southern seas together and visit . . ."

Ben Absedik gently shook his head. "No, my brother. This England is where thou belong, for home is where a man's seed be sown. I thank Allah for this voyage; I have learned much from thee, and from the Frankish priest of the noble heart and even the old one with the wooden leg. These are things I shall never forget, yet . . . the land of my fathers calls, and I am sore of heart."

"Then, by God, if you desire to go home, you shall!" vowed Magnus.

"Ah, but *how?*"

Magnus laughed. "Hast forgotten the gold below? Why, man, we'll buy you the fleetest ship in all England and send you off as befits a prince! Depend on it!"

The cheerful cry from the masthead interrupted. *"Wind a-comin'!"*

The galleon began to move with that majesty inherent in wooden ships, and the thin blue mists parted, as curtains on a stage, to curl themselves gracefully around the summit of Mont Edgecombe. Despite himself, Magnus felt the tears well into his eyes as they rested on the beauty. He had not realized how lovely England was. Then the gray stone buildings of Plymouth appeared, etched against the dark green background, and on the higher land, the sunlight dappled the lush fields.

As they rounded St. Nicholas Island, a fleet of small boats came out, like flower girls, to lead them in and the guns of the fortress belched a thunderous salute. Old Tim proudly returned the courtesy with his cannon, and the galleon swept onward to the quay.

"Damme!" muttered Tim. "It reminds me o' the time we came 'ome wi' 'Awkins in seventy-three. Must be they mistake us fer Drake. Yet, 'tis a brave scene, I own!"

It was indeed. The immortal Hoe was jammed with eager townspeople, as for the homecoming of a hero. The clear cold trumpet calls floated across the water, interspersed with musket fire and the deep bass roll of cannon. Even the galleon seemed attuned to the mood, for her progress was slow and queenly. Every man not actually needed to work the ship was perched upon her yards, hungrily scanning the shore for glimpse of friend or family.

Magnus was a trifle puzzled by the ovation, but he decided Tim's guess came close to the truth. Doubtless the fisherman had bungled the message, and he was being mistaken for Sir Francis Drake. He sighed resignedly. He would tell the truth, and if they wanted to hang him, well . . . he would have only one regret—that he hadn't discovered his true love in time.

280

From his place above the whipstaff, he conned the ship close to the mole, then sheered off smartly, and let the tide ease him alongside.

The first man aboard was Sir John Hawkins. Gruff and unsmiling as ever, his opening question was of Drake.

Magnus grinned. "He got away, sir. Ere this, no doubt, Cartagena has fallen to him."

"Thank God!" growled Hawkins. Although guards had been stationed across the mole to control the eager crowds, the noise was deafening. "Let us go to the cabin where we can talk," Hawkins commanded.

In the comparative quiet of the cabin, Hawkins looked narrowly at Magnus. "You say Drake 'got away'? Did Hardy find you, then?"

"Aye, sir, but I took the liberty of parting company from him."

Hawkins snorted. "On my oath, you're a slippery knave, Carter! How was it possible!"

Magnus summarized the story of his escapade, while Hawkins leaned back in his chair and thoughtfully tugged his beard.

"And so," Magnus concluded, "I decided to come home, Sir John. I've had a bellyful of running away. You warned me I might not be believed, yet 'tis my wish that the Queen should hear of the treason of Duane and Beckles, even if it cost me . . ."

Hawkins cocked his head. "'S'death! You mean you haven't yet heard what's happened?"

"I've heard naught but that the Queen wanted my head!"

Hawkins laughed sourly. "'Tis ofttimes said the Queen changes her mind right easily, and to that, I'll naught say nay. Why, bless you, lad, Duane lost *his* head a month agone!"

"For treason? But how, since the letters were destroyed?"

"Ah, but they were *not* destroyed! That pretty little wench of the Prettymans saw you hide them and recovered them. When word got around that Hardy had left to find and hang you, she brought them to me in tears. It appears she meant to give them to you, but there was a misunderstanding of some kind betwixt you two."

Magnus could barely keep his voice steady. "A misunderstanding, in all truth, my lord!"

Hawkins stood up. "Well, you can patch it up later," he said gruffly. "At the moment, we have more important business. The Queen—God bless her!—is impatient to know if you survived. She ordered me to bring you to her presence if, perchance, you were lucky enough to get home. Come—I have a carriage waiting. We'll leave for London at once."

Magnus shook his head. "I cannot leave until I settle another matter, Sir John."

"God's life, young man!" thundered Hawkins. "You cannot keep the *Queen* waiting!"

"Aye, sir, but there is another queen waiting, who has waited much too long! She comes first with me!"

L'Envoi

THE common-room was larger than the old one, and freshly scrubbed and painted. Tim was very proud of it. A highly polished *robinet*—a small one-pound signal gun salvaged as a souvenir from the *San Philip*—stood like a sentry at the entrance to the tap-room. The plate rail was decorated with tankards, mugs and flagons, and the paneled walls bristled with swords and halberts. Despite the old man's grumbling protests, the tables were gay with flowers.

Tim himself hobbled up and down the room, as fussy as an admiral on inspection. He paused to flick an imaginary speck of dust from the counter, then stooped to breathe on the little cannon before rubbing it with his rag. He had not changed greatly. True, the once iron-gray fringe of hair had mellowed to a gentle silver and his girth was wider by a hand-span, but contentment can do much to stay the hand of time.

Suddenly, he straightened and cocked his head, as he had done a score of times throughout the day.

"Kat-tie!" he bellowed. "*Kat-TIE!* W'ere are ye?"

The girl appeared, flushed and breathless, at the head of the stairs. The candlelight made a golden crown of her blond hair.

"Marry! What is the matter with you now, Master Timothy?" she laughed. "Sure, it sounds like old times to hear you caterwauling like a lonesome calf!"

Tim grinned sheepishly. "Blast me, I think I 'ear 'im comin'!"

"You've been 'hearing 'im coming' all the livelong day, you old goose!" she chided. "Now give me time . . . Oh, dear God, he *is* coming!"

She plunged headlong down the stairs, adjusting her apron as she came. "Heaven help me, I'm all a-twitter!" she gasped, racing to the fireplace where a large fowl was turning slowly on the spit. "Lord, I hope it is done!"

Tim was stomping aimlessly around, bawling for the Moor. "Abu! Abu! Damme, where's the bloody 'eathen?"

Ben Absedik appeared in the doorway of the tap-room, looking like an oriental potentate, with his black beard forked and his hawk's head swathed in a turban of cloth of gold.

"Peace be on thy tongue, friend Timothy!" he said with a smile. "What excitest thou?"

" 'E's comin'!" yelled the old man.

They could plainly hear the carriage rolling down the hill, and Tim began jumping hither and yon like a frog on a hot rock.

Kate stopped basting the goose. "Stop wuzzling!" she snapped at him. "Can't you two useless men light the candles on the tables? For all we know, he may be bringing Sir John with him from London town!"

"Hold yer puling tongue, lass! Sir John don't 'ob-nob wi' commoners such as us!" grumbled Tim, but he and Abu lighted the candles as she bade them. "The coach be stoppin'! Get the wine, Katie! 'Urry, else by Neptune, I'll . . ."

He scuttled toward the door, but it opened before he reached it and Magnus strode into the room, with John Hawkins right behind him. Tim started for Magnus, then recognizing Hawkins, caught himself and made a leg. As Kate paused to curtsy, Magnus ran over and grabbed her in his arms.

"God's life, my sweet, this week in London seemed longer than the voyage to the Indies! I hungered for my little wife!"

"Aye, darling!" sobbed Kate. "It was an age, in truth! Did you actually see the Queen?"

"See her?" crowed Magnus. "Wait until you hear our news! Abu gets a fine ship to take him back to Islam and I . . ."

" 'Ere, 'ere!" protested Tim brusquely. "Let yer billin' an' cooin' wait a bit. Look to yer manners, me girl, an' get Sir John a spot o' wine!"

Kate disengaged herself from Magnus' arms, and started toward the bottle and glasses on a near-by tray. But gruff old Hawkins got there ahead of her.

"Permit me to serve you, Lady Carter," he said, taking the bottle from her hand.

Kate stopped short. "What jest was that, sir?" she breathed.

" 'Twas no jest, my lady," chuckled old Sir John, carefully pouring drinks for all. "Your husband was knighted yesterday by the Queen of England!"

As Kate stood frozen in awe, Magnus crossed over and put his arm about her.

"Only as an indirect way of rewarding you, my lovely Katie!" he whispered.

284

While she leaned in his arms, with the tears blinding her, the men clinked their glasses.

" 'Ere's 'ealth an' 'appiness to Lydy Carter!" Tim bellowed lustily. "The best damn barmaid in all o' England!"

"Aye, aye, to that!" roared John Hawkins.

"*Ameen!*" echoed Abu Ben Absedik.

But Sir Magnus couldn't drink the toast to "the best damn barmaid in all o' England," for Lady Carter's lips were on his mouth.

Afterword

V ERY often, on reading a novel, I have been curious as to what prompted the author to choose the particular period and locale he did, or to conceive the characters involved. I have wondered, too, how closely he adhered to actual history. From the frequency of the letters I receive following the publication of a novel, I discover this inquisitiveness is not a mere idiosyncrasy of my own. Since a foreword seems hardly the place to reveal these points, I am violating precedent by the use of this informal *after*word.

There are certain eras which exude a strange fascination for some of us. Why we should be drawn so irresistibly by one period and not another, I cannot say; it is enough that it is so. To me, the days when Hawkins and Drake sailed the Main seem among the most adventuresome and romantic epochs in recorded history. These men, and others like them, established the principle of the "freedom of the seas," and dedicated their lives to that purpose. That they enjoyed themselves in so doing in no wise lessens their greatness.

So, while *Magnus the Magnificent* is strictly a piece of fiction, and intended to be read only as such, I have endeavored to be as truthful to the period and to the few actual characters involved—such as Drake, Hawkins, et al.—as careful research made possible. For example, the letter from King Philip to the *corregidor* of Biscay (quoted in the story) is factual, as is the fact that Drake and his little fleet sailed in reprisal. And if "Magnus Carter" never existed in name, he did in effect, for England owes her very existence to men of similar caliber; and the "Tim Prettymans" of history have long been the backbone of the British navy.

As for "Brother Diego," he is a composite of some Catholic priests I have encountered in my travels; he is also the result of a personal revolt on my part against so many of the namby-pamby priests of fiction. That there were men of his capacity is revealed in the records of the Holy Inquisition. Incidentally, some of the dialogue used in the trial of Magnus was taken verbatim from such records.

287

To append a bibliography would be a lengthy and superfluous chore, and such has no place in a novel.

While it is something of a relief to write *finis* to a long piece of work, it would be base ingratitude to do so without expressing my heartfelt appreciation to those "silent collaborators"—Helen, my wife; Paul R. Reynolds and Oliver Swan, my patient agents; and, perhaps, even to "Inkwell," the little black library cat, but for whose affectionate heckling, this book might have been concluded two weeks earlier.